Mystery
in Mactown

Mystery in Mactown

Second Stanza of the Crescent

Moon Chronicles

a novel by K.E. Robinson

atmosphere press

This book is dedicated to those who K.E. met along his journey but will not be able to see it all the way to the end. Those who were with him for a time but not a long time, at least not long enough. May your memories continue to reside in our hearts the way they will forever be etched in our minds. Rest in the Pieces of our memories that we are honored for you to occupy: Nyhlia, Bull, Carson, Butta, Domone, and Phil.

Introduction

"Crescent Moons: Premiering the Crescent Moon Chronicles" was all business...this time...it's personal! Once the biggest assassination in Crescent City was seemingly resolved, the mysteries were only beginning! One hero has fallen, the other is missing, and the lid is ajar on the presumed open and shut case!

Grab ahold of the second installment of the Crescent Moon Chronicles as the people of Crescent City will be forced to face their fears. In life we are guaranteed few things: taxes, death, and somewhere in between...a *meeting with our monsters.*

Chapter 1

A Warrior's Dream

Julissa sits in her living room, completely shaken at what is taking place outside her door. Mother Rampart stomps about the yard with two female collectors in tow. Julissa's mascara is smeared and running down her face while she sweats profusely. She sits next to Judy's bed, but no child is exposed as they are tucked under the covers. Julissa pulls out her phone to make a call:

"Renaldo, I don't know where you are or what you're doing, but we need your help! Pick up the damn phone, Renaldo. I'm not gonna call you again! This is serious!!" she pleads.

Julissa slams her thumb down on the end call symbol in utter disgust. She hears a window break downstairs. Julissa instantly locks the windows in Judy's room, slides a bookshelf in front, and hauls ass out the door. She locks it on her way out. Julissa places her palm on the knob as she hears the scurrying of multiple feet below. She plants a gentle kiss on the door, knowing it barricades what The Brood came to confiscate.

"Oh Leeeeeeeeeesa," Rampart calls, "There is nowhere for you to run. We need to collect. Pay what you owe, selfish harlot!"

Julissa defiantly chuckles as she turns her eyes towards the stairs. She pushes off the entrance and begins to strut down the hall. A collector ascends the stairs, dressed in all black clothing with a white shawl over her head. Julissa hastens her prowl at the sight of the collector.

"Well, don't make it easy for me by leaving it open. I welcome a little exercise," threatened the collector.

"You gotta get there first, Sister Sledge," Julissa poked back.

Julissa entered full gallop as she launched herself into the air and drop-kicked the collector's torso. The collector crashed into the wall violently, causing a small clock to fall and tumble down the stairs. The collector caught Julissa's hand with her own, stopping the pending haymaker from landing. The collector then shoved Julissa into the wall and followed up with a snap punch to the kidney. With Julissa clearly distracted, the other collector scaled the stairs to approach the room. Julissa saw the second collector and lunged toward her to stop her forward momentum. Julissa received a kick to the solar plexus for her trouble, temporarily ceasing her breath. Both collectors scurried to the room door. They displayed obvious frustration at the realization that the door is sealed. Julissa quietly laughed while grimacing in pain. Julissa mustered enough energy to roll onto her back and watch the collectors aimlessly try to pry the door open with a knife.

"Mother commands you to open this door, little girl. You wouldn't want to disappoint Mommy, now would you?" a collector shouted to the room.

"She won't be disappointing *her* mother at all, because she ain't opening shit for your sorry asses!" Julissa scoffed.

The collectors paused their pursuit as their attention returned to Julissa. One collector let out a "hiss" before darting at Julissa. The other began to kick the door. Julissa dodged the heckling collector to tackle the one attacking the room. While on the floor, Julissa landed a right, then a left hook across the face of the collector. She then clasped her hands together and drove them into the collector's forehead, knocking her unconscious after the back of her skull met the ground. The other collector placed Julissa in a chokehold and maneuvered onto her back as she wrapped her legs around Julissa's waist.

"Hush little Lisa, don't say a word; Mother's gonna get whatever child she prefers. If you think there's some mistake, we'll be gone long before you wake," the collector antagonized.

As the other collector remained motionless, a disturbance developed downstairs. The entrance to the residence is swung open furiously and closed with a rumble that rocks the house. Footsteps scramble across the pane before a voice emits:

"What are you doing here?" Mother Rampart alarmed.

"Returning a call. What are *you* doing here?" a man's voice repeats.

"Taking what is owed to me, my dear. Now you be a good boy and run along before I add you to that tally," Mother Rampart warned.

"I think you owe the state more time in the pen, Rampart. How 'bout I make you fulfill that request first?" suggested the man.

"Well," Mother Rampart began as she slipped a hand into the pocket of her tunic, "see no evil, speak no evil!"

Rampart tossed a dust-like substance at the man. He

side-stepped the particles but not the coffee table next to him. He stumbled over the table, onto the floor as Mother Rampart vanished into obscurity.

"Damn Rampart!" the man said from his seated position.

The collector released Julissa and ran downstairs as Julissa gasped for air. Her boisterous inhale was enough to startle the unconscious collector near Judy's room. As the other collector reached the base, she was intercepted by the man on the ground floor. The collector attempted to strike, but she was in for a rude awakening: a missed swing from the right, ducked one from the left, and received an uppercut that lifted her from the floor. Her landing was less than graceful, as she rolled her left ankle and crashed to the floor. The collector upstairs began clambering to her feet.

"You hit like a bitch. And you smell like one, too," the grounded collector mocked.

"Yes, today's ass whipping brought to you, courtesy of Curve," the man teased.

The male proceeded to the stairwell as he brushed past the plunged collector. Julissa, now curious about her mystery teammate, clawed at the floor to pull herself toward the staircase. The other collector utilized the banister to aid in returning to her feet. As she gazed upon the man coming up the stairs, her eyes nearly bolted from her head.

"Ya-ya-You...You ain't suh-suh-suh-posed to...you ain't supposed to be here," the collector uttered nervously.

"I beg to differ, miss. I was invited, how about you?" the familiar voice asked.

Julissa looked up at the man and shared the shock of

her antagonist: *Franc*!! How in the hell did he get here? And right on time? Julissa didn't really care. She knew if Franc was there, she wouldn't be losing a child tonight. Her renewed confidence elevated her from her supine position and locked her view on the standing collector.

"Yo, Lisa. Heard you had a few unwanted guests. How's the baby?" Franc articulated while maneuvering up the stairs.

Julissa nodded, indicating things were fine. The collector between them turned to Julissa, now startled that someone was behind her and made a beeline toward Ju. Franc wanted to cut off the collector, but the other made her way upstairs and clung to his ankle. Julissa, not to be taken off guard, dipped the clutches of the charging collector, wrapped her arms around their thighs, and rolled her weight into the banister. The collector fell headfirst into the railing and now lay unconscious, again. The remaining collector slit Franc's calf with the knife cloaked in her sleeve.

"What in the actual fuck!!" Franc screamed, pulling his leg away.

Franc lifted his foot and attempted to plow it back into the breastplate of the last collector, but she dodged his kick, struck him to the scrotum, and drove her left elbow through his chin as she rushed back upstairs. When she reached the top, she locked eyes with Julissa. They matched strides toward one another until their hands were braced onto one another's shoulders. With her mate still on the floor near the banister, the collector shifted her momentum toward the casing, nearly knocking Julissa over it. She did enough to get Julissa's feet off the ground with one leg over the guardrail. Julissa wrapped the inside leg in the rail to maintain balance. The collector took no exception to this as she punched Julissa in the mouth, then the chest. Julissa's leg unraveled from the railing as her shoulder landed on the other side of the banister before plummeting toward the floor. Franc was already down-stairs to catch her but dove for good measure. PLUNK! Julissa landed and rolled right off Franc's back. The impact from the fall was enough to render her motionless.

The collector tried to wake her fallen peer, but it was of no use. A few slaps to the face and some choice words were not enough to draw a breath from her partner. She looked down the hall to Judy's room. The collector arose from her crouched position as she let her comrade's shiftless body plop along the floor. She trampled back to the room door and banged on it five times, loudly.

"Get up, you little bitch, and open this door," she began. "I mean, little dear. Please come open the door for Mother. Don't make me huff and puff and tear your world down!"

"You don't sound like my mommy," Judy called.

"Oh no, I am far superior to her. I *broke her*. But don't worry, we can share my mother. My mother is the greatest of all," the collector taunted.

"You broke her? You hurt my mommy?" Judy repeat-ed, clearly confused.

"Yes. She was weak. And I won't let that happen to you, little dear. We're going to make you strong! Now open the door so I can introduce you to your new and improved mommy," the collector suggested.

Judy sobbed at the thought of Julissa's demise. She fell to the floor in her room and packed herself into a fetal position. The collector, clearly growing impatient, backed away from the door before running full speed into it with her shoulder. She bounced off the door and held her newly battered shoulder with her right hand. She turned her back to the door and drove her foot into it twice. As she became weary, she dropped her head and cussed at herself before she brought her eyes up again. She faced the door before feeling a hand on the back of her neck. She gulped as the hand drove her face first into the door and then flung her back towards the stairs. As her lifeless body slid across the carpeted floor, she realized her attacker was Franc. She slowly gathered back to her feet and as she charged for the door again, she was speared in her obliques by a highly pissed Julissa. Julissa climbed on top of the collector and battered her until Julissa's hands were bloodied. Franc saw this onslaught and wrestled Julissa away.

"That's enough, Julissa!" Franc called to her while dragging her away.

"It won't be enough until my baby is safe. It ain't gonna ever be enough!" Julissa shouted back.

"Walk away, Julissa. It's over. We'll get the police to get these two out of your house and pick up some of this stuff in the meantime," Franc ordered.

"Didn't one of them slice your leg open? You should have let me kill her when I had the chance. These bitches are just gonna come back and try to collect again.

"You were given the task of being a giver of life. Don't sour it by trying to take one," Franc preached.

Julissa reluctantly followed Franc's request. Before conceding, she pulled her hand away from him and nailed him in the shoulder. As she walked back towards Judy's door, Franc paced near the stairs and looked over the guardrail. He took one more look at Julissa as she let Judy out of the room and held the child in her arms. They disappeared back into the chambers as Franc nodded his head and brought one collector down the steps. Julissa held Judy near, with tears still streaming down her face.

"What did those people want, Mommy? Why were they trying to break the door down? I thought they broke you!" Judy asked.

"They wanted you, baby. They know how precious you are and how much you mean to me. They just can't make anything as lovely as you, so they tried to take my one and only," Julissa attempted to assure.

The flashback comes to a halt as Julissa is interrupted. The nurses re-enter the room where she, Cortissa, and the unnamed infant remain. Julissa is still in shock, and tears, following Renaldo's departure from Westbank Medical Center. She knew what she had done, and could no longer deny, with the evidence currently cooing in her arms. She looked down at her baby boy again as Cortissa called out to her:

"Lisa! Do you not hear the hospital staff talking to you? Are you going to name the child or are you waiting on Naldo to come back?"

"No," Julissa squeaked through her tears.

"No what, dear?" Mrs. Cortissa Monroe asked curiously.

"No, I'm not waiting. I don't think he's coming back," Julissa admitted.

"Why the hell wouldn't he be coming back? What happened that fast?" Cortissa inquired.

Julissa glared at Cortissa faintly. Almost as if she were looking *through* her. Julissa sunk into the hospital pillow as she looked down and cracked a small smile at her son. She remembered the journey of how he came to be and knew she would have to protect him the same way she protected Judy. Though thoughts of The Brood concerned her, she couldn't deny the joy it gave her to witness the cracking wisps in her son's eyes.

"Mrs. Brown. Are you ready to name the little bundle of joy?" the attendant asked.

"I'm sorry, ma'am. Yes, I believe I am ready," Julissa conceded.

"Okay, what's his first name?" the attendant queried.

"Peerless," Julissa answered.

"Oh, that's unique. What about the middle name?" the attendant continued.

"Paul!" Cortissa began. The attendant and Julissa looked at Cortissa, who then continued, "What? I'm telling my phone to call your father."

"You know what," Julissa stated toward the attendant. "Paul will do just fine."

"Guess what, baby, the middle name is gonna be Paul," Cortissa repeated into the phone.

"And Brown as the last name?" the attendant assumed.

"No, not Brown," Julissa clarified.

"No?! Okay. Then what shall it be?" the attendant requested.

Julissa paused momentarily, looking up from her newborn to her mother. Her leg began to shake a bit while she flashed a nervous grin. Julissa released a sigh before saying

"Tatiano."

Cortissa's phone fell to the floor and slid a couple inches past her feet. She looked over to Julissa, completely baffled. Julissa glared at her mother and didn't spare a word of explanation, feeling the approved print would be self-explanatory.

Chapter 2

Rude Awakening

Renaldo awakens. He blinks his eyes several times, but the view doesn't change: Utter darkness. "DUH-DOOMP" Renaldo hears as his body lifts then crashes back down on the surface. *He's in a car?* He now hears the engine as it continues to accelerate down what could only be a road in The Boot due to the constant wallops he felt below. This sadly provided some form of temporary relief. Renaldo started to breathe a little heavier when he realized he was bound and trapped. DUH-DOOMP! This time Renaldo rolls onto his back but bangs his head on an unfamiliar object. The impact disorients him again as he tries to decipher why he is in the trunk of this vehicle instead of driving his own.

"This ain't so bad—a little bumpy for my taste, but you get what you pay for, I guess," he joked.

Renaldo notices a smidgen of light coming from his left. He looks over to see there is a slight patch of moonlight sneaking through the surface. Renaldo's curiosity reaches a climax. He attempts to swing his feet toward the light but misjudges the construction of the trunk.

"DOMP!" His feet sound off against the frame of the vehicle.

The car begins to decelerate on the highway, until it reaches a tire-screeching halt on the shoulder of the road. Renaldo feels a sense of reprieve since he will come face-to-face with his captor. He hears the trunk pop open, but the sliver's not enough to observe any light. He forgets he is blindfolded, until the wind from the trunk being lifted violently registers in his ears.

"Who are you? What the hell do you want from me?" Renaldo pleaded.

There was a brief silence, before Renaldo heard an object being moved near him. As the sound disappeared, so did Renaldo's nervousness. Then, Renaldo's face is rudely greeted by the blunt object, rendering him coma-tose again. The trunk closes as the abductor returns to the driver's seat and continues the voyage.

Hours later, Renaldo stirs with a splitting headache. He looks around to find himself seated in a tiny booth. He looks to his left, realizing he has full access to his vision now, though a little blurred. He sees a solid wooden wall with a screened box. The seat he occupies resembles a miniature pew. He scales the wall with his hand to lift his torso marginally.

"Do you have something to confess, son?" a voice asks from the other side.

"Wh-what? Who asked that?" Renaldo requests.

"I am but a vessel. If you have anything you would like to profess to your Lord and savior, this is an opportune time," the voice responds.

"This...is...a confessional? Am I in a church? Or some reality TV show?" Renaldo pondered.

"I assure you, son, there is no camera. Just you, me, and your thoughts," the voice reassured.

"How? Why? Why am I here?" Renaldo asked.

"Maybe someone wanted to help you relieve a burden," the voice answered.

"Why *here*? Why now? Why *to you*?" Renaldo fired.

"Well, it's possible I could help you with your indiscretion, considering you helped rid me of mine," the voice concluded.

Renaldo did a double take as he stared at the screened portion box, separating him from the man he babbled to. He was curious about the appearance of a man he allegedly aided. As Renaldo leaned forward, the man slid a small sheet forward, blocking the square. Renaldo's eyes rolled to the back of his head as he reclined into his seat. Renaldo laughed to himself as he winced and grimaced, trying to find some form of consolation between his hurting head and the hard bench.

"Why so shy, sir? I usually like to accept my 'thank yous' in person. Makes it real to me, y'know?" Renaldo prodded.

"Oh son, be not in a great hurry to see me. I am but a vessel. Who I am does not matter to you. You should be more concerned with who *you* are," the gentleman persuaded.

"But I have no question about who I am. You and I both seem to know me. The real mystery is: *who...are...YOU*?!" Renaldo exclaimed.

"Perhaps," the gentleman began, "perhaps you are correct son. Maybe knowing who I am would help you know what it is you have DONE!"

The sheet that once covered the screened area is quickly pulled back as the gentleman leaned into view. The gentleman turns to his right and peeks at Renaldo through the partition. As Renaldo leans forward again and turns to his left, he discovers a fairer-skinned male with a peppery mustache. As he leans against the screen, he notices the guy is older and dons slicked back hair that reaches the middle of his neck. The clothing is hard to decipher as everything the gentleman is wearing is dark and the screen compromised the visuals. Renaldo lies back after viewing the gentleman, knowing he has seen him somewhere, but uncertain of where or why.

"I'm sorry, you're going to have to remind me of your name. Your face seems somewhat familiar, but I don't know why," Renaldo admitted.

"Don't be sorry, son. We were only briefly introduced. We did not meet under the best circumstances," the gentleman advised.

"(Sigh) In my line of work, it hardly ever is," Renaldo chimed.

"Understood, youngster. Although, I don't believe we met while you were on the job. At least, I hope the demise of an individual was not a part of the job for you. You are sworn to serve and protect, and that would extend to your friends, I would hope," the man stated matter-of-factly.

Renaldo's eyebrows crinkled. He tried to open them widely but pressure from wincing made his head pound. The dim light within the booth may have been his only respite as he sat dazed and confused. He recalled the features of the older man in the other stall but was having the darndest time recalling where they met. Renaldo contemplated whether trying to recall such a trivial thing was increasing his pain.

"Sir, you have anything for pain? I kind of have a splitting headache," Renaldo inquired.

"Ahh, yes. Sorry about that, young blood. My driver's methods are a bit...barbaric. Perhaps he didn't believe you would come quietly," the man stated.

"All he had to do was ask," Renaldo joked.

"Hahaha," the man laughed. "Well, you are a brave man indeed. Very few men would willingly go before their panel and atone for their transgressions."

"You have anything prescribed for pain, sir? Once things clear up, I might be able to recall who you are, and ultimately, why I should be here," Renaldo requested.

"I shall grant you the potion that heals all wounds: Time! I too have taken a dose of it to deal with the burden you rid me of," the man advised.

"We've been going in circles about this for a while now. I am no closer to knowing why I'm here or what I helped you with. Don't you think it would be easier if you just...told me?" Renaldo pleaded.

"Silly me, Mr. Brown. I was under the impression that not much got past you. *Nothing more than what you'd allow,*" the man admitted.

Just as the man completed his statement, Renaldo heard a door close nearby. He bowed forward to look into the screened area and found the other side bare. He shook his head and lay back onto the hard bench. Renaldo peered to his right to find what he believed to be a narrow door. Renaldo pushed the door, but it wouldn't budge.

"HELLLLLLLLLLLLLPPP!!" Renaldo screamed to dead silence.

Renaldo shuddered as his head began to ring. He felt a tingle in the depths of his belly just before he vomited onto the booth floor. Renaldo attempted to clean the rim of his mouth with his shirt, but he noticed red streaks around the cusp. He hurled more of what should have been noth-ing more than hospital food from hours prior. *In those hours where he thought he was on top of the world. Hours before it all came tumbling down!*

Chapter 3

Lie to Me

Julissa rushes down the road after leaving her parents' house. She's furious she hasn't heard from Renaldo. Where could he have gone all night, without a trace? Julissa speeds along I-10 until she reaches the Westbank. Her mind is racing nearly as fast as her car. "We have a damn daughter to think about. Why won't he at least think about *her*?" Julissa questions. Julissa exits I-10 in Metairie to look for Renaldo in the only place she believes he'll be.

As she exits Clearview Parkway, she makes her way to the Moon Light Apartments. Renaldo frequented this complex to work with a close friend. Julissa was no stranger to the location, but she had only come here in the past with Renaldo. As she parked her car in the lot, she prayed her husband would be there as he had before. If Renaldo was here, he was safe, he was cared for, *he was alive.* Julissa peered at the streetlight nearby, which flickered as fireflies wove in and out of its gleam. She slammed the car door shut while strutting up the walkway and into the building. Julissa sashayed upstairs and took a right. She walked down to door number 524 and banged heatedly.

The occupant swung the door open, bewildered by Julissa's presence, especially considering the time of her arrival. He wore a light blue wifebeater and navy track pants. He donned a fresh light brown stain on his shirt, probably from whatever aroma escaped into the hall. He leaned into the door seal as Julissa commenced her frantic clamor.

"Where is he, Franc? Is Naldo here?" Julissa asked.

"No. I don't know. He's not here. Did you call him?" Franc reacted.

"The hell do you think?! He didn't pick up. He even sent me to voicemail, which he only does when working a case. But—here you are. So, where the hell is he?" Julissa questioned.

"Julissa, you are aware that there are some cases Renaldo works without me, right?" Franc asked.

"Yeah, but I would assume you know which ones he needs you for and when he is working them," Julissa stated while slanting her head.

"Most times I do, but sometimes I don't. What's going on? Where's Judy?" Franc inquired.

"She's with my parents. I didn't want her to witness me killing her father. Didn't want to doom the child with years of therapy," Julissa scoffed.

"Girl, what you round here acting crazy fa'? You know if he is on a case, he probably got his phone on vibrate so he won't disrupt the scene. You know this," Franc defended.

"What I know is I called and he ain't answering. What I know is he gonna come home tonight and tell me he was 'busy' or something like that and there won't be much more discussion about it. What I know is—," Julissa stopped.

Julissa's eyes turned to the door frame. She fought off the inevitable as long as possible. She carried it with her from Destreland, to Harrahan, and now to Metairie. The heft of her load became insufferable, crash landing upon her psyche in one fell swoop. Julissa's dismay oozed from her pores like the skin's natural oils.

"—I'm tired," Julissa finished, hanging her head.

Franc witnessed her apparent fatigue, taking it upon himself to provide assistance. Franc knew he could not send Julissa back into the streets in her turmoil, as her threat on Renaldo's life may not be satire. He knew he had to brighten her spirits, or at the least, prevent her from performing in her lowliest state. He looked down at Julissa as she grazed her fingertips across her forehead repeatedly.

"You, umm, you like Yaka Mein? I'm sure you did some running around before you came out this way. You had a chance to eat?" Franc probed while pointing to the kitchen.

"I love Yaka Mein! Do you know what you doing? I've seen people mess up Yaka Mein," Julissa replied.

"I might know a lil' something 'bout it. I know my way round that kitchen, baby. I ain't no new jack, ya heard me?" Franc defended.

"Well okay, Mr. Tatiano. You have a name that sounds kind of *Boyardee-ish*. I'm gonna talk about you if your food tastes like meat and broth though!" Julissa pestered.

"Well, come on in and I'll let you judge for yourself. I've never been one to shy away from an honest challenge," Franc complied.

Franc steps aside so Julissa can enter. He walks

through his living room and dining area directly into the kitchen. Franc motions for Julissa to have a seat at the dining room table while he prepares her plate. Julissa looks around Franc's moderately decorated abode and begins to feel somewhat better. The parts she can see are well-kept but presented only a few photos featuring Franc and possible family members. She smells the roux from tonight's menu, but she also smells a slightly sweetened wooden aroma resonating from the living room as well.

"Here, I didn't want to imply anything by giving you too much. You are more than welcome to get seconds, if you want," Franc declared while placing her plate on the table.

Julissa obliged and took a scoop of the noodles from the bowl. She dipped the spoon again to gather up some of the egg and a portion of the beef. Julissa lifted the spoon to her lips and sipped the broth to test the temperature. Julissa then blew on the remnants of her spoon prior to ingesting.

"Shit!" Julissa said.

"Is it bad? Is it too hot?!" Franc fretted.

"No," Julissa began as she wiped broth from her lips. "This is actually pretty good. Your mama must have taught you that."

"Nah, man. My mama used to make some bomb ass Yaka Mein, but I done researched this here and made my own," Franc boasted.

They laughed as they continued to enjoy their dinner. The more Franc engaged Julissa in conversation, the less she considered Renaldo and his whereabouts. As the scent of the dinner faded, the subsequent fragrance became more pungent. She lingered in Franc's ambiance as if he was the aroma itself. She wasn't sure why, but Julissa became increasingly relaxed over time.

"What is that lovely smell? And I don't mean the food. It's something...minty," Julissa interviewed.

"Oh, that's the candle up there by the bar. One of my personal favorites: cedarmint," Franc answered.

"Well, that shit smells like Christmas!" Julissa exclaimed.

"Glad you like it. I know what to get y'all for the holidays now. Now I just have to worry about Judy," Franc clamored.

"Well for now, you can't go wrong with anything related to princesses," Julissa confirmed.

"Well, that narrows it down," Franc said, sarcastically.

"Anyway, why are you up here watching these mystery shows? Don't you get enough of this in real life?" Julissa wondered.

"Well," Franc began, "I guess I like keeping my mind sharp, y'know? I can always learn some more techniques. A man with a student mentality will always improve."

"A what you say? What is that?" Julissa asked.

"The student mentality? That's when you know that there are things you *don't know* and you decide to seek knowledge rather than indulging in self-ignorance," Franc detailed.

"Oh, okay. Kind of like how you made the Yaka Mein? You sought the deep knowledge of beef and broth?" Julissa teased.

"Yeah, yeah. Joke if you want, but there is no denying the wealth of self-investment," Franc preserved.

"Naw, I guess I can't front on that," Julissa conceded.

Julissa was admittedly impressed with Franc's frame

of mind. *Intrigued even.* She was tempted to pick his brain further. Julissa was curious about the inspirations for Franc's décor, as she considered modifications for her own home. Then her phone rang.

"Maybe it's Renaldo!" Julissa said aloud, scrambling for her phone. Much to her chagrin, the caller ID read otherwise.

"Yes, ma'am?" Julissa answered coldly.

"Is everything okay? Did you find him?" Cortissa asked.

"Honestly, I was hoping *you were* him. I hope whatever case he is working on won't take him all night. Worse thing that can happen is he finds what he's looking for and has to write a report," Julissa expressed.

"Well, dear, you know how I feel about that, but I won't harp on it. Are you okay? Seems like you are in better spirits than when you brought Judybug over," Cortissa noticed.

"I really was doing a little better, mom. Went by a friend and ate some good food. Just was hoping Naldo was done with whatever it is he's wrapped up in," Julissa revealed.

"Well, darling, if you like it, I'll tolerate it. Call me or Daddy whenever you're on your way here or when you make it home," Cortissa shared.

"Will do," Julissa agreed as she hung up the phone.

Julissa put her phone to the side. She peered at Franc as he remained seated in the dining area, watching the television. She wondered *"Isn't this like working at home for you?"* Julissa then picked up her phone to check on Renaldo one last time. It rang a couple of times, and then there was silence.

"Hel-hello?" Julissa answered.

"Hey, babe. What's going on?" Renaldo asked.

"I been trying to reach you all night. I went looking for you, and of course, I couldn't find you!" Julissa expressed.

"You know how the job is, baby. Sometimes I get so wrapped up in what I'm doing, I don't even hear the phone," Renaldo spilled.

"Oh, what kind of case you working on? Anything big?" Julissa questioned.

"Yeah, yeah. Me and Franc got our work cut out for us with this one," Renaldo said.

"Oh, *do y'all*?" Julissa entertained.

"Yeah, this seems like one of those cases that requires some extra man hours," Renaldo began. He paused for a second to discreetly address someone nearby.

"Babe, let me call you back later. Seems like we got more digging to do," Renaldo finished.

The phones disconnect before Julissa can utter another syllable. She looks befuddled, knowing that some portion of Renaldo's statement was untrue. *Franc was sitting right in front of her* and looking particularly good. She must have misunderstood what Renaldo said, she thought to herself. There is no way he just implied Franc was with *him*. Did he? Her uplifted spirits subsided as she was returned to her initial somber demeanor.

Chapter 4

To Chore or To Cherish?

"What was that all about?" Franc requested.

"You...uhm...you have a twin brother?" Julissa prodded.

"Nooo," Franc answered, confused. "What makes you ask that?"

"I talked to Renaldo," Julissa stated numbly.

"Oh, really! Well, that's good, right? Now you know where he is. You can rest easy," Franc misspoke.

"Not quite," Julissa murmured.

"Hnah? What did he say?" Franc asked.

"He said that y'all were working on a case," Julissa continued.

"Oh," Franc paused "He must be syphoning info."

"Oh yeah," Julissa judged, "Precisely which case is he working on?"

"Umm...I uh...I really ain't sho'," Franc acknowledged.

"Yeah, that's what I thought!" Julissa commented.

Julissa picked up her phone hurriedly and rose from the couch. Franc noticed Julissa's fervor and pushed his chair back from the table. The scraping from the chair was enough to draw Julissa's attention during her attempted exodus. Franc lifted his hands to shoulder level and stomped toward her.

"Whoa, nah! What's the problem, Ju? It was all peachy a minute ago, now you trippin'," Franc interrogated.

Julissa squinted her eyes at Franc before scooting toward him. She rotated her neck and poked her left index finger directly into Franc's chest. Julissa held back tears.

"Renaldo said he was so entrenched in the case that he didn't feel his phone ringing. Then he said that *y'all* had your work cut out for ya and it was going to take some extra time to work on the case!" Julissa cried.

"Well, maybe he—" Franc began.

"I don't wanna hear that shit, Franc! He sat up there and told me a boldfaced lie. I could hear him talking to somebody in the background and I know damn well it wasn't you. Don't you sit up here and defend Naldo and whatever it is he thinks he is doing. DON'T YOU DARE!" Julissa declared hysterically.

Julissa dipped her head as the tears began to roll down her face. She turned away so Franc wouldn't see. Her head slowly trembled side-to-side as her right leg quivered. Franc, well aware of Julissa's pending waterworks, headed toward the bar to secure some napkins. Julissa delayed prior to dashing for the door. Franc ripped a paper towel off the roll and sprinted toward a dejected Julissa. She was close enough to reach for the door, but Franc grabbed Julissa by her shoulders and tilted her back slightly. Julissa barely maintained her balance from the unexpected jolt, but his support helped her recover from a near stumble.

Franc stretched his arm past Julissa's shoulder so she would notice the napkins. Julissa reluctantly accepted the gesture. She crumpled the napkins in her grasp as she brought both hands to her face, whimpering into her palms.

"Maybe it ain't what you think. You don't need to go back out into the world in your current condition. It might lead to rash decisions and things you'll have to apologize for later. Just chill," Franc advised.

"I'll be fine. Just let me be on my way, Franc. This is not your problem," Julissa implored.

"If you walk out there and do something you live to regret, that being the best-case scenario, it will be my problem because you could have cooled off," Franc reasoned.

Julissa raised her eyes to Franc's. She inhaled deeply and exhaled just as profoundly. Her lips were tucked as she peered through her messy bangs. Julissa removed the hair from her view before addressing Franc again.

"Look, I don't know what the man is doing; but if he'd rather be God-knows-where doing God-knows-what, he can have it! I can't keep somebody who don't want to be kept. That's attention I could be giving to our child," Julissa opted.

"Ju, you don't know that. You do know he works hard on his cases. He's dedicated to his craft," Franc defended.

"So dedicated, *he hardly noticed the clock* was missing from the wall. Took him a week to realize it was sitting on the coffee table and a couple days after that to ask if I wanted him to hang it back up," Julissa spouted.

"It was a small clock," Franc endorsed.

"The clock may be one thing. But for him to come in that night and be completely oblivious to everything? He didn't even notice how achy my body was the next morning. It's almost as if he didn't care. *He doesn't care*,"

Julissa settled.

"Of course he cares, Julissa. I don't know where his mind was that night, but I don't believe it blocks out years of good," Franc claimed.

"You ever feel unwanted, Franc? You ever wake up next to someone and wonder if they meant to be there?" Julissa pondered.

"Ehh, not so much since my early 20s. Even then, sometimes I would wake up wondering if I was supposed to be there myself," Franc joked.

Julissa chuckled at Franc's wit. She wiped below her nose and looked up at him. Julissa shook her head as she placed her forehead into an unoccupied hand.

"What I mean, fool, is have you ever wondered if someone was with you out of love or obligation?" Julissa clarified.

"Well," Franc opened, "if someone does love you, should it not be their obligation to stick around?"

"In a manner of speaking, yes. However, love is purest when it feels like the cure; instead of the chore," Julissa rendered.

"The cure? What is it that makes you sick in the first place?" Franc questioned.

"You, Mr. Tatiano, are a trip," Julissa stated as she placed the napkin into her pocket. "A cure can be spiritual as well as medicinal. The love that is cure will uplift you; that of chore may bring you to your knees. The chore type of love is the one you just do, because you must. That of cure is the one you mustn't go without!"

Franc was taken aback by Julissa's account. He was immensely enthralled by the clear differences in the art of amour. Julissa leaned her head to the side, peering plainly at Franc. Julissa held herself securely with one arm resting on top the other. Each set of fingertips caressing the opposite elbow.

"Well, lil' mama, I can't argue with that. But for real though, ain't no way Naldo's feeling like you are a chore. I just can't see it," Franc denied.

"Okay. Well, tell me how you figure?" Julissa challenged.

"Man, that boy tell me how you always look out for him and make sure he is taken care of on multiple levels: physically, spiritually, mentally, emotionally...all that! He says you are a great mother to Judy, and you try to fill in where he is lacking instead of y'all just occupying the 'traditional roles,'" Franc proclaimed.

"He—He really said all that?" Julissa marveled.

"Here and there, in so many words," Franc revealed.

Julissa's face showed contemplation of progress, before she turned away. She tussled with her thoughts briefly before addressing Franc again.

"Well, it's worse than I thought," Julissa wilted.

"*Hnah*? What you mean? It's obvious he knows what he has," Franc gathered.

"Did you hear what you said? Everything you just stated was about what *I do* for him. Not one word you mentioned highlights how he reciprocates or shows appreciation *for me*. He may know what he has, but what has he been doing lately to preserve it?" Julissa summarized.

"I can't say I have the answer to that," Franc conceded.

"I understand, it's not fair to ask you about what another man would or should do. So how about you?" Julissa directed.

"What about me? What ABOUT *me*?" Franc inflected.

"If you had someone who supported you the way I support Renaldo, what would you do to show your gratitude? Granted, I know I get on his nerves occasionally, maybe more than occasionally, but some disagreements are to be expected," Julissa digressed.

Franc leaned his head as he gazed upon Julissa. He placed both hands to his sides and fully peeped her face. He noticed how she curled her bottom lip while staring back at him. He saw the dried trails of tears and noticed how instead of blemishing her appearance, it made Julissa glisten. She beamed, even in his dimly lit dwelling. After witnessing her suffering through a personal storm, he instantly recognized that Julissa shimmered brighter than anything around. She replicated any other precious gem: *Complex. Well-rounded. Stunning!*

"If I...If I had support so abundant...I would...do my best not to break it with my indiscretions. Instead, I would brace it. *Embrace* it. *Fortify. Cherish* it," Franc yielded.

Franc graced his index finger and thumb along Julissa's chin. She tilted her chin upward. He then cupped Julissa's lower jawline between his thumb and fingers as he guided her closer. Julissa draped her arms over Franc's shoulders, tugging downward along the back of his neck. Their lips intertwined gently, at first. They detached their faces momentarily following the initial peck. They locked eyes in their perplexed state, each silently desiring permission to go further. They inaudibly agreed to cross oral orifices once again. This time the smooches were smooth yet deliberate. The inevitable was now *the intentional.*

Julissa cusped Franc's face in both hands. Franc's hands moved from the small of her back to the cup of her buttocks. He picked Julissa up with an aided hop. They continued their sanctioned lip-lock as Julissa's inner thighs bordered Franc's pelvic crest. As Franc placed her against the wall, he experienced a moment of clarity. *What have I done? This is another man's wife. My good friend's wife!* Franc reversed his momentum as he reluctantly tore his face from hers. Julissa opened her eyes once she bore the cold air on her lips. She slid down from Franc's waist as she used her digits to swab her mouth. Julissa looked at Franc and let out a slow exhale as she located her phone and stormed to the door. Franc stared at the floor until Julissa passed him to exit the apartment. They exchange a lasting glance, and without a word, Julissa departed from Franc's place. As she walked toward the staircase, Franc stood in his doorway and ogled until she was out of sight.

A brief smile graced Julissa's lips as she thought back to that day. As she waited for Peerless' next feeding, she recalled the moment he became a possibility. More than anything now, she missed Franc's warm personality, heart ...and lips. Julissa looked in a mirror across the room and took notice of the white streak in her hair. She found it to be peculiar: and she loved it! She joked to herself that it would limit her choices in hairdos, but it was something signature, nonetheless. As Peerless woke, Julissa scooped him up in her arms and danced with him, while she sung to calm his tears. Peerless didn't carry on for long. The sound of his mother's voice secured him more than his receiving blankets. Little did he know, this was just the first layer of mother's fortification...

Chapter 5

The Scenic Route

It's drizzling in Tunneltown. The sun called in sick for the day. The sky's obscured by clouds. Customarily, this early in the day, the parking lot at *Nina's* is empty. Oddly, there are three vehicles present: Lucinda's blue Impala, a black marked Tunneltown Police Department SUV, and a white Chevy Camaro, property of the Gretna Police Department. Sitting at the bar are three individuals, but none with libations. Not solely due to it being midday or the location being technically closed; it was more so because the only person not on the clock during this meeting...was the bartender herself.

Lucinda Maroney, the most beloved bartender of *Nina's*, was asked to fulfill a request that wouldn't involve inebriation, despite how she may feel afterwards. She sat there with two men, both familiar faces, none ever propositioning her the way she had been today. *Nina's* was a lowkey establishment where locals went to jam out to oldies but goodies. They didn't have the trouble that some of the more rambunctious clubs experienced, largely due to the lack of appeal to younger audiences. The two men who sat before her stopped in for drinks occasionally, *off duty of course,* but everything about this meeting was far from the norm: no music, no spirits, and hardly any lights; aside from those close to the bar offsetting the lack of sunshine.

Lucinda sits in her usual location, behind the bar, while the two law enforcement representatives are separated by a couple of stools on the other side. Lucinda's flirtatious facade is nearly phantom under these circumstances. In fact, having to show up to work hours before she normally does makes her more sinister than seductive. The honey-blonde honey from around the way stands to be questioned on events that took place a few weeks prior.

The temperature on the other side of the table is a little—frigid. Though the event in question occurred in Tunneltown's jurisdiction, the result of said incident concluded an open case for Gretna P.D. *Or at least that's what the public was told.* However, after finding some discrepancies, Detective Rance McDonald is unconvinced the discoveries were entirely accurate. The two officers sit with the bartender who was present the night The Recluse was revealed, and apparently, killed. Rance has been mulling the peculiar events of that night for a few weeks, and personally, he suspects foul play.

"Well, Miss Maroney, I'm sure you are aware of why we asked you to come here today?" Rance asked.

"Cuz y'all ain't got nothing better to do than to bother a middle-aged black woman on her free time? Is that it? Should I keep guessing or nah?" Lucinda guessed.

"Not quite, Miss Maroney. We just had a few questions about the ruckus from a few weeks ago," Officer Morgan comforted.

"Officer, I run a bar. You gonna have to be more

specific as to your definition of 'ruckus' round here," Lucinda chimed.

"Surely, ma'am. We mean the shootings that took place in the rear section of your building here. Detective McDonald had some...concerns," Morgan clarified.

"Nothing a little liquor wouldn't help!" Lucinda joked.

"While I appreciate your vibrant humor, Miss Maroney, I believe the matter may be slightly more dire than that," said Rance.

"Who you telling? You know how hard it is to get my normal crowd back in here after something like that? We don't usually have any foolishness and carrying on. We play our old school music to keep those young punks from coming in here and ruining a good time," Lucinda admitted.

"Yes, ma'am, we are sorry for your losses; your customers and the business," Morgan empathized.

"Well, ain't you a sweetheart. I would give you a kiss, but your friend here might ticket me for fraternization," Lucinda mumbled sarcastically.

Rance snickered at Lucinda's comments as he pulled a small case out of his pocket and laid it on the bar. He then took out a manilla folder and placed it next to the case. Rance tapped the tip of his fingers on the desk twice before taking a deep breath and leaning back in the barstool. Lucinda rolled her eyes then shifted her head to the side. Officer Morgan let out a deep breath, perturbed he had to be there. Only thing remotely holding Morgan's interest on this gloomy day was Lucinda's sunny disposition.

"Miss Maroney, I am aware that some of the men who were shot that night were regulars at this establishment. Do you have any recollection of what led to their demise?"

Rance prodded.

"I have no idea. I was right here, serving drinks to the less problematic attendees," Lucinda poked.

"Yes, but were they ever up here in the front? Were any of the men involved employees here?" Rance proceeded.

"No"—Lucinda rolled her eyes—"none of them worked here."

"Miss Maroney, if this line of questioning is boring you, we could easily shut down the location for a few nights to conduct a 'more thorough' investigation to find the answers you are declining to give us," Rance threatened.

Lucinda shifted her eyes toward Officer Morgan as if to ask, "Is he serious?" Morgan read her gaze and simply nodded as he shrugged his shoulders. Lucinda reluctantly returned her sights to Rance as she delivered the cheesiest smile she could muster.

"Now why would you want to do that? An old gal like myself can't just be sitting at home all day and night. I might get cobwebs. Who is that gonna help?" Lucinda charmed.

"Well," Rance began "in that case, Miss Lucinda, I would like to ask about the one guy who may not have been as familiar to you, Detective Renaldo Brown."

"Re-what-doe who?" Lucinda responded.

"He was the gentleman that was here with Avon and Demone Lazlo. The man who is credited with finding The Recluse," Morgan clarified.

"Oh, the big news hero? Yeah, what of him?" Lucinda recalled.

"Would you happen to know why he was the assumed

object of ire amongst the patrons that night?" Rance asked.

"Probably was the best dressed. These older guys just let it all go once they reach a certain poi—"

"What he means, Miss Maroney, is did you hear anything that may have led to the dispute?" Morgan explained.

"The only parts of conversation I heard were with Avon and his cute ass friend he bought the drinks for. I assume that's the detective you're referring to. He kept calling him 'gumshoe' or some shit like that. Excuse my French," Lucinda described.

"Can you describe him to us? For clarity?" Rance requested.

"Well, he was about 5 foot 9, stocky but not too cocky. He was a sexy little Hershey's Kiss of Ebony Goodness. Had one of those nice fades and actually knew how to wear a tie," Lucinda recalled.

"Well, I'm not sure how cute he was, but I can venture to believe we are referring to the same guy," Rance advised.

"Comforting," Lucinda uttered.

"Can you tell me a little more about what transpired here at the bar?" Rance requested.

"If you must know, Avon and the detective were having a good time. Then Demone came over and started a conversation with his cousin. A little while after that, a few people dragged the nice-looking specimen to the back. I didn't know what they were doing, but I was hoping they left enough of him for me!" Lucinda described.

"Thank you for that vivid, yet disturbing, description of events. Did you happen to see or hear anything else?"

Rance interrogated.

"I was focused on the floor in front of me. I was the only one working that night. We weren't expecting such a 'raucous' crowd," Lucinda clarified.

"I'm sure you have been made aware that the men were shot. Did you happen to hear any gunfire yourself?" Rance dug.

"Yeah, it's the last thing I heard before I told everybody to get the hell out. I wasn't sure where it was coming from. I just knew where it bet' not be going!" Lucinda gathered.

Rance chuckled at Lucinda's recollection. Officer Morgan excused himself from the table to use the restroom. Rance then pushed the small case across the bar to Lucinda. He slowly removed the top from the remainder of the case. Within the case was none other than the identifying accessory of The Recluse: The Recluse Vision glasses. Lucinda looked less than impressed with the spectacles in the little blue case. She briefly inspected them before restoring her attention on Rance.

"Is this a joke? I tell you I didn't see what happened and you decide to bring me glasses? Well, ain't you just a sweet motherfucker!" Lucinda responded.

"Hnah? Wait, no Mi—" Rance initiated.

"I'm gonna tell you like I tell my daughter: If I was intended to see it all, God would have given me better vision. He gave me all these curves because he'd rather me be seen!" Lucinda gathered.

"Umm," Rance began, fighting back laughter, "I was just going to mention that these were found on Mr. Avon Lazlo. Did you happen to see anybody wearing these on the night in question?"

"No, dear. I think I would have noticed those if I saw

them on any face in here. Avon didn't usually wear glasses, at least not in here," Lucinda revealed.

"Hmm. I guess they do look a little...'peculiar.' I wonder what the hell they do," Rance divulged.

"Well, have you tried putting the motherfuckers on?" Lucinda suggested.

Rance was initially apprehensive to Lucinda's recommendation. A few seconds passed before he smirked and leaned the top of his noggin towards Lucinda while removing his spectacles. He smoothly slid his prescription glasses into his coat pocket while removing The Recluse Vision glasses from the case. Rance brought them to eye level, then carefully inspected each side of the frames, as he had so many times since the night he encountered them. He caressed the earpieces between his index tips and thumbs. He carefully inspected the notches he'd noticed along the handles. Rance slowly sauntered the glasses towards his face until they sat on his ears. He pushed the nose pads into position until the glasses were snug.

Rance searched along the outer handles for one of the notches that were nearly microscopic to the human eye. He slid his middle fingers along the side of the frame until he felt a tiny inconsistency in the center of the handle. He took his left hand and tried to find the spot parallel to it on the right. Rance watched Lucinda while pressing the two notches inward. The outer border of the lenses darkened. As he slightly angled his head to the left, he could see the objects along the wall moving in the outer frames.

"Whoa! This is some sci-fi grade shit here. What else can these do?" Rance marveled.

Rance began to slide his fingers forward near the

hinges. "There's another notch up here. I know there is," Rance thought to himself. He must have missed something. He reached the hinges with the tips of his fingers, to no avail. He decided to slide his fingers backward at a slower rate. *There it is*, he thought as he felt a nook along the left side within an ant's reach of the hinge. He brought his right hand along the other side until he found the accompanying notch. He forced them in until the outer lens now recorded a heat signature. As he turned to the opposite side of Lucinda, he was able to lock in on Officer Morgan. He viewed Morgan flushing the toilet and then walking toward them before he presumably turned up the hallway. Rance, who was clearly amazed by the specs, straddled the handles of his glasses again to turn off the Recluse Vision. He brought his hands back to the foreground, staring in utter disbelief of what he witnessed. Morgan re-entered the bar area. Rance glared at Morgan in utter disgust.

"Hey, did you wash your damn hands, man?! You ain't learn about biological warfare in the academy?" Rance accused.

Officer Morgan looked down at his hands, then back up to Rance. He took two slow steps backwards before eyeing Lucinda. Lucinda rotated her head to the side and stared at Morgan in disbelief. Officer Morgan noticed the displeasure of the room and disappeared into the hall from whence he came. Rance reluctantly placed the glasses back into the small blue case. As he closed the clasp, he noticed he had Lucinda's attention. Lucinda leaned on the counter with both elbows as she carefully inspected Rance.

"You have time on the weekends to come be a bouncer?" Lucinda asked.

Chapter 6

Meeting of Monsters

When Renaldo regains consciousness, his eyelids are slightly ajar due to the lone dangling lamp. The single light doesn't illuminate the room, but it occupies his head with a worrisome clang. He snaps his eyes shut, grimacing to himself. Renaldo's nostrils are infiltrated by a rank stench that makes his belly quake with discontent. The light flickers, then shuts off. Renaldo, noticing the absence of illumination, opens his eyes to view the dark room from his back. He hears something scraping along the cement floor in the distance. The light flickers back on as Renaldo looks over to his right and notices an iron bucket within reach. He extends his right arm and grasps the lip of the bucket between his palm and fingers. As he drags the pail toward himself, the light goes out again. Renaldo is startled by the darkness and tips the pail over unintentionally.

Renaldo's ring and pinky fingertips are touched by a wet and grainy substance. The rotten stench becomes robust as it bombards his senses. There went the sound of scraping concrete again. The shaving away of the surface lasts longer this time. When the sound ceases, the room is visible again. Renaldo has reluctantly solved two mysteries that plagued him in the dark: the bucket and the awful smell in the room. The bucket had previously been filled with vomit, presumably Renaldo's. It flowed toward him and already covered two fingers. He gasped for air as the foul odor overwhelmed him. His eyes began to water at the sight! Squeezing his eyes shut only increased the intensity of his migraine. Renaldo scrambled to his feet. He tried to identify other objects in the room, but the light flickered and failed again.

The scraping sounds are closing in. Ironically, the scraping seems to have shifted locations. It was now, *behind him*? "What the fuck is that?" Renaldo asked himself. He focused his ears to the sound and started to stumble toward it. The grinding across the floor was nearly rhythmic. When the light rekindles, Renaldo is standing 10 feet from another man. A freakish example of a man! The man's eyes are trained upon the floor as he breathes heavily in place. He's draped in nothing more than what looks like a grey curtain-turned-toga. His hair is sparse around the crown of his cranium, his skin bright but sullen, and his hands wrapped in chains at the wrist that are connected around the back of his toga. One hand drags behind the melancholy figure while the other holds the chains.

The beam depletes and the room is again filled with the loud scraping of metal upon the concrete base. Renaldo can hear the inaudible breathing of the man in between the rhythmic scraping. The light flickers and the character is within four feet. The man looks up with his seared mug and lets out a croak in Renaldo's direction. The light buzzes and ceases. Renaldo staggers backwards to avoid the unknown man. The grinding metal rings loudly regardless of where Renaldo retreated. The lamp brightens the room with a "pop." The figure is gone, but the scathing noise continues. The sound is coming from an unfamiliar region of the room. It's *behind him!* He somersaults to the left as he hears the croak of the figure's throat. Renaldo turns to his rear to notice the disfigured individual in mid-swing of his metal appendage. The hammerhead crashes viciously to the ground, cracking the surface it defaced.

The disfigured man realizes his mistake and locates Renaldo as he gives chase. The lamp shorts and Renaldo makes a beeline towards the mysterious figure to catch him off guard. Renaldo dives to tackle the man but completely whiffs. He didn't even touch the guy. *But he also couldn't hear him.* Then he hears a short scrape behind him and a chain nearby. Renaldo turns toward the echoes and lifts his hands in front of his face as a broad stick lands perfectly in his hands; the momentum from the swing still floors him. Renaldo quickly scurries back to his feet before the next blow comes crashing down. The core-shattering sound is followed by long grinding screeches across the base. Renaldo decides it's better to travel away from the sound than toward it, well, at least he thought. As Renaldo tries to blindly remember the little he observed about the room, he hears a door open. He then hears a call from a strangely familiar voice.

"Baron! Baron? Baron, are you in here cracking up the damn floors? Boy, get your ass out of here immediately. And why the hell is the light off?" asks the voice.

There was another croak and slurred speech. The room is once again illuminated, and Renaldo now recognizes the man in the doorway from the confessional. Renaldo was so fixated on finally figuring out who the man was, he nearly fell victim to the swing of the pale figure and his hammer. The hammer ricocheted off the brick wall as Renaldo grasped the shaft on the rebound. Renaldo and his adversary struggled for control of the sledgehammer until Renaldo was shoved back into a wall. The disfigured man screamed in Renaldo's face as he pressed the shaft of the sledgehammer against his chest. Renaldo grabbed ahold of the chains and wrapped one around the edge of the hammer. When Baron heard the sound, he inspected his weapon long enough to receive a headbutt from Renaldo. Baron let out a gurgled scream. He then batted Renaldo across the face with the butt of the sledgehammer. Renaldo grabbed his eye socket with both hands as he dodged an incoming strike. Renaldo then placed his back on the floor and sent the heel of his right foot through Baron's groin. Baron froze in mid-swing as he let out a babbled cry of sheer agony. Renaldo attempted to follow up with a left stomp, but Baron caught the ankle, swung Renaldo in a circle, and flung him onto the unforgiving concrete surface.

"Baron! That is enough, boy!" the older man shouted.

"CROOOOOOAK, Click-Click-Click-Click," Baron responded.

"Just go! I didn't ask you to come down here yet. Why are you so impatient?" the older gentleman asked.

Baron glared toward his elder, then back towards the flailed carcass of Renaldo. Baron raised his sledgehammer and began to march towards Renaldo. The senior gentleman strolled toward Baron while Renaldo watched in disbelief. Baron gathered the sledgehammer in both hands and circled his shoulders, about to gain momentum. The old fella stepped into Baron's path, preventing him from landing the life-altering blow to Renaldo's already battered body. Baron was infuriated by the old man's courtesy, until the man whispered something in his ear. Baron closed his eyes, took a deep breath, whipped the hammer over one shoulder, and slowly strolled out of the room. As Baron exited, the older man walked over to Renaldo. Once beside him, the older man kneeled next to Renaldo's shiftless physique. Renaldo squinted at the senior gentleman; he even lifted his head to get a closer look. Renaldo was no more confident about how he knew the man than he was in the booth. All he accomplished from the short inspection of the older man was seething neck pain.

"Wha-Who-Why the fuck was that guy?" Renaldo requested.

"Oh, Baron? Well, *he* is also a man freed of a burden, thanks to you," the geezer answered slyly.

"I assume no good deed goes unpunished around here," Renaldo retorted.

"Young man. You have much to learn. There are no treasures of this world that are painless. For one to gain, another must lose. It's the everlasting circle of life," the gentleman gathered.

"No disrespect to you sir, but after hearing that I have to believe you have never partaken in the pleasure formerly known as a threesome," Renaldo joked. The senior laughed at this account before he leaned down to Renaldo's eye level.

"Well, there's three of us here, as you can see. Maybe you can show an old dog some new tricks, hneh?" the senior whispered.

Renaldo's eyes widened more than they had in days as he rolled over to the shoulder opposite of the aged citizen. He pressed his palms into the ground and willed himself to his feet. *He moved too fast. Bad idea, detective.* Renaldo covered his eyes to stop the room from spinning. Bad idea again, as he was covering the wrong part of his body. He spewed more of his insides out into liquid form along the floor.

"Aww, come on, man! I gave you a bucket for a reason. Sheesh. You young boys can dish out jokes but you sure can't take 'em," the geezer reveled.

Renaldo wiped residue from the perimeter of his lips. He glared at the old man but froze when the light flickered. The lighting was dim for a short period. When the bulb returned to full capacity, Renaldo released a relieved sigh. The old man chuckled at the detective's newfound insecurity.

"That damn light doesn't bother you, old man?" Renaldo protested.

"No, young blood. Not nearly as much as it shakes you," the older man returned.

"You okay with that burn victim tearing away at the foundation of this building?" Renaldo wondered.

"But of course. He doesn't have a problem with me. He's quite fond of me, if I do say so myself," the older man gloated.

"I wish he was that smitten with me," Renaldo cited.

"Takes time, youngster. Me and Baron go way back. He's an okay guy once you get to know him," the older man defended.

"You want to formally introduce us someday? Preferably in a well-lit setting," Renaldo requested.

"Oh, you prefer to see him and not hear him. That's awfully complementary of you, sir," the older man chimed.

"It would be nice," Renaldo conceded.

"Well, I really must introduce him to you. He obviously already knows you," the older man stated.

"I've never met that guy before in my life. He doesn't look like anybody I ever encountered," Renaldo recalled.

"You ever 'encountered' the man who takes the taxes out of your check, detective?" the old man questioned.

Renaldo peeked at the old man through tightened eyes. His squinting was more so from confusion than brightness. He trampled to a corner of the room to decipher where he was. As he closed in on a shadowy outskirt, he noticed brown boxes sitting upon poorly painted steel shelving. One read "504," another read "225," then "337," and "985." Renaldo originally found the numbering system to be a bit peculiar, considering there was no identifiable sequence.

"From the looks of these boxes, I would assume you are the man who collects my taxes. Should I peek into the box marked 504?" Renaldo prodded.

"Take a crack at it, whippersnapper. If you find your name in that box, you owe L-O-R-D, not the I-R-S," the older man clarified.

"Fair enough. So, I guess I have not in fact met Mr. FICO himself," Renaldo conceded.

"Yet, you feel he has wronged you in some way. Because he takes something from you that you hold dear. Am I correct?" the gentleman dug.

"I guess you can say I feel cheated in a sense, yes. I often wonder where that large, yet minor, percentage of my money goes and why they think I can't use it," Renaldo admitted.

"So maybe you would understand that you took something important, valuable, theoretically irreplaceable from Baron. He is not as forgiving as myself. He's also a little younger and not as wise," the gentleman detailed.

"Oh yeah, that's right. I apparently did something to you too, didn't I. Funny thing is, I vaguely remember you, or someone who looks like you. I know damn well I haven't met that Baron fella," Renaldo defended.

The older man shrugged his shoulders at Renaldo's claim. He walked toward the wall where Renaldo once stood and nonchalantly pointed at the imprint from the sledgehammer. The older man searched about the room for some unknown object. He then walked toward an eclipsed portion of the room and stopped near one of the shelves. He knelt gingerly and reached under the shelf. The older man came back up with a brown-molded stick. Renaldo attempted to get closer to the old man to better ascertain what he possessed.

"Don't worry, whippersnapper. I think you had enough solid objects thrown at you for one day. This is just my special cane," the older man explained.

"I appreciate the courtesy, sir," Renaldo sarcastically began. "I didn't think a guy like you needed a cane. You got to Baron pretty fast before he could bash my head in."

"That was from pure instincts. *Or adrenaline.* Either way, I did what I had to preserve you, young man. We both owe you. I want to make sure you get exactly what you deserve for your troubles. No more, no less," the older man expressed.

"Well, how do we get out of here to a room with

better...accommodations. We obviously have much to discuss," Renaldo pried.

"Yes! We do, but first you have a task to complete. It must be handled immediately to preserve the sanctity of the room," the older gentleman explained.

The older man walked off into the shadows and beyond the shelves. Renaldo couldn't tell if he left or not. He looked up at the single lamp of the room and hoped it wouldn't faulter anytime soon.

"HEY! SIR! Where are you going?" Renaldo called into the abyss.

"Oh, sorry. I'm going get you some paper towels and Visqueen. I need you to clean that throw up off this floor before it gets in the vents. I'll be back," the older man yelled.

"Why can't I"—Renaldo called out before the door slammed—"come with..." Renaldo finished quietly.

Renaldo became frustrated with the older man's antics. He darted towards the dark corner where the older man disappeared prior to exiting the room. "There has to be a door over here," he thought to himself. Renaldo ran past the shelves and into the shadows. What Renaldo found would bring him resounding unrest: *no door*. He looked to his right and there was utter darkness. He looked to his left and found the same. *How did "Baron" and the old guy get out of this room*, he asked himself. Once again, Renaldo was left in obscurity. What Renaldo found to once be a cloak of comfort as a detective, now shrouded him in insecurity.

Chapter 7

Bittersweet Release

Julissa looks out on Mactown from the hospital window. Peerless is healthy and she is anxious to return home. Maybe Renaldo will be there, maybe he won't; either way, she is sick of hospital food and has been gazing at the same four walls for over four days. The newborn suffered a slight form of jaundice along with issues drinking from the bottle. His grandpa Paul joked it was because "the kid just don't suck." This comforted Julissa during those days she wondered if she'd ever leave. Once they found a different nipple to go on the bottle, Peerless fed successfully.

"Hey, little P.P. That's grandma's little P.P.," Cortissa fawned.

"Mom, would you just stop. Stop calling him that. You are going to give him a complex," Julissa instructed.

"Child, this my grandbaby. Besides, you named him Peerless Paul. You don't think I'm gonna call him Peerless every time I need his attention, do you?" Cortissa defended.

Julissa looked at her mother and rolled her eyes. Cortissa's phone rang. She stepped away from Peerless for the moment to answer. Julissa went to Peerless' bedside and smiled at him. He cooed at Julissa. There was a knock at the door just before it opened.

"Hey, Julissa, it's finally time for you and little Peerless to get out of here, honey!" Dr. Muhammed advised.

"Hey, Moo, baby, how you doing?" Cortissa addressed the doctor.

"I'm fine, dear. You can now enjoy your grandchild at your house, instead of being within the confines of the great Westbank Medical Center," Dr. Muhammed shared.

"Yes, he is 8 pounds, 7 ounces and has radiant eyes, child," Cortissa stated into her phone. "Okay, dear, I'll see you around at the club then, okay?" Cortissa said to Dr. Muhammed.

Julissa was taken aback by the description Cortissa provided of Peerless. As she gathered her things, she focused her attention on her mother's conversation. Cortissa's back was turned to the rest of the room, with her banter muffled.

"Come on, Julissa. Let me and Nurse Thatcher help you with some of your things. Seems that your mother is a tad...occupied," Dr. Muhammed offered.

"Umm, yeah. I think that will be fine. Thank you, guys," Julissa accepted.

Julissa sat in the wheelchair, while Nurse Thatcher pushed. Dr. Muhammed went over to Cortissa and nudged her shoulder. Cortissa acknowledged the doctor's alert and instantaneously picked up her items. They exited the room to the hall near the nurse's station. As the caravan moved toward the elevator, Cortissa continued her dialogue.

"You are going to love him. He is just the perfect little bundle of joy. And I ain't just saying that because he is my brand-new grandbaby," Cortissa bragged into the phone.

The listener on the other end laughed with Cortissa and made a quick comment. The group got on the elevator and descended the medical plaza. Cortissa remained on the phone as they reached the first floor.

"He has such precious features. He is the perfect blend of his mother and father. I hope he is as mighty as his father when he grows up," Cortissa described.

"Mama, who are you selling my son off to? Is this some kind of advertisement for a baby auction or something?" Julissa asked.

"Hnah?" Cortissa uttered after a few seconds.

"As you always would tell me, Mama, 'if you can hnah, you can hear.' WHO are you raffling Peerless off to?" Julissa repeated.

"Girl, you are so crazy. Don't interrupt people when they are on the phone. I'm talking to a friend of mine," Cortissa defended.

"Whatever you say, lady," Julissa forfeited.

Mr. Paul Monroe pulled the car underneath the breezeway. He hopped out to adjust the baby seat. As the party approached, Mr. Monroe reached toward Nurse Thatcher to retrieve Peerless.

"I got you all ready to go, lil' Paul, come on and ride with your Pau-Pau," Paul stated.

"Daddy, his name is Peerless. Are you ever going to call him that?" Julissa pleaded, jokingly.

"Well, his middle name is Paul, and for some reason, that is easier for me to remember," Paul clowned. Julissa found this to be especially hilarious.

"Daddy, wait!" Julissa pleaded. "Can you take me to the parking lot by the emergency room?"

"Sure, JuJu. What's going on over there? You feel

okay? Need some Tylenol or something?" Paul wondered.

"No, Daddy. I just wanted to check something. I ain't been able to reach Renaldo, and now his phone goes straight to voicemail," Julissa revealed.

"Well, JuJu, it's very possible he is still upset. He stormed out and told me he has no son. I could tell he was torn to pieces. You might have to give him some time, baby girl. Instead of being swollen with pride, he is probably deflated. Unfortunately, where pride goes, a man's mind may follow," Paul petitioned.

"I understand that, Daddy, but it doesn't make me any less concerned about him. I even tried calling Mama Brown to see if she heard from him. *Nothing*. He might be pissed with me, but he wouldn't avoid contacting Judy. He can't be *that* broken," Julissa explained.

"You would be surprised, darling. A man's pride is overwhelming, and at times, overrated," Paul warned.

"Wait, right there, Daddy. That's his truck. Pull over!" Julissa demanded.

Mr. Paul Monroe obliged his daughter's request. He pulled his car perpendicular to Renaldo's truck. Julissa checked for any passersby then opened the door. Peerless made a little grumble that grabbed Julissa's attention. She went to the other side of the car and watched him through his passenger window. Peerless flashed a slight toothless grin. She placed her hand on the car window and watched Peerless saunter in his seat.

Julissa turned away from her parents' car to face Renaldo's truck. She found it odd the car was in the same spot he parked it in so many days ago. "Did he take an Uber back to Destreland?" Julissa pondered. Julissa clasped her hands into a circle, pressed her face against her hands, and peeked into the truck.

"*Everything is the same.* Nothing moved from when we came here the other day," Julissa observed.

She scoured the back of the truck and saw nothing missing from the bed. Nothing had been moved. Julissa then approached the driver's side of Renaldo's truck. Before she could take a step, she discovered a couple small red specks against the dark asphalt. She slowly kneeled, still in pain from delivery, to further inspect the area.

"JuJu, don't bend your body like that! You are still in recovery. What are you doing?" Cortissa called.

Julissa waved Cortissa off as she studied the ground near the driver's side. She began to crawl on the hot asphalt to search for more clues. Julissa noticed a small rectangular object just below the driver's door: *Renaldo's phone.* She reached beneath the car and held the power button. *Nothing.*

"Shit!" Julissa muttered.

"Hey. Hey. Hey. Get up, baby girl. Let's go ahead and get the baby out of this sun, hnah? Let's get you home so you can get something good to eat," Paul suggested.

He had his hands placed on Julissa's shoulders and guided her back to her feet. Julissa eye formed a solitary tear that trickled down her face. Paul took notice of this and placed his arm around Julissa as he escorted her back to the car. Paul felt awful for Ju, but he also understood Renaldo's frustrations. Though somewhat conflicted, Paul's plan of action was clear: *protect my daughter*, as any other good father would have done. He watched Julissa as she took a seat while he offered to put her seatbelt on her. She declined the proposal but was no less grateful for her father's kindness.

"JuJu fruit, do you need me to drive Renaldo's truck for you?" Cortissa offered.

"Umm, no, Ma. I don't even think I have my keys. Thank you for asking though," Julissa declined.

Julissa batted her eyes at Cortissa. She wondered why her mother would offer such a thing. Julissa then took Renaldo's phone and placed it in her purse. She fiddled her fingers through her bag looking for another object. Julissa took a deep breath once she discovered Renaldo's truck keys. She nodded her head before removing her hand from the bag and sealed it rapidly. She had her doubts about Renaldo's whereabouts, but she now knew he hadn't deserted them on his own accord. Julissa groaned as she clutched her phone.

"Shit!" Julissa muttered again to herself.

"Whatchu say, JuJu?" Mr. Paul asked.

"Oh! Nothing, Dad. Can you turn the music down some? I have a call to make," Julissa requested.

Chapter 8

Claims to Victory

A few days have gone by. Renaldo returns to the confessional booth. This time under his own free will, sort of. Aside from the black bag covering his head as he was led down the hall by Baron, everything was completely his idea. Renaldo requested, loudly, from the shrouded storage room that he be allowed to meet with old man who held him captive. After being there for a week, Renaldo still had more questions than answers: essentially the theme of his life over the past half year.

The older gentleman obliged this request by sending Baron to retrieve Renaldo. After a few days of muffled dialogue between them, Renaldo was able to understand Baron through mere gestures. What Renaldo learned more than anything else: stay within the light. Baron was most dangerous among the carpeted areas, where the sledgehammer was quieted along the surface. Baron's chainmail-clad toga was no aid in locating him in the shadows, it was only an added inconvenience for your hand to get wrapped in, as Renaldo learned a couple of days prior.

Once the concussion symptoms subsided, Renaldo determined he would go another round with Baron to secure his freedom. However, just as Renaldo studied Baron, Baron studied him. Baron swung low at Renaldo, knowing he would dodge the blow if he saw it coming. A hammer to the ribs was never on Renaldo's bucket list, but it ensured his vomit pail was reinstated for a few days. The shot floored Renaldo and he escaped a head-pounding finish by rolling into the abyss and tipping one of the shelving units onto his adversary.

"I got that motherfucker," Renaldo mouthed to himself.

Detective Brown may have been slightly premature in his enthusiasm. Baron was clearly pinned to the floor by the shelving when Renaldo attempted to wrestle the hammer away. It was such a bright idea, at least until the light flickered.

"Son of a bitch! I see you! I don't give a damn if that light does go out, I have you—," Renaldo claimed.

It all went pitch black. The room. The scenario. *Renaldo's momentum*! In a matter of seconds, Baron turned the tables, or shelves rather, on Renaldo. Renaldo resumed prying the mallet away from his opponent, but to no avail. Baron screamed before he shoved the hammer's head directly into Renaldo's gullet. Renaldo fell onto the shelving unit headfirst and banged his forehead across exposed steel. He felt the unit shift underneath as he fell to the floor. When the light returned, Baron had vanished. Renaldo remained sprawled along the canvas whilst he contemplated his next step. For the time being, the rivalry had subsided.

Today, Baron escorted Renaldo along the halls of the facility without incident. Though Renaldo had full use of his hands, the cloak resting upon his face kept him at bay.

In the event he ever felt brave, Baron occasionally scraped the sledgehammer along hard surfaces to keep Renaldo humbled. Despite Baron's obvious advantages over Renaldo during their excursion, he dared not strike. Through their battles, they'd developed a rigid mutual respect for one another. Enough respect for Baron to make sure Renaldo reached the booth without incident, injury, or inconvenience.

Currently, the older gentleman has just taken his seat on the other side of the booth. He is clad in a black blazer and pants, along with a grey shirt and a black tie. He leans forward to take a gander at Renaldo, who appears to be in better spirits than days past.

"To what do I owe this special request, youngster? Are you here to file a complaint about the accommodations?" the older man tempered.

"Ha-ha-ha-ha," Renaldo cackled. "Surprisingly, the food has gotten better around here. I wish the water was a little warmer in the showering area. I know you are supposed to frown on things that resemble hell, but you wouldn't promote naked skiing either, I presume."

"Heh-heh-heh. Well, I'm happy things have improved during your stay. It shows that patience truly is a virtue," the older man imparted.

They each chuckled for an instant. The older man was honestly confused by Renaldo's jovial state. He didn't know if this was the onset of Stockholm Syndrome or a setup.

"Well, what brings you to the confessional today? Are you here to atone for your transgressions?" the older man asked with one brow raised.

"Sure, I'd be willing to admit to some of my mistakes,

but it's not exactly what I'm here for," Renaldo declined.

"Okay. Then what is it that you seek, son?" the older man entertained.

"Baron," Renaldo muttered.

"What do you mean? He brought you down here. You could have spoken with him in your chambers," the older man proclaimed.

"Yeah, but I don't understand him. I mean, I don't understand anything he says. It just sounds like...noise...to me," Renaldo admitted.

The older man sat back along the bench while he pondered Renaldo's interest in Baron. Renaldo surprised him with his thirst for knowledge. He was somewhat impressed with Renaldo's gall. He also believed he could help Renaldo see the error in his ways if he engaged him in "friendly" conversation, as allowing Baron to pound him into submission hadn't quite worked.

"It is not his speech that is completely unclear, nor is it the fault of your ears, youngster. The true issue is within your soul," the older man judged.

"Excuse me? You're telling me Baron does not sound like an adult frog when he speaks? I'm just imagining that from the depths of my soul?" Renaldo questioned.

"What was Baron doing when you first encountered him?" the older man quizzed.

"Dragging a damn sledgehammer across the floor. What does that have to do with my hea—" Renaldo began. The older man placed his hand into view with one finger pointed towards the sky.

"What else did you notice?" the older man continued.

Renaldo groaned at the question. He closed his eyes to recall what he saw in his concussed state.

"His face was disfigured, and he dressed like a character at a haunted house," Renaldo admitted.

"Mmm-hmm," the older man chimed.

"Mmm-hmm? What do you mean?" Renaldo wondered.

"Your eyewitness first impression of Baron resembled that of a monster, or something less than human," the older man deemed.

"I heard him long before I saw him. What else am I supposed to think of a guy whose first move was to strike me with a blunt weapon?" Renaldo questioned.

"All I have heard from you are possible negative aspects of Baron. Are you not trained to see the entire picture, Mr. Brown? Or is your work jaded by your negativistic views of those around you?" the older gentleman queried.

Renaldo became agitated with the older gentleman. He leaned forward to the screen opening and peered into the other side of the booth. He wanted to look the man directly in his eyes, but the screen complicated it.

"Now look, sir, I believe I have the right to defend myself against anything that poses a threat to me. You gonna suggest I turn the other cheek or some bull like that?" Renaldo rattled.

"I'm gonna suggest you start looking for the answers instead of highlighting the problem," the older man stated.

"I beg your pardon?" Renaldo snapped back.

"You can't understand Baron because you haven't tried!" the older man reiterated.

"Yet you understand him, and I can understand you. I came so you can help me understand him, didn't I?" Renaldo pieced together.

"Fair enough, youngster. So, what troubles you about dear old Baron?" the gentleman entertained.

"What happened to him? Why is his voice altered?" Renaldo interviewed.

The older man grimaced while reluctantly tilting his head. He wasn't sure Renaldo was truly ready for what he sought, but there was no compelling reason to delay.

"At one point, his voice was quite the contrary. It was still deep when he spoke," the older gentleman began. "However, once he graced that choir stand, he bellowed the smoothest tunes this side of the Mississippi," the older man described.

"People would flock to this church from miles around. Everybody wanted to experience the spectacle known as Victor Baronne. 'Young gold with an old soul,' they called him. This church stayed afloat from the various tithes and offerings from members and visitors alike. However, all money ain't good money," the older man professed.

"Let me guess, somebody got jealous of him and wanted to teach him a lesson, so they singed his vocal cords?" Renaldo butted in.

"Just like a young whippersnapper. No patience, and more importantly, wrong. The story ain't quite that simple. I know you may have seen many common crimes in the great Crescent City, but have you not experienced those, with let's say, variables?" the older man chastised.

"I guess you're right. Forgive me for my insolence. I suppose I did request to speak with you. It's not like I have anywhere to go today, I don't think, anyway," Renaldo retreated.

"I appreciate your splendor, sir. There may be hope for a tortured soul like yours yet," the older man squealed.

"Now, where was I?"

"I believe there was money involved, sir," Renaldo chimed.

"Ahh, yes," the older man called. "You do listen. I am thoroughly impressed,"

"I do what I can, good sir," Renaldo stated cynically.

The older gentleman took no exception to Renaldo's snide remarks but also knew how important it was to capitalize on Renaldo's curiosity. He restructured his thoughts and continued with Victor "Baron" Baronne's biography.

"Some of those visitors coming to the church weren't there for praise and worship. Even worse, they wanted to take Victor and his crooning voice away from here! He was so young, so naïve, so damn gullible at the time, Victor would believe anything told to him if it sounded good enough. Typical youth, believe in all the glory without recognizing the necessary work," the older man complained.

"Was he not just a boy with a dream?" Renaldo interjected.

"Yeah, we all are technically. Until we reach that which we want most, everything else we desire is merely a dream," the older man rationalized.

The older man leaned forward to the screened box. Renaldo took notice and leaned forward as well. Renaldo intently gazed at the face across from him; it was becoming more familiar, despite the obvious obstruction between them. The reason behind the familiarity had yet to strike Renaldo, but he was reverting to his former self.

"Victor was just like anybody else. He wanted to be wherever he was appreciated, not tolerated. There were certain individuals who became envious of Victor and his apparent stardom of the Sunday solos. Victor was young but he was no fool, not completely anyway. He could sense the disgust of those less talented than him every time he graced the choir stand. So, when some visitor approached him about possibly dipping into R&B, he didn't bat an eye. Victor took a meeting with the guy, and they began working together. They had a deal in place," the older man revealed.

"That sounds so good so far. Not about the holy folks, the judgmental mentality is nothing new, but being considered for R&B, that sounds great!" Renaldo commented.

"Yeah, but his secular friends were suspect. His mother tried to warn him about those guys, but he just couldn't see past what was in front of him. She had good instincts about people. I really wish Victor had given heed to her warnings. He might still be crooning the halls of this sanctuary today if he had," the older man stopped.

The older man took a handkerchief from his pocket and wiped a single tear streaming down his left cheek. He was interrupted with an abrupt cough. The older man gazed into his handkerchief as he held it in both hands rested upon his lap. His left leg began to bounce as he rocked his upper body back and forth. Renaldo viewed the discomfort in the older man and quietly wondered why he ceased the story...

"Sir, are you alright? I would get you some tissue, but I haven't had the formal tour of this place," Renaldo stated.

"I appreciate the sentiments, detective, but I am quite alright. Just tears me up to think about what those savages did to Vic. After about a year of singing in different local clubs and playing hood celebrity, Victor wanted to call it quits. Victor was content to return to the church and sing in the choir, a simpler form of life. He realized he didn't desire the worldly possessions as much as, well...inner peace. After all the things he saw at a young age while his family lived in Crescent City, he only sought peace," the older man suggested.

"Breach of contract?" Renaldo asked.

"*Big-time*! But there's a huge difference in breaking contracts with litigious guys and street rats. Unfortunately, Victor was running with the latter. He tolerated it for a while, but he always knew they weren't his cup of tea. Victor was a humble fella, and these fools were flashy. And *loud*. Sadly, Victor was a victim of his own dominance," the older man described.

"Dominance? On the stage?" Renaldo quizzed.

"There, anywhere. Just in life. Victor was an all-around good guy, he could sing, and he was built like a healthy college two guard. Them lil' street rats ain't wanna chance getting outdone in a round of fisticuffs with the boy. Oh no! They decided to attack him another way, through his stomach," the older man reported.

"Yeah, I can see what you mean. He could be physically daunting to the common man. But are they the ones responsible for his complete...transformation?" Renaldo doubted.

"They were the beginning of his slow demise. They decided to invite Victor out for 'one more drink with the guys.' You know, try to see if meeting in a relaxed environment would change his mind. Victor should have never taken the meeting but he is one of those guys that doesn't use the word 'no' enough. Victor says he went to the bathroom during the meeting and came back. He thanked them for their time and hospitality, but his mind wasn't going to change. They expressed phony well wishes and encouraged him to sit down, at least to finish the drink he'd ordered. They pretended as if things were all good, as they watched him sip until it was gone. He said he felt funny while drinking it but just thought maybe the alcohol was watered down. Turns out those punks expected him to say 'no' and they were prepared to do something about it," the older man detailed.

There was an elongated silence in the booth. Renaldo peered through the screened box yet again to find the older man now squeezing his temporal lobes. Renaldo was intrigued as to what happened with Baron, but he also did not want to come off as insensitive. Renaldo waited until the older gentleman was composed enough to proceed.

"Sorry about that, youngster. Some things are hard to believe, even once you've seen the result for yourself," the older man apologized.

"No worries, sir. I got time," Renaldo comforted.

"Well, Victor felt so bad that he went home and went to sleep, or at least tried to. He woke up in the middle of the night in his own puke. His face and portions of his arms were burning from the vomit. He was losing the ability to talk and was gurgling fluids in his throat. His mother called 911 and rushed him to the doctor. She called me and I met her up there as soon as I could. The doctor dropped a bomb on us that day: *Hydrochloric acid*! Those bastards practically poisoned Victor to make sure he wouldn't sing anywhere else—or for anyone else, for that matter!" the older man belted.

"Well, shit. Doesn't the human body produce hydrochloric acid? Like in the digestive tract?" Renaldo inquired. The older man pointed in confirmation.

"Smart man, Mr. Brown. It's one thing when the body produces it and forces it up your throat through acid reflux. It's another issue when it's a larger amount passing through your body with alcohol, and it doesn't sit well in your stomach. Technically, Victor burned himself inside out from buying that drink. His puke torched whatever parts of him it touched in that concentrated amount. His vocal cords took the brunt of the damage. Somehow the acid seeped through his trachea," the older man concluded.

Renaldo cringed. He was also a little choked up at the story. He now understood why the older man was so protective of Baron. *Or was he?* Sure, it was a touching story, but what did the gentleman have to do with any of this? Where did he come into the picture?

"I don't want to further agitate you, sir," Renaldo provided, "but whatever happened to those guys that poisoned Victor?"

"Fortunately, nothing. Even if Baron attacked one of them, he would only want to hurt the one responsible for pouring the acid. He asked around but no one would give him a straight answer on who applied the poison. He knows the guys who went out with him, but there were like, four or five of them," the older man clarified.

"That's completely fucked up. Excuse my French in the house of the Lord, sir. I sincerely cannot believe somebody would do that, over music?" Renaldo spilled.

"It's a fact of life, youngster. Every man will face a trial by fire and when they do, one of two things will occur: *he will be burned, or he will be forged in solidarity,*" the older man prophesized.

Renaldo drooped his head momentarily. He contemplated the story provided and partially sympathized with the disfigured being he had come to blows with over the past few days. The older man viewed the discourse in Renaldo's expression and decided to address it as best he knew how.

"Snap out of it, whippersnapper. Baron is a Victor, not a victim. There's no pun intended. He withstood his trial by fire and now stands before us a better man than he entered the bar that night. He may not ever sing again, but he still has a voice," the older gentleman attempted to reassure.

"So, now he carries around a sledgehammer as his equalizer or means of protection?" Renaldo asked.

"In a way, yes. The significance of the hammer goes back to a date just after the incident. When he was real young, he and his family suffered through Katrina. All those neighborhoods, businesses, even people, submerged in that toilet bowl they call a city!" the older man declared.

"Hey, hey, heyyyyyyy, sir. Crescent is still one of the most popular places in America, maybe even the world. We may have some flaws, but what large city don't?" Renaldo defended.

"What you have is a poor levee system and a lack of leadership in the government offices. It was true then, and to a degree, it's still true now!" the older gentleman fired back.

Renaldo humbled himself for the moment. Deep down, he knew his elder was correct. So many suffered what would have been avoidable for most if they had just one extra day of warning. One extra day to evacuate. *One extra day's notice that the city could not withstand what was to come.* The end result was a city underwater, and people removed from the only place they knew. Sure, some were able to come back, if they chose to, but others had to decide between rebuilding what was lost or paying a new mortgage in a new town. Even worse was the price gauging set by gentrification. Those who deeply held pride for the city came back to find their neighborhoods torn down and memories torn asunder.

"Anyway, youngster," the older gentleman returned, "around eleven years later, there was some serious flooding from constant rain. Red Stick was one of the hardest hit areas. All that water and all those people. He remembered how the people of Red Stick embraced him and his family once they were displaced there after Katrina. He remembered all those people that had to be housed in the shelter over there and always knew he would want to repay them. Once some of that water subsided, Victor worked with a crew dedicated to going into apartment homes and searching for tenants who may have remained. Victor saw many things while busting down the doors of those homes, most of which would further haunt him."

"Yeah. I believe many of us are still suffering some form of psychological dismay from Katrina itself. Every possible tropical storm, depression, or hurricane after that is a constant reminder of possible damage to come," Renaldo agreed.

"He scraped that hammer across the walls and hard surfaced floors of some of those homes to let any possible 'refugees' or 'squatters' know he was there. That initial sound was his way of giving them an ounce of hope, if they were still fortunate enough to hear it," the older man settled.

"Well, I can assure you it is less reassuring of one's safety when he is dragging that thing across the cement in the dark," Renaldo declared.

"Truthfully, my friend, he does it for the same reason. He understands the fear of not knowing where you are or how to move about, so anytime that light flickers, he grazes his hammer across the hard surface, to let us know he is there," the older man declared.

That last jewel shared by the older man provided miniscule solace to Renaldo. He had to rethink his entire initial encounter with Baron. *Baron*? Why in the world did they decide to shorten his surname and call him Baron? Baronne was a traditional name, at least to Crescent City patrons, why not with Victor?

"I have one last question about Victor, something that really puzzles me," Renaldo shared.

"What is it, youngster?" the older man entertained.

"Why do they call him 'Baron'? Are people just that lazy or is that the best nickname they could come up with for the poor guy? He deserved something more commendable, don't you think?" Renaldo dug.

"Well, he actually liked the name, considering its origins. He was a baron of sorts on the microphone, when he still had a voice worth hearing," the older man explained.

"Iiiiiiiiiiiii-heeeaaaarrd-yoouuuuuuuuu," a voice croaked from the confessional's exterior. Renaldo was shocked he could make out what Baron said.

"I wasn't whispering, was I?" the older man fired back.

"Doooonnnnnnnnnn't-get-cuuuuuuuuuuuuuute," Baron warned.

"Heh, heh, heh. Yeah, alright," the older man began.

"Anyway, detective. The name Baron is a tribute to his mother, Lavender. However, you may know her as 'The Baroness!'"

Renaldo's eyes widened as he located his entrance of the confessional. He darted out of the booth without a second thought, blindly navigating himself around the building. Once aware of the direction Renaldo traveled, Baron slowly pursued, knowing he would not find a way out. The older man laughed heftily while grabbing his cane then exiting his portion of the booth.

Chapter 9

Vested Interests

"Ladies and gentlemen of the Greater Crescent City, we come to you with disturbing news today. Only a couple of weeks after solving the case of one of the most infamous murders in this area and days after welcoming a new addition to his family, Detective Renaldo Brown has gone missing. After receiving a call from his wife, Julissa Brown, our reporters arrived on scene at his last known location, the Westbank Medical Center here in Mactown. We have reason to suspect foul play, as Mr. Brown may be gone but his registered vehicle remains. Reportedly, he left the delivery floor in a dash and no family members have heard from him since. As this occurred days ago, there are no feasible witnesses to what may have occurred and tapes from the parking lot cameras are being reviewed for any possible leads. If anyone has any information regarding the whereabouts of Detective Renaldo Brown, please call this station. Mrs. Julissa Brown would appreciate any info or help, but she is also currently nursing a newborn son," the Channel 4 news report stated.

The report rang throughout the Crescent City Police Department for nearly a week. While many didn't expect

Renaldo to return to the precinct for another month or so, they now wondered if he would return at all. Street officers and detectives alike were given special instructions to *search every crevice* of Crescent to find Renaldo. The order extended to all local towns and municipalities. However, without a perpetrator to focus on or even a vehicle, the man chase became an organized duck mission.

It was as if the brothers in arms were searching for a ghost. No one had seen or heard anything from Renaldo since he departed the hospital. No one from his usual hangout spots knew anything. His known associates had not been contacted and his own mother was none the wiser of his destination. Aside from his cell phone and the miniscule blood splatter on the parking lot pavement, Renaldo was missing without a trace.

Detective Rita Barrios sat at her desk, still distraught from the news. For many reasons, it was the last thing she needed to hear. She was already losing ground in the cases versus Tony Nguyen and Vashon Hall of the Fifth Ward Hogs. Officer Remy Daniels failed to convincingly recall key moments of the events that took place in City Park. Did Tony and the other Hog *shoot first? Were they the ones responsible for shooting an officer and a couple of civilians?* Attorney Ashley Archibald strategically questioned the officers' accounts of what happened, and he now had the court considering possible dismissal of major charges. The public shared their distrust for the police, noting how Renaldo chased Hall down and physically threatened him at gun point. Renaldo was able to properly verbalize his actions in the initial pre-trial hearing, but if he didn't return to testify, *what would the jury base their decision on?* Nothing more than a police report and witness statements from those present at the scene. Truth be told, Rita herself didn't know who to believe.

Rita heard the dense footsteps of a middle-aged man's clunky loafers traipsing along the precinct tile. She instantly exited the Channel 4 webpage, betraying an article she viewed so many times before. As she looked up from her desktop, she saw two silhouettes creeping past her blinds. The first figure was undoubtedly Lieutenant Morial, but the other? Rita squinted, as if it would be any aid in peering through the blinds. She was unaware she would get a closer look at the figures momentarily.

Lieutenant Morial and his less than favorable physique entered Rita's quarters first. He had done so many times over the last few weeks, rendering Rita unaffected. However, a six foot-plus, slender built, mocha machismo of a man in a high-cut fade and designer frames followed him in. Rita knew not of the second being, but her interest was piqued.

"Hey, Barrios, what you got going on?" Morial asked.

"Just reviewing some notes on the case with the Hogs, Lieutenant. It's become a daily ritual now," Rita fibbed.

"Well, depending on how you look at it, I may or may not have a little relief coming your way," Morial offered.

"Oh, really? You have another detective willing to take on this investigation or go to court?" Rita suggested, with her eyebrows raised nearly to her curly mini afro.

"I have a few cases of my own I wouldn't mind skipping court on, but I don't think you want to trade," the unannounced male declared.

"Try me," Rita responded matter-of-factly.

The man chuckled to himself as he grinned and looked toward Morial. The lieutenant was less enthused about the exchange. The visitor had arrived unexpectedly and Lieu-tenant Morial personally was focused on more than casual banter amongst his current and former detectives. The visitor read the grimace on his face and placed a hand on his shoulder prior to volunteering his attention to Rita yet again.

"Okay, maybe you would like to trade. But I believe we have a common friend in common cases. I recently discovered some info that could possibly link the two. I just wanted to stop by and see if a fellow detective had any interest in exchanging pertinent information. Would that be of any interest to you, detective?" the man asked.

"Depends on what you have, Detective...Detective...I'm sorry, I don't believe I caught your name," Rita replied while scoping the visitor from top to bottom.

"He's—," Lieutenant Morial began.

"Rance! Rance McDonald, Gretna P.D. Lieutenant Morial here was my boss once. Well, more than that. He was more of a mentor," Rance introduced.

Rance extended his hand to Rita to complete his intro-duction. Rita extended a hand back, palm down, allowing Rance to grasp the length of her fingers. They exchanged glances minutely before detaching extremities.

"Well, Mr. McDonald, I hope you have something worth my while," Rita expressed.

"I'm pretty sure we could come to some type of arrangement, Miss or Missus Barrios?" Rance questioned.

"Miss. Miss Rita Barrios," Rita clarified.

"Well, that was really sweet of you kid," Morial began sarcastically. "Since you all appear to be very chum and I know Rita would shoot you before she allowed you to cause any trouble on my floor, do I have to stick around here for this stakeout or can I continue with some other pressing matters?"

"I know where to find you if your protégé gets out of order, Lieutenant. You'll hear from me if there's a problem," Rita ensured.

"Sure thing. Okay, let me get to my office. Rance, don't be a stranger, but don't forget how to use a phone either, right? If either of you require my assistance, I'm right down the hall," Morial said as he exited.

Rita watched as the lieutenant quickly departed the room. He trekked full speed to his domain. Rance's body faced where the lieutenant once stood as he studied his departure as well. Once Morial cleared the blinds, Rita slowly brought her attention back to Rance. She quickly examined him before he set his eyes upon hers again. She met his gaze with one of query. She wondered how much relief Rance could truly provide. Historically, Rita had enough men disappoint her over the years; she had no rooting interest in welcoming a new parasite.

"So, you just going to stand there or are you going to provide me an awe-inspiring presentation?" Rita encouraged.

"Forgive me," Rance chuckled. "My attention must have been elsewhere."

"Well, I hope you didn't miss any details along the way in your case," Rita teased.

"Actually, I believe there may be something I discovered. I just need a little assistance sorting it all out," Rance stated.

"So, Mister...McDonald? How might I assist you?" Rita explored.

"For now, if you have any footage from the motorcycle

chase a few months back, I would be sincerely grateful," Rance answered.

"Oh, 'for now' you say. I'm not too fond of men who plan ahead to ask me for favors. It doesn't tend to end well," Rita admitted.

"If I ask someone for a favor, I always plan on reciprocating, sometimes even tenfold," Rance declared.

"Alright nah', detective. Now I'm intrigued," Rita replied while fluttering her eyelids.

"A few weeks back, Renaldo hinted to me that he didn't believe the Fifth Ward Hogs showing up to the burial was an accident. I understand there was a shooting at City Park involving the Hogs as well. I want to examine the film to see if any of those weapons match any of the ones we found the night Avon Lazlo and his buddies went down at *Nina's*," Rance explained.

"Oh, did he? I didn't know you two were that close," Rita began. "Well, I guess every little bit helps. If you wait a second, I could get you directions to our annex. That's where you can pick up the footage," Rita agreed.

"I'm umm...I'm somewhat familiar with the place. That's how I know Lieutenant Morial. I used to be in his unit, too. It had to be before you got here, though. I'm sure I would have remembered you," Rance flirted.

Detective Barrios peered at Rance with a small smirk in the left corner of her mouth. She picked up her phone and made the call to the annex building, advising them a Gretna Police Department detective would be gracing their presence in a few minutes. She asked for any and every piece of footage from the motorcycle chase on the day of Franc's funeral. She hung up her office phone and looked at Rance before she addressed him again.

"Detective McDonald. The footage you requested will be waiting for you in the annex. Is there anything else I can do for you at this time?" Rita checked.

"Naw. It's my turn to assist you. Thank you for all you have done so far. I am indebted to you," Rance recited.

"Well, I guess I'll be here, waiting on your rebuttal," Rita indicated.

"I sure hope so," Rance responded as he tapped the desk with his fingertips and turned away.

Once Rance cleared Rita's door seal, he glanced back at her through the blinds and walked to the elevator. For the moment, Rita forgot the world was searching for Renaldo. She took succor in the possible relief to come at the hands of a stranger. For an instant, Rita had a sense of relief, combined with a sudden urge to move forward.

As Rance exited through the hallway, he crossed Morial's line of sight. He waved to Morial as he continued down the hall and on to the elevator. Morial nodded to his former detective, then brought his attention back to his desk. In his view was the Crescent City Chronicle article outlining the career and probable capture of Detective Renaldo Brown. The lieutenant was heavily concerned about the future of Crescent City with the crime fighting duo evaporated in a mere matter of months. Yeah, there were plenty of other officers, and Barrios was a star in her own right, but she was also consumed with the Fifth Ward Hogs. Morial was less concerned about the day-to-day unsolved mysteries, and now more concerned about the larger-than-life criminals who had been in hiding.

Morial tossed the newspaper to the side in utter dismay. Now there were two files staring back at him. *Two young men shot to death in a car*. Would have been pretty cut and dry, had there not been shots that entered from outside of the vehicle as well, according to crime scene investigators. The only thing that was certain was that the music of a local rap artist, Pelli Kanisus, was still blasting through the speakers when the paramedics arrived on the scene:

"Hit 'em up for no reason/I'm watching my 6 cuz/It's pelican season/His shorty look decent/Few shots to his body/Free work for the precinct..."

Chapter 10

Holding Court

Renaldo runs down the eclipsed church halls, hoping to escape the fate he and Franc designated over a year ago: Renaldo and Franc had captured the Baroness, Lavender Baronne, after a series of car fires starting in 2015. Though none of the owners were ever harmed, their vehicles were not as fortunate. All four of the vehicles belonged to males. They were all buddies, pals, *business partners*! Renaldo and Franc caught on to the pattern and prevented it from happening to the man at the top of the chain: DeSean Jenkins, CEO of Chop It To Ya' Records. Lavender was caught red-handed with a lit Molotov and the crowbar she used to break the driver side window.

Baroness was silent in her arrest, as she often was. When Renaldo placed her in cuffs and sat her down into the car, she made no form of protest. It was during the ride that they witnessed Ms. Baronne in all her splendor. The lady of limber slowly slid the cuffs down the length of her legs, underneath her feet and up to her chest. She slowly shifted her body to her left before shooting both heels to the car window. The sound of the cracking glass was enough to make Renaldo and Franc pull the vehicle over.

When Franc leaned over to put the seatbelt back on the Baroness, she rewarded him with a headbutt to his chin. She then wrapped the cuffs around his neck and attempted to strangle him. Franc was able to slip his hands inside of hers enough to take the pressure off his neck, before he slammed his head back into her face, rendering her unconscious.

Lavender's marquee performance came courtesy of her trial when defense attorney, Ashley Archibald, advocated she be sent to a mental health hospital instead of the Parish Prison. The defense pled that Lavender suffered from PTSD, considering the events that occurred in the city during 2005, and her own personal issues with the near death of her son. The judge ruled in her favor, but as she was carried out, she cried "They tried to kill my son! He will never be the same again!" No one understood her outcry or even cared to ask what she meant. Now, Detective Brown knew what he should have desired to know all along: *C.I.T.Y. Records ruined Victor and his mother wanted to settle the score.* This went undiscovered the way the cries of many mothers go unnoticed: *pure apathy by the men around them.* And then the inevitable happens, somebody hears the story from a different angle, and then they understand. A result that is almost predictable, but never desirable.

The day of the hearing, Lavender Baronne was ordered to check into Beech Grove Manor. What was done to her is what had been done to many of those who proved to be a problem in the Greater Crescent City Area; she was placed behind a wall far away from society...and told to never return.

Renaldo was able to blindly navigate himself down the

hall to the only speck of light that wasn't coming through the tightly shuttered curtains. Renaldo bursted through the slightly ajar door to a copious amount of sunlight. He walked through the door and leaned over, gasping for another breath. Had Renaldo finally broken out of his personal hell? Would he escape the consequences of his actions *yet again*? Maybe, just maybe Renaldo had done enough to escape the questions Baron had for him, but, what about that of the older man? He still didn't understand what it was he had done for...or...to *him*.

Renaldo looked up at the sun and noticed his eyes were not affected. He took another look around the premises. He discovered why the brightness of the sun was nullified: enclosure. The cement floors in the room were for nothing more than a basketball court. The high ceiling resembled that of a sunroom. Renaldo had found the indoor basketball court. He was disappointed yet inspired, as he knew there had to be a door nearby. Renaldo paced to the far side of the court. The light jog slowly transitioned to a profound stump when he saw no way out. SPLACK! An object careened off the back of Renaldo's head and fell behind him. Renaldo dipped forward from the momentum but he was able to remain upright. Renaldo didn't have to turn around to know he'd been cornered. *Deep down, he knew it would happen all along.*

"You interested in a game of '21'? Hmm? Maybe 'Horse' is more of your speed. Cuz if you throw another ball at me, Baron, you better be ready to check-up or boot up," Renaldo threatened.

"Booyyyyyyyyyyyyyyyy, yoouuuuuuuu aiiiiiiiiiiiiiiiiin't gawwwwwwwt nooooooooooooo hahhhhhhps. Annnnnnnnd iffffffff Iiiiiiiii throwwwwwww sssssssssoooooomethiiiiiiing aaaaaaat youuuuuuu, iiiiiit wiiiillll beeeee thiiiiiiiiis haammmmmerrrrrr," Baron croaked.

"WHAT THE HELL Y'ALL WANT FROM ME, MAN?! I been here God knows how long and ain't nobody gave me no other reason for being here besides me doing my damn job!" Renaldo bellowed as he turned toward Baron.

"Iiiiiiii wannnnnt t-t-t-oooooo fiiiiiiiind myyyy muuhhtherrrrrr!" Baron replied.

"What do you mean? She's not in the Beech Grove?" Renaldo replied, confused.

Baron snarled as he picked up his sledgehammer and walked towards Renaldo. He placed both hands around the shaft and rested the steel head of it over his broad shoulder.

"Iiiiiiif sheee wassssssss, wouuuullllllld Iiiiiiii neeeeeed tooooo asssssssk youuuuuu?" Baron snapped back.

"Well, I didn't move her! What makes you think *I would know* where she is?" Renaldo asked.

"Waaaaaaaaanceeee uh-pauuuuuuun a tiiiiiiiiiiiime, yooouuuuu puuuuuut herrr innnn a plaaaaaace toooo maaaaaake suuuuuure everrrrrrrrryyyyyyyywaaaaaan waaaaas saaaaafe. Iiiiiiii hoped yoouuuuuu moooooooooved herrrrrr thiiiiiiiiiiis tiiiiiiiime toooo maaaaaake suuuuuuuuure sheeee waaaaaas saaaaafe," Baron declared.

Renaldo was taken aback by Baron's recollection. He wanted to inform Baron that a judge placed her in the mental facility, but he didn't want to dash what little understanding had developed between them. Renaldo had no idea how to help Baron, but he did not want to experience the result of disappointing him.

"No, Baron. I don't know where she is. I didn't have anything to do with her being moved. We thought we placed her in the best possible place. I..I...I have no clue where she could be. Have you guys asked around?" Renaldo interrogated.

"Whoooooooo izzzzzz gohhhhhhhhh-innnnnng tooooooo undurrrrrrrr-st-t-staaaaaaand meeeeeee? No-Nooooo-Nooooooo waannn eee-vin triiiiiiies. Theyyyy treeeeeaaat meeeee wurrrse thannnnn ahhh mannnnnn weeeeeeeth ahh st-st-stuhhhh-terrrrr," Baron revealed, clearly choked up.

Baron looked at the concrete court as he gripped his weapon of choice at the base. Baron released his right hand from the base as he cradled the hammer near the steel and pointed toward the sun. When he reattached his right hand to the bottom of the shaft, Baron swung the hammer in a full rotation before striking the surface mightily. He maintained his striking pose until he fell to one knee and looked toward the sky once more. Baron's eyes lowered to his hammer as his head sunk into his chest.

"I thought you boys were starting to play nice. What's got Baron with the long face?" the older man asked from the court entrance.

"Of course," Renaldo muttered to himself. "Well, it appears that Victor here wants me to help him find Baroness. For some strange reason he thinks I know where she is. You know anything about that, mister?"

"Yes, it's part of the reason you're here. Though you and your justice system prevented her from killing someone, you all technically took Baron's mother away from him. It would only be fitting that you helped him to...recoup...her. Don't you think?" the older man advised.

"What about you? Aren't you familiar with the lady? Can't you voice Baron's concerns to nearby patrons?" Renaldo interrogated.

The screeching sound of steel scraping across cement commenced. A perplexed Renaldo peered upon the sky again, curious as to why Baron was scraping the sledge-hammer across the surface in broad daylight. Baron crept to the entrance with his head down and his eyes shut. Despite the coveted sunlight that filled the indoor court, Baron's ray of hope dissipated when Renaldo denied any knowledge of his mother's whereabouts. One of the few people on earth dedicated to understanding him, vanished into thin air.

The older man stopped Baron at the entrance and grabbed him by both shoulders. The older gentleman inspected Baron head-to-toe, mostly because he had yet to lift his chin from its sunken state. The older man pulled Baron in for a hug, which nearly caused him to drop his hammer. The older gentleman released his hold on Baron and sidestepped the entrance to allow the distraught young man to pass. The older man watched Baron exit prior to taking a few short steps toward Renaldo, who now stood near center court. The gentleman picked up the basketball and fiddled with it in his hands.

"Well, my friend, that's just the thing. I'm well known by certain audiences in the Greater Crescent City region. I can't linger too long in the area without there being some humbug," the older man admitted.

"So, you take a chance on asking a black police officer to do it? You must be out of touch with recent events. There ain't many people willing to help us out like that, at least not anymore," Renaldo expressed.

"Maybe so, but have you not found a way to get things done anyway, detective? Do you not have a knack for 'closing the case,' per se?" the older man inclined.

"That's a fair assessment. But why didn't you just come and ask me for my services instead of, you know, ambushing me?" Renaldo requested.

"Let's just imagine Victor walked up to you and asked for your help; would you have obliged him, or would you have cast him aside simply because he appeared... different?" the older gentleman quizzed.

As Renaldo approached the older man, the gentleman looked off to his right. Renaldo inspected his features enough to breed familiarity, yet, not well enough to recall his name. It appeared the older gentleman wanted to remain a mystery for a little longer. This whole charade seemed amusing to the gentleman. Renaldo made a mental note of these behaviors before he continued.

"Hmmm. Maybe you're right. I can't really argue with your assessment considering the initial meeting between him and me. However, why should I be the one to help him? I haven't seen Miss...Baronne...since the night she was placed into Beech Grove," Renaldo professed.

"Because, if you help him, it is like killing two birds with one stone," the man informed Renaldo.

"Carry on," Renaldo urged.

"If you are willing to atone for your follies by aiding Victor, I will be inclined to settle our tab as well," the older man declared.

"That sounds mighty generous of you. Does that mean I will get to leave or are you rewarding me with continued room and board?" Renaldo asked.

The older man chuckled as he replied "No, no. After you help Victor, you will serve no purpose to us. We will make sure you are taken care of."

"No shit, hneh?" Renaldo pondered. He gazed upon the filtered sky just prior to returning his peepers to the man. "Well, I suppose that's a bargain, considering I still don't know what it is I owe you for."

"Now that you have seen the light," the older man stated as he pointed toward the gilded sun, "you have all that is necessary to complete your task, detective. Allow me to give you a better tour of this place as we get ready for our excursion."

The older man placed the cusp of his hand on Renaldo's shoulder blade and guided him back into the building. As they hiked the hall, the older man turned on varying fixtures throughout. The building was still in good condition: well lit, clean, updated furniture, and *programs*? "Wait a minute, this place is still active?" Renaldo wondered. While roaming the halls, the older man led Renaldo into a gaping door. Within the space was an organ and a few music stands. Baron was cradled in a fetal position in the far corner.

"Victor! Victor! Get up, boy. The detective agreed to help us. Get up so we can get our affairs in order," the older gentleman disclosed.

Baron removed his hands from his head and stretched his neck toward the older man's voice. The older gentleman nodded his head in confirmation. Baron sprouted up from his feeble position and rushed to his feet. A slight smirk formed in the corner of his mouth as he staggered to them. When Baron was within arm's reach, he slung the sledgehammer over his left shoulder and extended his right hand to Renaldo. The detective flared his nostrils at the gesture, before eventually giving in. As Baron entered the hallway, Renaldo took one more gander at the room, thinking to himself, "The music room, of course this is the first place Victor would go."

Chapter 11

Clarity & Clearview

"Where are they? I know they have to be in this shot somewhere," Rance mutters from his kitchen table.

Rance meticulously examines his laptop. The reflection from its screen is the only light in the room. He hasn't touched his meal, which was nothing more than chicken breast with a side of rice. He made his plate and sat it down an hour ago but hasn't looked at it since. His cellular device rumbles on the glass as he presses the screen to silence it. He has no patience for distractions right now. He needs to take in every frame of footage he received from the C.C. P.D. He mentally digests the motorcycle chase from each angle provided.

The current frame in focus comes from a traffic light on Canal Blvd., following the departure of the mausoleum grounds. Rance repeatedly presses the fast forward icon, hoping to progress the footage without missing a thing. He notices the two Hogs are beginning to split into their respective directions as Renaldo pursued. Rance is still puzzled while trying to zoom in.

"It's gotta be on him somewhere. How else would he have pulled that off?" Rance assures himself.

Rance removes the disc from the drive, places it into a case, and slides it to the other end of the table. Rance sees the next disc and places it into the drive. He impatiently waits for the media player to display the content. He looks to his left and notices a case marked "Clearview Pkwy." Rance lets out a slight "hmmm" as he recalls the news station advising shots were fired on Clearview Parkway the day of the funeral. Rance ponders whether what he sought would be easier to detect at the culmination of the chase, but he returns his attention to the screen just in case.

Rance rewinds the portion he missed so far. He smacks his teeth at the lack of substantial evidence to back his claims. He snickers to himself as he ejects this disc from the drive and returns it to the casing, prior to tossing it onto the nearest couch. He palms the next disc in the lineup but is intrigued by the disc marked "Clearview." Rance stretches his left arm to the quagmire of a case and removes the CD. Once Rance places the CD into the disc drive, he patiently awaits the details. The video opens to a red and black motorcycle turning onto Clearview Parkway hurriedly, followed by another. Rance partially recognizes the trailing individual and decides to slow down the transmission for a closer look.

"Wait, what was he reaching for? I gotta play that back!" Rance utters.

The detective rewinds the video until he pauses it on a still shot. Prior to Renaldo turning the corner behind Vashon Hall, he took a hand off the handle. He reached up to his face and seemingly pointed near his ear. Renaldo would then take out his weapon and send a warning shot for Hall, as could be seen in a later clip.

"Bingo, motherfucker!" Rance exclaimed to himself.

He'd finally found what he sought for. It was enough to make sense of the entire fiasco Crescent City endured over the last few months. It was obvious Renaldo shot in the direction of Vashon with no intention of injuring him, but he also was attempting to stop a reckless motorist with limited command of their vehicle. Rance slowed the video down enough to discover Vashon's bike beginning to swerve before Renaldo pulled the trigger. *Maybe he didn't cause the accident.* However, what Rance also believed was what he suspected all along: Detective Renaldo Brown was The Recluse!

Rance borrowed the traffic light footage from the Crescent City Police Department in search of one detail: The Recluse Vision glasses. When Renaldo turned onto Clearview Parkway, the dark lens tint that accompanied him in prior videos was no longer present. Rance's suspicions were further confirmed when he recognized Renaldo's finger in position to press a button on the spectacles. The final piece of the puzzle came when Renaldo removed the glasses from his face as he stood over the injured Hall.

"Yeah, we'll have to see what little Miss Barrios thinks about all of this. Maybe I'll give a shoutout to ole Morial too," Rance expressed.

Rance slid some discs to the side as he grabbed Rita's business card. He twisted it between his fingers, debating whether he should call and leave a message at her office. Rance laughed to himself as he sat the card down and gazed upon the screen again. He picked up a glass of brown liquor, swished it around and took a sip before returning it to a coaster. Rance removed the disc from his computer and placed it separate from the others. He got up from the table and entered a dark hallway. Rance ventured into a room along the hall. He turned on the lamp sitting on the nightstand. Rance opened a drawer and pulled out a clasped parcel, then placed it on the bed next to himself. Rance unclasped the parcel and removed the eyeglass case. He opened the case and snickered as he looked.

Chapter 12

Little Red Lie

Julissa stands outside of her parents' home in Harahan. Peerless is inside with Mr. and Mrs. Monroe, becoming more spoiled by the minute. Julissa awaits Mama Brown, who's bringing Judy over for the first time since Julissa checked in to Westbank Medical. Julissa's spry with anticipation. Sure, she has Facetimed with Judy over the period, but she can't wait to squeeze her little girl again. Julissa wanted to introduce Judy to her little brother. Though she feared she may eventually have to take them on herself, in a moment, she would be surrounded by the people who mattered to her the most, for the most part.

For now, Julissa enjoyed the scenery of the neighborhood. Large, illustrious homes with boisterous, robust gardens. The Monroe home was a red-bricked fortress wrapped in leafy greenery. Cortissa, like many of the patrons around her, took pride in the presentation of her home, maybe even more so than relations with her children. Julissa's sister, Ramona, had pretty much isolated herself from the rest of the family. Sure, Ramona would occasionally call Paul, but she wanted nothing to do with Cortissa or the sister closely resembling her.

Julissa's train of thought is broken by the appearance of a car closely resembling Mrs. Brown's. Julissa hops up in excitement, only to be disappointed as the car continues past the residence. Julissa shrugs her shoulders and grasps her phone to call Mrs. Brown. As she finds the number, she recognizes her impatience and presses the button to clear her screen. Suddenly, a similar car to the one Julissa just witnessed is backing into the long driveway from the opposite direction. Julissa jumps from the porch bench and scurries up the walkway. Even through the tinted windows, Julissa can see Judy's excited silhouette. When the car parks, Julissa runs to Judy's door to open it. Judy instantly unbuckles her seatbelt and jumps into her mother's arms.

"Well, did you have that bad of a time with Granny?" Mrs. Brown jokes.

"No, of course she didn't. I miss my little twin and she misses me too, Mama Brown," Julissa spews.

"I know, dear. I'm just messing with little ole bug. How you feeling, girl? Shouldn't you be inside right now, trying to heal?" Mrs. Brown asks.

"I know. I just couldn't wait to see my bug. I missed her so much!" Julissa replies.

"It's okay, Mama. I'm always going to be you and daddy's favorite. Perry is just going to have to understand," Judy declares.

"Wait," Julissa began laughing "What did you just call him, baby?"

"Perry! What's wrong with that?" Judy wonders.

"Baby, your brother's name is Peerless," Julissa clarifies.

"Oh," Judy utters, slightly disappointed. "Well, I'll call

him Perry for short."

"Well, you and 'Peerless' can talk about that when you go inside," Julissa settles.

Judy ran up the walkway and into the front door. Julissa and Mrs. Brown watched as Judy provided her best Jackie Joyner-Kersee impression. Mrs. Brown then turned her attention to Julissa.

"Julissa...Have you heard anything at all from Renaldo?" Mrs. Brown asked.

"No. No, ma'am. Not even a peep. Found his phone outside his truck at the hospital," Julissa revealed.

A look of complete horror stretched across Mrs. Brown's face. She clutched her keys as the ring nearly slipped through her fingers. Julissa wrapped an arm around Mrs. Brown to keep her stable. Mrs. Brown looked at Julissa with her mouth agape.

"Huh-huh-how do we know how he is, Ju? Where is my boy?" Mrs. Brown asked, restraining her sob.

Julissa winced as she looked toward the sky. Rays of sunlight peeked from behind the home. Julissa sighed as she searched for a suitable reply. The most assuring thing she could think of was the last thing she heard from Lieutenant Morial.

"He has got to be up and running somewhere, Ma Brown. There's too many men looking for him and not enough places to search. If they haven't found a body somewhere, there's still a speck of hope," Julissa professed.

"Oooh, child! Well, I guess I'll grab on to that little speck, too. Take me inside so I can meet little Percy," Mrs. Brown requested.

"Yes ma'am. I'll take you to see Peerless," Julissa

corrected.

"You know what I mean!" Mrs. Brown snapped back.

Julissa obliged Mrs. Brown's request as she escorted her into the home. They entered a small foyer, then the living room area. When they entered, they saw Paul hanging on the play pen as Judy hovered over Peerless. They each giggled as Peerless cooed and squirmed in the tiny playpen.

"Whatcha' doing there, lil' Paul. You got some ants in your pants?" Mr. Monroe teased.

"You silly, Pau Pau," Judy answered.

"Yes, he is, Bug. Very foolish indeed," Mrs. Brown answered.

"Hey there, V. How you holding up? Come take a look at this grandbaby of *ours*," Mr. Monroe invited after he noticed her in the room.

"That's why I'm here! Let me have a look-see at the little man," Mrs. Brown agreed.

As Mrs. Brown closed in on the playpen, Judy retreated to Julissa. Paul pulled up a chair so Mrs. Brown could sit next to the playpen and watch the show. Mrs. Brown found Peerless to be precious at first sight, yet somewhat peculiar.

"Mama, where's Daddy? He still hasn't called me yet," Judy asked.

"I don't know, bug. He's out there somewhere. He'll be back though. I'm almost certain of it," Julissa stated.

"But how is he going to play with Perry if he doesn't come back? How is he going to play with me?" Judy whined.

Julissa contemplated her next move. She knew to be careful of what she told Judy, but she also did not want her disappointed every night until Renaldo showed up. *If he shows up.* She grabbed Judy's hand and escorted her to the formal dining area. Julissa pulled out a chair and motioned Judy to sit. Judy held a puzzled grin on her face as she scooted to the back of the chair and giggled at her dangling feet.

"Okay, Bug, let mommy be honest with you," Julissa began.

"Okay, Mommy," Judy complied.

"Okay. So, when Daddy left, he was pretty upset with mommy. He had good reason to be, but I think he meant to come back. If he comes back for anyone, it will be you, dear. I'm almost certain you are his favorite, even more so than me now," Julissa shared.

"Where did he go, Mama? Why didn't he come and get me?" Judy inquired.

"I uhh, I—don't know, Bug. I wish I could tell you. I just don't know. Nobody knows," Julissa uttered with a single tear streaming down her face.

"I want my daddy!" Judy wailed.

Julissa leaned over to Judy's chair to console her. Judy latched on to her mother as she soiled Ju's shirt in a pool of tears. They leaned into one another.

In the den, Mrs. Brown had to satisfy her urge to pick Peerless up. She brought the newborn in for a closer look.

"Well, ain't you something beautiful. You remind me of someone, but for the life of me I can't put my finger on who," Mrs. Brown remarked.

"Oh! What you say, Cortissa? I'll be glad to help you out in the kitchen!" Paul shouted.

Paul instantaneously jumped up, grabbed his glass, and departed the den. Mrs. Brown watched his antics and simply shook her head. She reverted her eyes back to the baby.

"That grandfather of yours is a strange little man, Percy. Well, your father's dad really ain't much better," Mrs. Brown concluded.

Paul entered the kitchen and noticed Cortissa was just about finished with dinner. He figured she'd been in there for a while, but she was uncharacteristically quiet. He would usually cherish hushed moments, but Paul was willing to do anything to avoid the awkward discussion regarding Peerless' origins. Consequently, Paul had become more interested in the background of Franc posthumously than he ever was while he lived.

Paul crossed the kitchen floor into a hallway leading to the master bedroom. He picked up Cortissa's voice in the room. Paul slowed his gait as he pushed the door to check on his wife. Paul spotted Cortissa standing near the window facing the back gazebo. He took notice of her loose posture as she leaned one thigh on the nightstand. Paul rethought venturing further.

"Yes. You are going to love him. He is such a precious little angel. Sometime after he gets his shots and Julissa gets moving about, you have to come see him for yourself," Cortissa stated.

She straightened her stance to turn around. Cortissa noticed Paul standing in the doorway. The slight smile she held slowly transitioned to a smirk. Cortissa focused on the statements of the individual on the opposite end before she decided to wrap up the interaction.

"Sure thing, honey. Did you get the pictures I sent?" Cortissa asked.

Paul leaned his head until it nearly touched his

shoulder. Cortissa glared back at him while dipping her head to the side. Paul, who is no stranger to Cortissa's contrary demeanor, gracefully bowed out of the stare off.

"Okay, girl, let me tend to these hungry folks in my house. I will speak with you again soon," Cortissa assured as she hung up the phone.

Though Paul was essentially going to get what he wanted, he was still unsettled. He intended to leave Cortissa to her devices, but curiosity had overtaken him. He whipped his cranium back around to address the query weighing on his mind.

"Corty, who were you talking to? You seem prouder of Lil' Paul than Julissa is, and I know that ain't so," Paul addressed.

"A grandmother can't be excited by an addition to the family? What? You want me to hate him or something?" Cortissa returned.

"I want you to give JuJu a chance to brag about him too. Who were you trying to auction him off to this time?" Paul inquired.

Cortissa folded her arms and leaned to the rear. She twisted her neck matter-of-factly and snickered at Paul's concern. Cortissa slowly sauntered toward her beau and playfully "fixed" his collar. She then loosened the middle button of his polo and stared directly in Paul's eye.

"If you must know," Cortissa began, "I was speaking to our long-lost daughter, Ramona. Should I not tell her about her nephew?"

"What? She called *you*? I mean...why didn't she ask to speak with me?" Paul asked curiously.

"Oh, are you mad, dear? Daddy's girls don't have to dismiss the womb they came from just to remain in your favor, do they?" Cortissa accused.

"I don't mind sharing no spotlight with ya, Corty. Especially if it's on the dance floor. But I have a hard time believing *my* Ramona called you instead of me," Paul concluded.

"Well, Mr. Monroe, if you are willing to help me with the dinner crowd, I would love to share some more of my secrets with you," Cortissa reported suggestively.

Cortissa worked her hand into the opening of Paul's shirt, as she tenderly groped his pectoral. Mr. Monroe closed his eyes for a moment before he grasped her hand and nodded his head. Cortissa stared at Paul with pursed lips as she raised her eyebrows twice. He left the room without further hint. Cortissa watched as her husband moseyed down the hall to the kitchen. She trailed slowly behind him before she realized her phone was unattended. Cortissa returned to their bedroom. She viewed a text message alert on her phone. Cortissa opened the message to find a picture of Peerless. She smiled at the photo with a loving grin. The next message in the conversation was a dark photo with a reddish splash covering it. Cortissa pressed the phone against her chest as she folded her lips internally. She looked at the phone again before sighing and departing the room...

Chapter 13

Sliver in the Shadows

Renaldo was awakened to the hymn "Victory is Mine" ringing through the church. In his groggy state, he nearly grabbed the broom to start sweeping the storage room floor. For an instant, he imagined he was back in Crescent City on a Saturday morning. He reminisced on the tunes Mama Brown would play when he and his brother cleaned the house. He stood up from his air mattress and moved closer to the sound of the music. He laughed to himself, now reflecting on Sunday mornings in Baptist churches; the choirs nearly performed a song per each verse read.

Renaldo walked back to his corner and sat atop the bed. He pulled out his commission wallet and dug into the back fold. Renaldo pulled out a photo of himself, Julissa, and an infant Judy. He smiled at the sight of Judy, his last will and testament in this strange barren land he was tasked to navigate. When he focused on Julissa's image, he bit his lower lip as he slowly grazed his teeth across it. He clenched his jaw as tears began to fill his ducts. Renaldo hunched over his knees while trying to contain himself. He didn't know how long it had been since he had heard their voices, but he knew it had been long enough.

Renaldo stood up and stomped toward an adjacent corner. He needed to speak with the old man, *and he needed to address him now*! Renaldo picked up one of the boxes numbered "337" and launched it to the shoulder of an empty metal shelf. The shelf slid a little, but no additional effect. Personally disgusted with his living arrangements, Renaldo began to rotate his shoulders as he intently eyed another shelf with boxes. He methodically backtracked a couple of steps to help build momentum. Renaldo then plowed forward as fast and hard as feasible. He dropped his left shoulder into the corner of the shelf as they each went tumbling over. Renaldo clutched his left shoulder as he lay alongside the shelving.

The shelving met the floor with a loud thud. The abrupt crash supplied a satisfying tune to Renaldo's ears. He knew someone close by would hear and if he could get to his feet again, he would tackle a few more shelves. He decided he should find some shoulder pads and possibly a helmet first, as the old metal shelves had very little give. That shelf was less forgiving of him in that instant than Julissa had been over the years. While writhing in pain, Renaldo really thought back to the things he had done: stepping out on Julissa, taking her for granted, and allegedly driving her into the arms of another man. *Even if only for an instant*, what he was sure had transpired between Julissa and Franc around a year ago afflicted him more than the sum of what he suffered in that church building so far. Yet, if he ever wanted to receive an explanation for what happened, he would need to get off that floor and back to society.

Renaldo rolled to his right side and attempted to push himself up to his knees. The initial effort was an utter failure. His left arm was still tingling from the self-inflicted collision, and he had to wait for the feeling to come back before he could try again. He slid his knees and feet underneath his chest as he used his right hand to separate himself from the ground. Once Renaldo returned to his feet, he roughly massaged his left shoulder until he heard a voice in the hallway.

"I'm going up yonder (going up yonder), I'm going up yonder (going up yonder), I'm going up yonder, to beeeee with my lorrrrrrrd," the male voice sang.

"HEYYYY! HEYYY! OPEN THE DOOR!" Renaldo commanded.

The singing stopped expediently. Renaldo was sure the person heard him but had no idea which direction they would enter from. He looked around for another object to throw into the dark shadows of his surroundings. Renaldo's shoulder began to throb again. He winced constantly through spotty pain.

"HELP ME! Please! Please," Renaldo echoed as he slipped back to one knee, fading into unconsciousness.

"If anybody asks you, where I'm going, where I'm going, soooooooon," the male voice boosted as if it were present in the room.

Renaldo lifted his head and shifted his eyes back and forth to each side. He gazed into the abyss before him, not truly sure of where this man could be. Renaldo heard light footsteps to his rear. He gingerly brought his head to the posterior to find the older man traipsing from the far opposite corner of the room. The older man came to a stop once the front of his shoes were basked in the light. The rest of him remained shrouded in mystery.

"I love what you've done with the place. I have a few

pews upstairs that might need some remodeling if you have time," the older gentleman jeered.

"I'd love to come up there and listen one of these Sundays. Seems to be a fine collection of songs you guys sang today. Did one of the songs get stuck in your head?" Renaldo interviewed.

"Not exactly. *'Going Up Yonder'* is a classic and a personal favorite. At this point in my life, it really resonates with me, young buck," the older man clarified.

"Nothing like some of that southern Baptist gospel music, hnah, sir?" Renaldo patronized.

"You got that right, jack. Do you have any requests for the choir next Sunday? Any personal favorites you would like to hear?" the older man entertained.

"Before you walk the crystal stair, could you please take me out of here. I have agreed to help you and Baron look for his mother. Why in the hell am I still in this storage room?" Renaldo requested.

"Simple, my friend. It's the biggest room in the building, aside from where services are held. You are in a prime location, young buck. Don't let a few inconveniences ruin your sight," the older man attempted to convince.

"I'd prefer you take me to a small room with a real bed and a lamp that doesn't suffer from Tourette's," Renaldo snickered.

"You are very uptight and unappreciative. You need to loosen up a bit. You must be one of those Pentecostals or something like that?" the older man prodded.

"Naw, I'm more extreme than that. I lean more toward the teachings of Islam," Renaldo poked.

"Ohhh, you one of them righteous brother mans from the motherland types, eh? Victor thought he saw you throwing away that bacon we gave you. What a waste. That was applewood too," the older gentleman joked.

"It was under cooked. Tell Victor to spend less time on the eggs and more on the red meat products, if you don't mind," Renaldo entreated.

"You get up and tell him yourself, you little shit. This is a church, not Denny's," the older man fired back.

"Whoa, whoa, whoa. Language, my good sir. I believe it is you who has forgotten where we are," Renaldo patronized.

"Excuse me, son. The Lord forgives; I don't know if your savior 'Allah' is as considerate," the older man stated sarcastically.

Renaldo crouched over and laughed hysterically at the plight of the older man. He struggled to his feet, but the laughter shrouded the agony of his shoulder. He walked toward the older man, who took one step back into the shadows. Renaldo became suspicious of this movement and decided to engage the older man further; he hoped to distract him enough to divulge his intentions.

"Honestly, sir, I was just kidding about my religious affiliation. I consider myself a Christian," Renaldo declared.

"Well, thank God for that, I presume," the older man chimed.

"Tell me something, mister. I've been exposed to several religions, in one capacity or another. They all appear to praise one individual. Is it not entirely possible they are all the same man?" Renaldo outlined.

"Hmm, never pondered that. Funny *you* would mention it. Considering you are both the great detective Renaldo Brown and *The Recluse*," the older man ousted.

Renaldo's eyelids widened. He stared the older man down as he dashed across the room. The lights flickered twice then ceased. Renaldo plowed forward without interruption. There was the expected scrape across a hard surface nearby. The light came back dimmer than if left. At least it appeared so before Renaldo turned around and noticed he stood in the murkiest section of the room. He stomped back toward the light district.

"Who the hell are you, old man? I'm getting a little sick of playing these games with you and Victor. Bring your ass back here and face me!" Renaldo shouted.

The lightbulb dimmed considerably, then flashed back on. Renaldo circled about in place waiting on Baron to cross a threshold, so he knew where to run. He anticipated the light going out again in a matter of seconds. Renaldo zeroed in on the buzz.

"Come on, Vic. Bring your ass in here; I wanna play a tune on your face, you fugly motherfucker!" Renaldo baited.

The glow lessened but would not dissipate. Renaldo seethed internally for someone to engage him. All he needed was a small opening and he would be sure to rip a hole through it. *Or through them.* The beam depleted. The concrete began to snore. Renaldo ran toward the sound… and directly into a metal shelving unit. His knee banged into the unit so hard he whipped around to its rear and crashed shoulder blades first onto the surface. The scathing scratching of the surface was in earshot. Renaldo flung his leg out and hit a human calf. He tried to punch at the object, but the owner dodged his flailing fists. Suddenly, there was a loud thud across Renaldo's forehead that floored him. The hum of steel danced within his vicinity.

His head drooped to the side of his body. He was left motionless from the strike.

"Nooo! Dohhhhhhhhn't dooooo iiiiiiiiiiit!" Baron's voice rang.

The room was slightly illuminated again. Renaldo slowly turned his head to the opposite side to notice the older man and his cane being held off by Baron. Renaldo ascertained he had been struck by the dense handle portion of the cane, its thickest part. The older man continued to tussle with Baron until eventually yielding. The older man pulled away from Baron, nearly tumbling over. He adjusted his collar as he stared directly into Renaldo's eyes.

"Heeeeee cannnnnn't hellllllp ussssss ifff heeee's deaaaaaaad, unnnc," Baron reported.

"He can't help anybody but you, Victor! My burden is gone. LONG GONE!" the older man exclaimed.

The older man pointed his cane toward Renaldo's chest before walking off into darkness. Baron sighed at this display, then turned his sights to Renaldo. Baron reached his hand out to Renaldo, to which Renaldo denied him. Baron shook his head at Renaldo's hesitation. He took four steps toward the opposing end of the room. He then came to a halt.

"Therrrrrrrr izzz sommmmthiiiiiiiiiing youuuu neeeed toooo see," Baron shared.

"Fine. Give me a second to—," Renaldo began.

Before Renaldo could finish his statement, the room blacked out. Metal loudly scathed the surface for five seconds before the sound completely faded. Renaldo crawled to his feet to trail the sound, but he lost the trail. There was an abrupt "dink" off to his right before the light restored. Renaldo scanned the room to find that there wasn't another soul present.

"Of course he left," Renaldo commented.

Renaldo squinted his eyes as he noticed a small black pouch sitting on the floor near a shelving unit. The closer he came to the pouch, the easier it became to recognize: his credentials wallet. Renaldo picked it up and wondered how it had escaped his pocket. He attempted to flip it open but soon realized he was holding it upside down. He pondered momentarily, before turning his body the direction his shield pointed to. He stood up and carefully shuffled into a portion of the room the light refused to touch. Renaldo scanned the dark void for any sign of an exit but did not depart from the path he had been conveniently assigned. Renaldo stubbed his toe on a heavy object to the front. He leaned over to grab his foot and banged his forehead against a cold steel knob. He set himself upright as he felt around for the knob. Once Renaldo secured the knob, he twisted it and pushed it open. He entered a dim hallway.

"Well, I'll be damned, Victor still pulling smooth moves, even without his voice," Renaldo gathered as he smiled and continued down the hall.

Chapter 14

Peeks and Valleys

He's sitting by the phone, contemplating whether to make the call. His left thumb is pressed into the flap of his lower lip while his fingers scale his beard. The fingers on his right hand tap the table around his phone. He has contemplated it for a week, though it was obviously necessary to deliver on his promise. He grips the phone with his fingertips and locates the number. He found it instantaneously; however, he remained reluctant, even after pushing the call button. Then he hears the voice and realizes there's no turning back!

"Crescent City Homicide Division, Detective Barrios," Rita answered.

He quietly chuckles at her. His nerves have slowed his reaction time but amplified his hearing. He can hear the air around her, the stillness around him, and his own breathing pattern. He inhales deeply, releases a sigh, and proceeds with his greeting.

"Yes. Hello! This is Detective McDonald with Gretna P.D. How are you doing today, lady?" said Rance.

"Oh," Rita uttered, apparently confused. "I am okay; how about yourself, detective?"

"I do okay. I'm a little better now," Rance flirted.

"Oh, really? Why would you say that?" Rita challenged.

"Heh-heh. I've been holding on to some tidbits I found in that video surveillance you released to me. I believe you might find these findings 'interesting,'" Rance returned.

"Do you now? What makes you come to that revelation, sir?" Rita regaled.

"Well, I believe I may have noticed something you missed in the footage. I don't know if you thought of this already, but if you hadn't, it may help in court with the Hogs," Rance explained.

Rita released a breath of relief. She spun around in her office chair and looked to the sky outside, wondering if this was the break in the case she'd been waiting for.

"Okay, I'm listening," Rita uttered.

"I was actually hoping to meet up with you so I could show you precisely what it is I found. I would hate for you to have any doubts or concerns about my assistance," Rance declared.

"I have seen the different streetlight recordings. I'm fairly certain that if you refresh my memory, I could figure out the rest," Rita stated firmly.

"If you insist," Rance replied.

"I certainly do," Rita returned.

Rance laughed at her tone. Rita took no exception to Rance's assumed cockiness. She wished she could "huff and puff and blow" his house down. Instead, she awaited his answer.

"Okay. I understand. I was just thinking that since I must return the videos, we could go over them before I give them back," Rance revealed.

Rita cut her eyes to the left and shook her head in

disgust. "Typical" she thought to herself. She was a serious detective trying to complete a serious task, and here comes a man apparently trying to make a love connection.

"When you turn those videos in, sir, you would be doing so in a different wing of this police department. That is a task that will not require us to cross paths. However, if you would like to see me in person, that is a different conversation, for a *different phone*," Rita scolded.

"I had no idea the conversation was on the table. Unfortunately, I don't have another number to explore that option," Rance hinted.

"And mister, Rance, was it? There is a reason for that," Rita clarified.

Rance chuckled absurdly at Rita. Rita wasn't sure if she should join in or feel insulted. She looked at her phone as if she could see his face on the screen. She lifted her eyebrow in utter confusion. Rance settled down long enough to quell her query.

"Well, fellow detective, from what I gathered in the footage, it would appear subject Hall was losing control of his bike prior to Brown firing in his direction," Rance shared.

"Really?! You may be right. I don't believe I saw that the first time," Rita responded.

"That is fine. If you review it again, tell me what you think, okay?" Rance requested.

"Maybe I will. Maybe I won't. But I am sure you will hear about it either way, kind sir," Rita concluded.

"Hospitable as always; I appreciate that, detective," Rance replied.

"Don't be so formal, sir. It's *Miss* Barrios, remember?" Rita tarried.

"Ahh. Yes indeed...miss. Let me know what you find; I hope I was of some assistance. Good day," Rance vacated.

Detective Barrios gingerly placed the receiver back on its dock. A miniature grin briefly graced her lips. Rita whipped her chair around to find a male figure present in her domain. Rita's eyes and mouth were both agape in shock. Her chair slid back as she pulled a pistol from her desk and brought it on target. Upon recognition of the visitor, Rita dropped her arms, closed her eyes, let out a sigh, and gnawed her lip.

"Remy! Do you not know to announce yourself to let a lady know you have entered the room?" Rita exclaimed.

"Sure I do! Just didn't see a lady," Officer Remy Daniels chimed.

Rita cut her eyes at Officer Daniels for his snide remarks. Remy appeared unmoved by Rita's expression and less entertained by her tone. He donned a nervous yet overbearing scowl.

"Well, I wish you were that blunt about what happened in City Park. Somehow all the hot air fills your lungs when you address most women, but not so much in front of Judge Burgess," Rita said.

"I told you, all of you, exactly what happened. After repeating a story so many times, you start to wonder if people are dumb or if the story is simply unbelievable," Remy rebutted.

"When you are certainly telling the truth, there is no room for doubt!" Rita challenged.

Officer Daniels glared at Rita. The uptight individual took no exception to the detective's precise wit. Rita noticed Daniels' blank stare but felt no remorse for the man whom her entire investigation would hinge upon. She felt like he was hiding something, though she desperately hoped he wasn't. Something about Daniels did not sit right with her, but she couldn't quite put a finger on it.

"Well, did you come here to startle me or does your presence serve a purpose?" Rita goaded.

"I wish your memory was as long as your hair. Maybe becoming a detective made you forget what it was like being on the streets for critical incidents. Is it possible that having an office with a window view has taken your mind off the struggle we endure in the street?" Remy accused.

"First of all," Rita began as she looked down and shook her head, "my ability to perform on the street is exactly why I don't have to do it daily anymore."

"I bet!" Remy chimed.

Rita laughed to prevent shouting. She was no fan of Remy's insinuations, but she knew he was just like most other guys who couldn't become detectives. "She had to be sleeping with someone" is what some would tell themselves to excuse their own shortcomings. Humans were notorious for their crab in a barrel mentality.

"Well, maybe if anything you did in the streets was memorable, for even you, officer, you might be able to look out the window and *conveniently* avoid the strife out there, potnah!" Rita clapped back.

That struck a chord. A silent stare off ensued. Remy's right fist was clenched atop one of the office chairs. Rita had been standing and leaning forward on her fists since she'd advised Remy of his less than stellar accolades.

"Now, if there is anything I can help you with, then proceed. Otherwise, you can get back on that elevator and return to your floor with the rest of the street beats you are so fond of," Rita advised.

"I just came here to ensure you I will be more than ready for the next hearing. I was wondering if anyone heard anything from Detective Brown," Remy shared.

"No, I have not. You know something that I don't?" Rita replied.

"Naw," Remy chuckled to himself, "I was just looking for a little clarity. That's all."

Remy slowly backpedaled from Rita's desk while his hands were raised in the "surrender" position. Remy released an ominous cackle before spinning around and departing the office.

"Dumbass!" Rita claimed explicably.

The door to her office crept closed as air filled the space between the seal and frame. Rita walked over to the door, flipped the lock with fervor, and stomped back to the window overlooking the parking lot. She returned to her chair as she sunk slowly while sulking. The frustration flowed from her eyes like a waterfall. Unfortunately, her sobs were less than soothing to the ears. *Had she not done everything to prove she deserved her position? Was she not taking on one of the most controversial cases Crescent City had ever seen, with style and grace, nonetheless*? Though Rita knew her efforts were of gracious intent, the repeated doubt of her peers often kept her up at night. As life would have it, Rita spent more time proving she was deserving of her title than performing in it. Why were her credentials being questioned? It was not she who held the reputation of the C.C.P.D. in a testimony. Yet, Rita constantly felt the weight of the world on *her* shoulders. Little did she know, her hard work was hardly unnoticed.

Chapter 15

Writings on the Walls

Renaldo scoured the hallway for a functioning light switch. By his estimation, he'd spent more than enough time in obscurity. It all suddenly dawned on him: His only way to freedom was through the tunnel of his own darkness. Renaldo stopped at a switch on the wall with a hand-written note attached. He flicked the lever only to saturate the area in dull lighting. Renaldo inspected the note which read: *The road to our salvation is often uncovered by the recognition of our own faults.*

"What does that even mean?" Renaldo wondered.

Renaldo continued down the darkened hall in search of another panel. He located one on the opposite side of the walkway. Renaldo ignorantly flipped the switch, removing the sparse lighting he'd previously unveiled. He struck the knob into the opposite position but to no avail.

"SKRRRRRRRRRRRTT," went the stone scraping across the tile.

Renaldo raced back to the initial panel above the written memo. The grinding intensified with the duration of dusk. Renaldo hit the switch and was immersed in limited illumination. Those scathing scratches continued for a couple of seconds, then ceased. The silence soothed Renaldo amidst the hissing of the bulb. He released a vast groan.

Once he collected his breath, he resumed his journey along the hall. His eyes diverted between light control panels to search for little notes. The quaint light provided was just enough to furnish a gleam in the distance. He traveled three feet into the shadows before encountering another yellow sticky note. He flipped this switch to the tune of a brighter yet flickering light. He snatched the message from the wall with disdain. This one read: *An undisciplined boy never truly becomes a man.*

"Oh, I got a 'boy' for your ass. Just wait til I get my hands on this damn wordsmith!" Renaldo threatened.

He trudged the hall floors as his eyes frantically hunted the next clue. He figured the next letter would be stuck to a panel beyond the well-lit region. Renaldo's pupils contracted on the disclosed area ahead. He penetrated the zone until he was nearly covered in darkness. Detective Brown peered to his rear to realize he had traveled an ample distance from the plainly visible vicinity. He pondered his path but convinced himself the next hint was forward. Renaldo sightlessly sought a note. Suddenly, a yellow sticky note came into view. Renaldo flicked the switch to find another written note: *Have you covered all of your bases? Do your steps remain uncompromised in the sands?*

"A beach vacation sounds really good right now. But what the hell are they talking about?" Renaldo pondered.

In all his confusion, he nearly missed the door stationed at the end of the hallway. "About damn time!" he thought to himself. He placed his hand on the golden handle to the glossy wooden door. Renaldo twisted the knob only to be met with resistance. He was initially in disbelief. *That disbelief became anger. That anger was followed by rage!*

"No. No. NOOOOOOOOO!" Renaldo panicked as he wrestled the knob.

Renaldo banged upon the wooden obstruction with the base of his fists. His head drooped as he began to whimper with discontent. Behind him, he heard the familiar scratching of the surface. He whipped his head to the background to learn the error in his ways: *the dark territory?* Renaldo was startled by the buckling of the door from a blunt force strike on the opposite side. He released the handle while stumbling backwards. Another rap upon the door convinced Renaldo to voluntarily sprint toward the eclipsed patch of the floor.

He traversed the route blindly until he reached the lit region around the curve. Renaldo slid to a halt prior to reversing his momentum again. He whipped his head side-to-side as he navigated the cloaked segment. *SCCCRRRRRRPP! SCCCRRRRRRPPP!* The floor sounded like it was separating beyond the door. Renaldo panicked as the reverberation plagued his ears. He searched each wall until he found yet another note. Renaldo rapidly turned on the accompanying switch. He read the note while it remained secured to the wall.

"Sometimes we must take one step back to go two steps forward," Renaldo read aloud. He considered this omen. He then heard a "click" of the door. The door crept open a smidgen while the hinge lightly creaked. Renaldo began to dash forward until he heard a scrape in the distant background. He foolishly ceased his gallop to investigate the inconvenient disturbance. His naivety would be his downfall. Detective Brown ignorantly paced himself toward the former end of the hall. Discretion came in the form of a loud scour ahead. As he shifted his mass toward the laminated door, he ran chest first into the oversized head of steel. His own momentum sent him careening posterior first into the nearby wall as the affected shoulder struggled to remain in socket. The ligaments may have been lodged back in place by their forceful encounter with the border.

As Renaldo slumped into a seated position, he slowly scanned the author of his pain. Dirt-drenched boots accompanied by tattered and filth-splattered cream-colored khakis. Further observation captured the hem of an untucked white and blue striped shirt; one long sleeve hung past the waist and was graced by an unkempt hand. Renaldo already knew who had abruptly interrupted his suicide sprints; however, he'd never seen Victor in anything more than his feebly fitted toga.

"How long have I been here? Is it almost Easter again? What's up with you and the new digs?" Renaldo insisted.

Baron inspected his own attire and offered Renaldo a half-hearted smile in exchange for his compliment. The smile faded swiftly as Baron pressed the crown of his hammer firmly into Renaldo's chest. Baron's eyelids tensed as he leaned on the sledgehammer while subtly twisting it along Renaldo's pectoral.

"Shiiiiiiiiiit! Was this a damn cat and mouse chase for you! Let off the steel will, ya?" Renaldo screamed.

"Iiiiiiiiiiii did-d-d-d-d-int doooooo thiiiis. Youuuu diiiiid!" Baron expressed.

Baron slowly retracted his hammer from Renaldo's

battered body. Baron then directed Renaldo's attention toward the hallway door. He deeply inhaled the still air as Renaldo tried to recoup his own.

"This feels like 'Shutter Island' but I ain't borrowed nobody's smokes. I know damn well I'm not hallucinating or setting myself up for elaborate traps. You gonna have to try harder than that, Victor," Renaldo defended.

"Youuuu haaaad alllllll yoouuuuu neeeeed-ed... yehhhht youuuuuu stillllll diiiiid nahhhhhhhhhhhht havvvve theeeeee paaaatiennnnnsssssse tooooooo securrrre the liiiiiiiight toooo the briiiiiiighterrrr paaaaaath," Baron explained.

Renaldo was exasperated. He determined Victor showed him the way out in order to track him down again. *Was this some sort of game?* Baron reached his hand toward Renaldo, knowing the detective desperately needed assistance. Renaldo's face shriveled at the sight of Victor's outstretched appendage. He threw his weight to his right side and braced himself up slowly until eventually gathering his feet beneath his tenderized carcass. Renaldo stared into Baron's eyes as if to challenge him but noticed the metal appendage draped over Baron's shoulder and thought better of it.

"You ain't so tough without your metal shield," Renaldo boasted.

"Maaayyyyybeeee naaaaaaaahhhht, buhhhhhhttt, yoouuuuu cerrrrtaiiiinlyyyy arrrrrrrre naaaaahhhht azzzzzzzzz smaaaaaaart wiiiiiiithowwwwwwt youurrrrrr eeeleck-triiiiiic waannnnnnnn," Baron fired back.

Renaldo's eyes widened as he nearly gave himself whiplash to fix his sights on Baron. Baron placed a hand onto his shoulder and willed him in the direction of the laminated door. Renaldo began to ponder what was ahead. Whatever it may be, he hoped it would be less volatile than what he'd experienced thus far. Baron used his hammer to pry the door open as they approached it. Time slowed down for Renaldo as he cringed at the possibilities awaiting beyond that door seal.

Renaldo slowed his gait as he finally cleared the demoralizing foyer. Much to his surprise, Baron guided Renaldo into a stairwell. Were his trials finally over? Was this the lighter path transcribed in the notes? Renaldo began to ponder his affiliation to the older man. *What had he taken that could not be returned*? They climbed the stairs to the next floor, where Baron escorted Renaldo directly into the church corridor. Renaldo decided he was ready to take on the old man for the last time, and *this time*, he wouldn't leave his sight without the answers he desperately desired.

Chapter 16

The Forbidden Fruit

For the first time in what felt like awhile, Renaldo experienced an ounce of relief. The laminated tile floor seemed like socks out of the dryer in comparison to the concrete jungle Renaldo had been subject to over the undisclosed period. *Tile*? The blood- and water-soaked tile at *Nina's* in Tunneltown; Is that what this was about? Was the old man one of the Lazlos or somehow in cahoots with that crew? *Shit*! That would make sense. "How else would he know about The Recluse?" Renaldo pondered while still being ushered around the sanctuary.

Baron's eyes didn't divert from the path. It was as if the walls were infused with the powers of Medusa. His neck didn't sway in either direction, and even when his body did, his head remained aligned. Believe it or not, it was the strangest thing Renaldo ever encountered. At least it was until they passed the door nearest to the church's altar.

"No cramming in the confessional?" Renaldo inquired.

"No," Baron answered rather simply yet stoutly.

"Oh, is this the tour I requested?" Renaldo continued.

Baron shifted his eyes in Renaldo's direction momentarily. He released an agitated sigh and returned his eyes to the path. They approached another set of stairs, now at the rear of the church, before Renaldo received an answer.

"Thiiiiiiiis tiiiime, heeee izzzzzz nahhhhhhhht exxxspec-tinnnnng yoouuu," Baron revealed.

Renaldo was shocked! He would finally have the upper hand. His confidence quickly dissipated into concern. *"Why is Victor trying to help me?"* Renaldo wondered but dared not ask. Was this a set up? Would this be the last ambush before they dumped him in a nearby river? Renaldo's anxiety was put on hold once he started to hear *"Going Up Yonder"* ahead.

Baron stopped in front of the door as the melody seeped into the hallway. Baron utilized his hammer to widen the opening. Baron placed his hand between the shoulder blades of Renaldo and shoved him into the office. Renaldo barged into the room clumsily enough to nearly knock over a chair. The older man looked up at his guest, and with full display of displeasure on his face, reached over to his phone and increased the volume of the music. Baron snickered to himself while Renaldo appeared aloof. Renaldo nervously glared at Baron, who simply shrugged his shoulders. Renaldo took Baron's nonchalant demeanor as an indication he would not receive interference on his behalf. Renaldo took a deep breath and positioned himself directly across the table from the older man, whose head was down, trained on some paperwork.

"What is it th—," Renaldo began.

"I'M GOING UP YONDER! I'M GOING UP YON-DERRRRRR," the older man began to recite, loudly.

"You damn sure are if you th—," Renaldo started again before further interruption.

"To be with my Lord, LO-OHH-ARRRRRDDD!" the older man continued.

The actions of the older man simply incensed Renaldo. He suffered as much as he would take. Renaldo placed his hand over the phone and effortlessly slid it down to the far end and off the table. The older man watched the phone fall into the nearest chair then heard it crash onto the floor. The music continued to play but it was nearly muffled by the distance. The older man tightened his lids as he chuckled at the detective standing across from him. When the older man looked up, Renaldo was finally able to get a good look at him. That tingle of familiarity crept up his spine once more. Renaldo's eyes enlarged until they bulged out of each socket.

"This all makes sense now. You have me locked up all this time in one of your churches. And for what? What I do to you, old man? What is up with all these notes and riddles you left for me downstairs?" Renaldo inclined.

The older man's eyes bled with obvious perplexity. The gentleman slowly transferred his attention to Baron, who still stood idly by the entrance. Baron was unmoved by the older man's bladed stare. The older gentleman understood what had transpired but felt no need to dignify Renaldo with an explanation.

"It is not I who left any notes for you, anywhere. I never pictured you venturing into any hallway, much less being present here on the upper deck of this building. So, Mister 'Recluse,' as I referred to you earlier, who in the world do you think you are?" the older man chastised.

Following this recollection, Renaldo gazed at Baron as well. Renaldo snorted at the claims of the older man, but also understood what happened along the way: *Baron was the author of those riddles*. That's how he knew when to strike. But how did he know where to place each note? Renaldo reassessed who was the undisputed mastermind among the pair. That was a matter to be determined later. Presently, Renaldo had a bone to pick with the older man and there was no confusion about that.

"What you want with me, Father Maxwell?" Renaldo now remembered. "Yeah, I knew I'd seen you around before. You have that same stupid look on your face that you had when Mrs. Lafitte told you to kick rocks. You felt played or something, old man? One of them old-fashioned guys who think a woman can't speak up for herself, even when mourning a son?"

The older man's face filled with pure contempt. He began to grit his teeth at the hard accusations the detective hurled. Renaldo busted the man's chops so thoroughly; he could no longer sit. He leaned upon the plate glass tabletop, bearing all his weight on calloused knuckles. Baron abandoned his corner to get a better angle on the verbal spatter.

"Well, what is it? Hmm? What did I do to you, Mr. Maxwell? Did I hurt one of your little buddies that came through? You got some kind of connection with the Fifth Ward Hogs? Hmm? Is that what you wanted to talk to Mrs. Lafitte about? You had a change of heart and wanted to warn her because those young punks were too stubborn to call it off?" Renaldo interrogated, one allegation proceeding another.

"Boy, what did you call me?!" the older man thundered.

"Forgive me. I mean *Father Maxwell*," Renaldo corrected himself.

"Is that what Jennifer told you to call me that day? I can hardly remember. That was such an eventful day," the older man rebutted.

"Who you tellin'?!" Renaldo exclaimed.

The older man's lip quivered as he separated himself from the desk. He adjusted the collar on his suit jacket as he watched Renaldo intently. The older man walked over to a dry erase board and removed his cane from the extended border. Renaldo stood up as well, assuming the older man would attempt to flee.

"Where you think you're going, sir? It's about time we settle this. That family did not deserve what happened to them! If you had a beef with them, you could have settled it on *a different day. At a different place. At a different time*," Renaldo instructed.

"Trust me, son, any 'beef,' as you young punks say, I had with that family was settled before I stepped foot in the mausoleum. And that is thanks to none other than YOU!" the older man emphasized.

"What the hell does that even mean? Man, I had not even heard of you until that day! It looked like the Lafittes didn't want anything to do with you. I just came over to see what the issue was. I was there to help Mrs. Lafitte. NOT YOU!" Renaldo clarified.

The older man traveled to the other side of the room. He became disgusted with Renaldo and all his self-righteous babble. He grew tired of Renaldo's "hero" mentality, as if he were not a fool sitting in a glass house. The older man knew the one thing Renaldo apparently thought he could forget, so he was prepared to cast his stone upon Renaldo's entire world.

"It is not me who wronged Jennifer, not that day. In

fact, once I saw you, I knew *you* were an issue. I tried to warn her, but she was overly emotional, and rightfully so. The only son she had in this world. Stripped from her. And you could have stopped it, 'Recluse.' You could have prevented it all, the same way you did when my sister tried to choke him to death in your car. But what did you do? Hmm? You sat by and you let that woman's son die in your presence! How many times did he sit by and watch you crumble to *your demise*?! Hmm? How many!! You jacked-up piece of shit? By the simple fact you are allowed to stand here and make these silly assumptions to my face, I would have to say NONE!" hollered the older man.

His sister? Who was his....? Renaldo set his gaze upon Victor as he thought back. Didn't Victor affectionately refer to the older man as "unc" while they were in the storage cellar? The connection was beginning to make sense now. The older man was the brother of Lavender Baronne?! *He was the blood relative of The Baroness? This is why Renaldo was here.* He was brought here to help unite the older man with his sister, and Baron with his mother.

"Yeah, well, you may have been a concerned party, but you have no grounds to judge me. You weren't there that night! You have no idea what you would have done in that situation," Renaldo defended.

"I damn sure wouldn't have let my partner die. That's for certain!" the older man fired back.

"What's it to you, anyway? He is the other guy that helped put your sister into Beech Grove. You suddenly feel remorse for him? You brought me here and told me I helped relieve you of a burden and now you are talking to me like I owe you something. Which one is it, old man?!" Renaldo demanded.

"*The sins of the father will fall upon the child,*" the older man whispered.

Renaldo froze. He remembered the note from Franc's apartment. The wording was eerily similar if not verbatim. Renaldo's mind went into a tailspin. Was this the man who left the note at Franc's place? He was at the funeral and now he was quoting the words left on a note in the dead man's abode?

"What the fuck did you say to me, old man?" Renaldo requested.

"You heard what I said, young buck. Even if you didn't, you most certainly read it somewhere," the older man stated.

Renaldo stood still as the older man scooted around him. As the elder appeared to be planning an exit, Baron placed himself in front of the door. The older man snorted at Baron and raised his hands in surrender. Renaldo then turned to the older man, albeit in sheer consternation.

"How would you know what I've read?" Renaldo questioned.

"Because the police came looking for me after they received the note. Funny thing is, the only person who would have been able to make the connection between Franc and I, should have been Jennifer. Who else would Jennifer have trusted with that information, besides you?" the older man clawed.

Renaldo squinted at the older man. SHIT! Now that Renaldo had been in close quarters with him, the man did happen to look like an older...

"In case you are still confused, young buck. I am *Mack Wellington*! And I have been hot on your trail ever since you put the police on mine! I had to put two and two together and almost got twenty-two, but you the fo' fasho', Detective Recluse!" Mack resolved.

That was it. That's what this was *genuinely* all about. This whole time, Renaldo was a captive of *the Mack Wellington*. Somehow, all of Renaldo's efforts to take the heat off himself came collapsing down. Mack was correct about one thing; his so-called burden was gone. Dead. *Buried*. At least physically. However, Franc's name found a way to keep popping up ever since the burial. First it was Julissa's child and now, now it was Franc's father. Renaldo was bound to be haunted by Franc's lineage. Not only the lineage, but the extended family as well?

Renaldo then abruptly recalled Lavender's words, which were nothing more than a murmur amid choking Franc: "*You really gonna do this to me? ME*!?" Renaldo reacted so quickly that night, he never processed the possible relationship between them. If Franc knew what happened to Victor, how come he never mentioned it? Franc never uttered a word about his cousin. He only hunted crime. *An entity*. An empire that needed to be vanquished. Some days, it seemed as if crime was coming to a close. At least until Franc's last night on Earth.

"You done got mighty quiet there, Mr. Brown. You were a lot more verbal on that television screen some months back. You appeared to be awfully proud of yourself after you shot all those people in that bar. Pretty slick shit, if I say so myself," Mack advised.

"Well, if you witnessed that, then you also know The Recluse has been captured," Renaldo rebounded.

"Oh yeah? Well, I'll tell you like this, detective: If my son died with you around, *you might as well have put that bullet in him yourself*. Either way, you may not be able to bring him back, but YOU WILL reunite my nephew and sister. I guran-damn-tee that!" Mack professed.

Mack tapped his cane on the table before pointing the base towards Baron's chest. He then shooed him to the side. His nephew validated his silent bid by leading him into the hallway. Mack grabbed his coat from the chair near the exit, as he looked Renaldo over once more. Mr. Wellington aimed the tip of his cane at the dejected detective for a moment that lingered like an eternity. Without uttering another word, Mack put his cane beneath his armpit and forsook Renaldo to soak in guilt.

Chapter 17

Treading Muddy Waters

The original hue covering the walls of Westbank Parish Prison was bland as unsalted fries. Over the years, the barriers had been graced with the blood, sweat, and tears of convicts and correctional officers alike. The mixture of bodily fluids created a less than abstract glaze upon the enclosure. The place was once run by the Avondale Armada; now it was left to those young punks who relied more on trigger fingers than the might of heavy hands. Within these confines, their physical and mental will was tested regularly. Some inmates found issues with the guards while others were infamous on the yard. Nevertheless, one man had been relatively unopposed since entering the jaded gates: Scottie Bridgewater.

He was the known lone survivor of those who conspired to slay Francisco Tatiano. While some of the other inmates respected Franc, all of them knew his absence would make it easier to conduct "business" on the outside. They may not have all been fans of Scottie, but they were benefactors of uninterrupted commerce. Others were interested in only one thing: sheer chaos!

A Westbank Parish correctional officer leads Scottie to

visitation. Scottie emanates befuddlement, knowing damn well he received visitation two days ago. He doesn't complain though; Bridgewater relished the opportunity to vacate his work duty for a bit. It wasn't as if he was being paid top dollar, nor was the prison going to put any of his labor on his résumé. You could find many things within a cell wall, but nothing that helps prepare you to efficiently survive a return to the community.

Scottie enters the room to find a single stranger sitting amongst the tables. Scottie believes this is some mistake, so he pauses. The C.O. places his hand on Scottie's shoulder and nods for him to continue forward. Scottie wasn't convinced, considering his relations with law enforcement recently, but he reluctantly obliged.

"The fuck is you?" Scottie quizzed as he lowered himself to the small circular seat on his side of the table. His eyes toggled the visitor's features until he found a badge.

"Somebody willing to help you...if you prove willing to help yourself," answered the mysterious figure.

"Man, I have zero interests in cooperating with the police. Your kind ain't got no love for me on the outside, what make you think I give a fuck about anything you got to say in here?" Scottie fired back.

"Well," the figure began, "if you maintained that type of attitude while you were on the street, you probably wouldn't be here today, now, would you?"

Scottie raised his eyebrows and slowly turned his chin towards the correctional officer, being careful not to let the strange male out of his sights. Scottie quickly glanced at the C.O. before he committed contemplation to the opposite side. Scottie directed his entire torso forward while carefully leaning towards the stranger.

"Oh. I already know wassup," Scottie whispered.

"Really? Well, humor me!" baited the man.

"You done asked for the wrong guy. I can't be who you came to see. Like I said before, I don't roll with no boys in blue, ya heard mey," Scottie settled.

The antagonist tilts himself toward Scottie as he removes a case from his pocket. He produces a small folder and opens it to a photo of Avon Lazlo. The gentleman slides the photo over to display one of Demone Lazlo. The next two photos are that of the other two men shot at *Nina's* over a few months ago. Scottie takes a deep breath, then slides the folder and its contents to the floor while still staring at his visitor. The man chuckles at Scottie's display of arrogance, while Scottie stares in disbelief.

He takes no exception to the stranger's humor and suddenly eyes the case. The gnarly braided Bridgewater shrivels his face into a grimace as he outstretches his elongated digits to the small case. The officer's hand swats Scottie away before he can lay a finger on it. Bridgewater hops up at this perceived disrespect and flinches at the officer. Nothing. The officer doesn't falter. He just sits. And cackles. All while looking dead into Scottie's cold and ruthless eyes.

The offended offender now fills with contempt. He has been embarrassed for the last time, or so he thought. He hurls his upper body across the table whilst clutching for the officer's collar. The officer retreats into a standing position as he takes both of his palms, flattens them across Scottie's neck, and drives his forehead firmly into the wooden table. Scottie's neck whips back as his head ricochets off the desk and he nearly, perfectly, slides back into the seated position on his chair. Scottie grasps his head in his palm and peeks at the officer though one eye. The C.O. considers moving closer, but sees that the visitor has everything handled.

"So," the officer began as he adjusted his tie and collar, "shall we start over and try this again?"

"I'm about to start my time over once I get my hands on you...pig ass bitch!" Scottie exclaimed.

"Ahh, well, I guess you have no idea who I am or what my name is. Hi motherfucker, Detective McDonald at your service," Rance identified.

"McDonald? *McDonald*?! That sound like the name on the warrant that put me in here, man. Why the fuck would I help you?" Scottie wondered.

"Because I didn't pull your name from thin air. In fact, I got it from an eyewitness. The only problem with that is, the man who rolled on you is walking around free, you are in here, and everybody else is dead," Rance outlined.

Scottie's upper lip quivered, eyes tightened and chin dipped as if he needed to scratch his chest. Scottie took a deep breath as he leaned back on the stool, donning a stone-hinged scowl. Rance acknowledged his antagonist's closed demeanor and knew he had to raise the stakes. To do just that, he arose from the chair and started to gather his display items from the table.

"I tell you what, Mr. Bridgewater. Since you like taking the brunt of the weight for something that probably wasn't even your idea, you can sit your ass in here until you're ready to talk. Besides...murder? You got time, right?" Rance enticed.

Bridgewater stilled every portion of his body aside from his eyes, which simply followed Rance as he scurried toward the exit. Bridgewater took in a deep breath and let out a sigh as he looked down and slowly shook his head side-to-side. He placed his hands along the table as he considered his predicament.

"What's it to ya?" Scottie murmured.

"Excuse me, Mr. Bridgewater, what was that?" Rance answered.

"What does it mean to you. What you gain from helping me?" Scottie posed.

"The truth!" Rance answered emphatically while returning to the bench.

"What good is talking to you going to do me? They got me locked up for it and everybody they tried to get me to flip on is dead. Who else y'all gonna throw in here with me?" Scottie declared.

Rance placed the worrisome case back onto the tabletop. He slid it in Scottie's direction. Rance stopped the box long enough to pry it open and turn it toward Scottie. The Recluse Vision Glasses were on display yet again in their matted blue case.

"Do I need these to look at something in particular? Are they 3-D glasses or something like that?' Scottie questioned.

"Not exactly. These are identified as the glasses of The Recluse. They don't appear familiar to you," Rance deciphered.

"Nah, not particularly. Can't say I rock with anybody that wear those," Scottie declined.

"Hmm," Rance pondered as he gently grazed his beard. "Well, tell me this: what was Avon's beef with Francisco Tatiano? What could he have done so horrible that Avon wanted him dead?"

"Shid, I can't call it! Maybe that boy owed him some money or something. I don't even much know," Scottie claimed.

Rance peered at the spectating corrections officer, then back to Scottie. Scottie dug into the table with his elbows as he towered over folded arms. Detective McDonald was more amused than enthused by Scottie's attitude, but he knew how to break it. He just had to dig a little deeper.

"So, you a flunky? You in the parish prison cuz you running around here like a flunky?" Rance teased.

"I ain't never been on no flunky shit, ya heard me. You talk mighty tough for a guy who know these people watching me on camera," Scottie defended.

"Oh really?! Well, what else you call somebody that chance his life to take somebody else's and don't even know why?" Rance proposed.

"Man, I'm gon' tell you like this here: That fool bust through the door on us; we was defending ourselves," Scottie shared.

"Oh really?! If y'all were standing your ground, why didn't you stay until the police arrived?" Rance examined.

"Because we already had one dead black man, we didn't need five more," Scottie retorted.

Rance rolled his eyes at Scottie's buffoonery. Rance was honestly offended by the audacity of Scottie's recollection of events. He contemplated walking away again but wanted to give Scottie one last shot at deliverance.

"Funny how you were only worried about black lives when the police were involved. Not a moment before, when two good citizens walked in the room. Not the moment that one was put down like an old thoroughbred sent to pasture," Rance retorted.

"Them heroes wasn't about to put me in no cell. At least not that day!" Scottie claimed.

"That's ironic. Heroes? If that was the case, how come y'all only shot one of them. It wasn't because there weren't enough bullets; the gunman fed Franc three. What made y'all let the officer walk away?" Rance pressed.

Scottie hesitated to respond. He knew there wasn't an answer he could provide that wouldn't further scar the names of his deceased friends. Honestly, he hardly knew Renaldo enough to care what happened to him. Regardless of this fact, he could not make himself snitch. Once he was done circling the area in front of him with his index finger, he looked back up at Rance.

"Man, I honestly don't know why it went down like that. I wasn't even in the room. I helped rough them clowns up, but I wasn't nowhere round no gunshots," Scottie asserted.

"Flunky! Flunky! Flunky!" Rance cheered while guffawing at Scottie.

Scottie sprung up from his seated position and banged the base of both fists onto the table. The correctional officer closed in on the standoff but was waived away by Detective McDonald. Scottie veered himself around and stomped away from the meeting.

"Let me up outta dis' bitch, C.O. I ain't got nothing else for clown ass Five-Oh," Scottie shrieked.

"Surely you jest, Mr. Bridgewater. You ain't told me nothing I didn't already piece together. Well, besides the fact you taking a heavy charge for somebody that's deceased or still running around. But you the only person around that knows that. Ain't it, man?" Rance dug.

Rance arose from his seat, gathered his items, then returned to the door leading to the foyer. He shrugged his shoulders as he watched the correctional officer face Scottie to the opposite door while searching for his key. Scottie tilted his head back and peeked over his shoulder towards Rance.

"He said it was his best friend!" Scottie shouted across the room.

"Hnah?" Rance uttered.

"Vonny. He said the hit was ordered by ole dude best friend," Scottie cleared up.

"What's with the change of heart?" Rance implored.

Scottie inhaled deeply as he turned his attention toward Rance. He motioned to the officer to close the door. Rance stood idly, awaiting Scottie's rebuttal.

"So, check this out. My ole lady came to visit me a couple days ago. She was acting real shady, you know? She was trying to play it off, but I could tell something was up. One of my homeboys probably trying to get at her or some shit like that. Either way, I need to give myself a chance to get up outta here, if that's even possible," Scottie admitted.

"Well, conspiracy may hold less time for you than pulling the trigger. While we're on the subject, who actually was the trigger man?" Rance investigated.

"A dead man," Scottie answered.

The officer opened the door and ushered Scottie through. Rance's eyes remained directed towards the correctional officer as he knocked on the visitation door and awaited the buzz. After Scottie and the officer departed through the opposite side, the door sounded to release Rance. He walked along a breezeway until he reached intake. Rance and his belongings were thoroughly searched before he was granted departure.

As Rance walked across the front lawn of Westbank Parish Prison, he reached into his jacket and pulled out a small piece of paper. Within the frame of the paper was a full colored photo, where a few vehicles appear to be approaching a stop light. The photograph is of a white Escalade, being driven by Terry Bender; accompanied in the passenger seat by who appeared to be Demone Lazlo. Rance looked at the prison once more as he put his paper away. He thought to himself how the word of a man facing a death sentence is minimized within a court testimony, but it speaks volumes to what he already believed about Renaldo Brown: *He was absolutely The Recluse.* Bit by bit, Rance was determined to prove it.

Chapter 18

Breath of Fresh Air

Enough time passed for Julissa to return to Destreland. She missed her home, though she knew it would be frequented by memories. Julissa was aware that she slowly needed to return to her level of normalcy, which would also mean returning to work, even if some of it was to be covered remotely. She enjoyed her time with Mr. Monroe and appreciated Cortissa's constant love of her grandchildren, but Julissa did not leave Harahan with intentions of moving back.

"JuJu, you know I can turn this car around and take you back home with me and Paul. It's really no problem," Cortissa offered.

"I appreciate that, Mama. I really do, but it's time for me to get back to this house and get everything in order," Julissa claimed.

"Well, alright. I'm really gonna miss my grandbabies. I don't see you around as much since you got married to Waldo. I don't want to only see them during the holidays!" Cortissa expressed.

Julissa looked over at Cortissa, inspecting her from lip to limb. She shook her head before returning her gaze to the road. Cortissa peered over her shoulder toward Peerless. She grinned at him quickly before reestablishing her focus on the highway.

"It's a good thing you are bringing me here instead of Daddy then. Maybe now you can navigate yourself over here to your grandbabies whenever you're ready," Julissa retorted.

"I know you have that little white streak in your head, but you are no wiser than you were the day before you gave birth to little Paul. Respect your elders, Julissa," Cortissa contended.

"Me not agreeing with you is not a sign of me arguing or being disrespectful, ma'am!" Julissa defended.

"Unless you want to walk the rest of the way and have me and the babies wait for you at your house, I suggest you keep your little smart remarks to yourself!" Cortissa returned.

Julissa glared at Cortissa, whose attention was trained on the road. Julissa bit her lip as she rolled her eyes to the sides of the sockets before turning her view ahead. As they turned the corner of the block, Julissa could already see her house and the long green grass surrounding it. After nearly two months of no one tending to the residence, Julissa was pleasantly surprised the lawn was not higher. The mailbox appeared gluttonous, as it was hardly latched.

"I know a guy, to help out with that yard," Cortissa offered.

"Yeah, I used to know one too," Julissa muttered.

Julissa froze in the moment. The last time she was there, she was in a heated argument with her spouse. Now she returned to her abode with questions that were raised as high as the weeds sprouting from her garden. *Where the hell is Renaldo now? How did I leave with two parents and child and come back to two kids and one mother?* No matter the query, Julissa would not find the answers inside her mother's car. She looked back at Peerless, who was now asleep. She looked at Judy, who stared back at her. Julissa mustered up the feeblest smile she could bear, hoping to mask the overwhelming anxiety upon her face. Finally, Julissa brought her eyes to Cortissa, who was glaring back at her.

"Changed your mind, JuJu? It's not too late," Cortissa pleaded.

"No," Julissa sighed. "It's time for me to come back, Mama. It doesn't look all that great right now, but it ain't nothing a little T.L.C. can't fix."

"If I said it once, I've said it a million times: Do what you want because it's the only way you will ever be satisfied. You can get out but leave the grandbabies with me!" Cortissa chimed.

Julissa disregarded her mother's request as nothing more than banter. She advised Judy to remove her seatbelt while she tended to Peerless. Cortissa looked back and made googly eyes at Peerless as his mother unstrapped him from the seat. She noticed her daughter would have her hands full and she jumped out of the car to help detach the car seat from her rear seats. Cortissa grabbed Judy and gave her kiss on the cheek. Judy hugged Cortissa before sprinting to the front door. Julissa attempted to juggle Peerless, her bags, and the car seat attachments all at once. Cortissa tapped Julissa on her shoulder and motioned for her to open the front door of the home. Cortissa continued with the chair until she had freed it from the vehicle.

"Hey, little one," Julissa said to Peerless. "Welcome

home! Gonna give you the tour when you awake. Just let me get my key, baby."

Julissa dug around in her purse until she located her key. She pulled it out and entered it into the doorknob. There was a temporary struggle to turn the lock, but she does it. Julissa pushed the door open and was greeted by an unfamiliar musk. "Is that the trash?" she thought to herself. Her transport to the hospital was unexpected, resulting in the home remaining in the same condition for approximately two months.

"Baby, go turn on the air conditioning. It might get some of that funk out. I'll sit this baby seat down and check on your kitchen," Cortissa offered.

Julissa didn't verbally respond to her mother, but she obliged the advice. Julissa quickly prayed the air would still come on, considering no one addressed that bill in the last couple of cycles. Julissa eyed the panel, and thankfully noticed the switch was slid to "off." Julissa exhaled vaguely. One checkpoint reached and now came the finale: Will the system respond when I turn it to cool? Julissa gulped the little saliva resting in her jaws as she pushed the notch over to the desired setting. *Nothing*! No warning clicks as it rested in the designated section. Julissa's mind was met with uncertainty as the only noise she heard was her own breathing. She slowly trekked down the hall as panic began to seep into her mind.

When Julissa re-entered the living room, she viewed Cortissa sitting next to Peerless on the sofa. Julissa ogled at her mother, in anticipation of having to accept her mother's offer. Julissa thought of different responsibilities in and around the home she required assistance executing. While she was excited to be back in her own place, it no longer felt like home. Had it not been for the pictures spread about the den area, she would hardly recognize it as her own. She looked over to her children, knowing that her pride would not prevent sweat beads from trickling down their faces. Unwilling to concede, but less inclined to be a fool, Julissa called over to Cortissa:

"Hey, Mama. I may have to take you up on your offer to...," Julissa began.

She was interrupted by a tiny rumble in the ventilation followed by the whistle of cool air circulating through the abode. Julissa displayed a grin that stretched from corner-to-corner of her lips. She suddenly understood what it was she needed to know the whole time: *Be patient.* Though it seemed her world unraveled in a day, she knew the road to prominence is never fast or easy. She was going to get her affairs back in order, *with or without* Renaldo. More importantly, she came to terms with the realization she no longer had a choice.

"What were you saying, dear?" Cortissa requested.

"Oh yeah," Julissa refocused, "I may have to take you up on the offer of coming to see the kids more. I believe Peerless has taken a liking to you."

"Oh, okay. Well, I'm going to head out. I put a new bag in the trash. You going to cook tonight or what you going to feed my grandbabies?" Cortissa rambled.

"I'll order something for me and Judy. You know Peerless still feeds off me," Julissa explained.

Cortissa gave a disapproving glare and shrugged. She kissed her grandchildren and exited through the front door. She didn't spare another word. Julissa, completely unaffected by her mother's hospitality, waltzed to the entryway and locked up for the night. She sauntered into the kitchen and opened the freezer. All available options required thawing. She didn't want Judy to wait that long. She whipped out her phone, searching Google for the nearest delivery restaurant. She decided on the one with the best fries and quickly ordered the meal before nourishing Peerless.

Once everyone's bellies were full, Julissa gave Peerless a bath, followed by a lotion lathering and a lullaby. The little fellow had seen enough for the day; he slipped out of consciousness with little fuss and lesser fight. Julissa serenely slipped from the room and quietly closed the door. She went down the hall to the room where Judy lay wide awake.

"Girl, what are you doing up?" Julissa wondered.

"I was waiting on you, Mama. I wanted you to tell me goodnight," Judy answered.

Julissa smiled and lay next to Judy in her twin-sized bed. They played and laughed until Judy dozed off. Julissa thought to herself, "Finally, a moment of quiet before the sun comes up." Julissa scurried back into her room, where Peerless remained sprawled across her bed. She tiptoed to the back of her closet and grabbed a Star Crunch from her secret hiding spot. Julissa plopped down into a legs-crossed, seated position. She indulged in a snack while leaning against the petite dresser. She had a second to gather her thoughts and plan her return to normalcy. She thought about calling Mr. Monroe to cut the grass tomorrow, knowing he wouldn't mind skipping church service with Cortissa. Now Julissa had to configure her permanent landscaping option beyond the next day. Once she finished her second Star Crunch, she traveled down-stairs to rummage through old bills. Julissa's intent was to gather any recent envelopes containing bills and take care of them immediately. Her plan was sidetracked by a shrill wail from the upper floor. She charged upstairs to find an Peerless squirming around on her bed.

"I can't do this all night," Julissa muttered to herself.

She recognized she didn't have much of a choice. Although Peerless' room was ready, his crib was not. Renaldo had been so wrapped up with work up until the day Peerless was born, he hardly had any time to put the bedding together. Julissa cradled the high-pitched infant closely while she looked at the disarray. Julissa clutched her eyelids tightly as she strolled about the quarter. Julissa silently prayed for *serenity*, as strength was not something she required. She asked for *virtue*, as the path of her life had been convoluted by tiny lies. She wept for *peace* because she thought it was the only veil of protection for the children.

Chapter 19

Transfer of Transgressions

Over in Tunneltown, the Westbank Parish Prison was especially raucous as two inmates were transferred from across the river. Allegedly, the new guys were quite a hit over on the East, notorious even. These two brothers were thick as thieves, but the only thing they ever stole—were lives. The younger brother got into a fight on the yard with another inmate and he'd gotten the best of his opponent. The antagonist wouldn't bow out gracefully. His constituents jumped in to rob the younger sibling of his victory. The elder brother spared no remorse.

The older brother dashed across the yard to enter the fray. The more his sibling was pummeled, the more upset he became. The more upset he became, the faster he moved. The fleeter his pace, the more dangerous his swing!

The older brother, Cyril, launched his body into the crowd. His sturdy frame took down three of his sibling's attackers. It temporarily made it a one-on-one engagement again. Cyril's little bro grabbed the opponent's foot in mid stomp, powered it upward away from his face, then twisted the foot swiftly at the ankle. The balance shift was enough to throw off his concentration. Rookie mistake. The younger brother shot up headfirst into the enemy's groin. When the opponent toppled over, he was met with a knee to the gut and an uppercut that took him off his feet.

Meanwhile, Cyril held off the other three assailants. He held his own until his younger bro came to even up the score. Cyril received a couple more punches to his kidneys before he could muster a haymaker of his own. Charles, Cyril's brother, landed a strike square into the jaw of one inmate, eliminating him from the remainder of the altercation. For the moment, Charles and Cyril secured an even matchup...so they thought. Charles' original opponent went upside his head with a closed fist. The blow stunned him enough for the other two to attack Cyril. Cyril saw what happened to Charles and threw all thoughts of diplomacy out of the window. The first guy that reached him instantly regretted it when Cyril swiped across his rib cage vigorously.

"AHHHHHHHHHH," the inmate's voice shrieked as he fell limp.

Cyril landed on the ground too. The remaining nemesis tried to put his foot in Cyril's throat but missed. Cyril quickly responded by ramming his closed fist multiple times into the unsuspecting man's calf. The opposition clutched his battered leg instantly, while Cyril made his way to his feet. Cyril noticed the man nursing his affected area, so he knew where to attack when deciding to stomp the injured leg repeatedly until it bled. Charles came from nowhere and kicked the maimed man directly in the forehead. *One opponent remaining.* That attacker swiftly left the squabble before guards came and brutalized all parties involved.

Guards attempted to carry the noticeably gimpy men away. Why wouldn't they be? They'd just gone toe-to-toe with the *Henderson Brothers*! Serving a string of life sentences for multiple brutal murders, the brothers were meticulous, methodical, and just downright murderous. What they did during the fight on the yard was no different than what they had done to opposers on the street. They would pound, injure, and ultimately *deprave all challengers*. That may have been Chuck's original intention when the fight started.

"That's okay, baby. Ain't no hard feelings. We all know nobody chucks like Chuck!" Chuck's opponent uttered as a guard escorted him back to his cell.

Charles attempted to flip the chastiser off, but each arm was occupied by a guard. The opponent blew a condescending kiss at Chuck as he was dragged into the building. Cyril was taken aback by the dialogue. As the correctional officers grabbed Cyril, he looked back at the damage he, and ultimately Charles, caused. A few droplets of blood speckled the dusty plot. The remaining inmates loudly voiced their discontent for having recreation cut short.

"Fuck y'all and your sorry ass rec time. Ain't none of y'all gonna be shit after an hour outside, anyway!" Cyril taunted.

He nearly incited a riot. *That was perfect*!! His outburst channeled enough uproar for Cyril to hide the *shank*. As guards focused on the perimeter, Cyril discreetly raised his arm just enough for the shank to slide down to his shoulder blade. When all eyes were away, he quickly secured the blade into his opposite hand and placed it within the interior of his collar. An officer snatched Cyril's arm and shoved it into his back as he marched him inside.

The Hernandez Brothers' display resulted in quite a stir at Eastbank Parish. It wouldn't be enough to place them in solitary confinement, the warden presumed. The unexplained puncture marks across their opponents and two fruitless bunk tosses later resulted in the brothers' transfer to the Westbank. While in tow, Cyril's curiosity had yet been satiated.

"Charlie, what was that shit about, man? I got your back, bro, but I ain't too happy about going to the Westbank. That sheriff over there don't play," Cyril dug.

"That was some bullshit, bro. Those guys have no respect, y'know?" Charles responded vaguely.

"Oh yeah? What was all that stuff about 'chucks like Chuck'? What the hell you chucking like that?" Cyril interrogated.

"These fists!" Charles stated plainly. "And my snacks, foo'. Them hoes owed me from the dice game and didn't wanna pay up. You already know how that go."

"Yeah, I know. You right," Cyril reluctantly acknowledged.

Presently, Cyril sat in his cell thumbing through a magazine. Along the common area, the inmates were loudly playing cards, slamming dominoes, and watching the news broadcast.

"This just in out of Thibodeaux: A man by the name of Jackson Feldman was found dead near his home. Authorities on the scene state he was slit from his belly to his throat, with multiple stab wounds on either side of the laceration. The belief is that Mr. Feldman died from profuse bleeding. Surgery precision aside, the oddest component of this slaying remains the perceived initials of 'C.B.' across the victim's forehead. At this time, the local authorities have no prime suspects, but a full investigation will be launched. If anyone has any possible information regarding this matter, please call the..." The news reporter stated in the broadcast.

"Hey yo, Chuck! That sounds like some Hernandez Brothers shit. Is that why they transferred y'all asses over here? Y'all like to gut people like fish now?" an older inmate harassed.

"Naw, papi. That ain't none of our handywork. Me and Cy been keeping clean," Charles denied while aiming his palms to the ceiling.

Cyril could hear his brother carrying on with other inmates on the floor, but he was in no mood to entertain. Cyril's mind was on another venture. While the inmates were content to joke and dwell on the brothers' past, he needed to plan for the future. Cyril stood up from his bunk and leaned on the frame of his entryway. He shook his head at the sad souls frolicking about. Cyril searched the floor for a familiar face among the crowd. When Cyril secured his target, he strolled up to a couple of guys standing near the stairwell.

"Yo, homeboy, you the guy that shanked ol' buddy Franc?" Cyril asked.

Scottie looked over his shoulder to locate the voice. He initially began to shoo the admirer away, as he was personally tired of hearing about Fantastic Franc. When Scottie turned around, he realized it was one of the recent transfers, to which his aggravation subsided. He'd heard stories about the Hernandez Brothers, and was well aware that if he had to fight one, he would need to defeat both.

"I ain't shank nobody, essay. What it mean to you?" Scottie answered.

Cyril crumpled his eyebrows as he scowled at Scottie. He truly wondered if the slovenly configured man sincerely stood a chance against Franc. Cyril and Charles had been in an epic battle but came up short against Detective Brown and the Fantastic One. Despite his impression of Scottie, Cyril knew the man standing before him provided at least a miniscule amount of value. Cyril's frown vanished as he fixed his expression to something less volatile.

"No issues, loco. I just wanted to meet the man who cut down a thorn in me and my bro's side. A foe of Renaldo Brown is a friend of mine," Cyril clarified.

"Fa' real?" Scottie relaxed, "What they ever do to you?"

"Stuck their noses in me and my bro's business. Took away our freedom. Stopped our artistic expression. What about you?" Cyril stated.

"My issue with them wasn't personal. Straight business," Scottie explained.

Cyril looked at Scottie's counterpart and nodded for him to excuse them. Scottie watched his associate follow the signal without question. Scottie was confused by the instant cooperation. He quickly returned his attention to the Hispanic male standing before him. Cyril then motioned for Scottie to lean in closer so they could avoid spilling information. Scottie carefully obliged the request.

"You already got some pull around here, don'tcha?" Scottie poked.

Cyril chuckled at the sentiment then shook his hand to say "so-so." Scottie, now oddly reassured by the notion, was more interested in what Cyril had to say.

"I think I have some use for a businessman, loco. You in the mood for a little revenge or are you pleased with your current neighborhood?" Cyril identified by pointing towards the cells.

"I don't mind a little come up every once in a while, but you do realize one guy is dead and the other one is missing, don'tcha?" Scottie explained.

"Oh yeah? Well, they got families, don't they?" Cyril adjusted.

As Scottie nodded confirmation, Cyril turned and walked away. Cyril stared into Charles' general direction and shook his head. Charles was jovial among the other inmates. Cyril was more lowkey, so he made few friends, and by the same virtue, fewer enemies. Scottie watched Cyril until he vanished into his pod. Scottie set his sights on Charles and his "friends." He hoped to understand Cyril better through studying his sibling. Scottie needed more than the vague background provided by Cyril if he was going to align himself with the Hernandez Brothers.

Chapter 20

The Tangled Web

The poster board etched into the wall is covered in copious amounts of photos and string. The title over the menagerie reads "The Recluse?" Rance has all his evidence situated, to include the centered photo of Detective Renaldo Brown. While other police units searched for a missing officer, Detective McDonald was on the hunt for a missing conspirator. The confession he recently obtained from Scottie Bridgewater was more than enough fuel to continue his manhunt. Rance had photos of the men leaving the warehouse, a verbal confession from the last known survivor, and photos of Renaldo Brown donning The Recluse Vision glasses, so, what more did he need?

Truthfully, he couldn't hinge an entire arrest on the statement of a man serving a near life sentence for murder. The photos of the men leaving the warehouse only showed the men in the front seat, none of which were the man who was behind bars today. The hero who avenged the death of his best friend to most was no more than a fraud to Rance. He was hellbent on making sure the world found out as well...*if the swindler dared to ever show his face again.*

Rance was so consumed in his control center setup, he didn't notice his visitor. A frail man with hair like sheep's wool watched the detective silently connect the dots of his own complex diagram. The onlooker sympathetically watched Rance as his mind outpaced his hands.

"You got other cases you can work on, you know?" the man reminded Rance.

"Maybe so, lieutenant, but this is the one that keeps me up at night," Rance defended.

"Maybe you should try weed. Some of the good peyote. Cali Kush?" Lieutenant Perilloux suggested.

Rance spun around to locate Perilloux. He couldn't read the lieutenant's expression to determine if he was joking. Due to his confusion, he simply squinted at him. Perilloux walked closer to the display board to take a gander at what Rance had gathered so far.

"Just kidding, Rance. Wanted to see what you might say. Gotta keep you on your toes," Perilloux teased as he pointed both index fingers toward Rance.

"Sure thing, boss. I bet," Rance half-heartedly acknowledged.

"You could use a getaway of some form, McDonald. You keep wrapping yourself up in this case. Man, it ain't healthy. You got a decision on it already. You going to run yourself insane if you don't learn to chill out," Perilloux warned.

"I can't let go that easy. Something don't seem right about how all this turned out. Why was he so determined to find The Recluse?" Rance offered.

"Probably because he killed his best friend. Now, if you want to, you can continue to run behind that other detective, but nobody knows where he is. The only way you may find him is if you go missing yourself!" Perilloux predicted.

"I don't think it will be that hard. I don't think it will be that hard at all," Rance voiced while focused on his desk.

"You are borderline obsessed with this case. Don't set yourself up for that whirlwind. Some men never return," Perilloux advised.

The lieutenant blinked at Rance briefly before pulling his phone from his pocket. Perilloux positioned himself about four feet across from Rance and told him to "look up." Rance did so off pure instinct and Perilloux pressed his phone until a click registered. The lieutenant then placed his phone into his pocket as he scooted to the office door.

"What the hell was that about? What are you doing?" Rance wondered.

"I'm taking a recent photo so I can post it around town when you finally get stuck in that wormhole you're about to go down," Perilloux poked as he exited.

Rance shook his head and looked down at a glossy pamphlet. He flipped to the back, noticing the name of the printing location was "Priceless Prints." Rance remembered Renaldo telling him he would assist with the funeral preparations. Rance took notice of the address and recorded it in his phone. As he placed the phone on the table, it began to buzz and vibrate. Rance flipped over the phone to view an unsaved local number. He flipped the phone back onto its face, figuring someone was asking him about his expiring vehicle warranty. When the buzzing stopped, he walked back to his board. The phone began to buzz again. When he retrieved his phone, the same number flashed across the display. Rance answered the phone this go around.

"Hello?!" Rance answered, perturbed.

"Yes, hello. Is this Detective McDonald?" a female's voice requested.

"Yeah, this is him. May I ask who is calling?" Rance demanded.

"You forgot about me already, kind sir?" the lady led.

"Maybe it escapes me. It might help if I had a name," Rance settled.

"Well, it's me, Rita. Rita Barrios from C.C.P.D.," Rita clarified.

Rance's heart sunk into the pit of his belly. He'd become so intertwined with The Recluse he'd forgotten the melody of Detective Barrios' tone. He tried to regain his composure. It may have taken longer than he thought.

"You still there?" Rita asked.

"Oh. Yeah. I'm sorry. Wasn't expecting to hear from you. How have you been, detective?" Rance recovered.

"Honestly," Rita paused, "I believe things may be going in the right direction for me. I have you to thank for that."

"Pourquoi?" Rance asked, confused.

"You would infringe on the small portion of French I understand," Rita admitted.

"Pardon, ma copain," Rance continued.

"Merci, merci. Now, enough with all of that. I'm not about to play with you on this phone all night, sir. I just wanted to thank you for the tip you gave me. I went back and watched the tapes. I saw the early hesitation by Hall also. I sincerely appreciate the extra pair of eyes," Rita expressed.

"No problem at all. Only trying to help out. When is

court?" Rance inquired.

"Soon. Like a few days!" Rita provided.

"Ouch. Well, I'm happy you were able to notice the error in time. I wish you the best of luck in your case," Rance informed.

"Well, I will have a little more luck thanks to you. I appreciate it," Rita expressed.

"As I mentioned before, absolutely no problem at all. I apologize for the initial confusion; I didn't recognize the number. If I knew it was you, I wouldn't have ignored it the first time," Rance divulged.

"Oh, sorry about that. It's my direct cell, I would have called from the office, but I'm on the move right now," Rita clarified.

"Well, that is nice to know. I hope you enjoy the rest of your day," Rance determined as he hung up the phone.

Rita was a little surprised Rance hung up on her so quickly. He seemed different this time around. She assumed Rance would try to expand on the opportunity to chop it up with her. *Not this time.* He was obviously preoccupied.

Rance placed his phone down and revisited the board. He didn't give the call another thought. He knew what he saw and knew he was right. The affirmation by Rita was nice, but it had nothing to do with his current main concern. Lieutenant Perilloux was absolutely correct about Rance's obsession with The Recluse: it undoubtedly consumed him! He had reached the point beyond professional accountability and now dug into personal egotism. He vowed to right the wrongs of the C.C.P.D. hotshot...he only needed to find him first.

Chapter 21

Breaking the Barrier

Pastor Wellington has not acknowledged Renaldo since the reveal. While Renaldo now enjoyed preferable conditions to the basement, he's still shut out of church services. One of the few things Mack has eked out any effort to share is "If anybody recognizes you, they may try to help you and turn you in. If they turn you in, so am I!!" Renaldo was not sure what that meant, but he believed it would only make things worse.

Due to the lack of commentary from Mack, Renaldo established a stronger rapport with Victor. The relationship blossomed, enough at least, for Renaldo to truly desire to locate Baroness. The time to begin the convoy was on the horizon; consequently, Victor was now required to lay out the plans for her recovery.

"Theee peeeeplllllee at Beeeeeech Grohhhhve haaaaavve noooooo iiiiiiiideaaaaa h-howwwwww she got owwt," Victor explained.

"You mean to tell me she just walked out of a high security mental home and nobody knows how or why?" Renaldo quizzed.

Victor shrugged his shoulders as he crumpled up an

old satellite map of the facility and surrounding buildings. Renaldo faced the counter as if the map were still there. Victor grabbed ahold of his hammer with the intentions of sneaking away. Renaldo picked up a pen and threw it toward the door.

"Where the hell do you think you're going? What are we gonna do with this? You practically gave me nothing," Renaldo called.

Victor chuckled. He then opened the door while peering back at Renaldo. He flashed a devilish grin at his counterpart before he shut the door to remain in the room.

"Weeee broughhhhhhhht youuuuu herrrrrrrrrrre toooo solllllllllve thaaaaaat. Iffffff youuuuu werrrre aaaablle to caaaaaaaatch herrrr beforrrrrrre sheeeee couulllld blowwwwww uuuuuuup a caaaaaaaaar, thennnnn youuuu cannnnnn finnnnnnd herrrrr agaaaaain," Victor explained.

"Well, I'm going to need to know a little bit about her. Where else would she go? Do y'all have any other family down there? What about your fah—?"

"Whoooooo giiiiiiiiiiives a daaaaaaaamn abouuuuuuuut hiiiiiiim. Heeee won't helllllllllp herrrrrrrr. Heeeee nehhhverrrrr hasssss!" Victor roared.

Renaldo was startled by the agitation in Victor's answer. He was astonished Victor refrained from putting his head through the plaster. Victor neared Renaldo, but it was merely to place the map back in his view. Victor's scowl vanished from his creased head as he pointed at Beech Grove Manor and turned to Renaldo.

"Iiiiii beliiiiiiiieeve weeeee maayyyyyy neeeeeeeed tooooooo staarrrrrrrrt therrrrrrrre," Victor uttered.

It was the "damndest" of decisions either way, Renaldo

believed. After giving it some thought, he realized it was best to hop on the cold trail; it was better than none at all. Renaldo tried to recollect how he and Franc tracked down the Baroness before. Where did she hang out? Who might help her escape? What could she be after?

Renaldo's train of thought was sidetracked by the hurried interruption of Wellington. Mack waltzed to a chest of drawers, rabidly pulled the top shelf open, and ruffled his hands around inside. He slammed the drawer shut while releasing some pleasantries under his breath. Mack peered at Victor, then checked out Renaldo long enough to scoff. Renaldo, while thoroughly entertained by the exchange, was in no mood for the continued stand-offish nature of his elder.

"Hey! When are we going to execute this suicide mission of yours? You have a date in mind or are you just playing it by ear?" barked Renaldo.

Mack's eyes were squeezed tightly but swelled with hatred; he contemplated utilizing his cane to ensure Renaldo would never suffer the sorrows of constipation. Mack knew that would not endear Renaldo to assist with the search, so he decided to humble himself, as much as he could stomach anyway.

"Do you two fools have a plan yet, or are you comparing the assets of your favorite video vixens?" Mack hurled back.

"First of all, nobody uses the term 'video vixen' anymore," Renaldo informed.

"Well, excuse the hell out of me," Mack replied.

"Secondly...you two didn't really give me much to work with. You have any additional information beyond what your nephew provided?" Renaldo asked.

"Information such as what, detective? If we knew where she was, we wouldn't need you!" Mack reiterated.

"Well, since she is your sister, maybe you can tell me who some of her friends are. You know, who might be hiding her out? What about your parents? Would she run to them for help?" Renaldo plowed.

Mack grimaced as he leaned his head to run his fingers through his hair. He stopped his hand as he gripped a portion of his follicles and shook his head. He nearly tore through his perfectly coiled mane as he lifted his eyes to Renaldo again. His lip twitched fervently as he studied Renaldo's mug in disgust.

"I have no contact with any of her friends. I'm not exactly welcomed by certain ones, anyway," Mack uttered.

"But you could at least get us close to some of them? Maybe I can go around and ask some questions?" Renaldo suggested.

"I doubt it, hotshot. You are a missing law enforcement officer. I would venture to guess your face has been blasted all over the local news. If anyone recognizes you, it could compromise the entire operation," Mack advised.

"Well, ain't this some shit? I can't be seen because it might draw too much attention. You can't be seen for some undisclosed reason, and Victor here may startle the common citizen with his appearance. No offense, Vic," Renaldo ascertained.

Victor smirked as he gave Renaldo the middle finger salute. Mack snorted at the exchange briefly then returned to his natural state of angst. Renaldo shrugged off Victor's displeasure as he scanned the panel for guidance.

"Yooouuuu aiiiiinnnnn't tooooo valuaablllllllle forrrrrrr tarrrrrrget praaaacticceee," Victor responded.

They all laughed hysterically.

"So, I guess we're starting at Beech Grove. How long will it take us to get there?" Renaldo gathered.

Victor gawked at Mack. Mack leaned back on a cabinet and extended his arms like wings with his palms toward the ceiling. He shrugged his shoulders when he brought his arms back to his side.

"Depends on the traffic. I guess we should saddle up soon and make our way to The Manor. Those damn homes give me the creeps," Mack advertised.

Mack stood up to depart the area. Renaldo appeared unphased but a thought entered his mind.

"Wait a minute, sir. Since we will be in the area soon anyway, can you let me make a phone call to my daughter? I'm sure she's worried sick about me," Renaldo suggested.

"Is that a damn joke?!" Mack accused.

"The fuck you mean?" Renaldo questioned.

Mack gingerly tarried toward the detective in case there was something off about the acoustics in the room. He wanted to make sure Renaldo could look directly into his eyes so he would know this was no farce. Victor inched closer in case another altercation broke loose. He watched on as four eyes burrowed through one another.

"Can you pick up a damn phone and call my son?! Hmm?" Mack pressured.

Renaldo's eyes slanted to the right as he dropped his head to his left. Mack slammed his hand on the table in a rage.

"Motherfucker, I'm talking to you! Can you call him up? Hmm? How about you tell *him* you're in danger. *He done saved your sorry ass before!* Can he do it again? Would he even want to?" Mack boasted.

"What the hell you want me to do about it? I can't bring him back, and this won't bring him back either. Besides, he would probably rather talk to me than you. He ain't had nothing for you!!" Renaldo shouted back.

"I stayed away from Franc as a necessity. I did it to save his life. You should know a lot about that—didn't you nearly get your family killed at a funeral?" Mack prodded.

"And nothing happened to them because I was there to protect them. What you know about that, old man?!" Renaldo fired back.

Mack bit down on his lip, likely to prevent himself from spouting any further obscenities in a church. He stared *through* Renaldo intensely as he searched his soul for Franc's murderer. Victor placed his hand on Mack's shoulder but was brushed off instantaneously. Mack turned to Victor as he stood up and walked toward the door.

"Call me when you're ready to look for Lavender. In the meantime, keep that ignorant bastard away from me. Only reason I ain't went 66 on him was because we need to find her before it's too late," Mack declared.

Mack left without another sound or gesture. Renaldo didn't respond to Mack but was curious about the threat in itself. He mulled the verbiage momentarily before he gathered the map and stood up to follow Mack. Victor positioned himself between Renaldo and the desired path.

"Youuuuu maayyy waannt too slowwww dowwwwwn," Victor warned.

"I want to find out what the hell he meant by that. I don't play that shit!" Renaldo cried as he tried to maneuver past Victor.

"Youuuuu arrrrrrrre froommmmmm Cressssscennnt

Ciiiityyyyyy, arrrrenn't youuuuuu?" Mack bellowed.

"Yeah, and if I get my hands on Mr. Wellington, I'm gon' second line all up and through his ass!" Renaldo embellished.

"Iiiiiii wouuuuuuuuldnnn't beeeeee soooooooo spryyyyy iffff iiiii werrrrrrrre youuuuu. Therrrrrrre's ammpllllle reeeeeeasonnnn f-f-forrrrrrrr his aaaaabsssssence fruhhhhhhhm Fraaaaaaanc," Victor contended.

"Said by a man who doesn't have kids," Renaldo snapped.

"Saaaaid tooo a foool whoo haaad it alllll, yehhhht still ma-mannaaaged tooo gammmble iiiit uhh-wayyyy," Victor replied.

Renaldo sneered at Victor's presumption. He perceived Victor to be naïve. "How could he judge me?" Renaldo mulled. He wanted to interrogate the man's expertise in the subject of family affairs but shelved the probe for another day.

"How about you bring me to your family and show me how it's done, Vic? You 'bout what you be talking 'bout?" Renaldo quizzed.

"Juuuuuust focus onnnnn nott getttinnnnng shohhhhhht. Unc haaaaas commmme a lonnng wayyy, yet, stillllll haaaaas farrrrr tooo gohhh," Victor carefully warned.

"So, he meant to say '86 or 187? Tell Pops to get more in line with the lingo!" Renaldo boasted.

Victor's face flopped in dejection. He detested the detective's ignorance. Despite Victor's indifference to the squabble, he felt it would serve everyone involved if he provided the impromptu history lesson.

"Unc wasssss ahhhhhh sixtyyyyyy siiiiixerrrr," Victor revealed.

"A Seventy-Sixer? I didn't know he used to hoop. Guess that makes sense. Did he play college ball for Wake Forest?" Renaldo gathered.

"Sixtyyyyy-Six...Six...Six," Victor reiterated.

"Oh!" Renaldo understood, "What happened in 1966?"

"Asiiide frommm being a yeeeeeear beyonnnnnd theee death ovvv Malcolmmmm X, nnnothinnnnng," Victor settled.

"So, he is avenging the death of Malcolm X? I thought he didn't like Muslims," Renaldo incorrectly assumed.

Victor let out an empathetic sigh for the uninformed detective. He looked Renaldo squarely in the eyes to see if there was anything residing beyond his irises. Renaldo studied Victor's glare while awaiting an answer.

"Theeeee Sixtyyyyy Sixssssers werrre a gannng ovvvvv mennn dest-tinnned toooo aaaaaavennnge theee Newww Orrrrleeeeans massssacrre ovvvv ehhhhteeeeen sixss-teeee-six," Victor divulged.

Renaldo was dumbfounded. He'd only heard of the New Orleans Massacre in passing. He didn't know any specifics; it was merely a footnote, if ever mentioned in Louisiana History classes. There was still one detail that left him stumped:

"What does any of that have to do with Huey P. Long and mafia activity?" Renaldo sought.

"Huuuuey P? Unc izzzzz not the thaaat olllld. Youuuu woulllld have toooo diiiig up his great graaaandfaaather forrr that," Victor detailed.

Chapter 22

Opening Remarks

The Eastbank Parish District Court reached full pandemonium on this odd October day. Despite their best efforts to keep the media away, the courthouse was filled with multiple community leaders and residents in anticipation of two important hearings on the docket: *State of Louisiana vs. Vashon Hall*, and *State of Louisiana vs. Tony Nguyen*. Both matters were continued hearings conducted more than a couple of months ago. Now, some life-altering, and possibly earth-shattering, decisions needed to be made for Crescent City to move forward.

Within Judge Burgess' chambers, Vashon Hall and Ashley Archibald sat at one table while Travis Carrington occupied the other in solitude. Vashon donned a black suit, white shirt, and red tie; Archibald wore a tan-toned suit with a burnt brown shirt. Their opponent was decked out in a black blazer and tie with a grey button-up and slacks. Carrington was overtly disconcerted this morning, due to the potential delay in the Hall proceedings. Due to the untimely abduction of Detective Brown, a status conference was scheduled in rhythm with the Nguyen trial.

"Your Honor, Detective Brown is not the one on trial

here; are we not able to reconvene in court soon to resolve this matter with Mr. Hall?" Travis pleaded.

"Your Honor, I tend to disagree with opposing counsel. Detective Brown is very pertinent to these proceedings, especially considering he may be more culpable for the events that occurred than my client is," Ashley undermined.

"Gentlemen," Judge Burgess began, "you are absolutely correct, Mr. Carrington, Renaldo Brown is not the man on trial; however, he is a key witness with testimony that would be key for the jurors, whenever he is found."

A twisted grin flashed across Archibald's thin lips. His posture lifted with his spirits at the judge's warning; Carrington's spirits slouched nearly as much as his spine in the brown leather cushioned seat. Ashley's margin of moral victory would be halved with Judge Burgess' next breath.

"As for you, Mr. Archibald, if you are looking to throw some financial responsibility someone's way, you will need those victims to file a civil suit," Judge Burgess assessed.

"Well, your Honor, if any of those that suffered at the hands of Mr. Brown share a desire to pursue damages, I will point them in the right direction," Ashley advised.

"Allegedly," Travis chimed. Ashley rolled his eyes.

"Pardon me, sir. Allegedly," Ashley mocked.

"We will hopefully resolve one of your contested hearings today. Considering what happened last time, I cannot promise you any more comfort than that," Judge Burgess commented.

"No reason to rush, Your Honor. My clients are certain the truth will be revealed in due time," Ashley suggested.

"That's where you may be mistaken, comrade. Time is usually not on the side of the wicked," Travis warned as he stood up from plush seating in the judge's chambers.

"Man, what the—," Vashon slipped before Ashley elbowed him in his bicep.

Travis stared at Vashon, with both eyebrows raised. Vashon's attention was set on his stinging bicep as he tried to massage the soreness away. Ashley's face tinged in disappointment at Vashon. Ashley flipped his expression to address Judge Burgess.

"My client may have been a tad excited, Your Honor. Would you happen to have a proposed date for the next hearing?" Ashley requested.

"I'll reset it within the limitations, but we need to get through *this* hearing first," Judge Burgess pledged.

All parties stood up and vacated the judge's chambers. Ashley and Vashon allowed Travis a head start. Judge Burgess sat at her desk a moment, searching out her window for what could be assumed as grace for her jury to make the right decision. After a brief period of seclusion, Judge Burgess traveled to the courtroom, where she was awaited by an audience.

Tony Nguyen sat in shambles as he waited for Ashley to return to the defendant's bench. Detective Barrios sat among the crowd as 12 jurors were seated along the box. The tension mounted as all awaited the direction of Judge Burgess. Tony Nguyen stood up as he watched the bailiff saunter past the witness stand. He spotted Ashley Archibald at the defendant's table. Tony leaned over to hug his mother before he continued to the opposite side of swinging doors. Tony's expression changed as he took a seat at the table and looked back. Quietly, he prayed it was the last time he would sit across a barrier between himself and family. The bailiff gave the order to the masses that Judge Burgess would be taking the bench, just prior to the honorable one ascending from her chambers.

"Order!! Order in the Court!!" Judge Burgess directed while banging her gavel.

The commotion silenced. In addition to the presence of the necessary parties sat longtime leader of the Fifth Ward Hogs, Reginald Joseph. He sat with the families of Vashon and Tony. Though Vashon would not proceed today, the Hall family remained for support. This was an example of the virtues Reginald was distilling in the younger Hogs. Reg had truly turned himself around; he had come a long way from the "hell on wheels" persona he earned from the early-2000s. While slowly becoming someone locals could adore, he remained regarded by law enforcement as someone to abhor.

"Now on the docket is the trial of the *State of Louisiana vs. Tony Nguyen*. For those not directly involved, especially those not providing testimony, I ask that you remain silent throughout this hearing so the court reporter and the jury may process and record information pertinent to these proceedings," the bailiff warned.

"Thank you for that, Chris. I will open the floor for opening arguments from the state. Mr. Carrington, if you may?" Judge Burgess invited.

Travis obliged Judge Burgess as he pushed away from the state's table and walked to the middle of the open floor. He provided a quick glance toward Tony to gauge his nervousness. Travis could tell the young man was uncomfortable in this setting, and he hoped to eventually capitalize on it. As Tony adjusted his tie, Travis displayed a smirk, then faced the jury box.

"Ladies and gentlemen of the court. We are here today to address a matter of public safety. Of course, our local law enforcement agencies are tasked with maintaining our safety, but we as citizens are inclined to uphold it. Not just for ourselves, but for our loved ones: friends, family, associates, or anyone else who may attend our own funeral. For our children who innocently frolic about, even in an open park, with no intention of causing harm. This defendant is brought before you today on charges from casually showing up to a burial site at a funeral he was not formally invited to. Then arriving at a park and compromising the safety of all its inhabitants: men, women, and children. All were unsuspecting and non-threatening, at least until Mr. Nguyen and his friends brought trouble their way. Today, jurors, we will present to you the facts of the case and allow you to decide whether or not Mr. Nguyen was within reason for the actions he portrayed," Travis opened.

Travis eyed Ashley while striding towards his assigned seat. Remy Daniels gave an approving nod to the litigator for his opening remarks. The senior Mr. Nguyen wrapped his arms around Mrs. Nguyen as she shuddered at Travis' description of Tony. That surely was not the young man she raised; not the way he was portrayed in Carrington's opening statement. Tony was a sweet and kind gentleman. At least, that was what her mind was programmed to tell her.

"Thank you, Attorney Carrington. Now, Mr. Archibald, would you like to address the people?" Judge Burgess invited.

"If it pleases the court, Your Honor," Ashley answered.

"Well, that's fresh coming from you, counselor. You hardly ever seem too concerned with pleasing anything more than your clients," Judge Burgess rebutted.

"Touche, Your Honor. Touche," Ashley conceded.

Even minimal laughter sliced through the multitude of tension mounting while jurors and onlookers alike waited. Ashley patted Tony on the back as he stood up and adjusted his tie. He then swiped his sport coat and bottoms before approaching center court. Before yakking, Ashley hiked back his jacket, placed his hands on his waist, and gazed into the crowd. Ashley deeply inhaled, followed by a suppressed exhale, before releasing his initial claim.

"First off, judge, jury, ladies, and gentleman of the court, I hope you are all having a splendid day. I hope when you woke up this morning your eyes were untainted, unfiltered, and unaltered...so that you were able to fully appreciate the beauty of the sun. I hope your sight remained in full tact as you got dressed, got in your cars, got on the road, and arrived here at the great Eastbank Judicial Court. If these things are true, you will be able to see the truth that this state looks to cloud just to secure a conviction! The man sitting at that table beside me has never been convicted of a crime a day in his life. He is a man of great potential, great upbringing, and great respect for the pillars of this city. He comes with a positive support group and no desire to jeopardize that which he has worked hard to attain. So, you see, court, what I plan to exhibit to you today is that this man has no motive, no method, and absolutely no room for malice towards local law enforcement nor a penchant to harm civilians. As your eyes were allowed to be opened by a higher power this morning, I hope you open your ears as we address these allegations. Thank you all," Ashley concluded.

Ashley sauntered back to his table without even peeking at the jurors. He stared Tony down until he occupied the chair alongside him. Tony's shivering eyes never left Judge Burgess' face, at least not until Ashley had been seated for a moment. Once Ashley plopped next to him, Tony ogled the entire right side of his face. Ashley beamed with confidence as he awaited the state's first witness.

"Mr. Carrington, does the state have any witnesses for testimony?" Judge Burgess invited.

"Yes, Your Honor. The state would call officer Remy Daniels to the stand," Travis answered.

A collective gasp cast over the back half of the court as Remy stood up, then approached the witness stand. Remy loomed on the stand with an external hubris of a man who commanded attention; internally he embodied the heat of each pair of eyes following him to the judge's side. There were *more eyes* than last time. *More people to impress.* More at stake. More...*pressure*!

Remy was asked to raise his right hand and recite *only* the truth. He agreed to do so while looking at the crowd. As Carrington adjusted his coat and approached Remy, Remy settled in his own skin. All he had to do is tell his side of the story. No more, no less...*no problem.*

"Mr. Daniels, could you please state your full name and occupation for the record?" Carrington requested.

"Of course," Remy began, "I am officer Remy Lavar Daniels, and I am employed with the Crescent City Police Department."

"Thank you for that, sir. For the pleasure of the court, could you please advise how long you have held that position?" Carrington quelled.

"Nearly four years now," Remy shared.

"Thank you, sir. I am pretty sure in that time you have come across some serious situations in your line of work, right?" Travis eluded.

"Yes. Yes, I have," Remy confirmed.

"Your Honor, the term serious is subjective, first. Secondly, what does this have to do with the circumstances of the case?" Ashley barged.

"While I appreciate your attention to detail, Mr. Archibald, I would say the presence of the 12 jurors over there may make this situation, shall we say, serious!" Judge Burgess defined.

Ashley sighed at the Judge's discretion and raised his hands in surrender. He then gestured toward Travis to continue examining the witness. Travis chuckled at Ashley's reluctant bow, then focused on Remy again.

"Officer Daniels," Travis continued, "why, precisely, were you present at City Park on the day in question?"

"I was dispatched to the location in response to two men on motorcycles, possibly armed, heading to City Park following shots fired at the mausoleum on Canal. A few officers had been gunned down and the suspects fled," Remy divulged.

"So, fellow police officers, who were technically not on duty at the time events began, mind you, were gunned down? *During a burial*? I am no genius, but I would say that's pretty serious, Your Honor," Travis chimed.

"He's right, Your Honor. He's no genius!" Ashley joked.

Ashley Archibald was in his purest form. He had once again cut the tension in the room with sordid humor. More to his intent this time, he was able to stir Remy's confidence until he was a bit shaken. The defense attorney found the result he sought from his banter and waited his turn to cross-examine the witness. Remy may have taken Ashley's jab more personally than Travis, the man it was originally meant for. Once Travis finished snickering at Ashley's snide remarks, he continued with the examination.

"So, Officer Daniels, you reported to the scene as directed. Given the description you were provided, did you find two gentlemen on motorcycles who were armed?" Travis led.

"Yes, with the help of a couple other officers who were also dispatched. I heard shots in the park upon my arrival and was told there were two armed motorists in the park with no regard for civilian patrons," Daniels declared.

"Seems to be pretty dire circumstances, Officer Daniels. Did you ever encounter the rumored motorists for your own account?" Travis queried.

"Yes, sir. I did eventually identify the reported motorists on the park grounds, near the old bumper cars track," Daniels claimed.

"Thank you for that specification, Mr. Daniels. Any idea what the alleged suspects were doing when you encountered them?" Travis inquired.

"By the time I noticed two armed gentlemen in red and black clothing, they were running around the premises on foot, nearly trampling over bystanders," Daniels described.

"So, the young men who were running around were in red and black. Consistent with clothing items synonymous to the Fifth Ward Hogs. Tell me, Mr. Daniels, would any of the men you encountered happen to be in the courtroom today?" Travis examined.

Remy nodded his head slowly as he faced the defense table. He lifted his right hand to point his index finger in Tony's direction. He squinted at Tony Nguyen as he slowly lowered his arm back to his side.

"For the sake of clarity, jury, Officer Daniels just pointed at the defendant, Mr. Tony Nguyen. The same Mr. Nguyen who was originally petitioned for two counts of first-degree murder, amongst other things. Mr. Daniels, can you describe the makeup of some of those people who were present in the park on that date?" Travis described.

"Everything was happening so fast! I couldn't focus on any one person more than the others. There were men, women, and children throughout," Remy detailed.

"Objection, Your Honor. It's a park, not an adult novelty shop! Of course there were children there; what is the relevance to this info?"

"Sustained. The jurors should be aware that parks are a known gathering location for men, women, and children alike," Judge Burgess ruled.

"Forgive me, Your Honor. Was merely illustrating the scenery," Travis advised.

"Understood, Mr. Carrington. Take the liberty to rephrase the question if absolutely necessary," Judge Burgess advised.

Travis flashed a stare at the jury to find they were all intently gawking back at him. He knew if he gained nothing else from the group, he at least had their ears and attention. Travis was content with his observation.

"No, Your Honor. It won't be necessary," Travis declared. "Officer Daniels, can you please describe your encounter with Mr. Nguyen and his counterpart?"

Officer Daniels grimaced as he adjusted the knot of his tie and his collar. He nodded in approval of Travis' request before continuing.

"Sure...People were running around and screaming while trying to get away from the Hogs. Some of the Eastbank Sheriff's Deputies came in to assist us with enclosing the two suspects to one area. Once the deputies showed up, one of the guys fired a shot into the crowd and people scattered," Remy testified.

"And, Mr. Daniels, are you aware of which suspect fired the bullets into the open park at the time?" Travis requested.

"They each had guns drawn. Multiple other shots followed the first, which resulted in multiple injured civilians and a couple of dead officers in the process," Remy described.

"Officer Daniels, forgive me if this question seems aloof, but considering the circumstances, did you in fact discharge your firearm?" Travis delved.

Remy looked down at his hands and then toward the jury. He looked at his hands again before focusing on the vested spectators beyond the bar.

"Yes, sir, I did," Remy calmly answered.

"Officer Daniels, can you please inform the jury of who or what your muzzle was pointed at prior to pressing the trigger?" Travis examined.

Daniels raised his eyebrows marginally before his shoulders sunk. He deeply snuffed the still air before allowing his lips to part.

"I aimed a step ahead in the direction the other believed Hog was traveling," Daniels answered.

"Of course you did. And did anyone cross between

yourself and the trajectory of your ammunition?" Travis inspected.

"No, sir. No bystanders were harmed by my fire," Remy defied.

"Officer Daniels, how long have you been a police officer?" Travis dug.

"Umm... about four years. Yeah...four and a half, maybe five," Remy answered.

"And you all still qualify with your firearms annually, at the very least, correct?" Travis requested.

"More like two, sometimes even three times a year," Remy confirmed.

"That's undeniably impressive, officer. And in those years of experience, have you ever not qualified with your firearm?" Travis proceeded.

"No, " Remy denied.

"So," Travis began as he turned away from his witness and traipsed toward the defense table. "We have arguably a thoroughly trained veteran officer approaching a likely explosive situation with no more knowledge than what was provided by dispatch. He goes into an open park with multiple civilians and has to utilize his firearm to salvage what little peace could be mustered under the disruption of two men who may have been brash enough to fire shots at a funeral procession. Is that what you are telling us, Officer Daniels?"

"Yes. More or less," Remy backed.

"Your Honor, I will tender the witness. I have no further questions," Travis rested.

"Very well, Mr. Carrington, you may be seated. Mr. Archibald, would you like to address the witness?" Judge Burgess directed.

"He hasn't been tendered. But he will be when I'm done with him," Ashley stated under his breath.

As Travis returned to his seat, he stared back at his witness, who was deciding to abandon his slouch by sitting perfectly upright. Travis subtly nodded his head at Remy as he took a seat. Ashley stood up while his pupils burrowed through his adversarial state representative. As he cleared the corner of the defense table, he disengaged the middle button of his suit while artfully whisking the tails of the coat to his rear.

"Yes, Your Honor, I believe I do have a few pertinent questions for Mr. Daniels if the court will allow," Ashley declared out loud.

"You shall proceed," Judge Burgess granted.

"Yes, indeed," Ashley accepted.

Chapter 23

Rifts in A-Minor

Shouting drowns out the bass-filled ballad blasting over the studio's sound system. The sound engineer neglects to shut off his equipment as his boss erupts into the studio in a foul mood. The booth has been vacated by an artist who is currently being verbally assaulted by a man who has never spit a rhyme in his entire existence. Chop It To Ya' Records is on the brink of a pivotal moment in their history as the "moneyman" was heated at his *money-maker*.

"Look, whoa...you got to get the fuck up out my spot with that shit, man. You on that bullshit!" the CEO screamed.

"Mane, what is you talking 'bout, chief? I'm in the booth doing what y'all pay me to do. Where you want me to do it at, YouTube?" the artist pondered.

"You spewing that negative shit, man. People out here buying into it on a whole 'nother level," the CEO declared.

"This is the same type of shit you brought me here to spit. How you gon' flip out today when you be in the back of the club vibin' to it?" artist Vernell Kane shouted back.

"Because they ain't just words no more. This shit

starting to play out in real life. People losing they lives behind this shit!" the CEO stated.

"Are you superstitious or slow? People been saying shit worse than me for years. Negroes been dying for years. How all of a sudden, it's all on me? How many artists do you have? I'm the only one spitting that 'negative' shit, so to speak? Man, you don't believe that yourself," Vernell defended.

The CEO nearly trampled his own shades as he launched himself toward Vernell. The engineer got in between them, mostly to prevent damage to his equipment or rupturing the sound. The engineer wrapped his arm around the CEO and tried to guide him backwards to a chair. Vernell was still bewildered from the boisterous entrance.

"The only thing that's about to be slow around here is the money unless y'all get this ignorant motherfucker out of my building!" the CEO demanded.

"Carter Boy, you been smoking that shit, man? You steady tweakin'. You pay me to be here doing just what I'm doing," Vernell pleaded.

Carter grabbed a nearby jacket and flung it at Vernell. He arose from the arm of the couch he'd been relegated to and knocked the engineer's flailing arm away.

"Only boy I see round here is you, muhfucka'. But not after tonight. You can take all your shit and get up outta here," Carter ordered.

"Bruh, I ain't no damn intern. I'm an employee and you gon' have to pay me whether I'm here and especially if I'm not. I'm under contract, dumbass. You actin' real loopy right nah," Vernell reminded.

"Forget that contract and forget you. Trying to make

up my mind about which one I'm gon' rip up first. You itchin' for it to be you though," Carter replied.

Vernell kneeled to pick up the jacket from the floor. He grasped it in one hand and folded it over the opposite forearm as he heeded Carter's request and walked toward the door. Vernell looked at Carter, then back at the engineer before he shrugged his shoulders, grinned, and let out a small snicker.

"You know what, Playboy, I'm gonna go head and get up outchea'. I'll link back up with you tomorrow when Carter boy ain't trippin'," Vernell suggested.

Carter grabbed Playboy's shoulders to shift him the adverse direction whilst he positioned himself in front of the exit.

"I think you the slow one, Kane! For the last time: YOU AIN'T COMING BACK UP IN HERE! You ain't 'bout to be spitting that vitriol all over my studio. We'll worry about the logistics in the morning, but there ain't nothing you need to come back on this property for. Keep it moving!" Carter relayed.

"Man, I'm spitting the same shit *you* said the people want to hear. I was on the streets releasing conscious flow, until I linked up with you and this damn label. It was all good when I was making money for y'all! What's the problem now?! Ain't shit changed since I walked through the door. Well...besides your twisted ass," Vernell declared in outrage.

As Playboy looked back at Vernell, he took note of his matter-of-fact tone coupled with Carter's decreased agitation. He realized he no longer needed to intervene, so he moved horizontally to lean on the soundboard.

"Losing my son was the first straw. I thought that shit

was incidental. I should have known better because my boy didn't bother nobody. I hoped it was a mistaken identity. Now three more members of the Chop It To Ya' family are gone, and you know what they found on the scene? *Your toxic ass lyrics!*" Carter berated.

"My music causing people to be violent? You on some other shit. You sound like the people in the media that's always blaming rap music for kids being bad or some shit," Vernell spewed.

"It ain't about what I believe. It's about what my eyes have witnessed for themselves! There's too much blood around this building, and you the common denominator," Carter settled.

Vernell unwrapped the jacket from his arm and placed it on himself. He slowly slid the first arm into the sleeve without breaking eye contact with Carter. Vernell blindly navigated the interior of his coat for the other sleeve until he found it and covered his remaining appendage. Vernell adjusted the coat along his trapezius before approaching the exit.

"You know what, Carter boy?" Vernell began once he reached the door seal. "I'm not gon' even stress on this shit folk. You wanted to get grimy but blame me because your hands got dirty in the process. That's cool. I'll catch y'all on the come up. This ain't the last y'all heard of me. Believe dat'."

"Don't come your ass back in here, that's all I know. If you come back through my damn doors, you will be the next victim of the family!" Carter threatened.

"It ain't never gon' come to that. One, nobody affiliated with this label gonna put they hands on me without pulling back nubs. Two, you can't see me as family if you droppin' me on some superstitious shit. Man, I woulda thought we was better than this. If I come back in this building again, it's gonna be to do what I always do up in here...serve these hoes," Vernell contended.

Playboy's palm was the barrier between the two combatants as the artist ironically left the booth. A couple of staff members who heard the commotion were in the hall staring Vernell down as he brushed past them without the slightest glance. The road between the studio and the main street where Chop It To Ya' Records resided felt like the greenest of miles to Vernell. There were voices directed at him, but he heard none.

Of course, he couldn't leave unnoticed, not after the ruckus that ensued. Not after all the late nights he'd spent blazing and amazing in the booth. Not with all the onlookers who could see there was something unsettled about the look on Vernell's exterior. The scorned scowl dragged his face into obvious distortion. His irises remained chained to the floor until he reached the final threshold of the establishment. Like the disappointed partner of a failed marriage, Vernell carefully studied the last barrier separating him from the fall gust. He peered to his rear for the conclusion of his tenure with the group that practically discovered him. Groomed him. *Made him*?! No, surely they did not. If they had, they would certainly have to do it again.

When Vernell comes to terms with the pending separation, he takes the hood of his coat and places it over his already clouded head. His eyes ignite with contempt, confusion, and calculated revenge. As the words "Pelli Kanisus" shimmer in gold across the upper back of Vernell's black coat, spectators at Chop It To Ya' Records may literally be witnessing the best thing that has ever happened to them, strolling right out of the front door.

Chapter 24

Mowing the Pawn

"So, officer, you stated you arrived at City Park via dispatch. Were you present at the burial of one Francisco Tatiano?" Attorney Archibald asked Remy.

"No sir. I was not. I was working that day," Remy answered.

"So, were there not some of your coworkers present who were also on duty?" Ashley dug.

"Possibly. I'm not certain. I wasn't one of them," Remy clarified.

"Hmm. That's a curious thing. You didn't go to pay respects to your counterpart, Mr. Daniels?" Ashley highlighted.

Reactions of onlookers varied extensively. Detective Barrios cringed at the line of questioning. As inconsequential to the case as the question seemed, she had a sense of what Ashley was attempting to do. *Show the mixed feelings of the department toward Franc.* If he could even meagerly expose this inconsistency, it might be enough to weaken the state's stance that the Hogs were the responsible party.

"No. I preferred to remain on patrol in my unit. In the

event someone needed my assistance, let us say, like what occurred immediately after," Remy advised.

"Your commitment to duty is commendable, Mr. Daniels, I will admit. However, it is also a bit, concerning? Considering the assistance Mr. Tatiano provided your department, and others mind you, over the years, one might suspect more law enforcement professionals would be in attendance," Ashley outlined.

"I did not believe, initially, I would serve any purpose to anyone while at a burial ground. It's usually not so eventful," Remy commented.

"Eventful, you say? Hmm, so there was not enough action for you at a burial, but you show up to a gunfight in a park?" Ashley baited.

"I object, Your Honor!" Travis interrupted. "Attorney Archibald is getting off kilter with his badgering."

"I'll allow it for now, Mr. Carrington. As long as Mr. Archibald plans on making a point sometime soon," Judge Burgess ruled.

A few of the jurors' faces lit up at the last question posed. They too found curiosity in the actions of Officer Daniels on that given day.

"Forgive me, court, it's not my intent to badger. Let me ask a simpler question if I may," Ashley requested.

"Proceed, *and with caution*, Mr. Archibald," Judge Burgess warned.

"With pleasure, Your Honor," Ashley began. "Now, Mr. Daniels, I understand you are not a fan of burials. So can you please entertain the jury and advise whether or not you attended the funeral of Mr. Tatiano?"

"No, sir, that was even further away from my patrol area than the burial site," Remy informed.

"That is a respectable reason for your absence from the funeral. However, you did state you'd been employed as a police officer somewhere between four or five years, am I correct?" Ashley deviated.

"Yes, somewhere in that ballpark," Remy confirmed.

"So, you witnessed the decrease in crime in the Greater Crescent City during the Fantastic Franc era, I assume?" Ashley pressed.

"I suppose that's fair," remarked Remy, non-committal.

"I find it hard to believe you wouldn't notice the significant improvements in the city. Especially considering the accolades you all received in the news by comparison to other states. Do you know what the difference was between this city and all the others in the state?" Ashley poked.

"No, sir. I'm not really a numbers guy; that's not my job," Remy replied.

"Sure, you're not. It's not necessary to what you do, but the answer is not in figures. It's simple: Fantastic Francisco Tatiano. *HE* is the difference, well, at least he was. By simple comparison, he made your jobs easier than any other police force in the world. And what did you give him? Not even a few condolences before his casket dropped?" Ashley described.

There was no instant rebuttal from Officer Daniels. Ashley shook his index finger in the air, then abandoned the area near the witness stand to retrieve an item from his briefcase. Ashley gave it one more looksee before presenting it to the witness.

"Mr. Daniels, would you happen to be familiar with this documentation I have presented before you?" Ashley completed.

"I hope so, sir. It's not quite in my handwriting, but I wrote it!" Remy poked. Ashley chuckled at the gesture.

"I believe you did too, sir. This is Officer Daniels' typed report of what occurred on the day in question," Ashley cleared. "In it, you say you received the info from dispatch roughly around 12:35 p.m.?"

"That sounds about right," Remy confirmed.

"I certainly hope so, officer, I certainly hope so. Is it also correct you informed dispatch of your arrival on scene at City Park at roughly 12:43 p.m.?" Ashley alerted the crowd.

"That too seems sufficient," Remy answered.

"Well, sir, that seems like a pretty quick turnaround. Would it be safe to assume you were somewhere in the area?" Ashley asked.

"I patrol the areas nearby," Remy clarified.

"So, you apparently have no love lost for Mr. Tatiano despite his history of assisting law enforcement; however, 'Fifth Ward Hogs,' like Mr. Nguyen here, showed up and paid their respects despite their checkered history with him. Call me crazy, but I find it slightly ironic that a man literally gave his life for free in the profession you get paid for, and some of you, at the very least, could not lend final regards?" Ashley suggested.

There was a delay in Remy's reply. "Good," Ashley thought to himself. With each passing second between Archibald's question and Remy's answer, the air grew colder.

"Your Honor, I object; whether or not the witness felt close enough to another hero has no bearing on what the officer saw in the park that day," Travis interrupted.

"Mr. Archibald, I will have to ask you to tread carefully, sir. His feelings towards a deceased member of our community bears no relevance in this matter," Judge Burgess cautioned.

"Understood, Your Honor. My intent was to show the jury there is a glaring aversion on behalf of public servants as far as the deceased is concerned. Such a reverence could have possibly led to improper discharging of firearms with perception of the slightest threat," Ashley included.

A collective "gasp" gathered from all corners of the room. Just like that, Ashley Archibald shifted the focus from his client to the C.C.P.D. It was one thing for him to be familiar with tensions some officers held against Franc. The impact was magnified when it was filled with a group of civilians who witnessed the multiple police brutality cases that arrived over the years. Vilifying the state's witness caused just enough smoke to cloud the judgment of those present, even if for a moment.

"Court reporter, please do not put that in the record. That was an unnecessary and nearly 'disbarring' comment made by the defendant's counsel. MR. ARCHIBALD!" Judge Burgess commanded.

"I apologize, Your Honor. That was not a question for the witness. I must have been thinking out loud. Forgive me, court. If I may proceed with my examination?" Ashley requested.

"Continue, Mr. Archibald," Judge Burgess granted halfheartedly.

"So, Officer Daniels, you immediately responded to a pursuit of possibly armed motorists in the park. How long were you there before you witnessed the first gun shots?" Ashley rerouted.

"I cannot answer that for certain; everything was happening so fast," Remy shared.

"Well, Mr. Daniels, I definitely believe that. I believe there may have been so much going on that it could have prevented you from seeing the full picture. As I take a step back to your earlier testimony, I could not help but overhear that you were not able to identify who fired the first shots, am I correct?" Ashley recollected.

"No, I guess I did not," Remy recalled.

"Thank you for that, sir. Now, Officer Daniels, you stated that the crowd of people were running from the Hogs; however, you are not sure where the shots came from that you encountered. What makes you so certain the Hogs were the object of everyone's excitement?" Ashley inquired.

Another miniscule delay in response. Another minor *plunge* in the officer's credibility.

"All of those patrons were scattering to each direction except towards the two suspects. They were wielding guns as reported by dispatch and were not moving in the hysterical fashion of all other inhabitants of the park," Remy solidified.

That was the stone-cold answer the jury needed to hear. It may have taken Remy a moment to formulate his words, but once they came out, they were clear and poignant. Unluckily for Remy Daniels, it was going to take more than soliloquys to waver the momentum of Ashley Archibald. This was already a game of chess in Archibald's mind, but now he viewed Remy as something more significant than a pawn.

"Thank you for that, Officer Daniels. Mr. Nguyen and his deceased friend may not have been affected by the mass hysteria in the park, especially considering how much energy they dispensed while being chased out of a burial site. But with you admitting you have no clear sight of who fired the first shot, how do we know that after all the Hogs went through, these two were not simply standing their ground? I mean, from the mausoleum on Canal to City Park, is it not feasible that they may have run enough for one day? You reported to that place like several other law enforcement officers; how certain are we that one of them was not the true threat?" Ashley painted.

"Because...because...hmm. As I advised before, I cannot affirmatively answer that," muttered the stumped Officer Daniels.

Checkmate. Ashley's series of questions were completely developed from Daniels' own testimony. A man under oath is a man limited on answers derived from wild guesses and gut feelings. What the officer knew, however, is today's hearing would not be solely based on his testimony. Still to come was one of the deputies from the Eastbank Sheriff's Department.

"Well, how could you be certain you were aiming at the right people? How do you know you should not have been firing at a quote/unquote pig, as some call you all on the street, instead of a Fifth Ward Hog?" Ashley nailed.

"That's simple," Daniels opened. "I was there to address the threat of two motorists who fled an earlier gunfight. They were present with visible weapons on the scene once I arrived. Their involvement in an earlier shoot-out, which they were not formally invited to by the way, shows probable cause they have a high likelihood of being involved in such activity again. Such activity occurred minutes later...at City Park."

"Same could be said for the C.C.P.D., Mr. Daniels!" Ashley instantly rebutted.

"In both cases, we were where we were asked to be. The same could not be said for the Fifth Ward Hogs, Your Honor," Daniels directed toward Judge Burgess, subconsciously attempting to nullify Ashley Archibald from existence.

Remy's court presence in this examination may have been enough to deplete some of the ire he acquired around the C.C.P.D. following the previous hearing. While not altogether dominant in his joust with the infamous Ashley Archibald, he may have been convincing enough to make sure the focus was more on proving Nguyen's innocence than Crescent City P.D.'s guilt.

"Do you have anything further, Mr. Archibald?" Judge Burgess asked.

"No, Your Honor, I believe I have heard enough," Ashley indicated.

"And you, Mr. Carrington? Would you like to cross-examine your witness?" Judge Burgess offered.

"No, we have no further questions for Officer Daniels at this time. Thank you, sir, you may return to your seat," Travis directed.

With this directive, Remy Daniels descended the witness stand and joined the masses on the other side of the swinging doors. For now, his job was done, and somewhat valiantly. Nevertheless, this hearing was far from over.

Chapter 25

Ample Opportunities

The night sky is clear and uncontested for most, aside from one home in Destreland. Cries fill the room in two varied tones. The loudest belonging to the youngest inhabitant, attempting to draw attention to a need he can't verbalize or fill on his own. Peerless only knows what has worked before, so he clings to ole faithful. Meanwhile, his mother weeps internally as she bares her exhaustion. *"Not again"* Julissa thought to herself. *"When will he sleep for a whole night so I can too?"* She begged the stars above. As the child wailed, she couldn't help but recall a more peaceful time in her life, a time between Judy learning how to speak and prior to Peerless' debut.

Julissa picks Peerless up as her head dangles about her neck. Her legs plop about the room like a toddler waddling through a swamp. "No more" Julissa begs of Peerless. His nightly interruptions were more inviting when she was still on leave; now, it was just a reminder of why she needed a partner to relieve her. She returned to the marketing firm earlier in the week. Things were relatively slow as they tried to ease her back into her role. Julissa was splendid with the art of spin. She could take anything given to her and make it beneficial. Sadly, she couldn't manage to convince herself she was going to survive one more night of her son's shrieks.

She remembered being able to rotate nights with Renaldo when Judy was born. One night she would be on duty for the late evening feedings; the next night would belong to Renaldo, so on and so forth. The realization set in that even if Renaldo was still around, he would probably be fairly reluctant to assist her in the rearing of Peerless, with good reason. As she hoped to comfort her son, the faint touch of his tiny paws slowly consoled her. She transported him to her room, where the bottle warmer sat upon the nightstand on the empty side of her bed. She moved her pillows to the other side as she leaned against the cushioned headboard. She then adjusted Peerless so that his head rested about the exterior of her bicep and his body along the length of her forearm.

"Hush, little baby, don't say a word...," Julissa began to croon.

Julissa carefully nurtured Peerless as she looked at the empty portion of her bed, now covered by pillows. She slid her foot to the pillows to feel as if there was something, *someone*, there. She peered into her child's eyes as he watched a tear slip. His lashes whisked while he succumbed to the succor of a pseudo filled belly. Julissa's despondency dispersed at the slyest smirk from Peerless. The smirk was reminiscent of a man she both once knew and hoped the infant would even marginally become. She couldn't help but to think of how the little bundle of joy was bestowed upon her. The accidental acquisition. The fruit of betrayal. The proof of infidelity. The...*blessing in disguise*?!

"Please, get here in a hurry! He may be in trouble! I need your help!!" Julissa faintly recalls Franc's plea.

"Okay, okay. I'm on my way; where are you?" she asked the rattled man.

"My place," Franc answered hurriedly.

Julissa brought Judy to her grandmother's house before she began her expedition to Metairie. Her mind was miles ahead of her car as she dreaded her husband was finally in a pickle he wouldn't be able to back himself out of. "I just knew he would chase himself to his own demise" she thought as she punished the highway, scorching the pavement with her tires. She gets there faster than anticipated, much faster than she had a couple of weeks prior.

Julissa jumps out of the car to careen up the stairs in Building 5 of the Moon Light Apartments. Once she reaches the second floor, she sprints down the hall, nearly tumbling through Franc's front door. She pounds the entrance with enough force to rattle some of the pictures clinging to the walls. Franc opens the door as Julissa nearly trips over his foot.

"Where is he? In your bedroom?" Julissa searched.

"No, he is...He is right here in front of you," Franc answered.

Julissa pivots as she looks about the floor for Renaldo. When she discovers the floor is bare, she squints at Franc, then marches into his kitchen. *Nothing. No one.* Her concern slowly diffuses into anger. She waltzes back into the living room while Franc stands near his barstools.

"Where is he? You said Renaldo was in trouble and needed help!" Julissa shrieked.

"I never said Renaldo was here. But I assure you, he is

occupied and won't be needing help anytime soon," Franc provided.

"Wha...what?" Julissa remarked "Why in the hell did you call me here? You damn near gave me a heart attack. If Renaldo doesn't need my help, then who the hell does?"

"Me!" Franc reacted "I do. I haven't been able to help myself since the night you left here. I haven't stopped thinking about you."

Julissa retracted her chin as her eyes widened at Franc's wild claims. She blinked while shaking her head and walked to the other side of the couch, creating a barrier between herself and Fantastic.

"Franc," Julissa bellowed while bracing the edge of the couch.

"Listen," Franc interrupted.

"No, you listen, Franc!" Julissa began, flustered. "What happened that night was a mistake. It never should have gone that far."

"You're right, it went further than anyone expected. But an accident? Nah, I beg to differ," Franc rebutted.

Franc departs his kitchen to join Julissa in the living room. She wants to walk away before he closes in, but her feet betray her. She lets out a small sigh, knowing her trotters only sought to engage in her wondrous desires. She couldn't allow herself to give in. She *shouldn't* allow herself to give in, at least.

"Franc," Julissa muttered, "I'm a married woman with a family. What good will I be to you? What more could you offer me?"

"Peace! The peace in knowing that your love is cherished, not a chore. The peace in knowing that I may be taking on their world so I can ensure the safety of mine," Franc offered.

"And what about you? What good does that do you?" Julissa requested.

"I was talking about me," Franc politely joked.

Julissa laughed while staring blankly into Franc's chest. He placed the cup of his index and thumb under Julissa's chin and lifted her eyes to his. It's the last thing she needed. *To look in the eyes of a man who just finished confessing his soul to her.* Could it be that the love she so desired was being packaged to her in fantastic fashion? "No, this shouldn't be," she tried to convince herself, only to have her heart settle the dispute.

Julissa dislodges her jawline from Franc's grasp, nearly twisting his wrist in the process. She removes her right hand from his chest, watching his expression droop, down to the disconnect of her last fingertip. She's finally mustered the sensation in her legs to sprint toward the door. One hand grazes her hair as the other reaches for the knob. Julissa's hand drops as she pauses before exit. She quickly glanced over her shoulder before reaching for the doorknob once more.

"I'm sorry, I just hoped..." Franc began as Julissa shook her head and continued on her path.

Julissa's left hand grips the handle emphatically as she twists her wrist. The latch releases but she doesn't pull the lever inward. Conversely, the index and thumb of her right hand meet the other along the latch and lock the door. She gazes to the side momentarily before she extends her right hand to secure the lock above. Franc is suddenly confused and thinks back to the night he aided Julissa against The Brood. He wasn't sure if he was being treated or trapped. Either way, he was now on guard.

Julissa switches her focus to Franc. She's hesitant yet anxious before finally following her gut. Julissa's dress sways to the rhythm of her hips with each methodic yet melodic step. As Franc watched her seemingly float, she watched his eyes immersed into her. She noticed how he never blinked, as if he was worried he may miss the moment. When she was within reach, she wrapped both arms around Franc, tunneled her head into his chest plate, and took in his natural scent. "Is this what pheromones smell like?" Julissa jokingly assumed. Whatever it was would be shortly lived, as Franc soon placed his hands on her to pry her away.

Julissa looked up, stunned, disgusted, and probably a little ashamed. Franc let out a sly smirk at the sight as he grasped the cup of her derriere and hauled her thighs into his forearms. They reacquainted mouths, this meeting proving more forceful than the last. They occasionally opened their eyes to confirm this was a reality. However, the authenticity was in what they felt, not in who they viewed.

"*Why*? Franc! Why?" Julissa whispered.

Franc discreetly shifted his elbows inside Julissa's knees and his forearms along the length of her thighs. He slowly removed his lips from the crevice of her neck and collarbone. With the cold air now canvassing the spot, Julissa's lids lifted to gaze upon Franc. He inhaled deeply before gingerly pushing it out through his nostrils.

"Because we both deserve better...and there's nothing better...than the best," Franc concluded.

Julissa was awestruck by his declaration, but immediately concurred by tilting her head and draping her arms around the back of Franc's neck. As she pushed his face towards hers, Franc launched Julissa's posterior up to his chest. While she remained stunned, Franc hoisted her up again to his chin, nearly disguising himself within her dress. She could feel him jousting with the fabric of her panties below until she felt a warm moist object flicker along her vaginal cavity. Julissa's eyes widened, thighs tightened, and her body nearly sunk. Franc felt the sheer relaxation in Julissa's body as he carefully carried her to the nearest high surface. Franc placed her spine along the nearest wall as he did internally now what he had only done externally in the past: *he lifted Julissa's spirits with nothing more than the whip of his tongue.*

Whether it was due to literally being on a man's shoulders or the culmination of all her emotions rushing through her psyche, Julissa finally felt as if she was on top of the world! Franc held no award or trophy as gallantly as he upheld his best friend's wife. And honestly, he regarded nothing more than he regarded her gasps and moans of satisfaction. Crescent City could be set ablaze for all he cared; to Franc, he was now perusing the softest place on Earth. He knew his time was limited, so Franc carried Julissa and all her splendor to the closest comfortable object and laid her down gently. Julissa's body quaked as her back graced the cushion. She'd seen and felt enough to know she wanted to go further.

Franc kissed and licked her clitoral palette in ways that made her contemplate her soul detaching from her body. She felt as if she and Franc set sail on a *"Voyage to Atlantis"* as described by the Isley Brothers. Because she felt so secure in his arms, so wrapped up in his charm, she truly believed he would *always* come back to her. Their sensational romance honestly left them with no sense at all. Julissa gripped Franc in areas that could not be witnessed by the human eye as he delved into her entire being, searching for nothing more than her approval and appeasement. With each stroke, the lines that separated Franc and Julissa slowly dissolved while their desires blurred. Within his tempo, she witnessed his adoration, appreciation, and near infatuation with pleasing her. In the heat of the moment, their inhibitions were disregarded by passion. They were so caught in the moment they unleashed and released upon one another that which should have been reserved specifically for significant others.

The only shortness of the encounter was the breath lingering in their bodies. Two satiated beings previously bound by association, now connected by near asphyxiation. Moreover, Julissa and Franc mused the arousal of their rendezvous while basking in saturated solace; at least until Franc's body began to jolt. What she believed was mere aftershock turned out to be more an adverse reaction. When his eyes rolled to the back of his head, she reached around for her phone. Knowing there was no way to explain her presence at the location, Julissa panicked and wrapped herself around him. Franc's seismic shiver slowed until it ceased. He sucked in a loud gasp and coughed while trying to sit upright.

"That's a hell of a post-sex reaction you have there," Julissa joked.

"Who you tellin'? That's never happened before," Franc admitted.

Those were the last words they stated to one another before Julissa noticed the time, gathered her things, and vacated the premises. Franc assured she did not have to leave, but they both were aware this was not entirely feasible. She knew she needed to return to Judy, and, well, her father too. Though Franc understood her obligation, he could not accept her dedication to someone who didn't fully cherish her.

Currently, Julissa looks in the wisping eyes of her son, knowing he was the immediate result of a night of emotion. No matter what she and Renaldo had done before or after that night, it had been obvious since his world premiere that Peerless belonged to none other than Francisco Tatiano. Their tears subsided, and Julissa hoped to enjoy what was left of a weary night.

Chapter 26

Route 66

Three men exit church doors, each toting a bag as they march across the parking lot to the lone vehicle. The detective slowly traipses behind Victor and Mack, not fully certain of the next step. The other two men are aware of his foot-dragging yet harbor no concern. They prefer making it to the vehicle before him. Victor takes the keys out of his pocket and pops the trunk. He and Mack place their bags inside while Renaldo tries to find some reference to their location.

"Hey, detective, we can take you on the tour once this is all over. You wanna pick up the pace a little bit?" Mack chimed.

Renaldo takes his attention off the night sky so he can nod toward the anxious gentlemen. The air is tinted by a light mill-like scent. That gives Detective Brown nothing to work with. There are mills in multiple areas of The Boot, a fruitless discovery at best.

"Muh-Muh-Mayybee we shouuld havve ta-takennnn himmm owwwt sooooooner," Victor surmised.

"Maybe you're right," Mack settled. "Say there, dick... let's get this show on the road."

Mack intended to make another comment but deferred to his rumbling cough. He clutched at his stomach as Victor provided support. Renaldo recognized the frequency with which Mack has started to favor his abdominal area. He sees it as a possible opening for a later opportunity.

"You alright there, Rev'? We may need to get you out of this polluted air," Renaldo empathized.

Mack looked at the handkerchief he used to cover his mouth. He bobbed to Renaldo that he would be fine and signaled for him to get in the car. He secretly wondered if Renaldo had sincerely contracted Stockholm Syndrome.

"I appreciate the concern, young buck, I really do; but I'll be quite alright once we make it to our destination," Mack replied.

Renaldo seeks to comply with the request, so he attempts to sit in the backseat. Mack grabs Renaldo's shoulders and points the crown of his head toward the front passenger seat. Renaldo returns a puzzled look at his elder, to which the older gentleman simply opens the rear door with one hand and nudges Renaldo forward with the other. With respect to his elder, Renaldo fulfills the request by joining Victor in the anterior.

Victor revs up the ignition and there's a slight pause before the bass and treble overtake the eardrums of the vehicle's inhabitants. Victor scrambles to lower the volume as he dodges the dirty looks from his passengers.

"Were you having too much fun kidnapping another unsuspecting citizen?" Renaldo states sarcastically.

"I waasn't thee laaast perrrson toooo driiiive," Victor advised.

Renaldo scrunches his eyebrows as he slowly turns

from Victor to Mack. Mack offers no more than a glance at his younger counterpart.

"You looking for some sharp edges, boy? You won't find none. I may be sanctified, but I ain't square," Mack declared.

Renaldo shrugs his shoulders while returning his vision to the road ahead. He slouches a smidgen. He rocks his head side-to-side before letting out a bold revelation:

"Well, that would explain a lot," Renaldo claimed.

"Oh, really, youngster?! Would you care to indulge me on what precisely the hell that's supposed to mean?" Mack quizzed.

The detective sneers at the elder's retort. He found much levity in Mr. Wellington's responses and relished each opportunity to ruffle his feathers.

"Hey, sir. Don't take it personal. According to the things I'd been told about you, I know you a lil' gansta'!" Renaldo pooled.

Mack flashes an award-winning smile as he takes in the view courtesy of his passenger window. Mack sniffles prior to grazing the tip of his nose with his index and thumb. He then crosses one ankle over the other knee before letting out another cough. Once he regains his composure, he decides to entertain the detective's comments.

"Is that right, Mr. Brown? Well, I'll be! I am just curious as to what precisely you have heard about a gentleman such as myself," Mr. Wellington inquired.

"As far as I know, you were involved with some pretty dangerous people who were linked to some very interesting people," Renaldo proclaimed.

"I am certainly intrigued as to what type of people a

detective such as yourself would find...interesting...as you so eloquently put it," Mack engaged.

Renaldo whipped his head to the rear of the vehicle for a quick inspection of the pastor. He ascertained Mack to have displayed a fairly casual demeanor as his hands rested on the knee supporting the opposing ankle. Though Mack wore his seatbelt, he leaned along the door as if he planned to jump. Renaldo took note of these features before proceeding with his observations.

"People such as Huey P. Long. Or at least the mafia's connected to him," Renaldo blurted.

Mack laughed boisterously at Renaldo's remarks. He found the basis to be profoundly ridiculous, considering the difference in age between himself and the former Louisiana representative. Despite his best efforts to contain himself, Mack's fancy had truly been tickled. Renaldo took no exception to the brandish cackling of Mack Wellington. Renaldo now wondered if he was absurdly off kilter with his revelations, or if Mack was attempting a coup.

"I'm happy to entertain you, pastor. I'm here all day," Renaldo shared.

"What I need you to do is pick up a book. What in your life makes you think there was anything gangster about Huey P. Long? His brother, on the other hand, that may be more my speed," Mack indicated.

"Maybe my sources had you pegged wrong," Renaldo conceded.

"Damn right they did! Only Huey P. I acknowledge is Newton," Mack commanded.

"Te-Te-Tell him buh-bout it, unc!" Victor instructed excitedly.

"Long was a poster boy compared to his brother, Earl. Now him, he may have been in some sort of mafia, if that's what you're looking for," Mack detailed.

Renaldo momentarily contemplated two paths: the origins of Mack Wellington and the route the car was taking to Beech Grove Manor. Though the roads ran parallel in their obscurity, they would have to cross if Renaldo wanted to return to the world he once knew.

"So, you telling me the Sixty-Sixers are something like the Black Panthers? Is that your angle? Out of all the people who believed the Panthers were dangerous, not many of them were black," Renaldo affirmed.

Mack leaned forward in his seat until the tip of his hat rested on the back of Renaldo's headrest. The menacing minister wanted to ensure the naïve detective heard him correctly.

"Every time a black man sparks a match in this world, they think he came to burn it down. It doesn't matter how absurd the speculation may be, and do you know why, Mr. Brown? Because despite how lowly the world wants us to appear, the strength and prowess of a black man with his head anywhere above his shoulders is a light none other could extinguish," Mack avowed.

Detective Brown sat silently, simply soaking in the word. However, he wouldn't allow the reverend's righteous rhetoric to render him reserved.

"So, you and a bunch of other righteous brothers just walked around beating up on descendants of the people involved in the massacre?" Renaldo investigated.

"You a trip, boy, you know that? Think we was just riding around with our ancestry checklists and swiping down clowns?" Mack insulted.

Renaldo's rebuttal was delayed by the scene ahead of him: the high rising bridge along the highway. It meant only what he should have known all along: *Charles Lake!* He had been held captive approximately three and a half hours from his home. His life was in the hands of this uncle/nephew combo for no less than the next four hours of his life. *"Fuck that!"* Renaldo thought to himself. The first opening he saw; he was going to desert the inhospitable shrews.

"Something wrong up there, detective, or are you just pondering the foolishness of your question?" Mack assumed.

"Mayyybeee heee waaantsss toooo joinnn theeee grouuuuup!" Victor jested.

Renaldo tuned back into the banter of his captors. Now that he knew where he was, he had a decision to make. Take the long ride back home and provide assistance in a futile search; or use these few hours to develop an escape plan.

"Sorry about that, sir. I was just trying to figure out where I am...in terms of my thoughts on the Sixty-Sixers," Renaldo deflected.

"Since you seem so *enthralled* in the subject, I'll make it easy on you: We didn't just go around avenging the deaths of those lost in the Crescent City Massacre; we protected the city to make sure it never happened again!" Mack alleged.

Victor detected Renaldo gazing at him and without taking his focus off the road, he simply nodded in concurrence of Mack's claims.

"So, that whole organized crime rep was just a misconception?" Renaldo posed.

"Less of a misconception and more a matter of misinformation. It's only a misconception when people care about getting it right," Mack defined.

Being a veteran of the law enforcement community, and a black one at that, Renaldo identified with such conundrums for years. Despite his familiarity with the subject matter, he remained wary of the two men accompanying him for the ride. More so Mack than Victor.

"You still have some buddies down in the city? Some who can help us track down Miss Baronne?" Renaldo sought.

"You can say that. I still have a few potnahs down there. They've been keeping an eye out for me. I got resources too, detective," Mack confirmed.

"We could all use a little help from time-to-time," Renaldo agreed.

"Nothing like your informants or anything like that. You can't get my guys to flip on nothing but the grill," Mack insulted.

The trio laughed at Mack's wisecrack. Renaldo was laughing to avoid crying. *What the hell have I gotten myself into?* he thought. This was primed to be nothing more than a wild goose chase, which would begin at a mental home, of all places. Still, he would have preferred to have been doped up on medicine that made him feel like a zombie. Numbness would have been a relief compared to what he experienced the last...the last... *SHIT*...he has no idea how long he has been away from his norm, but he'd felt every second of it.

"What's wrong with a few people trying to give back a little relief to a community they once plagued?" Renaldo posed.

"An old wise man once said, 'all help ain't good help,'" Mack quoted.

"Maybe not, but what good is NO help?!" Renaldo returned.

"You suit cops are something else," Mack began. "You come around with your shiny shoes and shiny dispositions, looking mighty sharp, I'll permit. But nothing is as sharp as your tongues!"

Victor nearly steered them off the road as he gaped at Renaldo, anticipating a retort. He returned his sights to the streets once he realigned the wheels onto the motorway.

"What's that supposed to mean?" Renaldo desired.

"What you think it mean? You already know!! Y'all don't wanna step in that fire for yourselves, so you convince some shady fool to do y'all a favor and you promise him one in return. Whole time, y'all could be lying your ass off. Or yet, *they could be*," Mack outlined.

"If I'm ever looking into somebody, I already have a feeling about what they're doing. May just need a little confirmation, that's all," Renaldo defended.

"Where exactly do y'all get off trying to get somebody to flip on they brother? Hneh? You boys in blue don't seem to have no qualms about encouraging folks to stab each other in the back for your conviction rates," Mack blamed.

Renaldo could feel himself seething at the pressing assertions. There was always somebody outside of a precinct that felt they had law enforcement figured out. *What do they really know?* The media always showed the fools who brutalized a citizen on the job, but they rarely showed the officers who go into the communities and helped people feel safe by riding around and talking to the residents. Were there that few of them left? *Was the lieutenant right*? Was the disconnect between community and policing now a gaping hole?

"Where does the community get off keeping quiet while mothers lose their sons and daughters? Hnah? You got kids growing up without parents, and for what? Some code? Some honor amongst thieves? While one robbing one side of life, those that know are robbing that family of closure! Plenty of unsolved mysteries were nothing more than a loud town turned ghost. Everybody in the neighborhood know what happen, but when we come looking to put the right person away, you can hear a rat pissing on cotton," Renaldo verbally unraveled.

The tension rose well above the bridge towering over Charles Lake. Victor couldn't formulate a joke swiftly enough. He raised the volume on the radio, but it was no use. The battlelines had been drawn clearly in the sand.

"Well, that's elementary, Jackson. For every so-called good cop, there seems to be two or three scared little punks who'd rather use their gun than their mind. Who are the people supposed to trust? The guy who only comes around when you call him or the guy who is always around when you need them?" Mack proposed.

"They could be one in the same if people start to open their mouths for more than complaining, sir. Closed mouths don't get fed and those without dough can't make bread," Renaldo fired.

"You think you some kind of smart, don't ya? You must have never heard of a paleo or keto diet!!" Mack harassed.

The senior member of the caravan did enough to get a smile out of his adversary. It was more than enough to soothe Victor's concern. For now, the three men were on the same page, seemingly. But with more than a couple of hours to spare, Victor could only hope tempers wouldn't continue to flare.

Chapter 27

Checking for Checkers

"Does the state have another witness, Mr. Carrington?" Judge Burgess inquired.

Attorney Travis Carrington stares down at his file while thumbing through his notes. With his head tilted, he extends his eyes to the most northern region of his socket before answering.

"Yes, Your Honor. If it pleases the court, I would like to call Deputy James Latimer of the Eastbank Sheriff's Office to the stand," Travis advised.

A man standing approximately 5'8", tan toned, and outfitted with a dual-shaded grey uniform ascends from the court crowd and slides into the aisle. The man presumed to be Deputy Latimer bows to several onlookers as he clears the turnstile. He enters the witness stand, is sworn in, and humbly takes his seat alongside Judge Burgess.

"Hello, Deputy Latimer. If you do not mind, could you please state your name and occupation for the court?" Travis requested.

"Certainly. My name is James Latimer and I'm a deputy of the Eastbank Sheriff's Department," Deputy

Latimer answered.

"Thank you for that clarification, deputy. Are you familiar with the events leading to these proceedings?" Travis led.

"Yes, sir. It's not exactly a day I could forget," Deputy Latimer answered assuredly.

"That is understandable, deputy. In what capacity were you involved in the matter?" Travis searched.

"We were dispatched to City Park in relation to two armed men roaming at-large in the presence of unsuspecting civilians. We were advised shots were fired at an earlier event and some ammunition had been released in the park as well," Deputy Latimer identified.

"And does the park fall under your jurisdiction, Deputy Latimer?" Travis asked.

"No, it does not," Deputy Latimer admitted.

"*Is that right*?! Could you please explain the compelling reason your department was dispatched there?" Travis questioned.

"Some of my coworkers were present at the burial site that day. They witnessed the Fifth Ward Hogs arriving at the mausoleum and the shots that followed. One of the men present for the events contacted dispatch when the remaining cyclists fled the scene," Deputy Latimer outlined.

"So, is that a common occurrence? Different branches of law enforcement assisting one another in routine arrests?" Travis hinted.

"No, that's part of the reason we have jurisdictions: clear-cut territories," Deputy Latimer defined.

"I see. So, there would have to be some pretty outstanding reasoning for various divisions of L.E.O.s to answer one call?" Travis surmised.

"Yes, sir. The circumstances would have to be fairly dire indeed," Deputy Latimer specified.

Travis' face gleams at the deputy's last statement as he glares at Ashley Archibald. Tony catches Travis' glance and he exchanges a wilted smirk for the prosecutor's confident grin.

"Despite there being clearly defined boundaries separating one division from another, two police departments were compelled to join forces to stop an obviously heinous threat?" Travis posed.

"You can say that," Deputy Latimer confirmed.

"Deputy Latimer, did you come into close contact with the defense?" Travis expelled.

"Yes, sir, I sure did," Deputy Latimer checked.

"Can you explain to the court precisely what you mean and what occurred, deputy?" Travis invited.

Ashley's head cocked to the side as his eyebrows rose. Ashley then looked down the table toward Tony, whose gaze was now firmly trained on the witness. Ashley squinted at Tony as he followed his visual track to the stand.

"Sure thing," Deputy Latimer began. "During the course of this matter, the gentleman at that table ran over to me to wrestle my gun away. In the midst of our tussle, my weapon discharged accidentally."

"Those are unfortunate circumstances, Deputy Latimer. Does anyone know if that misfire resulted in the injury of anyone else?" Travis sought.

"I can't confirm or deny that, sir. I was making sure this young man didn't walk away with my weapon. They'd caused enough disturbance with the guns they already possessed," Deputy Latimer professed.

Travis paused before proceeding with a further response. He silently soaked in the hushed whispers of the audience. A slick grin graced his face once he finished stalling.

"Your Honor, I have no further questions for this witness," Travis declared.

"Very well then, Mr. Carrington. Mr. Archibald, would you like to address the deputy before I allow him to step down?" Judge Burgess invited.

"Momentarily, Your Honor," Ashley accepted.

Ashley refastens a button on his blazer as he stands to approach the witness. The defense attorney glances at the locations and expressions of all the pieces, like a chess master plotting the next move. He carefully scans the witness, seeking any ounce of insecurity he could expose.

"Deputy Latimer, thank you for joining us today. I don't have much to ask of you, as I'm sure you have plenty of other things to do," Ashley opened.

"It's no problem, really," Latimer assured.

"So, Deputy, you advised earlier that the sheriff's deputies that intervened were in fact, *not* in their jurisdiction?" Ashley rehashed.

"That is correct, sir. We were aiding the C.C.P.D. in good faith," Latimer clarified.

"Well, were there not enough Crescent City Police Officers available at the time? What justifies the need to ask other agencies for assistance? Are the public's tax dollars being properly distributed or not?" Ashley interrogated.

The jurors and onlookers whispered alike. Deputy Latimer noticed the hushed exchanges and expelled the little breath remaining in his lungs. Latimer was less concerned but more careful in the wording of his answer.

"I cannot answer for the location of all officers within the C.C.P.D., but I was made aware of several officers attending a funeral of a partner to the community. Considering the location of the funeral, it is plausible some of those on duty may have been delayed in reporting back to their assignments," Latimer explained.

"That is understandable, Deputy. What I still have trouble comprehending is the need for Eastbank Sheriff's Office involvement. According to the police report, I may be short a witness due to the actions of your department," Ashley revealed.

A moment of silence sweeps the surface of Judge Burgess' courtroom. Even the judge's eyebrows are elevated in marvel. *Had the deputies deterred a witness from appearing on the stand*? How? Bribe? Bullying? *Burial*!?!

"Correct me if I am wrong, Deputy, but were there not two Hogs that entered City Park on that fateful day?" Ashley eluded.

"Per advisory, yes," Latimer conceded.

"Yet...only *one* was arrested? Can you explain to the court what the sheriff's department did with the other young man?" Ashley goaded.

"Oh, yes," Latimer started hesitantly. "The other young man was killed during the attempted detainment."

A couple of gasps disrupt the air. The collective curiosity of the room is satisfied, yet there is now more to be desired. Ashley was doing what he did so well on behalf of his clients: planting the seed of disbelief firmly in the jury box.

"Deputy Latimer, this is truly concerning to me. Now,

did you take the shot that killed Artemis Williams?" Ashley probed.

"No, I did not," Latimer denied.

"So, a few C.C.P.D. officers opening fire in a public park is not enough? The deputies needed to join the fray as well? How many guns does it take to stop two young men?" Ashley appealed.

"However many it takes to preserve the sanctity and security of the public!" Deputy Latimer replied.

The fiery rebuttal was met with mixed responses amongst the crowd. While some were prepared to applaud the officer for his commitment to service, others saw him as nothing more than a cocky, callous cop. Ashley, too, was taken aback by the statement. The delay in response wasn't as strategic as it would appear.

"Be it as it may, there's one young man who won't get to defend himself or his actions because a police officer decided to shoot him in the chest instead of a less vital portion of the body. I thought your job was to 'stop the threat,' not 'take the life,'" Ashley blasted.

"Unfortunately, there are rare occasions where they become the same thing," Latimer expressed.

"Rare that it's necessary, but not necessarily a rare occurrence," Ashley spoke. "Your Honor, I have no further questions."

"Very well, Mr. Archibald. Prosecutor, would you like to cross-examine your witness?" Judge Burgess bid.

"No, ma'am, I have nothing further," Travis concluded.

"Okay, Deputy, you may step down. Mr. Carrington, who is your next witness?" Judge Burgess asked.

The deputy lowers the crown of his head toward the

honorable one as he clears the witness stand. Travis scours his notes, then looks at the jury box. He briefly stares into the crowded pews at his rear. Travis nods to himself before meeting the gaze of Judge Burgess.

"The state has no further witnesses, Your Honor," Travis spewed.

"Are you certain?" Judge Burgess checked.

Though he could feel the multiple pairs of pupils piledriving the posterior of his cranium, he fought off his urge to look into the crowd yet again. He shrugged off the minor uncertainty.

"Yes, Your Honor. The floor is open to the defense. We shall proceed at your advisement," Travis confirmed.

"Fair enough, prosecutor. Mr. Archibald, is there anyone *you* would like to call to the stand?" Judge Burgess sustained.

It takes a moment for the judge's question to register. Ashley was certain there would have been another witness from his adversary. Ashely gathers himself after the minor derail.

"Yes, Your Honor. I would like to call Mr. Reginald Joseph to the stand," Ashley announced.

Reg Leg arose from his seat near the Nguyen family and hobbled up the walkway. Judge Burgess was lightly impressed by Reginald's choice in garments. In years past, Reginald Joseph would only come to court in a jumpsuit or casual clothes, but never in a business suit! The infamous Reg Leg was sworn in before woefully descending to his seat.

"Before you move forward with the examination, Mr. Archibald, I have a question of relevance for the witness," Judge Burgess advised.

"Fa sho', baby! I'm at the mercy of the court. Ask me anything you like," Reggie confirmed before Ashley could utter a syllable.

"For starters, I have to commend you on the attire, sir; you have come a long way since the last time you came into this building. How have you been, Mr. Joseph?" Judge Burgess surmised.

"I appreciate that, Judge Burgess. I'm just here trying to set an example for the next generation. It was my goal to make sure they never had to come here, at least not without being paid for it or something like that," Reggie relayed.

"Mr. Joseph, were you anywhere around the incident in question? I have a strange feeling your name would have come up if you had any direct involvement in what happened," Judge Burgess investigated.

"Nahh, I keep out of that kind of stuff, baby. That ain't my steelo' no mo', ya dig," Reggie stated.

"He is a character witness for Mr. Nguyen, Your Honor," Ashley clarified.

There it was: Ashley's big play would involve the testimony of the mentor. Just one more stunt to siphon the jury's sympathy.

"Thank you for clearing that up, Mr. Archibald. You may proceed," Judge Burgess observed.

Ashley unbuttons the blazer again. He gradually approaches the witness stand. Ashley looks toward Tony at the defense table as he begins to question his witness.

"Mr. Joseph, could you please advise the court of your role in the life of the defendant?" Ashley requested. Reggie looked at his hands while he rubbed the palms together before he faced the gallery beyond the tables.

"Tony there is one of the members of my Hog Tied program. Me and some local volunteers try to provide the youth with skills they will need as adults," Reggie outlined.

"Thank you for that, Mr. Joseph. If you don't mind, could you please elaborate on some of those skills for the court?" Ashley bade.

Reggie let out a small sigh and leaned his head to the side. He caught Tony's gaze, who sat agitated and alone. Reggie flashed a reassuring smirk to his young, unnerved pupil before proceeding.

"It's a small thing really, Judge. I done made some connections over the years, y'know. I know a guy who is teaching them about building credit, one who has spoken with them about budgeting, a guy who does some work on some cars, things of that nature. Even know some people at a few stores that are willing to help them get jobs," Reggie spewed.

"It appears to me that you have developed a fine program that helps young adults acquire skills many schools won't teach, Mr. Joseph. Can you relay to the court how you became familiar with Mr. Nguyen?" Ashley summarized.

"Yeah, I have known the family for a long time. I used to shop in their store, still do from time to time. I was choppin' it up with Mr. Nguyen one day and he mentioned he may want Tony to take over the family business one day, so he asked me a little bit more about the program and decided to have Tony join after school," Reggie outlined.

"But you mentioned Mr. Nguyen runs a store of his own. Was he not able to show Tony the ins and outs of business at his own leisure?" Ashley proposed.

An interesting question for his own witness. This type of question likely should have come from the prosecution, but that's exactly why Ashley asked first.

"I wondered that myself initially, but the truth is, Mr. Nguyen still has to work when he goes home at night. He was trying to get the ball rolling with Tony, but he felt like there were some things he was forgetting to tell him. He just wanted to make sure all the bases were covered," Reggie thoroughly explained.

"What I hear, Mr. Joseph, is that you were basically providing assistance for an associate in need. Very commendable, if I do say so myself," Ashley supported.

"I too find the efforts to be admirable, Mr. Joseph; especially in consideration of the past," Judge Burgess offered.

"Thank you...both of you," Reggie accepted.

"Mr. Joseph, in your time of working with Tony Nguyen, what kind of person has he presented himself to be, in your opinion?" Ashley queried.

"Tony is a genuinely nice young man. He was a little apprehensive when he first started coming to the classes, but he eventually opened up. These young cats, always wanting to look so tough and impress each other. I had to tell him ain't none of these other guys in here gonna help you get a job," Reggie advised while chuckling.

Tony's stone-faced expression crumbled into a gentle smile at Reggie's recollection. It was as if he was living the moment all over again, sitting in the Hog Tied program instead of the Eastbank District Court. The sense of comfort was short-lived.

"It appears you have established a rapport with the Nguyen family. But more importantly, Tony, would you have any idea why Tony and some of those other young men were present at the burial site of one Francisco Tatiano?" Ashley enlisted.

"A lot of young guys respected Franc. Tony was such a fan of the guy he even asked him to come and talk to the group about jobs in electricity. I'd be James Brown if he didn't eventually come and do it!" Reggie described.

"So, they were just trying to pay their respects like anyone else present on the site? You don't believe that any of them came with intentions of injuring police?" Ashley interrogated.

Another peculiar question coming from a defense attorney. Ashley Archibald was a piece of work, but this was odd, even for him. It's as if he was emptying the barrel of a gun before he handed it off to Travis.

"No, not at all. None of those boys had anything to do with any police. None of 'em had even been arrested. What issues would they have with the police?" Reggie barked.

"And for the clarity of the court, Your Honor, Mr. Tony Nguyen is a client of the Hog Tied program, not the Fifth Ward Hogs, correct?" Travis chimed.

"That's right!" Reggie emphasized.

"Thank you for your time, Mr. Joseph. I have no further questions for you. Your Honor, I tender the witness," Ashley settled.

"Very well then. Mr. Carrington, would you like to question Mr. Joseph?" Judge Burgess invited.

"It would be my pleasure, Your Honor," Travis accepted.

Travis stood from the state's table and waltzed toward the bench. At the same time, Ashley started to strut back to the side of Tony Nguyen. As they passed one another,

Ashley glared upon Travis. Yet, Travis didn't entertain the defense attorney. Travis' sights were set squarely on the witness.

"Good morning, Mr. Joseph; I'm glad you were able to join us today," Travis opened in earshot of the witness.

"No big deal, happy to be here," Reggie returned as he watched the Hall and Nguyen families.

"Good...good. Mr. Joseph, I couldn't help but overhear about the program you are running in the community. I have to tell you, that is quite a feat you are taking on. My heart goes out to you, sir. Tell me, is self-defense a part of the curriculum in your program?" Travis diverted.

"No, not really. Me and a few buddies of mine have a boxing gym, but we don't require the clients to participate," Reggie clarified.

"Understood, sir. Well, did you all happen to hold a session on firearms handling?" Travis dug.

"No, we don't do much of that either, I'm afraid," Reggie denied.

"That's puzzling. How about a motorcycle safety course?" Travis tunneled further.

"Now that," Reggie bought in, "THAT is more my speed. That is how the Hog Tied Program began. Me and a few of my old pals were teaching motorcycle classes and we spoke about some things that would be useful for the youngsters to know. Hence, Hog Tied."

"That's a bit of a relief. I was trying to understand why twenty-something-year-olds would arrive at a burial site in Fifth Ward Hog garb and motorcycles. That mystery has been answered. However, how do you explain most if not all of them having guns?!" Travis sought.

Reggie looked up to the sky as if the answer was going

to drizzle upon his face. He rolled his eyes and slowly exhaled before tackling the accusation.

"I have no idea. Like I said, we never held any classes on using guns. Maybe we should now," Reggie jested.

Travis lightly giggled at the comments himself before he looked at the jury box and mockingly cackled in their direction. His humor ceased when his vision returned to Reggie.

"Mr. Joseph. Don't you have a history of run-ins with the police as well as the deceased Mr. Francisco Tatiano?" Travis questioned.

"Yes, some years back. Been a long time since I had to put on the matching silver bracelets," Reggie concurred.

"Was it not the C.C.P.D. Detective Brown and Francisco Tatiano that put you and the original Fifth Ward Hogs behind bars the very last time you wore those bracelets?" Travis instigated.

"Yeah, they did. That's how I knew I had to retire from it. They actually caught me on my bike; nobody was ever able to do that," Reggie slighted again.

The court filled with chuckles and snorts despite everyone's futile attempts to remain serious. The bailiff too held a contentious smile on his face.

"Have you ever had to bury a friend or a loved one, Mr. Joseph?" Travis wondered.

"At my age, I've lost many people. Still, it's more than I thought I would have lost at this point in my life," Reggie confided.

"Definitely, sir. Even with all the advances in medicine and technology, we are still losing people much earlier than we hoped. Friends, family, co-workers, other associates: those are the groups of people which you have attended funerals for, I would assume," Travis incited.

"Many people...anybody I thought may have gone too soon," Reggie implied.

"Be that as it may, Mr. Joseph, how could we be sure you didn't utilize those young men to settle an old score with the C.C.P.D. once Mr. Tatiano was buried? I mean, you did advise that the group respected Fantastic Franc, yet he is no longer with us. What better place to catch several officers at one time than the one place they might gather to pay their respects to a man who aided them over the last few years?!!" Travis blurted with little to no regard.

"I object, Your Honor; how is he supposed to answer for the actions of others?" Ashley intervened.

"I will allow it, Mr. Archibald. The question is in regard to motive and we have heard Mr. Joseph testify to mentoring these young men as well as a checkered past of his own. Though there may not be a direct correlation, there is at least reasonable suspicion," Judge Burgess rectified.

"The answer to your question is no. I had no reason to instruct anybody to attack law enforcement. That was not their purpose for being there. They went to pay their respects. Simple as that," Reggie defended.

"Alright then. I have nothing further, Your Honor," Travis rested.

"And you, Mr. Archibald, would you like to re-examine the witness?" Judge Burgess offered.

"No, Your Honor; if it pleases the court, Mr. Joseph may step down," Ashley decided.

"Okay then, Mr. Joseph, you may be excused, sir," said Judge Burgess.

Without another word, Reginald Joseph descends the witness stand. Ashley finds Travis' last display to be profoundly comedic. Nonetheless, he has at least one more witness to approach the court before he is done for the evening.

Chapter 28

Background Check

"No, you don't need to do this—STOP!" a man screams in utter shock.

He twists his body to avoid the impending threat. He continues to mutter for mercy, but his pleas fall short of satisfying his assailant. He sweats profusely, knowing his demise is in short order. He manages one final cringe before a plunge to the floor...proverbially.

The man lifts his soaked torso up using his couch; sweat still making its way from his face to the furniture. He laughs while noticing his shirt is nearly transparent in certain spots. He then looks at his watch. He buries his head into his palms before horizontally rolling his face across each hand.

"Freaking overslept. Let me get my ass up and on the road," Detective McDonald chastises.

He presses his knuckles firmly into the cushions to lift himself from the couch. Rance disappears into his bathroom momentarily to bathe. Rance completes his shower and briefly ponders his attire. He settles on an outfit that reflects the night sky. He grabs the fedora on the nightstand and steals away into the darkness.

Rance jumped into the Chevy Camaro outside his home. He backed it out of his driveway and sped off without an ounce of consideration for his neighbors. The H.O.A. could fine him, but they had to catch him first. "A silly concept as it is," he thought to himself. "Paying a fee to follow rules on my own property," he continued. Rance pondered this phenomenon brashly yet concisely. For the time being, there were more pressing matters to decipher.

Rance makes his way into Crescent City, trying to make it to the East before he is too late. Rance flips to the back of a pamphlet resting in his front passenger seat and shouts "damn" to himself before laying into the gas pedal. The Camaro punishes the pavement along the highway; tires nearly leaving an imprint in their wake. Eight o'clock is approaching and Rance can't miss his target, not tonight. He captures a sign that tells him his exit is two miles away. Rance decelerates after about fifteen minutes spent weaving in and out of other vehicles.

"Come on, come on, come on!" Rance pleads silently to the vehicles between himself and his highway exodus.

Rance exits Morrison Blvd. and makes his way to his destination. From the main road he noticed the lights were already off at the desired location. "Shit!" Rance mutters. Rance goes into the parking lot to turn around and return home when he notices a green '72 Oldsmobile Cutlass Supreme appear from the rear of the building.

"Gotcha, motherfucker!" Rance exclaims.

Rance tries to quickly yet subtly turn his car around to trail the Cutlass. He narrowly avoids shredding his tires in a pothole. Rance is fortunate the Cutlass is stalled by the traffic light. He appreciates the assistance but won't enter the roadway until the light turns green again. His car faces the building until the light changes. As soon as a glimmer of green hits the rearview mirror, Rance whips the Camaro around to race into the roadway and through the light fading from yellow to red. The hasty pursuit nearly gave the detective away.

"Where are you going, where are you going?" Rance utters.

Rance watched as the car turned Westbound down Crowder Blvd until it reached I-10. With a purposeful delay, Rance eventually caught up to the Cutlass on the highway. Rance had no issues spotting the green machine under the lights. Once it turned westbound onto the highway, the Cutlass traveled the speed limit, if not slower. Rance began to ponder if his target was taking him back to the Westbank as he rolled onto Highway 90 without any indication of an exit or a remote care in the world. The detective wouldn't mind cruising if he knew exactly where they would end up.

Finally, there's a break in the monotony as the turn signal flashes about a mile before the Cutlass' exit. Rance gains a false burst of relief that this trail may be coming to a close. He's pleased the car is taking him into a part of town he is familiar with. In fact, as the car exits but goes past the first light, Rance becomes very curious about where the car is going. It's surely not going home, as it's near an industrial part of town with nothing but businesses, and...the *C.C.P.D.?*

The automobile is nearly half a mile ahead of Rance, seemingly by both design and individual scheme. True to form, the car goes to the next light, then makes a left, crossing back under the bridge. It goes into the far-right lane and turns down the next available opening. Rance watches as the car strolls along the exterior of the C.C.P.D. campus, until it reaches the final opening to the lot. The green vehicle turns into the lot and goes a short distance before coming to a complete stop. Rance utilizes one of the earlier entryways to join him. Rance contemplated driving around the lot before approaching the vehicle, but he thought better of it. He didn't want to risk the driver getting away. *He couldn't afford it.* No! *Not when he was this close.*

Rance illegally strolls through multiple parking spots while making his way toward the green vehicle, still motionless in the aisle. Rance stops at the last available parking spot just short of T-boning his target. There was visible disgust on the mark's face, with the lights of the precinct revealing the silhouette of his grimace. Rance walks up to the vehicle's passenger side and leans over to introduce himself face to face.

"Excuse me, sir, my name is Detective Rance McDonald. Would you happen to be Mr. Romero Meredith?" Rance introduced.

"Yeah, that's me. To what do I owe the inconvenience?" Romero confirmed.

"For starters, what made you come over to this precinct? I'm pretty familiar with this place and I don't think you work here," Rance bothered.

"You're right. I don't work here. But I know some people who do. One of them warned me if you have someone tailing you, stop at a police station. That way, you either scare them away or escort them to complete their paperwork," Romero cracked.

This exchange extracted a brief guffaw from the detective. While the subject was not meager, he was going to be mildly entertaining.

"And it just so happens that one of those people is the town hero Renaldo Brown, isn't it, Mr. Meredith?" Rance accused.

"Yeah, what's it to you?" Romero concurred.

"Well, I find the dynamic to be, let's say, interesting," Rance offered.

"You must not have a lot of friends. You don't seem too well versed on how it all works. There shouldn't be anything 'dynamic,' as you put it, about friends looking out for one another," Romero chastised.

Rance flashes his signature nervous grin. *It's not that he is uneasy*; it's all in the way his little smirk makes the viewer feel. Seemed like nothing anyone would say could upset him, at least not on the surface.

"Is that right, sir? Sharing secrets and tricks of the trade are all a part of friendship, hnah?" Rance insinuated.

"I think it's a good tip to know. You never know who is following you. Y'know what I mean?" Romero chimed.

"I get your drift. Now I wanna know if you're picking up on mine," Rance continued.

Romero shrugged at the detective's notion. He motioned a hand towards Rance, advising him to continue.

"I originally came here to chop it up about the funeral, but it's apparent you and Detective Brown are acquainted beyond that. Shed a little light on me, Mr. Meredith; Where has your homeboy run off to?" Rance digs.

"I don't know where he is. I wish I did. I haven't seen him in some months. Still strange he up and disappeared like that," Romero expressed.

"Really? You sure you're not hiding him out some- where, sir? As you said before, friendship has its dynamics," Rance suggested.

"The man left a hospital where his child had just been born and his wife was still laid up in the bed, and you think somebody is *hiding* him? Officer, you on some special type of bullshit, ain't ya?" Romero safeguarded.

Romero placed his hands on either side of his face with his palms facing inward. He bounced his shoulders and curled his lip before providing an explanation.

"You care to explain how a man vanishes out of thin air and nobody knows where he went?" Rance pressed.

Romero's eyelids tightened as he searched for the punchline in Rance's statement. "Is this guy for real?" Romero asked himself. His left hand clasped the steering wheel while his right hand lay flat on the arm rest.

"Look here, private eye," Romero began, slightly perturbed, "a man went downstairs after his wife had a child and never returned to the scene. His family has not heard from him, to include his young daughter."

"Desperate men do desperate things, Mr. Meredith. All he needed was to find someone willing to accompany him in his heist. Wouldn't be the first time," Rance ignited.

"Now you just wait a got damn minute, officer! You can't possibly have children of your own? There's no way. I don't give a damn what he had going on, a man of his caliber ain't gonna go too long without talking to his daughter. Now you can cash that shit and take it to the bank!" Romero remarked.

Rance distanced himself from the subject's vehicle. He knew he had gone far enough by Romero's widened eyes and boasts. He needed to ask one more question to taper his suspicions.

"Maybe you're right, Mr. Meredith. Of course, you

know the Detective better than I. I'm just trying to look for him and get him back to his family as well. We truly have a common goal," Rance embellished.

"Like I said, Officer, I haven't seen him. It's not like him to abandon his responsibilities, and I am sure Julissa could vouch for that!" Romero declared.

"Well...I'll just have to see about that. Thank you for your cooperation. I believe I have all I need for the night," Rance settled.

Romero wouldn't offer another word. He accepted the opportunity to finally leave the grounds of the C.C.P.D. Romero revved the engine of his restored vehicle to drive away abruptly. Rance contemplated Romero's advice while returning to his car. He had previously avoided contacting Julissa Brown due to the birth and necessary nourishment of a newborn. Rance now believed enough time had passed and he owed it to the missing brethren to conduct a "welfare check" on his family...

Chapter 29

Birds of a Feather

Julissa looks at her children's photos planted on her desk. A smile comes over her on what has otherwise been an overtly slow day. Magnolia Marketing was still drawing in plenty of business; that was never an issue. Truthfully, Julissa resumed her stamp on the advertising world as if she'd never left. Plenty of local businesses and professionals noticed for years, so she was never short on projects or customers. But now, Julissa was simply a victim of her own dominance: designing the marketing strategies came so easy to her that she no longer saw it as a challenge. One flip of the word here, a deletion of a word there, a simple twist of a phrase was usually all it took.

Julissa needed a challenge! Julissa's accomplishments, once driven by her will and desire, were now results of second nature. She'd performed her job at the highest level for a few years; to a consistency that prevented the fear of failing. No, she was never nervous now, not like those nights when she faced The Brood. *The butterflies in her belly. The flight of her feet. The hops in the heart's beat.* Aside from the love of her children, *these were the feelings Julissa desired the most.*

"Julissa! JULISSA!?" a voice slices through Julissa's trance.

"What?! What is it, girl? Why are you yelling?" Julissa shouted back.

"Because, girl, you act like you can't hear," her coworker responded.

Julissa laughed at her friend's sarcastic ridicule. "Caught again," she thought. Another day of her head in the clouds seeking a signature moment.

"Y'all don't be talking about nothing anyway, but what is it, Marisol?" Julissa returned.

"Girl! Somebody round here pouring up some hot tea!" Marisol informed.

"Well, don't just stand there, girl. Spill it!" Julissa employed.

And just like that, Julissa realigned with the rest of the planet. After spending nearly an hour with her mind in the stars, she returned to solid ground.

"Look! Don't tell nobody I told you," the pecan-tinged counterpart began.

"I definitely won't, especially since you ain't said much of nothing yet!" Julissa imparted.

Marisol gritted her teeth against her lip as she flipped her long hair and swiped at Julissa's shoulder. They hooted as they carefully watched another coworker stroll by. Marisol quickly placed a finger over her own lips while shushing Julissa, who still hadn't quieted. Suddenly, and on cue, Mr. Denver walks along the hall where the two comediennes are gathered. The mullet-wearing, often swearing gentleman from St. Bernard considered playing the Louisiana Lottery after lucking up and finding the two people he wanted to talk to together. The ladies are somewhat puzzled by Mr. Denver's presence, hoping they hadn't been reported for a disturbance during their roasting session.

"Are you happy to see us, Mr. Denver, or are you visually impaired?" Marisol scoffed.

Julissa tried as hard to hold her laughter as she did to grip Marisol's skin when she pinched her. Marisol let out an "eek" before covering her mouth and wrapping herself around Julissa's arm.

"Honestly, I'm quite satisfied to find both of you. It makes my job a little easier. Any of you ladies familiar with Chop It To Ya' Records?" Mr. Denver queried.

"Hel—" Julissa caught herself. "I mean, yes, Mr. Denver. Aren't you? They've been around Crescent for a while now."

"Yeah! It's nothing like salsa or zydeco, but they have the beats that get butts out the seats," Marisol seconded.

Marisol lifted her hands and began to slightly rock her hips until she received a slight nudge from Julissa.

"I was hoping one or both of you would be familiar with them. I—" Denver started.

"Wait, do they want us on the marketing team? They want to work with Magnolia Marketing?!" Marisol exclaimed.

"No, not quite. In fact, it's closer to the opposite," Denver denied.

"So, they want to work with the competition? Is somebody gonna end up releasing a diss track about us?" Julissa inquired.

Mr. Denver snickered at Julissa. He then pondered the possibility. Marisol and Julissa awaited the verdict while Mr. Denver attempted to compose himself.

"If any of their artists make a song about us at all, it means everything turned out just right," Mr. Denver expressed.

"Umm. I'm not sure we have anybody who could respond to a label full of talented artists, Mr. Denver," Julissa declared.

"Maybe not yet. But that's where you two come in," Mr. Denver shared.

The ladies are officially puzzled. Was it bring your drink to work day? What was Mr. Denver expecting these two to do? Form a hip-hop duo?

"So, should we start working on a mixtape or...?" Marisol questioned.

"Not yet. I need you two to ring in this artist first. A guy named Pelli Kanisus, if I'm saying it right? He's looking to go independent but is going to need help with ads, productivity, etc." Denver revealed.

"Wait! What!?" Julissa exclaimed.

"He wants to work with us? Pelli Kanisus? What happened at Chop It To Ya'?" Marisol wondered.

"He didn't give too many details on that. He said they have irreconcilable differences. He mentioned needing assistance with advertisements and such but didn't want to worry about working with a label who might get muscled by Chop It To Ya'," Denver outlined.

"You sure you want to work with that type of artist, Mr. Denver? I like some of his music, but he does get a little...grimy...at times," Julissa divulged.

"Well, he said he wanted to work his way into a new sound, but the bottom line says this guy is widely loved and streamed. It can't hurt to be affiliated with someone like that. Besides, I won't be working with him...you two will," Denver detailed.

Mr. Denver laid a folder on the desk marked "Vernell Kane" as he bid the ladies adieu. They sat down at the table as the suspense mounted. They were given the biggest assignment of either of their careers: link this company to one of the hottest artists in the state. This had to be it: *the challenge Julissa sorely desired.*

"Marisol," Julissa called.

"Yes, boo," Marisol answered.

"What was it you came to tell me?" Julissa asked, stiffly.

"Magnolia Marketing was bringing a bird to the nest," Marisol spilled.

They gave one another a brief glance before focusing on the folder again. Julissa's return to the file was a bit delayed as she found Marisol's phrasing to be a bit irregular. She didn't know if that was going to be Marisol's original delivery of the news or if was a summation of the events that just transpired.

"Look at that! Well, honey, I don't know who your sources are, but they be on it!" Julissa muttered.

"Yeah. You could never have too many good sources," Marisol confirmed hesitantly.

They were already familiar with Pelli Kanisus, as was most of Crescent City, apparently. They opened the folder to introduce themselves to Vernell Kane! A 20-something-year-old man with a smooth flow but rugged lyrics. For the last couple of years, he'd worked his way up in the ranks at C.I.T.Y. Records until he embodied star power. What was once deemed destiny has now been ravaged by misunderstanding. In the end, the fork in the road provided an opportunity for three parties to renew their brand.

Chapter 30

Shuffling the Deck

Scottie Bridgewater is engaged in a game of Spades with his newfound partner, Cyril. They've been accused of cheating by some sour inmates, but truth is they've become well acquainted in the last few weeks. For Scottie, it's been a learning experience: being groomed by a notorious convict. On the other hand, Cyril was getting to know a man who he presumed had gotten away with murder. Not just any murder, but one that would leave the streets open for he and his brother to prowl again.

While Cyril's connections were fairly calculated, Charlie was the social butterfly he'd always portrayed. Knowing the family's reputation, no one was going to tell Charlie he could only associate with his *own kind*. It was better to know a Hernandez Brother than to oppose one. Though Cyril enjoyed the perks of notoriety, he was becoming increasingly concerned that Charlie's congeniality was more curse than gift.

"Gimme fifteen. That's game, muhhfucker!!" Scottie bragged as he dropped the last domino onto the table.

Cyril recorded the score with a sly smirk. One opponent drops his head onto the table in disappointment while his partner slams his hand down as if he forgot to scream "domino."

"You can't be fucking serious! You can't read the board worth a damn, Booker. Go to medical and get you some damn glasses!" one opponent complained.

"Man, fuck you and these '*New York Undercover*' looking motherfuckers! If you played defense as well as you ran your mouth, we might have beaten these sorry bitches," Booker replied.

Booker, the senior of the assembly, walks away after slamming his dominoes on the table. Scottie hops up, taking no exception to his elder's gamesmanship, but Cyril places his palm in his path. Cyril bows his head to Scottie, suggesting he sit and let the sore losers depart in peace.

"You better watch it, fool. You ain't got no guns in here and ain't nobody 'bout to let you square off on ol' school either. Better recognize where you at, bruh!" Booker's partner warned.

"Man, go to the cot and map out a new way for y'all to lose," Scottie taunted.

Booker flashes the middle finger to Scottie as he engages another set of inmates. Scottie waves off the middle-aged man and washes the board. Cyril looks about the scene for his brother but can't spot him. Cyril's search ends abruptly with commentary from his despondent colleague.

"Man, whatchu' on, bruh? Them lil' fools wasn't 'bout no drama, man. You could've let me handle that right quick," Scottie boasted.

Cyril leaned back in his chair and whistled. He folded his arms across his chest, then slowly tracked his eyes to Booker's general direction. Scottie followed the path of

Cyril's irises back to Booker's location. Booker spoke with some other guys on the floor, a couple of which were looking back in their direction. Scottie noticed Booker speaking with his hands and occasionally motioning back towards the table where the game took place. Cyril allowed his index finger to guide the hothead a little closer.

"Last thing we need around here is anybody trying to blow up our spot with unnecessary attention. You been here a lil' longer than me, fool—how come you don't know your way around?" Cyril maintained.

"Man, that ain't nothing. I got people all up and through this bitch!" Scottie boasted.

"Oh yeah," Cyril began as he stared toward Booker. "Well, you better hope your people are really your people. Cuz' if they ain't, they're probably *his* people."

Scottie received the advice; whether he accepted it remained to be seen. Cyril tried to mentor the young goof but had to sharpen some rough edges along the way. The longer Cyril was exposed to Scottie, the more he questioned his significance in the assassination of Fantastic Franc. A complete hothead would not be capable of executing a plan that effective.

"Brother, you got a lot to learn about politics. Maybe it's convenient you have a little time on your head. A few semesters in the hard knocks might do you some good," Cyril estimated.

"According to you, we not gonna be here too long anyways, Big Hern. So, what you stressin' for?" Scottie asked.

"You have much to learn, my friend. Haste makes waste but grace creates space," Cyril professed.

"They have Dr. Seuss books around here or something? If you prefer to look at boy butt, you can just say that!" Scottie teased.

Cyril laughed while scanning the floor again. He finally caught a glimpse of Charlie coming out of a neighboring cell. Charlie outlined his mustache and beard with the tips of his fingers as he moved back into the common area. Another inmate walked behind Charlie and briefly tapped his shoulder before disappearing back into the bunk. Cyril threw a hand in the air to gather his brother's attention. Charlie was heading to his own cot until he noticed Cyril flagging him down. Charlie preferred not to be bothered at the time, but he also didn't want to draw any suspicion from his peers. Charlie is deliberate in his pace as he inches closer to the two men waiting.

"What you been up to, Chuckie Boy? We ain't seen much of you today?" Scottie commented.

Cyril is staring intently at his brother, awaiting his answer. Scottie's focus remains on the box of dominoes. Charlie sits next to Cyril but makes no eye contact.

"Been moving around, brother. Trying to keep up with the temperature around here," Charlie answered.

"Oh, you must be doing all that politickin' your brother always talking about," Scottie rebutted.

"That's how you learn the lay of the land, right bro?" Cyril incited.

"Whoomp, there it is!" Charlie ranted.

Three grown men burst into heehaws like young donkeys. It drew some attention from nearby tables, but they remained unchallenged. Cyril caught Booker peeking over his shoulder.

"Yo, Chuck, what do you know about the guy a few tables ahead of us with the bifocals and jacket?" Cyril scouted.

"I shot the shit with him and his buddies a couple of times. They don't really be saying much. Ol' school has a few war stories he likes to share," Charlie shared.

"Well, our congenial brethren almost became a new tale. We beat 'em in bones, then Bridge here almost started a fight," Cyril revealed.

Charlie posed a baffled glare at Cyril before transferring his confusion to Scottie's scowl. He looked down and shook his head side-to-side while stating "tsk, tsk, tsk."

"More like nearly incited a riot, bro. You gotta watch that," Charlie warned.

"Ain't my fault them cats couldn't play the hand they was dealt," Scottie meddled.

"Don't forget that when they bust you over the head at phone time," Cyril warned.

Scottie waved Cyril off while sliding the dominoes to the opposite side of the table. Charlie cracked a smile that only another wise ass could love.

"Y'all got beef with those guys or what?" Charlie sought.

"None I'm certain of but I surely want to keep it that way. You think you might be able to smooth things over with them?" Cyril propositioned.

Charlie's response was delayed as he gawked at Booker and others at their table. Charlie physically agreed to Cyril's request.

"Shouldn't be a problem. I might be able to talk a lil' sense into them," Charlie was convinced.

Charlie stood up and returned to his own quarters. He took one more look at Booker's table, then to his own brother, before ducking into the cell. Scottie's eyes followed

Charlie until he was out of view.

"To say y'all are some known killers, you motherfuckers are awfully diplomatic," Scottie chimed.

"And for that reason, brother, we got to be," Cyril stated as he stood up.

Without word or warning, Cyril gathered himself and walked to his side of the unit. Scottie held his hands out to his side, clearly baffled. Cyril caught a whiff of Scottie's confusion and winked. Cyril then vanished into his room. Scottie looked about the unit, just before the correctional officers came in to tell them it was time to go back into their cells.

"This fool must have a damn clock in his head," Scottie said to himself before throwing the cards down and leaving the table.

Chapter 31

Indecent Disposal

The sun has given way to the moon, without sparing much light in the exchange. Three men are on the downhill portion of their expedition, with the end squarely in sight. The Bonne Carre Spillway is as dim as it is lengthy. Conversation amongst the parties has been sparse for over two hours, until curiosity cuts the cloak.

"Those boxes with the area codes have anything to do with the Sixty-Sixers?" Renaldo bellowed.

"Yeah, a little something like that," Mack answered.

"Silly me. This whole time I thought you were running the Power Ball," Renaldo jested.

"Naaht quiite, buddyyy," Victor chimed.

"Well, I hoped not. Considering the sanctity of the church and all. What's the purpose of all those boxes?" Renaldo sought.

Mack attempts to answer but a hard cough replaces his words. He holds a finger in the air to excuse himself momentarily. Renaldo acknowledges the elder's silent request. With no intention of shying away from his naïve constituent's challenge, Mack decides to continue.

"Then you should assume whatever is going on in a

church is the work of the Lord," Mack answered.

The detective lifted his eyes before turning toward the elder. Mack received this contact with some confusion.

"That explains a lot. I assume I was supposed to be a sacrifice of a holy war?" Renaldo entertained.

Victor scoffed, nearly sacrificing control of the vehicle in the process. Both counterparts stared at Victor, questioning his crude sense of humor.

"Sawwry, thaat shiiit wasss funnyyy," Victor apologized.

"Ahh, yes. There it is. Entertainment was my purpose," Renaldo stated.

"You think I found pleasure in bringing you to your realization? I find no pleasure in having to bring one of my own to humility," Mack answered.

"I didn't see you shedding any tears on my behalf either. However, my original question was about the numbers, sir," Renaldo redirected.

Mack's eyeballs made a full rotation around the socket before settling on the back of Renaldo's chair. Mack cleared his cluttered gullet before engaging further.

"If you must know, Mr. Brown—nose, those boxes contained important documents from events all throughout The Boot," Mack said dryly.

"Ahh, my original thought, TAXES!" Renaldo joked.

Victor found much humor in Renaldo's monologue. Mack himself shared a miniscule smirk.

"Someone definitely needed to pay, but, nah, that's not it either. We Sixty-Sixers work hard to prevent 1866 from ever happening again," Mack informed.

"That's one hell of a commitment you guys are making. But you were born years after it happened, I'm sure. What makes you—and your friends—want to take that on?" Renaldo inquired.

"Youu really arre llimited, arren't you, myyy friend?" Victor declared.

"What?!" Renaldo paused.

"You familiar with Thibodeaux, Colfax, or Opelousas?" Mack proposed.

Renaldo wasn't sure if this was a joke or a test. Either way, he was in no mood for a riddle. Once more, he found himself in the position of having more questions than answers.

"I'm familiar with the towns, to some degree," Renaldo shared.

"Good! Means I don't have to waste time pointing massacres out to you on a map!" Mack barked.

Renaldo pondered the gems provided to him. *Were Mack Wellington and his constituents given a bad rep?* It was easier to believe a revolutionary gave his life to Christ as opposed to a mobster doing so. He still wasn't sure what any of this had to do with the mafia, but Mack made sense of everything, to say the least. Renaldo didn't know if the old man was being completely upfront about his dealings, but there also was no clear reason to doubt him.

"I would venture to guess you are familiar with Jena, or at least Jennings?" Mack suggested.

"That's a fair assumption, sir," Renaldo responded.

"Then you must be aware of the massacre the Jena 6 event could have become had it been exclusively left up to the town's people?" Mack proposed.

"So, you guys are responsible for the little justice those kids actually did receive?" Renaldo questioned.

"Responsible is a strong word, my friend. Let's just say

we are often prepared for the worse," Mack incited.

Renaldo soaked in the heavy information laid upon him. Just how did the Sixty-Sixers affect the results of the Jena 6 hearings? There were many people who protested on behalf of the events that took place in 2006. Was that their role? How could they have been anything more significant?

"Have you forgotten about Red Stick and the police shooting? The shooting of police that followed in Dallas. Then of uninvolved officers in Red Stick yet again?" Mack asked.

"Yes, those are all unforgettable," Renaldo conceded.

"You live in a red southern state, yet you have no clear and concise reason why there has not been another attempt to massively erase black people within these parishes since the early 1900s?" Mack allotted.

"Well, I guess that's that," Renaldo commented briefly.

As they continued to span the spillway, Mack began to cough ferociously. Renaldo had grown accustomed to the hacking, but Victor knew something was off. Victor looked over his shoulder to see his uncle visibly choking. He pulled to the nearly non-existent shoulder of the spillway, clearly in panic. He then looked out of his rearview window to notice lights of other vehicles coming up the road. Victor then punched Renaldo in the arm.

"Helllp him, please! He doessn't look so good!" Victor cried.

Renaldo decided he would deal with the disrespect later but right now he needed to race into action. *Or maybe he didn't.* After all Mack put him through, this may have been the only revenge Renaldo could muster without any possible interference from Victor. To this point, Victor had proven to be nothing more than a pawn in this wicked game distributed by Mack. On second thought, Victor had also featured some wit and grit of his own. He determined Victor would make a better ally than vengeful enemy. Renaldo needed to act, NOW.

Renaldo thrashed his door open and jumped out, nearly scraping the frame against the concrete barrier. He whipped open Mack's door and cradled him as he nearly fell out. The rear door was caught between Renaldo and his elbows as he struggled to maintain Mack. Another whooping cough nearly sent Renaldo into reverse, causing him to release his grip on Mack. The momentum was enough for the door to pivot into the opposite direction and nearly close.

Mack lay hunched over on the ground, still hacking away. Renaldo dashed to the elder. He gathered Mack by his underarms and attempted to lift the ailing man again. Victor finally made his way out of the car to assist.

"Calmm down, unc! Tryy to breeeeathe!" Victor called.

Mack's lungs wouldn't facilitate Victor's bid. As they lifted him to his feet, he continued to clear his passageways while leaning over the bridge. Victor and Renaldo each held a bicep to steady Mack. Once the coughing subsided, they encouraged him to inhale the night air. Mack uttered a deep gasp as he started to regain his stability. Mack pulled his arms inward and nodded so the men could release him. Once no longer hindered, he reached into his pocket and grabbed his handkerchief. Victor was still in shock as he too tried to steady himself.

"Doo you neeed mee to get you anyyything?" Victor questioned.

"No, I'll be fine," Mack muttered.

Victor placed a hand on Mack's back and scrubbed across the shoulders. Mack cleared his throat once more as he stared into the murky water below. He patted Victor on the shoulder to show he is going to be fine.

"You go ahead and get the car started back up, Vic. We don't have too much further to go, but we still need to get there," Mack directed.

"Surrre thing," Victor obeyed.

Victor walked to the trunk of the car and looked out for passing motorists. Renaldo walked back to the rear passenger door and opened it. Renaldo slipped between the door and the barrier to reunite with Mack. The senior's chin was still tucked into his breastplate as he watched the ripples roll on. Renaldo wrapped a hand around Mack's triceps to stabilize him.

"If you're alright, we can get you back into the car, sir," Renaldo advised.

Mack takes a deep breath as if he were taking in an inhaler.

"I think I'll be fine. Just help me to the car so I can sit," Mack conceded.

Renaldo obliged the man's request by attempting to guide him to the car. Victor wanted to assist yet again, but they both waived him off. Renaldo and Mack treked step for step to the backseat until Renaldo lowered him into a seated position. As Mack got comfortable, he motioned Renaldo away.

"I can get my feet in and my seat belt on, young buck. You just shimmy your way to the front," Mack ordered.

Renaldo shrugged his shoulders and followed the command. With Mack now seated, Renaldo narrowed the space between the elder and the door so he could slip by.

With the little energy Mack fostered, he drew back his right foot, then blasted the door with his heel. The impact was enough to send Renaldo off balance and onto the barrier. The "dink" was loud enough to draw Victor's attention. He looked to the passenger side but could not find Renaldo.

Mack mustered some energy as he grasped his cane and departed the rear. Mack peered over the ledge to monitor Renaldo's location. He found the officer, who dangled by a thread. Victor left his seat to investigate what was transpiring on the other side of the car. Mack's demeanor completely altered once he made eye contact with the flailing detective. The minister sported a sinister grin.

"On second thought, Recluse, I don't think we will be needing your assistance any further," Mack announced.

"UNC! NOO! Let him up!" Victor stated as he rushed to Renaldo's aid.

Mack took his cane and planted the base squarely into Victor's gut, knocking him off his path and momentarily out of wind. Renaldo silently fought to get back upon the highway.

"Now, now, nephew. You know you shouldn't interrupt me while I'm performing a service. Especially not one of this magnitude," Mack chastised.

"The fuck are you talking about, old man! You came to me for help. How is having me falling to my death your way of aiding me?!" Renaldo howled.

"You don't listen, boy. Your services are no longer needed. They spared you when they killed my son. You should have died right along with him, but now, I'm going to make things right!" Mack barked.

"Two wrongs never make a right! HELP HIM UP!" Victor screamed to his uncle.

Mack walked over to Victor and dug the dull base of his cane into Victor's hand. He heard a grunt from the railing. Renaldo was pulling himself up to safety.

"Who do you serve that would approve of this?" Renaldo challenged.

Mack stops his torture of Victor to gaze into his cane. He turns his torso toward Renaldo so his words may be clear.

"Perhaps you are right. No being fit to be a savior would ever approve of this," Mack settled.

Mack, while still staring at his cane, carefully trots toward a flailing Renaldo. Renaldo's eyes light up as Mack peers over the ledge and reaches out to him.

"However, my faith in man isn't nearly as abundant!" Mack switched.

He takes the head of his cane and buries it into Renaldo's. Renaldo's neck snaps back as he slides down the side of barrier. Mack catches Renaldo's hand with his wooden weapon.

"May you rest easy beneath the reservoir, dragged to your resting place by nothing more than the heft of your own sins. Consider this a final baptism! A dirty pool is most fitting for a filthy pig!" Mack exclaimed.

With one last haul, Mack leans over the bridge and deals a final blow to the detective's cranium. A boisterous "CRACK" disrupts the bare silence usually disturbed by passing vehicles.

"NOOOOOOO!" Victor roared into the pale moonlight.

Victor's last-ditch dash was far too tardy. The damage was done. And apparently, so was the detective. Before

Victor could gaze over the pier, his ears witnessed a loud PLUNK below. When he could finally investigate the unlit liquid beneath him, his fears were confirmed. His new-found friend was taken away from him, almost as instantly as their comradery blossomed. Victor ogled the lake for any visible signs of struggle beneath the water. There was nothing, not even a bubble. Victor looked over to his uncle, who now departed the lakeside view for a window seat.

"No sense in crying over spilled swine, my boy. We still have much to do," Mack directed.

"HOW?! How will wee find myyy motherr now?" Victor cried.

"Did you learn nothing from the detective? We will make our way to Beech Grove Manor, where it all began," Mack stated matter-of-factly.

What hit harder: Mack's last revelation or the frame of the door slamming into the car? The window's rattle nearly matched Victor's. He still looked on in disbelief. It was the story of his life: nothing worth having ever lasted long. It usually ended in some form of tragedy. Music. Mother. And now a *possible mentor*?

Victor's hearing goes inaudible to anything going on behind him. Cars are once again passing in the shrouded night. Mack is calling for Victor to get back into the driver's seat, but everything is muffled. Mack eventually discontinued his protest. Victor eventually realized his hope to preserve the private eye was nil. Victor's palms were beet red from grappling the concrete barrier so tightly. His face, however, had turned as dim as the road that remained ahead. Victor re-entered the car with one less passenger, and perhaps, even less patience.

"He was wounded for our transgressions, he was

bruised for our inequities: the chastisement of our peace was upon him," Mack blurted as Victor sat.

"Whaaat?!" Victor screamed back.

Meanwhile, the detective continues to sink to considerable lows, even for him. The impact of his body hitting the water from that height nearly paralyzed him. The light became more distant with each second, until it was nothing more than a memory. The will to fight escapes him with each passing breath. The desire to move on fills him with each fleeting thought:

"...all you can do is fulfill your promise..."

"Home, Renaldo. HOME!!....."

"Daaaaaaaaaaddyyyyy"

"...continue this fight in... honor..."

"THAT is what you MUST do!"

"If his partner can't finish the mission, then who?"

"It's a boyyyyyyyyyyyyy!"

"How many more close calls, Renaldo?"

"You still had to be the big shot!"

"I have no son!"

"Noooooooooooooo"

Chapter 32:

Hold These Truths

A bead of sweat crests Ashley's brow. He has one last trick up his sleeve but he's not sure the deck is cut in his favor. He's heard every word spoken from every witness willing to grace the stand. In his mind, the battle between he and Travis Carrington stands at a stalemate. He has but one shot to set Tony free of the allegations, while possibly setting the tone for Vashon's trial. Ashley knew his next move, and yet the final one, would have to be his best.

"Mr. Archibald? You were saying?" Judge Burgess urged.

Ashley peered up from his briefcase as he nodded, confirming intent to call a witness. He looked at his client, who sported a nervous scowl while staring blankly ahead. Ashley's been here before: bottom of the ninth, fourth quarter, the last hurrah!

"Excuse me, Your Honor; I was just giving the jury a chance to process everything Mr. Joseph just shared," Ashley recovered.

Judge Burgess raised a single brow while grimacing at the defense attorney. Ashley noticed the judge's displeasure and twisted his pencil between his fingertips. He released the pencil to the table as he took one more gander at Tony Nguyen. In a quiet courtroom, the metal surrounding the eraser plodded like a hammer to a nail. Archibald cleared his throat as he rose to his feet. Archibald made sure none of the buttons on his blazer were attached as he pranced in front of the defense table. With one hand placed on the table and the other on his waist, Archibald cleared his throat to call his last witness.

"Well, don't leave us all in suspense, Mr. Archibald. I'm sure we all have more to do this week," Judge Burgess jabbed.

"Of course, Your Honor. Shall I proceed?" Ashley requested.

"We would prefer it, Mr. Archibald," Judge Burgess declared.

"Thank you, Your Honor. Without further ado, I will call Tony Nguyen to the stand," Ashley announced.

Tony froze in his seat while his father sprang up from the pews. Travis flashed a puzzled grimace from the state's table. Judge Burgess poured herself a glass of water as her eyes were trained on the affixed witness. Tony mustered enough energy to stare Ashley down. Tony slowly rose from his seat, then trampled to the witness stand. While en route to the stand, Ashley lightly brushed him and stated "You're gonna be fine." As he was sworn in, Tony's expression remained stoic. Judge Burgess took notice of Tony and decided to break the ice.

"Mr. Nguyen, I want to be the first to remind you that you do not have to take this stand and submit yourself to any possible self-incrimination. It is the responsibility of the state to prove what you did, not for you to prove that you didn't," Judge Burgess advised.

Tony broke his stature, looked over to the judge, and feigned his comfort with proceeding. While the young man seethed, the remainder of the room's disbelief was quite transparent. "*Why would he put him on the stand*" thought those supporting the defendant and the prosecution alike. Tony Nguyen apparently was not prepared but was going to be a good sport. *What precisely did Ashley hope to draw from this?*

"Mr. Nguyen, could you please introduce yourself to the court? Please tell them your legal name and what it is that you do," Ashley opened.

Tony's obvious discomfort spoke louder than the words detained on his lips. The simplest questions sometimes draw the most difficult responses. Be that as it may, this would be the easiest question proposed to Tony Nguyen for the remainder of the hearing.

"Anthony," Tony muttered "Anthony Nguyen. I uhh...."

"It's okay, Mr. Nguyen. The state has brought up a very interesting case against you on somewhat severe charges. I do understand if the circumstances have left you a bit speechless," Ashley reassured.

Ashley's half-assed attempt at comforting his witness was beneficial. Tony visibly responded well to the prompt, as he corrected his posture and straightened his tie.

"Ahh, where was I?" Tony phrased to some faint amusement of the crowd.

"So far you have given us your name, Mr. Nguyen. I'm only waiting on your occupation or vocation," Ashley led.

"Sure thing. I am employed by the Bonneville Meat Market. I wear multiple hats there. My father wants me to understand all of the in-store positions, so I know what everyone is responsible for," Tony explained.

"Ah, a jack of all trades, I presume. One that comes from structure and stability. Would you agree?" Ashley proposed.

"Yes," Tony confirmed.

"From what it appears, you have a family that has instilled some prime values in you. Values that exude hard work and accountability. Things any good leader would have ingrained in their repertoire. And as we were advised earlier, your father even placed you in an additional community program to help you develop even further?" Ashley recapped.

"Yes," Tony confirmed.

"Your Honor, the state objects to this line of leading the witness," Travis interrupted.

"Overruled, Mr. Carrington. The defense has the right to confirm or deny prior testimony," Judge Burgess invoked.

Travis surrendered from his seat and beckoned the examination to continue. Ashley acknowledged the cue with a tilt of his head before gazing into the jury.

"So, Mr. Nguyen, it would appear your life has a desired path as long as you continue to follow it. Perhaps you would have more to lose than gain if you were to run into a crowded park and open fire?" Ashley trumped.

"I concur," Tony uttered.

"So, can you please provide the court with your account of what happened on the day in question?" Ashley invited.

Tony became apparently leery of the summoning. He adjusted his posture behind the witness stand as he leaned forward.

"We just wanted to pay respect to a guy who took time to kick it with us back in the G," Tony shared.

"Understandable. Admirable, even. Mr. Nguyen, if you wouldn't mind, can you give us your account of what happened when you showed up at the mausoleum?" Ashley inquired.

There it was: utilize a community member and the defendant himself to formulate his character, then let the jury decide. High risk doesn't always equate into high reward, but neither does folding. The man of the hour let out a muffled sigh before going forward.

"Honestly, me and a few of the guys from Hog Tied got together and rode to the mausoleum to see if it was all real. The stories we'd heard about Fantastic; the way he always seemed to stand out without ever saying a word. The threat of certain danger and an unsupportive police force couldn't stop him, so how the hell did a bullet?" Tony revealed.

"Thank you for your recollection, sir. From your statement, one would assume you were more so an admirer of Franc Tatiano. Probably even more so than the men he'd aligned himself with for years. So, you guys had no intention of going there and starting trouble? Can you share what actually happened?" Ashley outlined.

"That's just the thing: I don't know! We rode up to the cemetery and saw those people there. We tried not to cause a disturbance, but soon as police noticed us, shots rang out," Tony recalled.

An uncertain quiet came over the room. The entire story previously painted for the jury was now distorted. What was the likelihood neither the police NOR the cyclists fired the first shots?

"So, are you suggesting that neither you nor any of your comrades fired the initial shots heard?" Ashley asked.

"We were still riding up when we heard the shots go off," Tony shared.

"And what was your reaction to that?" Ashley questioned.

"We tried to get up out of there. They were shooting and some of my guys decided to bust back in defense. Three of us were chased out by this guy after he knocked one of my boys off his bike," Tony detailed.

"I believe that was Detective Renaldo Brown; an individual with a rather unique connection to the deceased," Ashley acknowledged.

"I don't really know who buddy was, but he chased us on some looney shit. I mean stuff, sorry, Your Honor," Tony blurted.

Judge Burgess shook her head at the defendant before flashing a pleasant smile. She gestured for Tony to continue with his account of the events.

"Forgive me for that line of questioning, Your Honor. I can see how having to relive a moment such as that can lead one to swear. If it does not cause you as much displeasure, Mr. Nguyen, would you please advise the court of why you ended up in City Park?" Ashley interjected.

"We were just trying to get away from that cemetery. We figured if we went to a public place, the maniac wouldn't run behind us. We didn't know he had already stopped following us," Tony explained.

"Well, when you are running to safety, it's only natural you don't waste too much time looking behind you. Could you please tell us what happened in the park? There were some unfortunate events that occurred, and I believe it would help the court to understand what happened," Ashley advised.

Here it was: *the moment the court had been waiting to hear*. Tony could make or break his own case with whatever came out of his mouth next. Tony was aware of the stakes and wouldn't proceed hastily. He swallowed whatever doubt remained in the frame of his mouth and pushed it to the lower depths of his belly, suppressed by a heavy heart and an iron gut.

He looked at his mother, who buried her head into his father's nearest armpit, as if she couldn't bear to watch. He then watched his father console his mother by draping both of his arms around her. Though Mr. Nguyen's body was wrapped around his wife, his eyes remained squarely on his son. It was the only pieces of him he could lend to Tony; so, with his son, they would remain.

"We went into the park, with no intentions of bothering anyone. We were hoping to just blend in, but we were surrounded by more police. I heard a gunshot go off and that's when people started scattering and running around. Before I knew it, Art was stretched out on the ground. He was just drowning in his own blood," Tony recollected.

"And can you please clarify for the court exactly who 'Art' is?" Ashley requested.

"Artemis," Tony nearly whispered.

The dejected look on Tony's face matched that of his mother's. While most eyes were on him, his were lowered to the stand in front of him. In just those few minutes, Tony relived a day full of emotional valleys. Nothing about that date was worth remembering, much less reviving.

"Artemis, as mentioned earlier, was the Hog Tied

member whose life was lost on that day. Your Honor, I have no further questions for the witness at this time," Ashley released.

Ashley watched Tony as he began to carefully back-track towards the defendant's table. Ashley eventually changed direction and caught a glimpse of Travis in the process. The assistant district attorney stood tall, awaiting the invite from Judge Burgess.

"Would the state like to cross-examine Mr. Tony Nguyen?" Judge Burgess proposed.

"Yes, Your Honor, we do have a few questions," Travis confirmed.

Travis was in stride before finishing his sentence. Travis was careful not to rush into the interrogation. He knew Ashley had just left the room teetering on emotion. Travis knew it was best to tread carefully...*initially*.

Chapter 33

To Be Self Evidence

"Mr. Tony Nguyen, sir, we are going to backtrack a little bit if you don't mind. I would like to begin with you all arriving at the mausoleum. Can you recite for the court what you all were wearing?" Travis began.

"Yeah, I had on some black jeans and a grey shirt," Tony stated.

"Is that all you had on? You all were riding on motorcycles, correct? For the sake of safety, you guys had to be wearing more than that. Could you clarify your full attire for the court, please?" Travis refreshed.

"I'm sorry. We wore jackets and helmets, of course," Tony confirmed.

"Thank you for that, Mr. Nguyen. Could you please describe the protective materials to the court?" Travis requested.

"Yes, we wore black leather jackets with black helmets," Tony answered.

Travis inched toward the state's table to retrieve a document. Travis inspected the paper carefully before moving any further. He then approached the bench as he deciphered his next question.

"Did that jacket or helmet have any other colors on it? Specifically, red?" Travis insisted.

"Yes, there are red stripes on each of them," Tony admitted.

"So, you have a black and red jacket with a black striped helmet. Are these not the same colors worn by the Fifth Ward Hogs?" Travis narrowed in.

"We object due to relevance, Your Honor. A character witness already stated the defendant was not a part of that group in an earlier testimony!" Ashley barged.

"Overruled, Mr. Archibald. The character witness is a well-known associate of the former and is running the latter. There is a blatant connection, sir! Mr. Nguyen, please answer the question," Judge Burgess ruled.

The obvious attempt to derail Travis' line of questioning did not fall on deaf ears. Tony slumped in his seat with his head lowered, rocking to and fro. Ashley sat with his legs crossed and head resting in one palm.

"From what I have heard, yes," Tony finally blurted out.

"From what you have heard, hneh? Have you heard of all the squabbles law enforcement agencies had with the Hogs? While Mr. Joseph was teaching you guys life lessons, did he ever tell you about his personal escapades?!" Travis grilled.

"Yeah, of course the O.G. did. He told us he did those things and learned from 'em, so we don't have to," Tony retorted.

"Good. But did you listen to him? How did you guys get the jackets and helmets? Are they commemorative? Attend 10 sessions get some garb free? What is it?" Travis badgered.

Tony's eyes widened but his pupils shriveled as he found the eyes of Reginald Joseph. Reginald leaned his head to the side in curiosity. He could tell by his pupil's expression that something was amidst.

"He didn't know we had them," Tony mumbled.

"I'm sorry, Mr. Tony. My ears must be failing me here. Could you repeat that so the rest of the court may hear you?" Travis instigated.

"Reg Leg......" Tony began.

Reginald Joseph shot up from his seat to interject. He instantly realized what had happened.

"I GAVE IT TO THEM!" Reginald shouted.

"MR. JOSEPH!" Judge Burgess startled. "You have been given the opportunity to testify already and a similar question was posed to you. As someone who wishes to be regarded as a pillar in the community, YOU WILL conduct yourself in an exemplary manner in this court or risk being arrested for contempt!"

Mr. Joseph deferred to the bench per the judge's order. Ashley nodded to the gentleman before returning his focus to the client. Travis gazed upon the Fifth Ward Hog a little longer, deeper, and more intently than his counterpart.

"Is that correct, Tony Nguyen? Did Mr. Reginald Joseph provide you all with protective gear?" Travis asked while still staring at Reg Leg.

"No, he didn't know. We jimmied the lock at the building to go in and get the jackets and helmets," Tony admitted.

"And the motorcycles? How about the motorcycles?" Travis included.

"Yes," Tony conceded.

A collective gasp overtook the room. Reginald Joseph

sank into his seat and shuddered his head. Mrs. Nguyen was now in full tears as Mr. Nguyen sat in utter shock and disappointment. Tony could feel his parents' displeasure, as it weighed on him like a ton of bricks.

"What about the guns, Tony? Hmm? Did you all confiscate those from the Hog Tied facility as well?" Travis dug.

"No," Tony denied.

"So, the only five guys who attended the funeral were guys with guns? Was that a criterion to appear? What exactly were you expecting to happen at a mausoleum where you all felt the need to bring weapons?!" Travis continued.

Tony now sat with his head in both hands. When he dropped his hands, he momentarily rocked back and forth in the seat. He muttered something inaudible to himself before looking up.

"Mr. Nguyen, why would you all need guns at a burial site?" Travis repeated.

"We didn't know what to expect, I guess," Tony stated plainly.

"I don't follow. You didn't know what to expect at a mausoleum. Did you guys plan on securing the premises after everyone left to make sure no one messed with the body?" Travis sarcastically proposed.

"That's not it. You *know* that's not it," Tony bounced back.

"Enlighten us, Mr. Nguyen," Travis lightly provoked.

"Then again, maybe you don't know. You don't have to worry about going out for a ride and being profiled, now do you?" Tony proposed while gawking at Travis.

Ironically, the witness stand transferred from the man

sitting to the one standing. Travis heard the statement but felt it was planned. He looked over to Ashley, whose face was about as plain as a bowl of vanilla ice cream. Travis had grown accustomed to Ashley's theatrics, but they were still less than welcomed.

"No, I don't believe I do, Mr. Nguyen. And while I apologize for your experiences, Francisco Tatiano, whose origins may have been riddling, is still widely regarded as an African American man. I do not find it weird that young Asian, Black or otherwise noted races would be present at his burial site. Now, if you were so concerned about police relations and attention, why would you show up to the site wearing the colors of the most notorious biker gang this city has ever known?" Travis retorted.

"We just really wanted to pay tribute to Mr. Franc. We didn't want no trouble," Tony redirected.

Travis scoffed at Tony's recollection. Travis waltzed near the jury stand before posing his next question. He thought carefully about his delivery but proceeded forward with relative ease.

"So, you guys were greeted with gunshots and a chase out of the mausoleum. I can see the issue with that. However, once you were in the park, you were in there with multiple innocent bystanders. Some of which could not testify today because they are deceased. One of which is an eleven-year-old girl missing her father. An eleven-year-old that still has nightmares about her father's white T-shirt slowly turning red in front of her eyes. You have any idea who Amber McGuire is?" Travis painted.

"Nah. I have no idea who that is," Tony conceded.

"You shouldn't. And because of that, I didn't put her on the stand today. But you know what? She knows you.

You want to know how? Because she can recall plain as day you and your friend running into City Park, pulling out your guns, and shooting at police officers. She can recite frame by frame her father taking a bullet from one of your guns and hitting the ground. And do you know why, Mr. Nguyen? HMM?" Travis accused.

"Your Honor, we object to hearsay. If the witness was available to speak, the state should have allowed her to do so!" Ashley defended.

"Sustained! Mr. Carrington, you have to tread carefully with lofty accusations, sir, unless you want to call your witness to the stand," Judge Burgess warned.

"What child would want to dream that up. There's no hearsay in the fact that Martin McGuire died on that date, it is in Eastbank Sheriff's Department police reports, Your Honor. More importantly, it's on replay in a little girl's head. The bullet found in him was a .50 Action Express. The bullets found in Deputy Harris were Remington 9mm Luger. My question to you, Mr. Nguyen, is which gun belonged to you? The pistol or the Desert Eagle?!" Travis barraged.

Tony's mouth moved but not a sound came from it. A tear formed in one eye as he switched his attention between the jurors and the onlookers. Tony looked at his mother; Mrs. Nguyen had gone completely numb. She was so distressed her head was slightly tilted, and her expression was nearly non-existent.

"THE PISTOL OR THE DESERT EAGLE, MR. NGUYEN?" Travis repeated boisterously.

"Your Honor, he is badgering the witness!" Ashley called from his chair.

"PISTOL OR DESERT EAGLE!" Travis asked again.

"ORDER, ORDER in the court. Mr. Carrington, I need you to CALM DOWN!" Judge Burgess demanded.

"He is avoiding the question, Your Honor. He is here on serious charges that the defense would like to have argued down. The jury deserves to know!!" Travis clawed back.

"The jury deserves to see you all conduct yourself as men instead of as fools! This has gone on far enough! Mr. Nguyen, you may step down and return to your seat," Judge Burgess hurled.

Tony wasted little time gathering himself and scampering back to Ashley's side. Travis' eyes followed the young man from one seat until he was firmly planted into the next. Ashley stood up as Tony sat down. The entire room remained on edge as they awaited the next order from Judge Burgess.

"Attorney Carrington. I'm going to give you some time to cool down. Mr. Archibald, if you have any closing statements, I will allow you to go forward at this time," Judge Burgess decided.

Ashley walks around the defense table to be near the jury. He raises a finger to indicate he accepted the judge's offer to speak first. He looks at the Nguyen and Hall families as they watch in anticipation. He gives them a quick wink before proceeding.

"Ladies and gentlemen, what you have just witnessed over the last several hours was a story. A story of young men who went to pay tribute to their *idol* and were met with resistance by people who responded first and asked questions later. Imagine you were actually able to meet your hero and build a relationship with them. A dream that we all only hope to realize. Now consider the nightmare, being familiar enough with the hero that you may actually *mourn* their death. In the midst of your tribute, you are confronted by men with guns. Not for what you personally have done, but instead, to punish you for their own personal traumas because, for a lack of better words, 'you fit the description.' You get chased from one place just to be surrounded by these men in a place you thought was safe. And what happens to cement your suspicions about your adversaries: they shoot one of your buddies down with no remorse. Ask yourselves not if Tony Nguyen is guilty, but rather, what exactly is he guilty of?" Ashley divulged.

Ashley poses momentarily for the jurors before moving along to the defense table. Travis, who was practically sitting on the prosecution table, now stands to address the court for the final time.

"Thank you, Mr. Archibald. Prosecutor, now that you've had time to compartmentalize, would you like to make one final address to the court?" Judge Burgess called.

"I surely would, Your Honor. Forgive me for my previous outbursts. I am somewhat concerned about the logistics of it all. *Why did young men need to attend a burial site with guns*? You usually don't see fireworks at a funeral unless the mistress wants to sit on the front row. Everywhere these young men went that day was altered forever. A mausoleum and a public park, two places where most might deem to be the safest, now attached to bitter memories. And why? Because a few young men came prepared for a gunfight. What were the true intentions of the young men from Hog Tied? Two deputies met their demise in the park and another man, Martin McGuire, died days later due to complications while in the hospital.

Others were seriously injured. Whose fault is that? Is it the officers who took time while on duty to attend the funeral of a fallen comrade, or a few young men who laid terror in their wake at every turn?" Travis enforced.

"Jury, you have heard all testimony and all opening and closing statements. Please take all you have heard into consideration and all the time you need to reach the proper verdict. Thank you all and please contact me when a final decision is reached," Judge Burgess alerted.

The boiling point of the most controversial hearing in the Eastbank had been reached. All vantage points were displayed, and all truths made available for the consensus of twelve jurors. The verbal jousting between two top tier contenders had been laid to rest. All that remained was a scorecard from the panel.

Chapter 34

A Bit of Advice

The fourth floor of the Crescent City Police Department is oddly...tranquil. A well-groomed gentleman walks the hall in search of an old friend. This time around, Detective McDonald's presence was requested. He traveled down the familiar walkway to an office he had only scurried past recently. Rance finds the door is slightly ajar, so he decides to peek in. He finds Lieutenant Morial looking down at his desk. Rance taps two knuckles on the door frame.

"Come right on in, Mr. McDonald. Come have a seat. You might want to sit for this," Morial warned.

Rance's lip shifted as he placed one hand over his chest. Morial caught the dramatic response and simply chuckled at his former protégé.

"Well, why would that be, sir?" Rance questioned, obviously concerned.

"Mostly because you've been doing a lot of scrambling on your feet lately. Now I want you to take a seat, so you have nothing to do except listen," Morial further advised.

Rance shrugged his shoulders as he carefully placed his hat and blazer on the bare edge of the lieutenant's desk. He sat in one of the two well cushioned seats and awaited

Morial's narrative.

"Well, Lieutenant, I'm all here and all ears," Rance lightened.

"Good, I almost considered meeting you at a bar in case I instantly began to regret this sit down," Morial joked.

Both men chuckled at this exchange of gab, but for very different reasons. Rance was anxious to find out why he had been summoned to the C.C.P.D. Was it about Rita? Renaldo? *Romero?*

On the other hand, Morial had brought in his former employee for a hard discussion. He made light of the situation with sarcasm, but he truly did ponder if libations would be necessary to quell the queries that lie before them. Like a father telling his son about the birds and the bees, he would expect things to be awkward at first, but ultimately, he hoped it all would stick more than it stung.

"I've had my ear out for you lately, son. Heard you been busy around this part of town. You getting bored over there on the Westbank?" Morial prodded.

"You know Gretna P.D. keeps me with plenty to do, sir. Even some of your stuff has trickled over into my jurisdiction," Rance defended.

"Yeah, maybe you're right. How are you coming along with that, by the way? We still haven't found Detective Brown yet. I thought maybe you would have," Morial poked.

Rance smirked at the comments but also read Morial's expression. Just how much did the lieutenant know about his current star detective? Rance immediately began to ponder if he was in for an intervention or an ambush. Rance abandoned his slumped and slightly sloven posture for a more upright and erect approach.

"Nothing to brag about yet, sir. I'm making some headway on it though. Just trying to piece a few things together to make sure it all makes sense," Rance implied.

"Sounds like good detective work to me. Making sure everything is in place before calling it quits. It's a good quality to have, but don't let that gift become a curse," Morial forewarned.

With the lieutenant glaring right into his eyes, Rance leaned forward in his seat. As Rance's jaw hovered over the desk, Morial remained locked-in to the detective's gaze. Rance knew what he had to do to get Morial's purpose out in the open.

"Lieutenant! You know this is standard procedure, sir. We may have closed the case with the deceased men at 'Nina's' but there were still some concerning facts surrounding your star pupil. Are you trying to get me to drop the case because you're afraid of what I might find out?" Rance boasted.

The lieutenant twiddles a piece of paper between his thumbs as he chuckles at the accusations. Without looking away from the document to acknowledge Rance's boasts, Morial lays the paper down flat and scoots it across his desk with the tips of his two fingers. Lieutenant Morial lifts his eyes to Rance after he removes his hand from the photo. Rance inspects the contents of the photo carefully. He sees a very discreet abrasion embedded through human epidermis. After analyzing the stitching thoroughly, Rance's eyes lift from the photo without ever moving his head.

"Frankly, I'm more concerned about what has already been discovered. They pulled this off the Jackson fella' that was found in Thibodeaux. After somebody cleaned it up and enlarged a photo, they were able to get a clearer view of the artwork left by the suspect," Morial suggested.

"Oh yeah? Who is 'LB'?" Rance posed.

"If that's what you see, you may need to flip the image. It should be more familiar to you than that!" Morial boasted.

Rance abided by the advice of his senior and spun the sheet 180 degrees. Rance's head hovered over the image until his eyes bulged. Morial sunk into his seat and awaited Rance's synopsis.

"I still don't understand who that is," Rance blurted.

"Really? Hmm. That's interesting! Doc Smith was able to match the initials with some past cases. He said once they cleaned it up, the scarring was quite distinct. I'll be damned if these marks ain't familiar to you, Rance. You chased after Cliffhanger for nearly two years before you took that job in Gretna!" Morial surmised.

Rance drooped his head and planted his hand on the back of his neck. He rocked in the chair before springing up from his spot.

"How is that even possible? I thought y'all put her away! How is she roaming the streets?" Rance requested.

"Stopped her, yes. Secured her in a prison, no," Morial clarified.

Rance contemplated whether this exchange was a cruel joke, but he could tell from his elder's dry disposition this was no farce. He hoped to not be distracted from one mystery with the pursuit of another.

"I have my own cases to worry about, sir. I never stopped to concern myself with what is going on in Thibodeaux. There's not much I can do about that," Rance dryly stated.

"Hmm. Maybe *you have* learned your lesson. I hope you eventually come to the same conclusion with the case you already closed!" Morial berated.

"The only reason you want me to close that case for good is because I know your star detective is a fraud and deep down...*you know it too!*" Rance clapped back.

The lieutenant covered his face as he laughed hysterically at his young pupil. He stopped for a moment, dropped his hand, and laughed more once he realized the younger detective's expression hadn't changed. Once calmed, Morial attempted again to appeal to the enraged officer.

"I want you to close that case for good because I don't want another precinct to lose you. More importantly, I don't want to see you lose yourself, *again*," Morial carefully explained.

"If you were that damn worried, why did you allow me to leave?!" Rance shouted back.

"It was better to watch you gallop off into the sunset than to watch you dig your own grave in this building; behind *her*!!" Morial launched back.

The men exchange stern glances that paired perfectly with the heated debate. Morial stood up from his chair, walked to the exit, and secured the door. Once locked, Morial walked away from the door and plopped down in the chair adjacent to Rance. The lieutenant leaned over and quickly double tapped his pupil's leg before reclining in the seat.

"Look, Rance, you can't afford to dig yourself into such a hole you eventually have to change offices, not again. Chasing cold cases is a high risk, low reward game. It's not one you can build your name on; you only chance hindering it. Do you understand what I'm trying to say to you, son?" Morial pleaded.

"But that's just it. She wasn't a cold case. I didn't get to track her down, but Renaldo and Franc did. They at least encountered her long enough to stop her from striking once or twice," Rance shared.

Rance rubbed one hand along the other as if he planned on cracking his knuckles. One leg bounced in anxiety while the other soaked in the vibration. His head rocked side-to-side until he forced himself to stand. Rance began to pace the short area near the two cushy seats.

"Look at her now! Had I kept it going, that guy in Thibodeaux might still be alive. If I could have just put her behind bars. It could have all been so simple," Rance doubted.

"Or...you could be just as dead as he is. You never know! You were going down a rabbit hole then and I see you beginning the same pattern now. IT. AIN'T. WORTH IT!" Morial reassured.

With hands out to his sides, Morial continued his pleas in silence. Morial looked up at the wandering detective with a gleaming speck of hope. Rance was so deeply entrenched in thought he hardly noticed the lieutenant's appeal. Rance stopped his sauntering momentarily, grabbed his personal items, and marched towards the exit.

"I've seen the way you look at her. Barrios, I mean! I would usually threaten someone's life for fraternizing with one of my top detectives, but I believe you both could use some good. Maybe you can surround yourself with someone good so you don't have to engulf yourself in the world's treachery. In exchange, maybe Rita can finally have the happiness *she* deserves," Morial projected.

"And you still don't understand, sir. I find more happiness in serving and protecting the innocent than watching lovers of lawlessness parading these parishes. I will keep in mind what you said about the lady though. Tell her I said hello, will ya?" Rance relayed.

Without awaiting a response, Rance opens the door and shuffles out into the hall. Morial remains seated while looking over his desk to his chair. He gathers his thoughts about what just occurred and considers what he could have done differently. He looks over his shoulder towards the door to determine if Rance remained in earshot.

"Sure thing, kiddo. I'm sure if you had it your way, you would tell 'em yourself," Morial mumbled.

Chapter 35

Rollercoasters

The Magnolia Marketing building is internally vibrant today. Though only two strategists are assigned for this venture, the entire staff is fully invested in the outcome of a highly anticipated meeting. Today is the day newly independent rap artist Pelli Kanisus comes to commence the marketing deal. Landing the high-profile free agent emcee would be one thing; having marketing success that rivals a music label would be something different altogether!!

Julissa surveyed her notes repeatedly to not miss a beat. She viewed past social media posts regarding Pelli and pondered ways he could be better promoted. Julissa was ready to lay everything out on the table and let Pelli decide his own fate. She only had a few criteria to satisfy first. Marisol walks into the board room, momentarily delaying Julissa's train of thought.

"Ju, are you ready? The guy is almost here, and Mr. Denver wants us to be on top of our game," Marisol reminded her.

"I am about as ready as I can get to deal with this guy. I just hope he doesn't have a whole crew full of 'yes men' coming in here with him. There's nothing worse than one guy trying to look like a giant by surrounding himself with ants," Julissa commented.

"It wouldn't hurt if a few of those ants are cute though!" Marisol teased.

"Agreed," Julissa confirmed as both broke out in laughter.

The ladies' hooting is interrupted by the phone. Marisol motions for Julissa to be quiet before she picks up the line. Julissa covers her mouth with both hands to avoid busting a gut.

"Yes...Oh really...okay, please have someone to escort them up here, please," Marisol conveyed to the administrator.

Marisol slammed the phone down and snatched Julissa by her shoulders. She guided Julissa to the corner seat of the boardroom table. Marisol quickly spun a chair near Julissa and sat.

"Where is Denver?" Julissa inquired.

"He trusts us to get started with everything. I think he received an important call right before I came down," Marisol informed.

"He better have that same energy when it comes to the commission," Julissa blurted.

Marisol chuckled along with Julissa and her hushed demands. Julissa placed her documents in order, admired them a moment, and then shuffled them again. Marisol watched Julissa repeat her anxious antics two more times before she planted her hands on top of Julissa's.

"Unless that's a part of your presentation, you might want to stop, girl. They're almost here," Marisol warned.

Julissa nodded her head in agreement with Marisol.

Suddenly they heard the hall fill with excited grunts and shouting. Marisol released Julissa's hands before straightening the folders. Marisol opened the binder containing the contract and nearly fainted at the figure proposed.

Julissa bumps Marisol in the shoulder to revitalize her. As Marisol assumes her normative posture, the door handle turned. In walks Pelli Kanisus with two other men neither marketing agent recognized.

"Oh look, he didn't bring the whole army with him, just a couple of worker ants," Julissa whispered to Marisol. They cackled as the constituents entered.

"I present to you all, Pelli Kanisus! You all may go join Ms. Sinclair and Mrs. Brown at that end of the table. Would you all need anything more than those waters we have provided?" asked Mr. Denver's assistant.

"We have what we need for now, sir. Thank you for these beverages," Pelli answered.

The young man left the boardroom without further instruction. While his two associates immediately took a seat, Pelli walked around taking notice of accomplishments, awards, and other accolades on display. Julissa and Marisol curiously observed the musician canvassing the scene.

"Mr. Kane, have you found something over there that piques your interest?" Marisol initiated.

"I'm digging all these plaques and such, ya heard me. Just trying to see who I'm getting in bed with, ya dig," Pelli responded.

"Now I don't know what Mr. Denver promised you, but ain't nothing mentioned in these contracts about getting in bed, sir!" Julissa reprimanded.

Everyone seated at the table smirked. Pelli provided a

half smile as he circled to join the group. He found a seat, but instead of sitting, he leaned over the chair and planted both hands onto the conference table. The smirk faded to a stone stare as he focused his attention on the ladies of Magnolia Marketing.

"Don't misquote me, love. I just take my contracts serious. I believe anything I sign my name to is something I'm bonded to. I don't mind the jokes, but I at least hope you all will take your representation and advertising of me more serious than this meeting," Pelli declared.

"Well, I hope your commitment to the brand will be far more tender than the lyrics you spew," Julissa sputtered back.

Marisol's head remained still but her eyes darted through Julissa. The two men seated at the table covered their mouths to avoid laughing directly in Pelli's face. Pelli elevated from his bulldoggish stance and stared at Julissa momentarily before pulling out a chair and settling in it.

"Hmm," Pelli muttered.

"Yes, Mr. Kane. Is something troubling you?" Julissa baited.

"I always find it funny when people attack the very lyrics they dance to. People act like conscious artists are not a rarity on the mainstream," Pelli regarded.

Julissa's eyebrows raised while she twisted her head slightly as if she was attempting to get clarity on what was said. Marisol sat up in the seat as she noticed the change in Julissa's disposition.

"Why do you believe that is, Mr. Kane or Kanisus, or whichever persona you are speaking from right now? Why do artists have to feed into those type of lyrics to get on the radio?" Marisol redirected.

"The labels won't promote what they know the radio won't play. You have to drop ten 'Hail Marys' before they play one 'Dear Mama.' And either name is fine, but you can stick to whatever you all are putting on the paychecks," Pelli inclined.

"Well, you are independent now, Mr. Kane. What do you plan on doing with your newfound musical freedom? Will you finally diversify your palate?" Julissa asked.

Vernell began to laugh at Julissa's notion and his two associates followed in unison. Marisol snickered at the men across from her, finding their particular brand of ignorance entertaining.

"I make the music that ties in with my soul. Regardless to how raunchy or rugged y'all find my lyrics to be, I always come from the heart with my stuff, ya dig," Pelli responded.

"So, we putting our brand name behind your bragging and boasting is what you are telling me?" Julissa questioned.

"Look here, shorty. If I wanted to deal with censorship, I'd go with one of these big record companies in one of those other states. You think nobody wanted me to sign with them soon as they heard C.I.T.Y. Records bought out the contract?" Pelli posed.

This small moment of quiet that followed felt like an eternity. The tension between the artist and the advertisers was thicker than thighs in the south. Julissa and Marisol couldn't think of a solid rebuttal to Pelli's claims of being courted by other music labels.

"But to answer your question, yeah, if you all had ever bought one of my albums or fully streamed them, you would notice there were some 'conscious' tracks on there.

As I said before, I didn't get to choose what songs were released, but I plan to have a bit more...*autonomy*...now," Pelli iterated.

"Well, in that case, I believe we all will...," Julissa began.

"Come in!" Marisol called to the knock on the door.

The door opens as Mr. Denver appears. He motions towards his employees to meet with him outside. Julissa simultaneously gestures between herself and Marisol.

"He's talking to you, girl. I can take care of these guys for a little, while you step out," Marisol deemed.

"Girl, how do you know he doesn't want both of us? Or just you?" Julissa inquired.

"Call it a feeling," Marisol responded.

Julissa looked at Marisol dumbfoundedly before settling on her request. She stood up from the table while uttering "Excuse me, I'll be back in a moment." Mr. Denver closed the door once he saw Julissa upright. Julissa pushed the door open to enter the hall, only to find Mr. Denver leaning against the opposite wall. Mr. Denver groped his face with one hand as he watched Julissa enter the walkway.

"Mr. Denver, what's going on? I thought you were coming in for this meeting?" Julissa questioned.

"Yeah, I did, too," Mr. Denver replied as he fanned his hand.

Julissa noticed Mr. Denver evading her eyes. He took a deep breath and found the discipline to look at Julissa without faltering.

"Mr. Denver, what's wrong? Is everything alright?" Julissa further delved.

"I umm...I just finished watching the news," Mr.

Denver answered.

"Oh no! Is there a warrant out for Pelli Kanisus? Maybe he really is living those lyrics," Julissa judged.

"No, not that at all. That would actually be a relief," Mr. Denver stated while cracking a subtle smile.

Mr. Denver's brief cheer was subsided by his uneasiness. Mr. Denver took a deep sigh in hopes it would make what he had to say flow easier. He would soon discover there was no comfort in the news he had to deliver.

"Mr. Denver, do you need me to get you something? I want to help, but we also have Kanisus here and I know how much this deal means to you," Julissa offered.

"Yes...yes. I'm sorry, Mrs. Brown. Authorities found an item floating in the lake near the Bonne Carre Spillway. It was...it was umm...," Mr. Denver attempted to relay.

"I'm not sure I follow, Mr. Denver. What was it that they found?" Julissa urged.

"A shield," Mr. Denver uttered.

Julissa mouthed Denver's answer. She did so multiple times as her eyes shrunk in confusion. She looked at Mr. Denver, hoping he could elaborate further.

"A shield, Mr. Denver? A shield of what? And for who?" Julissa requested.

"A badge. A C.C.P.D. badge. They confirmed the number matches Renaldo's," Mr. Denver stated.

Julissa's mouth widened as her eyes shut. She leaned on the boardroom door, internally crumbling. Julissa grabbed for the doorknob, only to turn to the door and hide the single tear streaming from her face.

"Did they find anything else? Anything at all? Do they know where he is?" Julissa pleaded.

"No, not right now. Some fishermen found the badge

floating while they were on the water this morning. Reportedly, they will be sending someone underwater to search for any other signs," Mr. Denver reported.

"Okay," Julissa squeaked through prohibited tears.

"Look, Julissa. If you need, I can go in there and finish the meeting if you would like to take the rest of the day off or just to get away until this all clears. We can have M—" Mr. Denver supported.

"No. No! I can do it. If you go in there and I don't go with you, they'll know something's up. Let's just go in there and wrap this up as best we can. We could use some good news. I know I sure can," Julissa detailed.

"Okay, I can go in there for now to help Ms. Sinclair. Just come in whenever you're ready, okay?" Mr. Denver arranged.

Julissa crossed the hall, allowing Denver to enter the boardroom. Denver opened the door and took one last look at Julissa before disappearing into the meeting. Julissa placed her head into her hands as she slowly slid down the wall. While crouched, Julissa contemplated Renaldo's whereabouts. She feared the worst, not for Renaldo, or herself, but for Judy. She'd accepted Renaldo may never want to speak with her again—but Judy, there is no way he would have stayed away from his daughter on his own. Despite her realistic outlook, Julissa's heart still skipped a beat when she heard the news.

Julissa gathered her thoughts first, then herself. Julissa wiped her eyes and slowly rose to her feet. She dusted herself off and walked to the door. She grabbed the handle and took a deep breath before deciding to twist the knob. She pushed the door open and heard pieces of the conversation in progress:

"I just want to be sure that you are not going to soil our brand with tasteless representation on your behalf, Mr. Kane," Denver advised.

"And I want to make sure your brand doesn't try to put a strangle on my creativity like you guys are getting in the booth with me or some shit like that," Pelli declared.

"My client has other places he could go if necessary. He thought a local marketing firm with some clout would be a good fit, but a talented artist deserves certain liberties. If y'all can't give us that, we can surely find a label willing to deal," Pelli's agent stated.

"What we cannot afford is to lose all of our other clients because this one guy who hasn't earned us a penny yet wants his creative juices to blow up in all our faces," Marisol defended.

The voices began to collide as they expressed their gripes. Julissa brooded on the arguments temporarily before bursting in. Julissa returned to her original seat as Mr. Denver remained standing. She knocked on the table lightly to gain everyone's attention, but no one noticed.

"Excuse me. Excuse me!" Julissa stated plainly.

The squabbling continued while Julissa reflected on the news she received a few minutes prior. She felt her world slowly coming apart before her eyes. As far as she knew, the two biggest heroes she had known were deceased. There was no one coming to save the day. Then again, she didn't need anybody to save her. *She never did.*

"EXCUSE ME!" Julissa shouted.

She finally got their attention. More importantly, she was able to get them all to be quiet. Julissa knew she had to work quickly to salvage the remainder of the meeting.

"Pelli Kanisus belongs with Magnolia Marketing and

it's not even close. Both are Crescent City made with mainstream flare. They could survive apart but would thrive together! Magnolia will trust you to make the music; that's where you have the expertise and proven accolades. Pelli just has to trust us to properly promote him. You can choose to release whatever song you want whenever you want, just trust us to bring the promotion to life!!" Julissa anchored.

Everyone in the room goes from staring at Julissa to gawking sporadically at one another. Pelli's agent leans over to him and whispers in his ear. Pelli's eyes remained on Julissa until he stood up and tapped the shoulders of each man next to him, signaling for them to do the same. Julissa's eyes drop to the table as Pelli's group walks toward them. *Did she say too much??*

"If you wouldn't mind, ma'am. Could you please show me which of these folders has the contract in it?" Pelli asked while leaning across the table.

Julissa's stoned face cracked into a smile as she opened a blue binder and handed it to Pelli Kanisus. Marisol wrapped her hands around Julissa's arm and kissed her on the cheek. Mr. Denver gave a slight smile to Julissa. He shook the hands of his new business partners and exited the boardroom. Once Pelli and company were done signing the necessary paperwork, Marisol escorted them to the elevator. Julissa sat in the chair and let all the feelings she experienced in the last thirty minutes rush from her eyes. She tumbled the tissue box over as she ripped the exposed cotton sheets.

She tried to force the snot out of her nose like the pressure built up in her chest. She could no longer determine if her sobbing was a product of joy or dejection. She may have signed the biggest deal known to marketing, but how was she to avoid advertising her grief? She may finally know where Renaldo is, but she would have preferred to be able to say goodbye. Either way, it wasn't enough. *Nothing was going to be enough*! Not the new contract acquisition; not the accolades on the wall; *maybe not even* the recent bundle of joy she brought home from the hospital. Until Julissa had the closure she desired, all the treasures of the world wouldn't amount to *enough*!!

Chapter 36

Requesting Fervors

Her eyes are bloodshot red; redder than the blood bubbling in her veins. How could they just discard him like that? *Why* would they discard him like that? *WHO* would dump Renaldo into the lake...like...*THAT*?! Who did he hurt? So many questions filled her mind and fueled her disgust. Unfortunately, the answers weren't nearly as accessible as the mountain of questions.

She couldn't explain how she felt inside. It had been some time since she saw his face and even longer since she desired to. Peculiarly, though, she wished they were on better terms. Maybe then she could be satisfied with the last words they uttered to one another. Maybe they would have been more pleasant. Probably? Possibly?

She swore the more she tried to forget, the more it appeared the news flashed updates on the search. She would be more at ease if the updates would provide something of substance. Hearing renditions of "we have not located the body" tends to get old after the fifth time. She turned the television off, hoping her displeasure would fade with the display. No such luck. Now she sat stewing in silence.

Rita's throat was so parched, she wished she'd left a cup on the floor to collect her tears. She questioned her own sanity. How foolish was she to be nearly in mourning for a man who'd led her on—then astray? She had forgiven him for it. Surely, she had. However, she could never forget what her former paramour had done. How he disappointed her. Ditched her! *Deserted her*?!

Rita vigorously rubbed her eyes as if the tears themselves were distorting her point of view. Rita felt it necessary to forego her own desires and replace it with the duties of Detective Barrios. Unfortunately, her task may require some assistance to be executed smoothly. Rita rose in the ranks in Renaldo's absence, but Morial's current orders would leave her reeling: complete a welfare check on the estranged officer's family. In essence, it made sense for the last surviving partner of a fallen officer to make the rounds. In reality, it would be completely uncomfortable for the main man's former mistress to deliver words of comfort to his wife. Feeling helpless as a newborn and hopeless as a penny with a hole in it, Rita decided to phone a friend. She contemplated hanging up multiple times before the receiver picked up on the other end.

"Hello, may I ask who's calling?" a man's voice invited.

"Hello. Yes, this is Detective Barrios with C.C.P.D.," Rita answered.

"Ohhh, Ohhh! I'm sorry about that. To what do I owe the call? Is the case over with yet?" the man inquired.

"The testimony is over, but the jury is still in deliberation. Thank you for your assistance with that. However, I may have another favor to ask," Rita indicated.

"You don't need me to take the stand, do ya? I try my best to stay out of those Eastbank District Courts. They give me the heebie jeebies," Rance jabbed.

"No. That won't be necessary. What I need is a little simpler, yet sadder than that," Rita chuckled.

"Oh yeah? Well, you name it and I'll see what I can do," Rance invited.

A hesitant sigh slipped from Rita. It was one matter to ask the favor; the possibility of having to explain it was another issue. Still, better to possibly be judged by someone from across the river than a comrade of the C.C.P.D.

"Well...umm. Have you heard? About Detective Brown?" Rita begun.

"Nah, I don't believe I have. Did they find him?" Rance requested impatiently.

"Maybe. Maybe not. Someone found his badge under the spillway," Rita reported.

The silence is deafening. Rita thought Rance may have taken it as hard as most people who worked closely with Renaldo. Sadly, Rance was only saddened by the prospect of another unsolved case. He felt as if he'd been jinxed, more specifically by Lieutenant Morial.

"Really?! Shit! I can't believe that," Rance voiced.

"I don't think any of us can. He was missing for months, and then...this," Rita indicated.

"Another hero gone? Always gone too soon," Rance uttered.

"Indeed," Rita blurted.

Rita's head dropped as a grimace formed on her face. Rance's disbelief slowly transformed into distrust. Was this the C.C.P.D.'s ploy to have Rance thrown off the case? Why call and tell him about these findings? It's not like he was especially attached to the detective. At least not *affectionately*.

"He's a decent guy. Really helped me out with that whole 'Recluse' thing. I appreciated his above and beyond approach," Rance noted with some disdain.

"Yes, he was," Rita implied.

"I'm sorry. I started running my mouth and may have gotten off topic. What was it that you needed me to do?" Rance asked blatantly.

"Oh yeah. I almost forgot. Lieutenant wants me to meet with Mrs. Brown and check on the family. Since his body has not been found and he wasn't on duty at the time he disappeared, it's a little awkward," Rita recovered.

"Okay," Rance began in sheer uncertainty. "I'm still not sure why Morial would have me assist you in that."

"That part wasn't his idea. Renaldo was a private person, and he wouldn't want any of the guys from this office to know any particulars about his family. His home is kind of far from the office, being out in Destreland. I thought we would stop by Julissa Brown's job. She works at Magnolia Marketing," Rita fabricated after biting her lip.

"I can empathize with that. Sometimes when people are too involved in your affairs, they tend to get comfortable giving unsolicited advice," Rance attributed.

"Umm, yeah? If that helps you understand it better, I guess that's a way of looking at it," Rita answered with some concern.

Rita pondered her companion's snide remarks on coworker relations but shook it off. Rance stewed in contemplation of the C.C.P.D.'s motive for having him tag along on this certain field trip. The question lingering in Rance's mind was the one Rita wanted to avoid the most.

"So, when would we be paying Mrs. Brown a visit?" Rance questioned.

"I'm kind of waiting on the results to come back in the case before I make a move. There's not a hard deadline because there's still a chance Renaldo is still out there... somewhere," Rita provided.

"Well, despite the circumstances, I would be delighted to join you on what might be a difficult visit. Please just give me some early notice so I can shift some things around if necessary," Rance requested.

"Sure thing. Be expecting my call sometime this week. We should have the verdict from the grand jury sometime soon," Rita ascertained.

After they hung up the phone, the two detectives experienced two very equal yet opposite emotions: Rita was relieved she did not have to reveal the details of her past with Renaldo, while Rance stewed in contemplation of his next move. Would Rance be forced to allow the case of 'The Recluse' to finally rest, or would he dare soil the image of the deceased?

Rita powered down her phone once the call was completed. She'd rather miss a few phone calls than to be hindered with any further negative news. If there was anything she needed to know, she would find out in the morning. Rance speculated if current events were a sign, he should return to the sport of his choice: *Chasing the Cliffhanger!*

Chapter 37

A Step in the Right Direction

One might attach the lack of conversation to the car being without its most inquisitive member. Sadly, that is not the sole reason for unrivaled silence. The uncle and nephew duo are avoiding a very pertinent conversation as they have taken their exit off the main highway and are now approaching Beech Grove Manor. Victor sat idly for as long as his temper would allow. He now needed to know what his 'genius' uncle had planned.

"Howw will weee get inn there to check on my mama?" Victor broke the silence.

The reverend snickered at the initial request. His initial attempt to answer was interrupted by a sound-shattering cough. Victor turned to check on Mack, but he was directed to monitor the road. With a hand covering his mouth, Mack composed himself while addressing Victor.

"The detective advised us we should start at the beginning, so that's what we're going to do, son. You have to take with the good with the bad. We took the little good there was in that terrible man and discarded the rest," Mack convicted.

"What was soo baad about hiiim? Shoullld hee not haaave diiiied with Franc if it was truuuly his dessstiny?" Victor challenged.

"HE LET your cousin die!! I don't care how you slice it, that damn apple seems rotten! In what universe does Franc die and a bastard like that deserve to live? Hmmm?!" Mack retorted.

"In a worrllld wherrre destiny is respected, eeeven when not unnnderstoood. In whaat riiighteous worrrld does a mannn of God find it fit to chaaaange the scriipt of hisss will?" Victor roared.

The hair stood on the back of Mack's neck as he fumed at the disrespect. He strongly considered slapping the youngster in the back of his head but couldn't chance crashing this close to their destination.

"You still have much to learn, Vic. That's okay though, it's by...destiny...as you would say...and I'm going to be here to teach you. Some lessons just come harder than others. Fear not the rod, for you can see it. Fear your own ignorance, for it is the sum of things you never allowed yourself to witness," Mack prophesized.

"We soooon shall see," Victor rebutted.

They pull off the roadway into what initially looks like a residential area. Before reaching the neighborhood, Victor turns down what appears to be an alley but most certainly is a long pathway through some trees. Victor flicks on the car's bright lights to navigate through the uncharacteristically wooded portion of Westwego. The pathway doesn't extend far before they come upon an elongated white building with a curt breezeway. Victor pulls into the quaint adjacent parking area and turns to his uncle for the next cue.

"Howww doo we get innnn therrre?" Victor posed.

"Well, for the sake of preventing an uproar, I will go in there myself. I'm not quite sure everyone is as accepting of your appearance as your dear old pal we left some miles back," Mack slighted.

Victor turned his torso slowly to gather a gander of Mack. His frown was understood, yet unmoving.

"Seeeeems I cann't keeeeep those whooooo unnnderr-staaand meee aroooound," Victor noticed.

"That boy didn't care about you. Not the way you think, Vic. If he cared about Franc, we might still have him today," Mack defended.

"Heee triiied to help us! Heee got usss herrre!" Victor contested.

"HE ONLY TRIED TO HELP HIMSELF! THINK ABOUT IT! First, they arrest Franc's killer, then, a bunch of other negroes end up dead and they were connected to it? The only denominator I see is if you hang with that mother-fucker long enough, *you die!*" Mack shouted.

Mack shot the base of his hand into the door frame. He nearly ripped the handle off kilter as he tried three times to vacate the vehicle. He flipped the lock up and shoved his way outside the car.

"Just wait here until I can find out where we should look next. It won't take me too long, I'm certain," Mack asserted.

"Iiii would haaate tooo see what woullld haappen if Iiiii angerrred youuuu," Victor replied.

Mack slammed the car door before disappearing into the night. Victor sat in darkness and angst while hoping his uncle would return with some light. Mack and his cane sauntered towards the entrance of Beech Grove Manor. As he reached the front door, he pressed the button on a panel.

"How may we help you?" a voice requested from the box.

Mack looked back toward the car where Victor remained seated. He registered a scowl as he returned his attention to the box.

"Mr. Wellington, here in search of Ms. Baronne," Mack announced.

The request is followed by miniscule hush. The attendees took a moment to review Lavender's file before proceeding with Mr. Wellington. The attendant watched the door as she pressed the button to open the mic

"Been awhile since we've seen you, Mr. Wellington. Please come right in," the attendant greeted.

The lock released as the door buzzed. Mack yanked the green door open to enter the foyer. To either side of the attendant's desk is an airlocked door requiring an identification card or remote access. In the lobby sits a few tall fake plants, some outdated magazines, and a couple of couches straight from a 1980s sitcom.

"Mr. Mack! How could we assist you today, sir?" the attendant requested.

Mack leans on the front desk and flashes a shy grin to the seated attendant. He drops his head and shakes it before placing an elbow on the table to support his weight.

"If someone could point me into the direction of Lavender Baronne, that would be an eternal blessing!" Mack explained.

The attendant's gracious smile faded into a grimace. She looked away from the older gentleman to search the computer system for any possible leads. Once she completed her search, she stood up and walked around the desk.

"If you wouldn't mind, I'm going to send you down this hallway to speak with someone in the nursing department," the attendant directed.

Mack nods his head in agreement as the attendant waves her identification card past the sensor. A beep sounds and a green light flashes before the attendant unseals the door. She stands back to allow an unobscured path for her elder. Mack obliges the sincere gesture and moseys beyond the checkpoint. Once the door secures behind him, the attendant fades from view.

Mack sauntered down the cluttered hall, mostly filled with the sounds of disenfranchised patients. The narrow hallway's only interruption came from the light so many feet away. As he approached the lit area, the shrieks and shrills of the sullen met in a symphony of sorrow. Pleas to return home played in multiple keys. Once bathed in the glow, Mack saw a spectrum of emotions across a span of a few meters. Some patients wanted to get out; some preferred to remain; others...well...didn't truly look like they were there at all. Mack looks about the location for someone who may know where Lavender is, but he has no idea where to start.

"Can I help you, sir? You appear a little lost?" a voice called from Mack's rear.

Mack rotated 180 degrees to find a fairer skinned woman with green eyes and long black hair flowing past the brim of her scrubs. Her ebony hair flowed fluently over the magenta scrubs; even those areas creased by her glasses. The only thing more inviting than the words wrapped in her southern drawl was the smile she held after they were long gone. Mack inspected the woman carefully before crafting a response.

"I, umm...I surely hope so, ma'am. I was hoping to find my sister here, but no one seated over there quite fits her description," Mack provided.

"That's awfully sweet of you to come and visit. Especially at this time of night. I would imagine you have something important to tell her," the technician determined.

"Yes. I truly do," Mack reiterated.

"Well, if you give me her name, we could look her up and see where she is located," the tech advised.

"Sure thing. Her name is..." Mack began but caught himself.

He turned away from the technician to scan the room again. A clear glaze of moisture covered the elder's eyeballs as the failure in his search became more apparent. When his eyes returned to her, he could do no more than shake his head.

"I'm sorry, sir, I didn't quite catch that name. Who was it again?" the technician requested again.

"No, apologies are all mine. I was temporarily distracted. I am here for Lavender Baronne. *THE* Lavender Baronne!" Mack repeated.

The technician glared at Mr. Wellington's request. She then forced a fraction of a grin while biting her lip and looking away. The technician shook her head in a manner similar to the dismay the pastor felt.

"As I am certain you are aware, sir, Ms. Baronne has been missing for quite a while. I really wish I could have been more helpful," the technician informed.

Mack pushed the disappointment out of his nostrils

and inhaled acknowledgment of that which he already knew: Lavender is long gone! Mack's lips formed into a near smile that served as a mask against his tears.

"I bet you are. Well, I guess I'll be going now. Hope I didn't trouble you too much," Mack conceded.

Mack spun himself toward the main lobby. Even with his back to her, the technician would not take her eyes off Mack. She fell victim to her own empathy as he reached the door and awaited the buzz. Mack raised his hand when he stood a few feet from the door. He waited roughly fifteen seconds for the technician to release the lock before he began to stroll back toward her station. The technician watched him return to the ignited portion of the room. He looked at the technician sternly before requesting his release.

"Did I forget anything, ma'am? Did you find anything regarding my sister?" Mack wondered.

"I personally did not; however, we do have a patient who she was fairly close to. She won't give us much, but she might be more willing to help you," the technician indicated.

Mack gaped solemnly at the technician for a time. He then broke his demeanor by shrugging his shoulders. Mack let out a vicious cough that rattled his lungs. Once composed, he was able to address the technician.

"Contrary to my wicked sinuses, I believe I have time on my side," Mack accepted.

"That's good to hear. If you sit here for a minute, I can have someone bring the patient in so you all can chat," the technician settled.

The technician directed Mack to a table somewhat secluded from the remainder of the leisure area. Mack glared at the technician before obliging her request. Once he reached the table, he sat and patiently awaited the arrival of his sister's peer. Mack watched the technician from the moment she picked up the phone to locate the patient until the moment she looked back at him and confirmed the patient was in route.

Chapter 38

Nature vs. Nurture

"I have no son!"

"I love you, JuJu!"

"You are a thrill-seeking vigilante, Renaldo Brown, and one day you might not be so lucky!"

"HOME! That is where you need to be, Renaldo!"

"Julissa!"

"I took an oath...."

"Have you?!"

"Julissa! Don't you hear me?"

"I was protecting you."

"Protecting me?!"

"JULISSA RENEE...Have you lost your damn mind?!" Cortissa's voice ripped through Julissa's flashbacks.

Julissa's upper torso whipped around frantically to face her mother. Even in acknowledging Cortissa's presence, she didn't utter a word. Julissa sat on her bed and looked out the window as if she was ready for something to return. *Someone* to return. Someway... somehow. She turned back toward Cortissa with a frown no more welcoming than a lump of coal.

"I'll take that as a yes," Cortissa assumed.

Julissa, expecting nothing less from her...dear... mother traced Cortissa's body with her eyes before she guided her gaze back through the pane. Cortissa, identifying her child's displeasure, unhinged herself from the door seal and unfolded her arms. She exhaled prior to joining Julissa on the far side of the bed. Before Cortissa could rest her bottom, Julissa scooted closer to the headboard. Cortissa feigned an attempt to place a hand on Julissa's shoulder but the descendent shrugged it off. Cortissa rolled her eyes at her daughter but eventually scooted closer anyway.

"I know you're hurting right now, baby. I don't know what I would do without Paul..." Cortissa began.

Julissa shot a look of despair to Cortissa. Cortissa inched toward Julissa and grabbed her closest hand. Cortissa squeezed her daughter's hand as she brought it near her own lap.

"Now look, I know we have not always gotten along, but that doesn't change the fact that you are my daughter, and I will always be here for you. You may be okay being couped up in here all day but let me take the kids so you can have some time to think," Cortissa suggested.

Julissa's forehead curled at her mother's suggestion. She gritted her teeth while one leg bounced feverishly. She sat on the bed nearly hunched over while one hand gripped onto the headboard. Her torso rocked back and forth before she settled and stared at Cortissa.

"Okay," Julissa squeaked.

Julissa stood up and gingerly trotted to the window. She then sat along the window seal and faced her mother, who remained supportive despite Julissa's icy disposition. Her eyes winced as she took another gander out of the window but saw no sign of what she desired. Julissa exhaled deeply as she held back tears. Though her mother could likely see her discontent, she did not need to confirm her sorrows.

"You know what, let us keep them a few days, dear. Me and ole Paul may get a room out here or something like that so Judy can go to school. Whatever we need to do to make it easier on you, honey, we'll figure it out. Just a couple of days, until Friday anyway, honey," Cortissa pled.

"Okay," Julissa muttered.

Julissa still stared on as Cortissa stood up and slowly came toward her. Julissa heard one of her mother's missteps and looked over her shoulder toward her. Cortissa noticed Julissa's defensive posture and placed her hands on Julissa's shoulders. Julissa preferred to not be touched at the moment, but she also had no desire to argue with her mother. Two of the last people she argued with were no longer available to provide a rebuttal. Personally, Julissa wouldn't mind such circumstances with Cortissa, but she also didn't know if she'd be able to stomach another person leaving her indefinitely.

"Do you have Halloween costumes for the kids? I'm sure I could find a potato sack or something for little Paul. That juicy little bundle of a man," Cortissa poked, attempting to lighten the mood.

Julissa delayed a moment before addressing her mother again. She'd prefer to have taken Peerless on his first Halloween outing herself, but she knew she was in no mood to go out into the world while she was still a mess on the inside.

"Yes, ma'am. They are in Peerless' closet in his room. Didn't want Judy to see what I got her until the day of.

Guess it wouldn't hurt for her to see it now, right," Julissa figured.

"Right, babygirl. I'll go and gather everything. You just take the time you need, okay. Give me your car keys so I can get the hunky potato's car seat," Cortissa gestured.

"They are right by the door. I appreciate you taking them for a little bit, Mom. I'll only need a couple of days to get my head straight," Julissa predicted.

Cortissa nodded at Julissa's claim while gently rubbing her back. She patted Julissa's shoulders just before she turned to exit the room. Though Cortissa discreetly closed the door, Julissa still heard the clasp lock. Julissa held both arms folded as she peered over her own shoulder to the barrier separating her from the rest of the world. Julissa looked back out of her window as she tightened the band on her robe. Julissa drooped her head and placed one hand on the window, as if she was soaking in the remaining remnants of the setting sun. She gathered what was left of herself emotionally and decided to exit her chambers. She nearly stumbled at the sight of the rail, remembering her last shouting match with Renaldo. She reenacted her steps to the banister where she stood in complete disgust the last time he was home. She blamed him then for not being more considerate of the family, and now blamed herself for letting him walk out of the hospital angry, confused, and possibly to his own demise.

Judy sprinted out of the kitchen towards the door as Cortissa hauled Peerless in one arm and a bag of milk in the other. The sight brought a slight grin to Julissa's face as she watched Judy move in excitement. Judy noticed her mother standing atop the staircase and flashed a big smile at her.

"Mommy, Mommy, Grammy is going to take us trick or treating. Can I eat all of Prentiss' candy? Can I? Can I?!" Judy gleamed.

Julissa held onto the railing and shook her head as she walked down to see her children off. She walked over to Judy and kneeled directly in front of her. Cortissa stood by with Peerless to capture the interaction between her daughter and granddaughter.

"That sounds great, baby. I'm sure he won't mind," Julissa joked.

They both laughed at the notion as Julissa played with Judy's hair. She then looked at Cortissa, gave a confirming nod, and stood to her feet, while gently cupping Judy's face.

"I need you to be grandma's little helper and make sure nobody gives Peerless anything he can choke on, okay? Show me how much of a big girl you are, okay!" Julissa encouraged.

"I got it, Mommy. Peter is going to be okay with me!" Judy reassured.

Julissa and Cortissa both laughed at the little girl while she butchered her brother's name. Julissa concealed her face as she nearly laughed herself into tears. Cortissa grinned as she picked up Peerless' carriage. Julissa then leaned over to kiss each of her children on the forehead. Afterwards, Cortissa guided Judy to the door and allowed her to open it. As Julissa attempted to assist with the children's belongings, Cortissa snatched the diaper bag from her and motioned for her to remain inside. Julissa complied with her mother's request as she watched the kids get loaded into the car from the front porch.

"Bye, Mommy!! I hope Daddy is here by the time we

get back," Judy called from the car.

Cortissa's facial expression was undoubtedly mortified. She stared back to Julissa and quickly shook her head while holding her palm out toward her daughter. She then strapped Peerless into his seat and gently tickled his belly. Julissa waived to the car from the moment Cortissa turned the key in the ignition until the vehicle cleared the driveway. Once they were out of view, Julissa walked in the house and shut the door. As she latched the last lock, she placed her forehead on the door and winced once more, this time at sheer silence.

Julissa turned her back to the door and slid down the frame, nearly into a stupor. She cried, discreetly at first, then boldly and loudly as if she wanted all to hear. Julissa then let out a treacherous wail that lasted nearly five seconds. She leaned her head over to her left hand and gripped the frontal portion of her hair as she drained the tear ducts a little longer. Julissa exhaled all the frustrations she felt inside and inhaled hopes of a better tomorrow. *Tomorrow. That's it!* "I just need to get through the night," Julissa thought to herself.

Julissa began to recuperate as she pulled herself up from her sunken place and walked into the kitchen. She opened up the pantry door empty-handed and exited with a bottle of wine. After Julissa found her bottle opener, she opened a cupboard to search for a suitable glass.

"Ehh. Fuck it," Julissa blurted as she shut the cupboard door.

Julissa shrugged her shoulders, gripped her bottle, and made her way back into the living room. Julissa looked around, this time taking more comfort in the silence before turning off all lights on the bottom floor. She sauntered up the stairs, nearly renewed but still feeling the effects of the last few days. On the way up, she caught a glimpse of herself in one of the reflective pieces on the wall. She noticed her snowy streak of hair had widened over the past few months. She initially appeared concerned, but a beaming grin proved otherwise. Overall, Julissa knew things were going to be okay even if they were nowhere near what they used to be.

Chapter 39

Trials and Tribulations

The day was here! After so many hours of delegation and discontent over what this could mean, not just for Crescent City but the entire Eastbank Parish, the hotly anticipated moment was on the horizon. The Eastbank Parish Court was steaming with eagerness. Who was to blame? Did the mentees of the Fifth Ward Hogs start this matter, or did they finish it? *Which is worse?* What came first? Though the decision was calculated by the jury, it was the judge who would be delivering the message.

Tony Nguyen sat alongside Ashely Archibald, for what most certainly should be the last time, and if not, hopefully for a long time. His family remained in the rear of the courtroom as Mrs. Nguyen tensely observed. She wrapped herself around Mr. Nguyen as if she was afraid the police could take him too. Reg Leg was present as well, dressed in a grey suit, blue shirt, and speckled tie. The Hall family wasn't present, but they'd sent words of encouragement through Reg Leg. The considerate gesture was appreciated yet ineffective for a mother on the most important day she never imagined.

Detective Barrios and Lieutenant Morial sat in a pew

off to the left. Barrios was interested as to whether the matter would truly be resolved, even once the verdict was read. It was genuinely a convoluted story that was now accompanied by further winding roads leading to a cliff.

"Any word on what Travis thinks might happen today?" Rita posed.

"Not even an inkling. His nerves are just as shot as ours. Did you visit the Browns?" Morial asked.

"Not yet, I—"

Detective Barrios was interrupted by the bailiff and his announcement of Judge Burgess' arrival. All parties stood and acknowledged the Honorable Judge Burgess before retaking to their seats.

"Good morning to you all and I thank you for taking time to be here today. I am aware the interest in this matter is at a peak and it also explains why the jury was very careful and selective in their deliberation. I would personally like to thank all of these jurors who were consumed with this decision for almost an entire week," Judge Burgess opened.

In the brief silence observed during a pause in the judge's delivery, the eyes of the crowd diverted toward the defense table in anticipation. While most participants wanted Judge Burgess to get straight to the decision, Tony was perfectly fine with a dialogue that would build further suspense by delay. It was his freedom on the line! His future! His *forever*?!

"It is important for all to realize that recently the State of Louisiana has made it mandatory that all jury trials are now decided by unanimous decisions, not majority," Judge Burgess informed.

As she educated the masses, most of the law professionals shook their heads in agreement. There were a few puzzled looks in the crowd accompanied by some sheer amazement. The former method had led to some pretty controversial rulings in prior cases of The Boot. With a unanimous decision, jury members were forced to truly look through all evidence provided as well as the preponderance of the law.

"With such a task, yet a burden, placed on jurors, I have the utmost confidence that the decision rendered is derived from dedication to justice, and not a designation to haste. I once again acknowledge the twelve jurors for the time they took and will recognize it as a testament to their commitment to make the correct decision," Judge Burgess announced.

With the closing of her statement, Judge Burgess looked over to the bailiff, who awaited the decision of the jurors with an open hand. A young lady with glasses and hair tied into a bun walked up to deliver a piece of paper containing the final word in the "Great Debate." Chris quickly passed the folded paper to Judge Burgess, who put her glasses on for the first time within the course of the trial. Judge Burgess inspected the document thoroughly as she masked her lips to avoid mouthing the verdict. Once she'd fully inspected the results, she carefully placed the paper on the desk and framed the edges of it with her fingertips. She then placed the tips of her left hand approximately in the center of the note as the palm mounted. The right hand deliberately slid the glasses from her face and placed them to the flank.

"I humbly order you all that I will need your complete cooperation as I read the verdicts. I would ask that you hold any expression, applause, or other noise until all charges have been read," Judge Burgess commanded.

Ashley nudged Tony to advise him to stand for the judge's recital of the verdict. Tony's eyes couldn't mask his initial hesitation, but he followed the directive of his counsel. Travis too stood for the delivery of the results. Judge Burgess took notice of the men's initiative and proceeded with a subtle smile and grin.

"Please listen carefully as the verdict is being delivered. On the count of disturbing the peace, the jury finds Tony Nguyen guilty. On one count of reckless operation, the jury finds the defendant guilty," Judge Burgess unveiled.

The reciting of the verdict was disrupted by a boisterous cry from the pews. Mrs. Nguyen was as confused as everyone else until she looked over to her husband, who tried to cover his face so Tony wouldn't know. To no avail; Tony heard his father wail similarly to when he thought he would lose the family business. It had been a long time since he heard his father weep so openly, and he hoped it would be the last time. Tony's vision became distorted as he almost accompanied his father with tears. Mrs. Burgess waited for Mrs. Nguyen to comfort Mr. Nguyen before reading further.

"Chris, could you please bring this tissue over to that family," Judge Burgess gestured.

"Sure thing, Judge." Chris complied as he grabbed the box of Kleenex and trotted over to the bench separating the participants from the onlookers. An elderly lady seated two rows in front of the Nguyen family strolled to the partition and retrieved the box. She then walked up to Mrs. Nguyen and gave her a soothing smile along with the box of tissue. Mrs. Nguyen tilted her head in appreciation before taking out a few sheets for her sullen husband.

"For the one count of resisting arrest, Mr. Tony Nguyen is found not guilty. And lastly, for the two counts of first-degree murder...the jury states the defendant, Tony Nguyen, is...*not* guilty!" Judge Burgess read from her card.

Chatters rattled through the room as Mr. Nguyen jumped up from his seat and embraced his wife. While some were happy for the Nguyen family, others were in pure disgust that multiple lives were lost and unaccounted for. Detective Barrios and Lieutenant Morial glanced at one another while shaking off the result. Even Travis peered back toward them in amazement, but the C.C.P.D. representatives were unmoved. The chatters were becoming rumbles before Judge Burgess intervened. She tapped her gavel two times before nearly splitting the cork on the third.

"Order in the court! ORDER!" Judge Burgess commanded.

Her force nearly clattered any item not nailed to the ground. The court's clatter ceased. The room was nearly silent aside from the whimpers of a young man who had just witnessed a miracle in real time. Tony's forehead was nearly buried in the table while mixed tears flowed from his face. His body trembled, with each breath he took becoming more difficult than the last. Tony lifted his head with reddened eyes and a moistened palate above his lip. He shut his eyes and began to breathe slowly while Judge Burgess addressed the court.

"Mr. Archibald, I ask that you make sure your client is here in the next two weeks to receive his sentencing. I also would like you to relay that the offenses he has been convicted of hold either a fine, time served, or a combination of both. Please further advise that if he is not present on the day of the disposition, there will be a warrant issued for his arrest and he will be detained for a period to be determined at a later date," Judge Burgess ruled.

Ashley places a hand on Tony's shoulder while nodding his compliance to Judge Brown. Detective Barrios and Lieutenant Morial had seen enough and decide to leave ahead of the crowd. Ashely leans over to share the Judge's orders with Tony. Tony tosses his head back, still damp from his own tears.

"Yes, ma'am. I mean...Your Honor. I will be here. Thank you so much. Thank all of you so much!" Tony exclaimed.

As Chris motions for those present to stand, Judge Burgess warns that "Court is adjourned." The mouths moved swifter than the legs of the attendees as chatter of bewilderment and confusion began to swoon. Some couldn't help but to peek over to the jury and wonder what went through their minds to not charge the young man with murder or resisting. As Judge Burgess vanished into her chambers, the clamors of the crowd became louder.

Rita and Lieutenant Morial made it to the ground floor of the court prior to everyone else. They'd exited the courtroom and now stood on the steps only ten feet from the front door. Rita is standing on the step with her arms folded while looking down at her feet.

"You okay, Barrios? You know you did really well with that investigation, don'tcha?" Morial examined.

"That sounds good, but I wish I'd done enough to have him convicted. Who's to say something like this won't happen again? What message did the court just send?" Rita documented.

"He wasn't charged with murder. Those other charges he took could result in some jail time or at least probation. He should be under somebody's thumb in a little while," Morial consoled.

Rita initially shook her head then nodded in agreement. A Channel 4 News truck pulled up at the foot of the stairs. Then herds of other media sources gathered on the stairs in anticipation of the reporting opportunity to come. Without much delay, Travis walked out of the door first. One reporter tried to mirror his movements down the stairs, but Travis declined an interview as he scurried away. Once Travis found Rita and Lieutenant Morial, he walked over for a briefing.

"Maybe not quite what we were looking for, but at least something stuck," Travis settled.

"Not a big deal; we lose some and we win some, right?" Morial directed at Rita.

"I guess," Rita uttered.

As they watched on, the media crowd became amped. They turned to find Ashley Archibald and his client exiting the courthouse. The media outlets surrounded the young man and his family as they all jockeyed for position. The rush of the crowd almost robbed Tony Nguyen of his breath; he felt as if the cameras were closing in. He attempted a gasp but received nothing in return. The questions came faster than his inhalations. Tony's parents were able to dodge the media circus, but his attorney and mentor stood firmly behind him.

"Tony! Tony! You must be relieved to not be convicted of murder, sir. Can you put into words how you feel?"

Tony heard clearly from one reporter.

Tony and his camp turned their heads to address the right reporter. A hand went up further into the crowd, but there was no sign of a microphone from the individual. Just a black male dressed in a T-shirt and jeans. He lifted both arms simultaneously while Reg Leg carefully watched. Tony is frozen by what he witnessed but Reg Leg knocks him forward before a loud "POW...POW-POW-POW" sounds off. While others scattered, Detective Barrios raced toward the gunfire. Detective Barrios slowed her pace once she gained sight of the man, nearly frozen by the familiarity.

The gunman noticed Detective Barrios and he turned to open fire in her direction. She instantly gained her nerve again and ran toward the weapon-wielding bastard. The assassin came on target just before Barrios was knocked out of the way by a mysterious figure. The intervener fell to the ground with Rita and rolled over while cradling her in the process. As Rita rolled away from the man, he stood up and shot at the mad gunman. The slayer took a bullet in his shooting arm, knocking the appendage out of the air and the firearm from his grasp. The momentary inconvenience was enough to distract the gunman as officers on duty surrounded him and drove him to the pavement.

Rita searched the area for the man who pushed her out of the line of fire. She looked around until she located him: a slender gentleman in a tan suit and peculiar glasses. A face she'd seen before with a scent she admired, even from afar. She wandered toward the acquaintance while on-duty authorities sorted out the mess.

"When did you get here? Why did you get...are you

here?" Rita posed.

"I was interested in the verdict. Seems I got here a little late though," Rance answered.

"Nah. I beg to differ," Rita chimed back.

Lieutenant Morial jogged toward Rita until he saw her rescuer. He slowed himself to a snail's pace as he watched their interaction continue. A hand tapped him on his shoulder, nearly frightening him. Lieutenant Morial spun around to face a uniformed officer. His eyes widened as he awaited the reason for the officer's interruption.

"Oh, I'm sorry to startle you, sir. I really believe there is something over here that you need to see," the officer advised.

"Okay, you lead the way," Morial huffed.

The officer led Morial back towards the stairs of the Eastbank Parish Court. Lieutenant Morial noticed with his own eyes that officers were still corralling the alleged shooter. Morial then canvassed the scene until he locked his eyes on Mr. and Mrs. Nguyen watching a body being loaded onto a gurney. Mrs. Nguyen bawled while Mr. Nguyen shielded his face. "Oh no," the lieutenant thought to himself. He rushed ahead of the escorting officer to the open ambulance.

"WAIT! WAIT! I work homicide for the C.C.P.D!" Morial shouted to the EMS staff.

The staffers came to a halt just prior to lowering the legs of the gurney and placing it onto the ambulance. Morial circled around the other side of the gurney to allow the EMS staff to shield the victim's face from the public. As they unzipped the body bag, Morial's eyes bulged. As Morial gawked at the victim, he could hear the whimpering of a young male nearby. Tony Nguyen was being held up by his parents as the tears streamed down his naïve mug.

"WHYYYYYYYY! HE DIDN'T DO NOTHING, MAN!" Tony wailed as his family fought to hold him away from the ambulance.

Morial looked over to the shooter to notice he was being checked out by additional EMS staff. He marched to the slayer, with tears forming in the ducts of his own eyes. As he closed in, Morial became incensed at his presence. Once in close proximity, Morial bumped the EMS dressing the wound out of the way as he came face-to-face with the handcuffed gunman.

"What the fuck did you just do?!" Morial gritted.

"They couldn't get away with what they did. They took down my brothers. I'm taking out some of theirs!" Officer Remy Daniels boasted ignorantly.

"Oh, I see...NEITHER ONE OF US ARE SURE OF WHAT THE HELL YOU JUST DID!!" Morial barked directly in Daniels' face.

The emergency staff began to dress Daniels' wound once again, this time silently requesting the lieutenant to back away. The supervising officers moved closer to ensure the safety of the decorated C.C.P.D. supervisor.

"And I'm gonna make sure it nev—" Remy began before a rude intrusion by Morial's flying fist.

Morial socked Remy well enough to knock him and the EMS staff off balance and nearly into the bushes. Morial's eyes had become engorged with rage and disgust. Two officers grabbed Lieutenant Morial and moved him away from the site. As he was being escorted, he thought he heard Remy laughing in the distance. Morial tried to pull away from the officers, but they kept him hemmed despite sacrificing their original position.

"Let me go, got dammit! Y'all just make sure to take his ass straight to the parish jail! Don't pass go or collect not two cents for that sorry motherfucker," Morial ordered.

The officers escorted Morial to the other end of the building so he would not have an opportunity to strike Daniels again. Morial jerked his arms away from the officers and threw them up in surrender. The officers accepted this feigned forfeit and left the lieutenant to his own devices. Morial searched for Rita and Rance, but they'd apparently departed the scene. He pulled out his phone and called Rita's cell. It rang multiple times before rolling to voicemail. Morial almost hung up but thought it better to leave a message instead.

"Rita, I don't know if you are aware of this, but we may have some trouble on our hands. Remy Daniels has gone rogue and may have damned us all to hell in his gullible plight for street justice. Reginald Joseph has been pronounced dead, and pretty soon, we will find out if the Fifth Ward Hogs truly cease to exist. So...get ready, this whole ordeal may be a long way from over!" Morial telegraphed.

Morial hung up the phone instantly, declining the option to review the message before sending. If Rita wasn't ready before to take on the biggest outlaws Crescent City had to offer, she may have been in line for a crash course. In consideration of everything that transpired to this point, Morial knew somebody would need to face the city's impending doom. If not the ranks of the C.C.P.D...then who?!

Chapter 40

A Piece of Mind

Mack sat patiently as he awaited the nurse technician's return. He peered over his shoulder, but there was no one coming back down the hallway. He inventoried the multiple personalities that were presented a few feet from where he sat: some appeared dead to the world, others looked like they were life of the party. Mack became surly wondering how people could survive in a place this dreary. Was the scene Mack witnessed the reason Lavender may have left them behind for good?

The tech walked down the hall with a frail younger ebony woman, whose hair was ruffled about her head. Mack stood up at his table as he waited for the two ladies to join him. As the technician neared, Mack stared until the ebony beauty was within his view.

"Hello there, dear. My name is Mack. I hope I'm not disturbing anything you may have had planned for the night," Mack introduced.

Mack stuck out his hand for a shake, but the stranger looked at it, folded one arm across her chest and combed through her hair with the other. Mack understood the possible discomfort and positioned the hand to instead invite the woman to have a seat. She looked at the tech, who reiterated the request. The woman obliged by sitting down. The technician then placed both hands around the woman's shoulders as they faced Mack.

"This lady here likes to go by 'Honey.' I believe she may be able to answer some questions regarding your sister, sir," the technician informed.

"Thank you for your help, dear. Do you believe that Honey and I can have a minute to speak, in private?" Mack requested.

"I can't exactly give you two a private room, you know, considering where we are. But I can return to my station while you guys catch up," the technician explained.

"That seems fine to me. How about you, Honey?" Mack insisted.

Honey lifted her eyes, and nothing more, from the tabletop to acknowledge the technician. The technician curled her lip and gave a slight yet confirming nod. She then walked toward her station, momentarily taking Mack's eyes with her. Once the technician was back at her post, Mack sighed and turned his face to Honey. Honey raised the remainder of her face up from the table as she stared off seemingly beyond Mack. Mack tried to trace her line of sight with his own eyes, but all roads led back to the technician. Mack turned his body Honey's direction to provide her with his undivided attention.

"Who is she?" Honey squeaked.

"I thought you knew her. You didn't ask her name wh—"

"No. Not her," Honey interrupted.

Mack looked back toward the tech but there was no one standing near her. He stared into Honey's eyes and tried to follow her line of sight yet again, but the results remained consistent. He wasn't sure if Honey was prone to hallucinations, but he was careful not to insult her.

"Uh. There's nobody else up there, dear. Who do you mean?" Mack inquired.

"Your sister. Who is she?" Honey cleared up.

"Oh," Mack began. "That's what you mean. My sister is Lavender. Lavender Baronne. Are you familiar with her?"

"I used to be," Honey answered.

"Seems we have something in common," Mack jabbed.

A feeble grin flashed fleetingly across Honey's otherwise bare face. Her silhouetted lips twinged before responding to the older gentleman.

"I had a family once," Honey blurted.

"Well, of course you do. You should still have one now unless something tragic happened," Mack responded.

"Yeah, something like that," Honey emphasized.

Honey's eyes returned to the table as she cupped each elbow in the opposite hand and leaned forward. She pursed her lips to blow away the smallest inconsistency resting on the table. Mack watched carefully as Honey discreetly disposed of the insignificant inconvenience that lay before her. He then gently planted his hand on the table, inadvertently distracting Honey from her chosen pastime. Honey adjusted herself upright, with her ankles crossed and the balls of her feet planted on the floor.

"Well, we can talk about your family first, if that would make you more comfortable," Mack gestured as he tried to gather her irises in his.

Honey offered her off-kilter smirk to her elder. This time her eyes were firmly planted on his peppered mug.

Mack took note of the attention and removed the pre-viously planted palm from the canvas.

"There ain't much to talk about. You win some, you lose some, you live to fight off another day," Honey recited.

Mack blinked rapidly at Honey's dissertation on family. He wasn't quite certain how to proceed.

"Well, fortunately we are all brothers and sisters in God's eyes. Jesus' bloodline is oft the only you can depend on to last for all time," Mack preached.

"So, how many of your sisters in Christ have you fucked? Brothers?" Honey poked.

Mack nervously scoffed at Honey's account. While his head dropped in amazement, Honey's eyes settled again on the tech. Mack noticed Honey's focused gaze as he now had her back in his sights.

"I do not mean to pry, young lady. I understand I am asking you for help, so I don't mind sharing some words that I hope would positively impact you along the way," Mack explained.

"Well, if you must know," Honey began with her eyes still on the tech. "My family found it easier to write me off than to help me righten my path."

Mack grimaced at this sad yet legitimate fact provided. He turned to his left as he lightly yet rhythmically tapped the base of his hands against their shared table. After-wards, Mack stroked the length of his forehead with his fingers.

"Do they keep in touch at all? Maybe come to see you in person?" Mack inquired.

"Not enough for it to matter," Honey stated bluntly.

"Be that as it may, I do believe we share someone who cared about both of us at one time: Lavender," Mack coaxed.

Honey's eyes returned to the elder while she checked for authenticity. She inconspicuously lifted her rump from the chair to adjust and leaned forward on the table.

"How do I know you really cared about her, though? I've seen you come in here to visit in the past. It don't seem like you ever had any intentions of helping her get out!" Honey accused.

Mack was taken aback by Honey's faulty insinuation. He gave her a thorough look over before parting his lips to address the lofty claim.

"Well, I don't know how you landed here, Miss Honey, but Lavender was court ordered to be here. It don't matter what I say. It's up to some goof in a black dress reading a few white sheets of paper, if ya know what I mean," Mack endorsed.

Honey placed her elbows onto the table and interlocked her fingers to support her chin. She smirked wildly as she glared into Mack's general direction.

"So, what else have you done to help her besides showing up here and probably making empty promises that 'everything is gonna be alright'?" Honey mocked.

"She and I had a plan to get her out of here. I always encouraged her to do what they asked so she could get out of this hellhole—excuse my expression!" Mack voiced.

"You'll hear no argument from me," Honey quickly chimed.

For the first time, Honey squeezed out a genuine laugh. Her pleasant expression began to alter as she viewed someone approaching from Mack's rear. Mack swung his head around to realize the tech advancing toward them. He peered over his shoulder briefly before turning back to Honey for his last-ditch effort.

"If you know where she might be, it would be a great service for you to tell me. I still plan on making the people who put her here pay! And dearly!" Mack described.

Just as he finished his statement, the tech impeded their vicinity and occupied a space near Honey. Mack looked at the attendant and grinned while Honey's eyes diverted to the table.

"I don't want to intrude on your excursion, mister... mister...? What is your name again, sir? I don't believe I caught it," the tech requested.

"Wellington. Mack Wellington, to be precise," Mack reiterated.

Mack closed his greeting with a painstaking smile, followed by an obvious frown. The tech provided a warm grin of her own. Honey's eyes traveled back and forth between the two parties as if she awaited the results.

"Of course. Mr. Mack, if you wouldn't mind, that is all the time we have for the meeting this evening. You are more than welcome to come back tomorrow or during our normal visitation period. You are aware of those hours, I presume?" the tech directed.

"Yeah, sure, I get the drill, ma'am. Miss Honey, I thank you for your time and conversation. I hope you enjoyed my company as well, despite the brevity," Mack complied while rolling his eyes at the tech.

Mack arose from the chair as the tech walked toward him to assist. He waived off her advance as he grabbed his cane from the chair. Mack twisted his lip as he stole one last glimpse of Honey, whose head faced the table but eyes sought the tech. Mack began his trek out of the common area before Honey addressed him again.

"I don't think she got too far," Honey blurted.

Mack and the tech each spun around to face Honey. Honey was now fixated on the tech.

"Excuse me, I'm sorry. What was that?" Mack asked.

"Your sister. I don't think she's run off too far. She might just be looking for a reason to come home," Honey divulged.

"Well," Mack began while smirking at the tech, "that is surely something to consider. I guess I need to work on that, don't I?"

The tech shrugged her shoulders and turned toward the exit as Mack followed suit. As they approached the tech station, Honey called out to Mack again.

"Where is he?" Honey asked.

"He who?" Mack questioned.

"Lavender told me she has a son. She used to talk about him all the time, but he's never been here to see her. She was losing her mind being away from him," Honey clarified.

The tech squinted her eyes at Honey while Mack stared at his cane. He looked at the tech and gave a brief grimace before adjusting his sights onto Honey.

"How much has she told you about him exactly?" Mack investigated.

"A whole lot," Honey answered plainly.

"Well, then you probably know why he hasn't been here," Mack fired back.

Mack looked to the tech once more, this time with a heightened inclination to leave. The tech took notice of Mack's frustration and aided him in his scurry.

"You know what?" Honey shouted as she stood up, staring in their general vicinity. "That Lavender was a true

Southern belle. You know one movie she always said she loved?"

Mack's interest was piqued as he sought to solve Honey's query. He took a moment and leaned on the nearest wall as he soaked in Honey's peculiarities.

"Lavender loved many movies while we were growing up. There are so many choices. How about you give me a hint," Mack conceded.

"*Steel Magnolias.* If I were you, I'd take time to check it out. You may be able to connect with Lavender well enough to narrow your search," Honey warned.

Mack was rather impressed with Honey's summation of Lavender's possible whereabouts. He rolled his eyes toward the tech as he gave a dim wave and bow. The tech pressed the automatic button under her desk to allow Mack to depart. Mack quickly meandered out of the section. He turned for one last gander of the area's inhabitants before the door sealed for good. Without further delay, Mack rushed out of the Beech Grove Manor entry door and into the Crescent City night!

Chapter 41

A Misty Brew

Luther Vandross' "Bad Boys" is playing through the speakers of the shotgun house in the lower Ninth Ward. A few men are gathered together for a night of chords, calamity, and cards. The fellows are having a good time talking shit and taking snacks...well, aside from one glum member.

"Hold up, chief. You can't have that book. You reneged! You ain't watch the board little boy blue?" a bald-headed man shouts to Lieutenant Morial.

"Man, prove that shit. You show me where I shoulda' played a club and I didn't. Where the proof?" Morial challenges.

The bald man reached over to Morial's partner and ruffled through a few of the books until he found the hand where Morial's spade took the hand of clubs. He slammed the four cards down on the table while snatching the newest book of cards away.

"Got dammit, we done been set! We ain't gon make enough books with these few lil' cards left!" Morial's partner exclaimed.

Morial hopped up from the table and tossed his cards

across it. He stumped out of the living room down the hallway to the kitchen. Morial's portly partner, Doc Smith, tapped the bald-headed guy on the shoulder and gently placed his cards on the table. Doc Smith stood up and followed Morial.

"He must've lost his mind throwing them cards down on my table like that. My mama gave me this table," the bald man reasoned to his partner. The partner nodded in agreeance with his claims while laughing at his shenanigans.

As Doc entered the kitchen, he saw Morial leaning against the fridge, with one hand draped over it. When the lieutenant noticed Doc enter, he removed his arm from the fridge, grabbed the handle of the freezer, and pulled out a beer. He tilted the can towards Doc to see if he also would like a beverage, but Doc Smith declined. Morial then closed the door and leaned on the fridge while popping the top off his drink.

"Man, you alright?" Doc Smith inquired.

Morial nodded his head before slightly sliding his back down the fridge. He took a sip of his drink and released a sigh.

"I'm fine, man. Just hate losing my money to Bill," Morial answered.

"Yeah, we all do, trust me. Still, in all, man, I ain't never seen you act like that over a few dollars. You sure you alright?" Doc checked.

Morial used his free hand to swipe his mouth of residual beer. He looked at Doc intently before taking another swig and repeating his wiping ritual. Morial stood up from his relatively relaxed stance, walked over to the kitchen table, and sat down. Doc watched him in all his infinite glory and decided to sit across from Morial. Doc and Morial exchanged glares briefly until they were interrupted.

"You simple motherfuckers coming back to the table or y'all gon' sit in here and drink up all my damn beer? You don't think you gave me enough money already?" Bill teased.

Morial shot a staunch look at Bill while taking a longer guzzle from the can. Doc shook his head and snickered at the homeowner while shooing him away.

"We'll be back out there, man, we ain't going no-where," Doc pled.

"Alright nah! I bet not hear that back door slam. I know where to find you two law abiding crooks," Bill poked.

Morial forced a brief grin as he gazed at the tabletop. Doc sat back in his seat with his arms crossed, laughing jovially at Bill's remarks. Bill chuckled, then did a little shimmy back down the long hallway to another room. When Morial finally lifted his eyes from the table, Doc was already awaiting him.

"You don't think I forgot, did you?" Doc spoke.

Morial rolled his eyes and got up from his seat to discard the empty can into the trash. Morial braced himself on the nearby counter, posturing and pondering.

"Been a crazy year, man. A really crazy year, that's all," Morial conceded.

"I'm sure for your department it's been a crazy *few* years. Ever since police been shooting people on camera, it's made a lotta folks defensive," Doc added.

"Yeah, that's true. You want a drink?" Morial deflected.

Doc Smith waived his buddy off and motioned for him to come back to the table and sit. Morial rotated his eyes as he agreed to the directive. The lieutenant sat sideways in the chair with one elbow resting on the table.

"There ain't enough beers in Louisiana to make you forget whatever it is bothering you, Mory. We both know that," Doc retorted.

"You wanna bet?" Morial clowned.

The two middle-aged men laughed heartily. Doc knew Morial was going to wall him off as long as he could. This was a dance these two old friends had done for years. Morial's tough exterior was experienced by his unit, but the laxer core was recognized by his pal Doc.

"Lay it on me, man. You know you can't lie to me. I see the pure disgust all over your face," Doc relayed.

"You heard about Reggie?" Morial proposed

Doc's eyes lifted as he released a sigh. Doc abandoned his relaxed position to lean on his elbows and cover his side of the table. He exhaled once more before addressing his pal.

"Yeah...yeah...I shole did. He literally went from living his life on the edge, to giving it up for the kids. I guarantee you he dodged plenty of bullets with the Hogs and he died from the one that wasn't even meant for him," Doc declared.

"You know what they always say, man. A man can leave the streets...but...they never quite leave him alone," Morial agreed.

"You ain't never lied," Doc concurred.

"The shit just don't seem right, y'know? Like, at what point has a man redeemed himself for the errors of his past. How much do you have to pay the piper just to avoid the reaper?" Morial questioned while scratching his forehead.

Morial slid down in the chair and stretched his neck over the top of it. He looked up at Bill's ceiling as if the stars were present in the kitchen. Doc watched his buddy with one eyebrow raised and the other curled.

"Mory, according to what people say, Reginald was not a victim. He was a hero. He gave everything he had to mentor those boys, down to his very last," Doc concluded.

"Man, you remember all that shit Reggie and the Hogs put us through back in the day? They ran up and down the streets for more than 30 years, until Renaldo and Franc put a stop to they ass," Morial reminisced.

"Let Reggie tell it, they only was able to stop him because he was getting old. Said he ain't been the same since he messed up his leg in that accident. That boy was a damn fool, I tell ya!" Doc jested.

Morial slapped the table in delight while Doc cackled at his own joke. Morial laughed until a thought ran across his mind. His joy converted to unease.

"Fifth Ward Hogs did a bunch of crazy shit, but they wasn't no gun-toting miscreants. These young guys they have now from that Hog Tied program...they scare me a little bit, y'know. They showed up to a funeral with guns, man. How you think they gonna act once Reg Leg is buried in the ground?!" Morial forecasted.

"It's gon' be alright. It's gon' have to be. You been doing this for years, Mo. Y'all gonna be able to offset those guys just like everybody else that done came along. Just watch, you'll see," Doc consoled.

Morial's eyes were glazed yet intense. He was staring at the kitchen door as if he expected Reggie to come walking through it.

"I hear ya, Doc, but this time things are different. It took two equally crazy bastards like Renaldo and Franc to take them down. Ever since those two have been off the scene, shit has gone haywire. I still believe in my people to handle the everyday crook, but the shit that's been creeping up lately. Everybody is coming out of the woodworks. We gonna be the murder capital again before too long," Morial projected.

"Oh, shoot. That reminds me. You remember what I said about that autopsy from Thibodeaux?" Doc Smith recalled.

"Yeah, I remember. That's another thing I have to worry about. What if that crazy ass girl starts coming back around the city. Rance don't work for me no more, but I can't help but get worried about him if that girl comes back around," Morial shared.

"Well, you might not have to worry about Rance..." Doc began.

"You probably right. He got his head so far up Rita's ass that he may not go apeshit while looking for Cliffhanger again. Whatever Rita is doing, I hope she keeps him occupied long enough for this to go away," Morial surmised.

Doc Smith tapped the table two times with his bent middle finger. Morial gave a puzzled look to his comrade, or more specifically, his hand then his face. Doc placed one finger in the air prior to rising up from his seat. He nearly walked out of the kitchen, stuck his head into the long hallway, and came back near the table to corral Morial.

"How well do you remember what I said about that autopsy?" Doc rephrased.

"I remembered what you said about the possible initials. Didn't you say they could have been 'LB' or 'CH' or a combination of other things?" Morial recalled.

"Right, well, there may be another possibility," Doc divulged.

Doc began to pace; Morial's eyes followed Doc's every step, to and from, back and forth, awaiting elaboration.

"Well, what is it?! You gonna lay it on me or make me take a guess? You not gonna tell me it was Reg Leg, is ya?" Morial urged.

"No, man, hell no! Reg Leg was many things, but he wasn't a murderer," Doc admitted.

"Just sit still and tell me what the hell is going on then, Doc!" Morial shouted.

Doc raised one finger to silence Morial while he looked toward the door. He shifted his attention to the back door once he was convinced no one was coming from the front of the house.

"You right. Cliffhanger and Reg Leg are many things, but they also ain't no damn wordsmiths!" Doc bellowed.

"Hnah?!" Morial muttered.

Doc looked at Morial with both eyebrows raised and the crown of his head tilted towards his friend. Doc sat nearly upright with his chest puffed up and chin raised, as if he was about to release some privileged information.

"They found a note *inside* the body. It was a little tough to decipher, with all the digestive fluids getting ahold of it. One of those damn cardboard stock ass cards," Doc described.

Morial's face frowned as he sat in pure disbelief. He then entered a range of phases, shifting his expression from one of shock to that of awe.

"Man, how far down could it have gotten? Did they shove that shit down his throat? What the fuck did it say?!" Morial rattled off, searching for answers.

"Chances are, that cardstock was his last meal. It would explain some of the internal bleeding he suffered. For all we know, the shots were just a cover-up for the real crime," Doc explained.

"What kind of sick motherfucker would shove a card down somebody's throat? Where y'all come up with this off the wall shit, Doc?" Morial sought.

"Somebody with a message. A message that needed to be embodied more than it needed to be heard," Doc gathered.

Morial dropped his head and delivered a nervous chuckle. The chuckle that began from discomfort turned into a guffaw that made his peer a little uneasy. Doc now had one brow raised and one finger lightly tracing the surface of the table.

"So, you mean to tell me there's somebody out there torturing people by shoving cards down their bodies, hoping someone gets the message?" Morial proposed after slamming his hand down on the table.

"So, you mean to tell me through all the shit you've seen, *that's* the hardest thing for you to believe?" Doc tossed back, unaffected.

Morial gritted his teeth as he slid the striking paw from the table. He leaned back in his seat while carefully studying his comrade. The lieutenant then shook his head "no" as Doc gave one nod and shifted an opened arm toward Morial.

"Forgive me for a little lapse in memory. I can only paraphrase what I was told, but I'll be damned if the shit ain't heavy," Doc warned.

"Well, don't keep me in suspense, buddy—let it out!" Morial encouraged.

Doc patted his pockets in search of his cell phone. He stood up to search his back pockets once he realized he wasn't holding anything in the anterior of his garments. Once he located his cell, Doc navigated through his contacts until he stumbled upon the conversation with another coroner. When he located the appropriate message, he opened it and relayed the information to his buddy.

"It goes a little something like 'Somewhere lay the wicked in waters long forgotten, cleansed of their transgressions, but still left to the rotted'," Doc recited.

Morial's face shriveled as he pondered the poetry provided by Doc. He grabbed the pen from his pocket, once used to keep score.

"Say that to me again. A little slower this time, if you don't mind, Smitty," Morial requested.

Doc Smith repeated the cadence two more times as Morial scribbled and scratched through his notes. Morial then delivered the sonnet to himself, while Doc sought to gain a peek of his notes.

"Cleansed of their transgression, but still left to the rotted?" Morial questioned.

"Something to that effect, Mory. I said don't quote me," Doc reminded him.

Morial shrugged his shoulders and continued to map out the words. He contemplated the many scenarios that came to mind, but none brought him to a suitable conclusion. Bill came crashing into the kitchen to express his displeasure with the current delay.

"Excuse my lack of hospitality, but umm, you two here to play cards or to sit and gossip like a couple of witches?" Bill questioned.

"*Witches*?!" Morial repeated as he remained focused on his blueprint.

"Well, I'm trying not to cuss as much—my ol' lady asked me to stop—but if you would prefer the old fashioned..." Bill began.

Morial's eyes lit up as he read the presumed words of the note again, this time assuming there could be some link between sorcery and the death in Thibodeaux. He shot up from the table as he now felt certain about the lead. He grabbed his things and darted towards the back door.

"Hold up, fool. Where you think you going? The card table is that way. Did we beat you so bad you lost your memory?" Bill poked.

"Nah, actually, you gave me a bit of clarity. Good looking out, Bill," Morial answered.

"That's great and all, but still, where in the hell are you going?" Doc demanded.

"Rampart!" Morial blurted, without mentioning another word.

Doc Smith and Bill watched as the rear door slammed behind Morial. Bill then looked at Doc, who could only lift his hands in surrender. Bill was pulling out his phone and beginning to dial a number when Doc distracted him.

"Let him go, Bill. He done got ahold to something and I don't think he gonna let it go until he is good and through with it," Doc advised.

"That's fine, but I clearly need to find you another partner. That boy is a gotdamn fool going through the back door when he was parked in the front! We obviously need to find you somebody with some gotdamn sense," Bill jokingly ridiculed.

Doc laughed at Bill's claims as he returned to his call in the living room. Once out of sight, Doc's smile wilted into a discerning grimace. He wondered what Morial was about to get himself tangled into. Whatever it was, he hoped the next time they met at a table, it would still be by their own free will.

Chapter 42

Down to Business

Julissa smiled as wide as she had in over a month. Of all the things she may have lost, she was quite content with the those that could never be taken away: her children. She stared into her phone while a pair of hazelnut eyes returned the courtesy.

"See, I told you I should have gotten him a potato costume. I guess this will have to do instead," Cortissa poked.

"He wouldn't need a costume at all, Ma, if you or Dad would stay home while the other one took Judy trick-or-treating," Julissa commented.

"It ain't gonna hurt Chubba Bubba to stroll around the block a few times. Hell, it ain't gonna hurt his grandpappy either," Cortissa gloated.

Both ladies dropped their heads while joining in laughter. Peerless peered up at his grandmother, likely because her hoots were in closest proximity. Julissa noticed the child's bewilderment and tried to conceal her amusement.

"Look, JuJu, this boy needs to get out the house and so do you," Cortissa directed.

"Well, I might go out with Marisol when we leave work. I don't know, kind of not feeling the likelihood of running into some masked weirdos tonight," Julissa shared.

"Well, I know you prefer your weirdos exposed...so... there's that. Whoops! time for us to go. Goodbyyyyyyyyye," Cortissa duped and dashed.

Julissa rolled her eyes at her mother as she waved to her infant. When they hung up the call, Julissa gazed at the computer monitor before looking down at some notes. Julissa carefully picked up two sheets from the pile, each wielding a former CD cover for Pelli Kanisus. She noticed that though each cover was artistically different, they both possessed a slight reddened overcast at the upper border. Julissa carefully returned the sheets to the desk as she examined them for further common details. Nothing else tied them together aside from Vernell Kane himself. Julissa considered looking up some of Pelli's local albums, but she was interrupted by a knock and entry at her door.

With the white hair entering before his tanned face, Mr. Denver graced Julissa's workspace with his wisdom. He planted himself at the furthest portion into the office where he could maintain contact with the doorknob.

"Julissa, how are things coming along with that Pelli Kanievel project?" Denver inquired.

"Kanisus?!" Julissa questioned.

"You know what I mean," Denver stated.

"Still trying to get a grasp of who he is. We could better advertise for him when we know his real message," Julissa concluded.

"That is absolutely true. Well, I don't intend to distract you. I just wanted to check and see how you are doing. The kids okay?" Denver asked.

"Thank you, Mr. Denver. My parents seem to have a pretty good hold of them. They seem to be enjoying themselves," Julissa admitted.

"That comes as no surprise. They did a pretty good job rearing you, in my opinion," Denver assessed.

"They don't deserve all the credit," Julissa jabbed.

Denver chuckled at her notion briefly while maintaining his grip on the door. A vat of silence covered the room as Denver's sorrowful eyes looked upon his most productive employee. He believed she'd gone through more than her fair share of grief in the last few months, but she still rose. Julissa glared back at Denver, wondering why he remained if there was nothing more to say. Once Denver gathered himself, he was able to rehash the conversation.

"Julissa, in case you are not aware, Magnolia Marketing sincerely appreciates you and all your efforts," Denver advised.

"Thank you, Mr. Denver. It's always good to hear it, although I didn't doubt it before," Julissa accepted.

"If you need anything at all—a few days off, a babysitter, or a really long lunch break—don't hesitate to ask," Denver offered.

"I'm fine for now, Mr. Denver. If I need anything, I will let you know. I promise," Julissa attempted to reassure.

"Well...alright. I'll be in my office if you change your mind," Denver conceded.

Denver slowly worked his way back into the hall. Julissa continued her examination of the previous album covers. She contemplated the likely reason for such consistent imagery until her eyes expanded. She picked up her phone and searched for a number before dialing and returning to the canvas. Julissa adjusted the phone from her hand to her shoulder while she waited on the party to answer.

"Umm, hello? Who dis?" the male subscriber asked.

"Mr. Kane, this is Julissa Brown, from Magnolia Marketing," Julissa answered.

"Oh..OH! My bad. I didn't know. What's hattenin' witcha, love?" Vernell accepted.

Julissa delayed a moment to turn her nose up at Pelli's request. Had she not been so homed in on the images in front of her, she may have entertained a discussion about the artist's phone etiquette.

"I had a question about some of your past albums," Julissa revealed.

"What, you wanted to see if they came in vinyl?" Vernell joked.

"Hardy-har-har, Sucker Bar. I mean the covers," Julissa answered.

"Oh. What? Would you like me to autograph some for you? Did you want to take my picture or something?" Vernell agitated.

"The only autograph of yours that I would ever need is on the contract! The revenue you bring to this company will be the real measure of your worth, Vernell!" Julissa stung.

"Oooooh weeeee!! You ain't got to do me like that, miss lady! I'm just trying to see what's to it, ya dig?" Vernell recovered.

"I hear ya, lil' juvie. But can I get my question out, please?" Julissa cornered.

As a void entered the conversation, Julissa chuckled to

herself while imagining the many responses that must have crossed Vernell's mind. While he gathered his thoughts, and likely his nerve, Julissa delved further into the cover art, looking for a suitable correlation.

"Aight then. Aight then. You got it, lil' baby. You all about the business. I can appreciate that. I hope you keep that same energy when it comes to putting me on the billboards or somethin', ya dig?" Vernell retreated.

"Well, that's what this call is about, sir. The best way for us to promote you is to know...well...YOU! Am I right?" Julissa proposed.

"I feel dat. I'm rockin' witcha," Vernell entertained.

"Okay then. So, I like how you made your cover art relate to the name of your albums. Some fine artwork you have. Are they done by the same photographer and/or artist?" Julissa questioned.

"Nah, I don't think so. You might have to check wit' C.I.T.Y. Records 'bout all that. I remember working with a different photographer for each cover, but I don't know about all that other stuff," Vernell revealed.

"Okay," Julissa began. "So, I have seen some albums from other C.I.T.Y. Records artists, and they don't have that red overcast on the cover. None of them do."

"Oh, that? Red is my favorite color, ma'am. It's my own little light on each album," Vernell confirmed.

"Own little light, hnah? It kind of reminds me of something, but I don't think that could be it," Julissa clarified.

"Like I said, baby, it's my own lil' thang. I can't even really explain it, but I always was drawn to the color, y'know. My own lil' way of telling the people keep ya eyes on the horizons, that's where you'll find me, ya dig,"

Vernell claimed.

Julissa stepped down from her figurative soap box and expelled a sigh of relief. She stood up from her desk and adjusted the lower edge of her shirt. She reassembled the items previously removed from the folder. As Julissa began to sort the documents back into place, Vernell interrupted the silence.

"Scue me, miss. I don't wanna cut you off or nothin' like that, but I need to run up in this studio session and make us all some money. You had anything else you wanted to know?" Vernell announced.

"No, sir. You are free to go, Mr. Kanisus," Julissa commented.

"Preciate it, love. I'm gon holla back atcha once we get this lil' joint mixed down. I'm tellin' ya, this shit here 'bout to be fiya!" Vernell exclaimed.

"Well don't let me hold you up, sir. As you were," Julissa bowed.

"Fa sho," Vernell simplified.

Vernell Kane ended the call midway through his transformation into Pelli Kanisus. Before she could acknowledge the phone's click, she heard repeated "clacking" in the hallway. Julissa walked to her office door to investigate what could possibly be going on. Just as she entered the hall, she was nearly T-boned by Marisol. Luckily for both, Julissa dipped back into her office while Marisol widened the distance between herself and Julissa's door.

"Bitch!! Where are you going? You almost gave me a concussion!" Julissa blamed.

"I love you, JuJu, but I done told you about that damn word. I literally cut off a fiancé behind that word!" Marisol reminded.

"You right. But you know I didn't mean it like that," Julissa plead.

"Mmm hmm. That's what he said," Marisol countered.

"Marisol, what is it? Why are you the only fool running down the hallway?" Julissa redirected.

Marisol ogled the direction she arrived from, her hair ruffled and nearly covering the length of her cheeks. Julissa called over to Marisol again, but her sights were dead set down the hall. Julissa reached over and tapped Marisol on the shoulder. Marisol jumped, turning toward Julissa while moving away.

"Something's coming," Marisol professed.

"Something? Like what?" Julissa asked.

"Something I can't even begin to explain," Marisol blurted.

Julissa glanced peculiarly at her friend before the sound of scurried steps increased down the hall. Julissa began marching down the hall until she jogged. As she reached the end of the hall, she noticed more individuals running toward herself and Marisol. Julissa had no idea what was brewing until she set her eyes on an individual she believed she'd encountered before...

Just outside of Magnolia Marketing headquarters, a white Chevy Camaro has come to a halt near a dented iron statue. The vehicles two occupants carefully inspect the large yet vulnerable object, mostly out of curiosity.

"Did a car jump the curb and hit that oversized flower?" Rance asked.

"I don't know if that's possible, but whatever it is must be inside," Rita ascertained as she pointed towards the entryway.

Rance trailed Rita's finger to a crowd of individuals evacuating the building. Rance darted up the long pathway with Rita in tow. When they reached the entrance, they noticed security personnel on the floor while others continued to evacuate.

"Is there a chance she ran out of there before everyone else did?" Rita asked.

"For some reason, I sincerely doubt it," Rance relayed.

They entered and noticed the toll taken on the occupants. Rita clamored at the sight before her, lending Rance the necessary time to switch out his glasses for the pair in the blue case.

Chapter 43

Impromptu Invasion

Julissa and Marisol scream at bystanders to clear the floor as all inhabitants are motorized by fear. Julissa finds that one particular elder appears to be stumbling along the path from their rear. The seemingly drunken man comes upon the door bearing Julissa's name plate and attempts to walk in after releasing a wicked cough.

"I'll get him out of there. They're gonna need you out here, dear. Just be careful," Marisol warns before dashing to Julissa's workspace.

Julissa nodded in agreement as she watched Marisol carefully trek down the hall. Julissa observed Marisol push open the door and slide into the room. "SCREEEEEEEECH" goes a wall nearby, causing Julissa to stir. Julissa gets a look at a disfigured being before the lights flicker. Her head swivels until she returns to the original position to find the being has disappeared. Julissa retreats toward her office until a gurgled shriek fills the hall. She then hears a scream from her office that signals Marisol may not be faring well. She bolts toward the door, but it locks before she reaches the handle. She hears a scrape of the surface as the lights dim for a longer period than the last.

Inside the office, Marisol tries to rip a cane away from an elder, who is hell-bent on deconstructing the space around him. He snatches the cane away from her and whips it across her face. The impact knocks Marisol into the wall, then bounces her onto the floor.

"Excuse my manners, ma'am. Would you mind pointing me into the direction of a Miss Julissa Brown? Show me where she is and I will grant you reprieve," Mack propositioned.

Marisol pushed herself up from the floor and swept a closed fist across her lips, checking for blood. When she noticed no discoloration to her hand, she smiled and glared at Mack.

"You may be a little old fashioned for her taste. Ladies today prefer flowers over brutality," Marisol deflected.

"You are not my target or transgressor, young lady. I have no problems with you, unless you have something to hide," Mack pried.

"You gonna have to beat it out of me first!" Marisol warned.

"Very well then, 'spare the rod' they say...'spare the rod,'" Mack accepted.

Mack then turned and struck Julissa's desk before dragging the cane across to knock all the items off. Marisol attempted to attack the elder with the slight moment of distraction, but he turned and struck her in the hip. Marisol winced in pain as she toppled over the edge of the desk.

"I don't take pleasure in this, ma'am. I did not come here for you and I prefer to leave you in peace than pieces," Mack pleaded.

Along the hall, Julissa trampled around searching for a

shred of light. She flipped the nearest switch but all she heard was a disappointing buzz. As she nearly escaped into the opposite hall, she heard a solid object dragging across the laminated tile. Julissa narrowed down the source of the wretched scraping to something behind her. She twisted around to her damnation as she walked chest first into an iron slab, nearly knocking her wind out! As Julissa gasped for air along the cold floor, the scrapes continued behind her. Julissa found solace in the nearest wall as she utilized a protruding block to pull herself upright.

A light flickered dimly enough for Julissa to confidently turn around to face her attacker: a tall, pallid man with altered skin pigmentation, bulging muscles, and a glazed look in his beading eyes. Julissa's mind ordered her to flee but her body forbade it.

"Wherrrre issss myyy motherrrrr?!" Victor roared.

Victor's croaking cry broke the trance that once occupied Julissa's limbs. She strained her eyes in disbelief as Victor stared. He lifted his hammer from its resting position and grabbed the base of the steel mallet with his off hand.

"Who is your mother? Everyone here knows how to use lotion," Julissa poked.

Victor sneered at Julissa's crassness before driving the crown of his sledgehammer into the wall near her head. She dodged the blow narrowly, almost getting her hair pinned in the process. She still felt the weight of the steel between her bosoms, not quite recovered from the introductory strike. She lifted her right foot from the ground while planting firmly upon her left. As Victor removed his plastered weapon from the wall, Julissa drove her foot through the outside of his knee. Victor buckled as one knee nearly knocked into the other. He immediately swung the hammer around in one hand but only managed to knock off a nearby lamp. Julissa occupied a fighting stance before delivering an ominous hook to the base of his chest plate.

"Oof!" Victor released in shock.

Julissa's office was in mere shambles as Marisol, now bruised and confused, held on against Mack. She bled from her nose as Mack held her captive against the wall, pressing the cane across her shoulders.

"Where...is...JULISSA?!" Mack requested once more.

"In...her...skin. When...she...jumps...out...YOU JUMP IN!" Marisol taunted.

Mack took no exception to Marisol's humor as he pressed the cane harder against her. He held on until he realized she was no longer fighting back. When he removed the cane from Marisol's carcass, she fell forward onto her hands and knees upon the floor. Mack walked back to the deconstructed desk and picked up some scattered photos.

"Is this ebony goddess the one I'm searching for?" Mack asked as he came across one of Julissa's photos.

Marisol's body still trembled from Mack's force. She lifted her head to indicate she heard her elder, but she offered nothing more in terms of a response.

"Very well then, may find this one and hold onto her for myself," Mack stated as he moved on to the next photo.

Mack took the picture and placed it into the breast pocket of his blazer. He granted a smile at the following photo, this one including Julissa, Judy, and Renaldo.

"Ahh, yes! It would appear I have found who I am looking for. Such a beautiful family. Well, it used to be,"

Mack snared.

Marisol heard the remark and shot a stare at Mack from her humbled position. She was fuming while also curious as to what the elder meant.

"Used to be?! The hell does that mean, grandpa!" Marisol jabbed.

Mack looked back at Marisol for a moment, shrugged his shoulders, and returned his attention to the photo. He turned to the next photo and was frozen. A picture of Renaldo and Franc, together. Mack gazed at a moment where his son was still doing what he loved, protecting Crescent City. While Mack was obviously occupied, Marisol slowly crawled toward Julissa's office door, unlocked it, then crept into the murky hall. She could hear footsteps from one end of the hall with scraping along the other end. She grabbed onto a protruding portion of the wall to return to her feet.

After admiring the photo for some time, Mack's face crinkled up and he ripped it in half, discarding Renaldo's half amongst the litter. He then peered at one last photo: the one photo that truly gave him pause. Mack discovered his last glimmer of hope in the face of a baby boy.

A little further up the hall, Julissa and Victor remained entangled in a battle to uncover loved ones. Julissa continued to deliver strikes and kicks to the formidable figure, meanwhile attempting to avoid his homerun swing. Victor feigned a blow to Julissa's head, which caused her to duck. When Julissa crouched, she received a front kick to the forehead, knocking her onto her back.

"AHHHHHHH!" Julissa screamed as the blanched area of her hair widened.

Victor hovered over Julissa as she grimaced in agony.

He looked down on her painstaking expression and thought of Lavender. *What if someone had done this to her? Would attacking the wife of a man he befriended truly help locate Victor's mother?* The remorse was short-lived as Victor ground the heel of his size 14 boot into Julissa's chest. The integrity of her hazel shirt was altered with each twist of Victor's lead-like foot.

"Who is your mother?" Julissa choked.

"Laaavenderrrr," Victor answered.

"Who?" Julissa asked once more.

"Barohhhhhhhne," Victor belted.

With tears dripping from her trauma-laden body, Julissa struggled to lift Victor's foot. With less than favorable leverage, Julissa's attempts were fruitless. She resorted to throwing multiple strikes through his ankle with the base of her hands, but Victor appeared less than affected. For a split moment—she gave up. Julissa figured if this is how it would end for her, at least her children were in the care of her parents.

The children. That's it! That's why she couldn't afford to falter. She was all they had!! With one's father buried and the other presumably below a body of water, she would leave them to be raised by their grandparents.

"Fuck that!" Julissa murmured to herself.

Julissa's body began to quake as she grabbed the toe of Victor's boot in one hand and the unoccupied portion of the heel in the other. Julissa strained as she let out another scream, this time releasing the tension from her body while slightly lifting the foot from her chest. Victor noticed his limb elevating and quietly panicked. He forced his foot back down momentarily, though not enough to fully discourage the damsel. With one more hurl, Julissa rescinded the foot from her chest and twisted at the ankle, taking Victor off his center and nearly dislocating the tendons. Victor crashed into the nearest wall while Julissa remained supine, circulating what little oxygen she had in reserve through the rest of her body.

The crashing thud from Victor's landing was heard multiple yards down the hall in Julissa's office. Mack discontinued his examination of the infant child's photo and turned toward the door.

"Hnah?" Mack mumbled as he realized he was in the office alone.

Mack hobbled to the agape door and peeked down the hallway. Marisol had vanished! Mack chuckled as he began to walk in the direction of the resounding crash. As Mack traveled the hall, it started to brighten. He began to doubt his sense of direction until he heard a scrape of the flooring ahead. Mack was going to turn the corner when he felt a hard thump across the back of his neck! It wasn't enough to floor Mack, but it did compromise his stability.

"POLICE! Put your arms in the air and place your hands behind your head," a woman's voice called.

"I am not resisting," Mack calmly spewed as he followed the directive.

Mack vaulted both hands into the air before bending his elbows to place the hands behind his head. He then felt a hand tracing the lining of his arms and shoulders.

"Spread your legs!" the female officer commanded.

"Now, is that any way for you to speak to your elder? What is your name so I may file a complaint?" Mack demanded.

"Rita! And you can speak with my supervisor directly when I bring you to the station!" Detective Barrios provided.

As Rita searched Mack's lower extremities, she saw the faint silhouette of his cane. Rita had no desire to find out whether or not the stick was hollow or dense.

"Sir, please drop your weapon to the floor," Rita requested.

"Sure thing," Mack complied.

As he released the cane with his fingers, he dropped his right hand to catch the cane just above his waist. Rita witnessed Mack moving his arm, so she glided to his left. Mack swung his cane but found no suitor. Rita grabbed the cane while Mack hung on. She brought it down so she could drive her knee through it, dislodging one of the elder's hands from its grip. Rita maintained that side of the stick and shifted the free end of the cane through Mack's jaw, spinning him headfirst into a wall, then ass first to the floor.

While Rita subdued Mack, Julissa continued to catch her breath from the ongoing battle with Victor. She'd finally recuperated enough to raise her torso from the floor. Victor took notice of Julissa's newfound momentum and decided he needed to disrupt it. Victor raised the hammer fervently, scraping it against the wall in the process. As Victor hoisted the hammer above his head, he heard two gunshots in the hall, one of which nearly sent the mallet backwards. Victor scanned the foyer for the interrupter, only to find a man with a bald-faded haircut and dark brown glasses standing across from him, occupying the isosceles stance with his weapon drawn.

Chapter 44

The Last Hurrah!

Victor's face twisted in disgust for the man standing with his own steel brandished between his palms. Though the dark-framed glasses concealed much of the man's face along the shaded hall, Victor still noticed the sweat forming around his brow. Victor raised the mallet again and moved closer to a battered Julissa.

"Alright, big guy. Just put your hammer down and nobody else has to get hurt," Rance reasoned.

"Youuu th-th-think Iiiiiii neeeeeed a weehhhhhponn toooo hurrrrt you?!" Victor proposed.

"Do I get a vote?" Julissa reconvened as she climbed to her feet.

While Julissa stabilized herself along the wall, Victor charged toward her. Rance placed himself between them until Victor bowled him over and ran into the wall. Rance's lower back was rammed abruptly into the protruding panels of the wall, causing him to double over from the pain. Victor stomped on Rance's back twice before kicking him in the obliques.

Victor wanted to attempt another stomp but was interrupted by another gunshot; this time the bullet pierced his arm, relieving him of the steel mallet. As the hammer graced the ground, Julissa attempted to confiscate it. While Julissa struggled with the deterrent, an elder gentleman scurried across the floor to Victor. As he rushed to Victor's aid, Mack noticed Julissa's ploy and swung his cuffed hands across her face.

"Dammit! Watch it, old man, or your pet here is gonna get another shot. The next one should put him down for good," Rita warned.

"Get up, Victor, and help me get these damn cuffs off!!" Mack cried.

Victor looked up at his uncle while grasping the handle of the hammer. Rita rushed to regain control of Mack, but he stepped beneath her whiffed attempt and guided her face-first into the wall. As she repelled the barrier, Rita swung her arm back and inadvertently decked Julissa in the face.

"Bitch!" Julissa crowed.

"I'm sorry, girl. I missed!" Rita apologized.

Julissa instantly returned the favor as she struck Rita in the mouth. With little strength remaining, Rance pulled Rita toward him by her belt loop, helping her to avoid a follow-up punch from Julissa. Julissa's fist sliced through open air. Her forward momentum aided in her falling into the cusps of Mack's cuffs. Mack yanked Julissa backwards until she plowed onto the floor.

"Nice to meet you, my dear. We have much to discuss," Mack stated to Julissa while attempting to drag her across the floor.

"LET HER GO!" a woman's voice called over an intercom.

Mack halted as he sought the voice. Julissa coughed

while retrieving what little air was available. Victor charged over to Julissa and Mack and swung his mallet upright, then it came thrashing to the floor. Julissa rolled away in the nick of time. As Victor loaded up for another swing, Mack stood in front of him, holding his cuffed hands up to Victor's eye level. Victor nodded at his uncle and motioned him to rest his hands on the floor. Victor slammed the hammer down twice more to break the small chains holding his uncle. Once his wrists were separated, Mack stood up, staring at the ceiling.

"Who speaks down upon us as if they are the almighty themselves? Hmm? What gives you the authority to speak upon us as if we were to glorify *you*?" Mack retorted.

"I am an employee here and I have a badge, sir. Why are *you* here?" the voice called over the speaker again.

"Mar...Mar...isol?" Julissa reasoned.

As Mack became enthralled with the hovering voice, Victor took it upon himself to rush toward the two detectives. Rita dodged the attempt, but Rance was clipped by the hammer. Rita kicked Victor in his obliques, but he didn't budge. Victor lifted his foot to plant it through Rita's chest, knocking her and the kneeling Detective McDonald to the floor. Mack heard the bodies collapse, which brought a deviant grin to his face. He looked up at the ceiling again and pointed at Julissa.

"That there is my reason to...let it all hang out. We are here for one lady and one lady only. Give us Mrs. Brown and the rest may go," Mack negotiated.

"She ain't exactly for sale, puta!" Marisol croaked from the loudspeaker.

Mack shook his head and walked over to the fallen Julissa, standing mere inches from the top of her head.

Victor attempted to stomp on Rance, but the detective rolled away like a child's crayon on a restaurant floor.

"The debt is not yours to pay, young lady. Since you want to sit somewhere and look down on us as a God, I would appreciate you understanding someone paying their dues. Her husband allowed my son to die. It's only right I walk away with hers!" Mack ordered as he pounded his fist into his hand.

Julissa's eyelids parted as she peered into Mack's gullet. She couldn't fully make out his profile, but he did seem familiar. Her mind was still a little cloudy. Rance was back on his feet adopting a boxing stance. Victor acknowledged the challenge with a grin and grunt. With one hand on the handle, Victor elevated the hammer above himself until he knocked out the nearest light. Rance remained shrouded in the darkness until there was a scrape across the floor.

"SLIDE TO THE SIDE!!" Marisol yelled.

"Hnah?" Rance muttered just before he took a steel block to the chest.

The nearest wall prevented his plunge to the floor, despite lacking a comfortable landing. Rita heard the thud but could see nothing more than Mack standing over Julissa's shiftless carcass. Mack looked down at Julissa's mug with an initial grimace that turned into a scowl. Rita noticed and began to inch toward them. While still concealed by the shadows, Victor swung his open palm toward Rance.

"DUCK! DIP! DODGE!" Marisol screamed.

Rance took heed to the warning and slipped Victor's errant swing. He jabbed at the opponent's bullet-pierced shoulder, which aggravated Victor more than it discouraged him.

"Take out his legs!" Marisol screamed.

Rance nodded at the command as blood escaped his nostril. He planted a front kick directly into Victor's nearest kneecap, drawing a groan. He then followed up with a haymaker across Victor's dome, causing him to take a false step to the side. Mack heard the blow and noticed Victor's frame dip into the dimly lit section of the hall. As Mack attempted a step toward the action, he was halted by a pair of hands gripping at his ankle. Mack slightly lifted the secured appendage and attempted to pull it away, but a twist at his ankle forced him to the ground in an awful tumble. Mack landed chest first onto the ground as Julissa rolled over his back and secured her calves under his chin. She maintained control of the ankle as she leaned back and placed her weight on it, nearly creating a bridge over Mack's trampled torso. Julissa pulled back with her calves while pulling down on the controlled ankle, causing Mack to flail all other extremities. Victor witnessed the scenario from the corner of his eye, encouraging him to rise to his feet and intervene.

"Take him out...NOW!!" Marisol commanded.

Rance tried to attack Victor's knees from the rear, but the Baron drove his enormous foot through the unsuspecting detective's chest. Victor's foot was still hoisted when Rita launched her entire body below his waist to the planted knee. Victor careened to the canvas, nearly folding over Rita's torpedoed body. Rita wrapped her hands around Victor's neck as he pulled her forward. Rita was brought to her feet by Victor's momentum as she used her forearms to administer a chokehold. Victor rolled his torso back and forth, but it only strengthened Rita's hold. She rode the bully for dear life until the back of his head connected with her forehead. Her grip began to slip as she weakened from the impact. They then heard a scrape across the floor, as Rance separated the steel core from the floor just enough to drive it into Victor's abdomen. Rance tumbled to the ground as Victor curled up into a ball, wincing from the gut check.

Julissa released her clutch on Mack as she too became wary. She rolled off his back and kicked him in his obliques, both startling and forcing Mack onto his back-side. Julissa straddled the elder as she took one more look at him. Julissa threw two stiff straights at Mack's closed mouth, breaking the skin of his upper lip. The blood dripped into his mouth, forcing him to cough. After his fit of coughs, Julissa pulled Mack up by his collar and stared coldly into his eyes. She gritted her teeth as Mack bared his, blood stained and all.

"You are much tougher than your husband. Maybe you should have been my son's partner instead," Mack hoarsely suggested.

Julissa's eyes crumpled as she glanced at the older gentleman. She looked over to Rita, then back to Mack.

"What partner? The only other partner Renaldo had was...," Julissa paused, examining Mack more thoroughly than she had previously.

"Yes. My son...Franc!" Mack confirmed through another set of coughs.

Julissa's eyes bulged as the confirmation arrived simultaneously with her recollection. Her fingers un-raveled Mack's shirt while his head plopped back to the surface. Julissa looked away from Mack, avoiding any remnants of Franc. Rance pulled himself up to observe the man; surprised a man he once sought now stood before him. Rita remained dazed from Victor's headbutt.

Julissa looked about the floor, noticing photos turned over near Mack's shoulders. She reached over to a shortened photo, only to find the face of Franc Tatiano. Julissa's jaws slumped as memories of Franc filled her mind. Mack noticed the temporary distraction and utilized the opportunity to toss Julissa from atop him. As Julissa rolled to the side, she corralled another item from the ground before landing on her spine. Mack rose to his feet, in perfect position for Rance to make a beeline toward him. Rance's attempt to reach the legend was intercepted by a last desperate lunge via Victor. Rance flipped himself mid-air so he could break the fall with his back. Rance rose from the temporary inconvenience, setting himself up to be speared by the Baron.

While Rance was being disposed of by the barren bully, Mack straddled Julissa and maintained a forearm in her throat. Julissa fought to slide the arm from her neck, but Mack forced his "old man" strength forward. He saw the object in her hand and ripped it from her flailing fingers. Mack then turned the object forward and flashed a cunning grin.

"Perfect," Mack whispered.

Victor lifted his foot and drove it through Rance's head to the wall. The echo of his skull against the barrier was nearly deafening. His torso slumped over his legs as the final blow busted a frame of his glasses. Victor then walked over to his uncle, who still pinned Julissa to the floor.

"We are about to find out just how loving of a mother you are. Victor, I'm going to give Mrs. Brown here until the count of three to tell us where her son is. If she doesn't budge, I want you to smash her head like Gallagher," Mack ordered.

"Isss thaaat necesssarrrrry? Cannn't weeee jussst asssk someonnnne elsse insssteaad?" Victor attempted to reason, trying to save his friend's estranged wife.

"Is it necessary that her husband let someone put a bullet in my son's head? Hmmm? You trying to protect her because you made friends with the little bastard? He don't give a damn about you and I don't give a damn about him, or her son!!" Mack howled.

"You? You took Renaldo?" Julissa pieced together.

Mack glared at Julissa without providing a response. She cut her eyes to Victor's face, whose solemn scowl told her all she needed to know. She suddenly began to tremble as she started shifting Mack's arm from her throat. He tried to push back against her, but Julissa was driven by rage.

"ONE!" Mack began.

"You ain't gonna do shit! I was better to Franc than you ever were!" Julissa taunted.

"The hell are you talking about, young lady. All you ever did was nurture a backstabbing son of a bitch who thought he was the gift to God's green earth! TWO!" Mack retorted.

Julissa forced Mack nearly upright as she shifted his arm off her. He leaned forward to subdue her again, this time allowing Julissa to wrap his arm around his own neck and fling him beside her on the floor. She then grabbed his other wrist and turned the photo of a newborn toward him. The stress of the battle caused Mack to break out into another coughing fit, giving Julissa further leverage. Victor scurried to Julissa's side to line up his strike, but the struggle between her and Mack made a clean shot nearly impossible. As Victor contemplated the perfect strike, Rita located her gun and pistol whipped him in the back of his skull. Victor's feet took him horizontally, but he remained standing. Victor rubbed his palm across the sore portion of his head. When he viewed his hand, he saw traces of his own blood. Victor's face twinged as he looked at Rita. Rita's eyes bulged and her bottom lip drooped while she watched Victor become enraged.

"Look at him! Who do you think this is!" Julissa called to Mack.

"A dead boy. THREE!" Mack directed.

Victor lifted his sledgehammer and charged towards Rita, with no regard to Mack's previous command. Rita held one finger on the trigger but didn't feel she had enough time to squeeze.

"Do you hear me, boy! Get this wench off of me!" Mack demanded.

Victor heard nothing more than the crash of his own body as Rance speared him into the wall before he reached Rita. His dome crashed into the head of his hammer, scrambling his thoughts. The impact repelled Rance backwards as he plunged to the surface as well.

"LOOK AT HIM! You don't want to see it! This is all *we* have left of Franc! This is your grand—," Julissa began before Mack freed his hand and planted the exterior of it across her cheek.

Julissa took the blow without blinking before she punched Mack with her free hand, then released his wrist with the other. Julissa lifted the elder by his collar, pulling him up as far as she could. She then maneuvered her hands until she was holding Mack by the back of his head.

"Take a good look at me, bitch. I am the only thing keeping your legacy alive! Sorry I can't say the same for you!" Julissa grizzled.

Julissa yanked Mack towards her as she dove her head into his and let the back of his cranium meet the tile. Mack's eyelids shut as his vision hazed. He released one more blood-smearing cough before lying dormant. Julissa stood over the battered man, as she empathized with his loss. She honestly was as upset with Renaldo over allowing Franc to be murdered as Mack was; *possibly more so*. Rita ran over to check on Rance, who hopelessly held the fractured spectacles in his hands. Rance's expression was rife with despair; he was nearly in tears.

"Hey, thank you, Rance," Rita expressed.

Rance wouldn't deviate his attention. He sat in dismay as the frames were obliterated.

"Rance? Are you okay?" Rita checked again.

"Hnuh?!" Rance relayed, startled.

"Are you alright? Are you hurt? Do you need me to take you to the hospital?" Rita explained.

Rance scrambled to gather himself until he stood on his own accord. His eyes never strayed from the glasses. He searched his pockets until he found his prescribed black frames. He placed them on his face and watched as Julissa applied her focus to a twitching Victor. As Rance followed her stare, he witnessed Victor attempting to revive himself. Rance took the tarnished spectacles and placed them in his pocket.

"Can you see now? Is that better?" Rita pried.

"Uh...no! I gotta go. I'm pretty sure someone's called C.C.P.D. by now and I don't know if you wanna explain to Morial why I was here. I'm gonna catch up to you later,"

Rance averted.

"I guess you're right. We'll catch up later then?" Rita accepted.

Rita squinted at Rance as he wandered down the hall and out of sight. Julissa walked towards Victor, but Rita placed herself between them. Rita gazed at Julissa's distressed face while Julissa attempted to push her out of the way.

"Give him the finger!" Marisol announced over the speaker.

"Wait a minute. Wait a minute!" Rita warned.

"I don't have a minute, Rita! They tried to kill me, and I want answers!" Julissa bellowed.

"Let me take him to the station and I can get those answers. Just let me take him in; you can even help me," Rita reasoned.

"Okay," Julissa agreed while staring Victor down.

As Rita spun around to place Victor under arrest, Julissa rammed Rita headfirst into the wall, disorienting her as she slowly descended to her knees. Julissa then kicked Rita forward into Victor, which caused him to brush the wall with his shoulder. As Rita fell backward, Julissa dug her middle finger into Victor's bullet wound.

"AHHHHHHHHHHHHHHH!" Victor cried as Julissa tunneled into his shoulder.

"WHO SENT YOU HERE?! WHY??" Julissa commanded.

"MAHMMAAAAAAAA!" Victor yelled in anguish.

"Where is your mama and what does she want with me?" Julissa interrogated.

"Iiiiii don't know," Victor wept.

Julissa squinted at Victor, not sure which question he

was answering. She released some of the pressure, hoping it would aid Victor in clarification.

"You just said she sent you here! Where the hell is she?" Julissa rephrased.

Victor's head sunk as he reminisced about the mother he once knew. At the advisory of his uncle, he showed up at Magnolia Marketing and scared off half the lot. He considered how he wasn't sure of many things; aside from the fact he had been the source of much pain.

"Iiiiiiii don't know," Victor sobbed.

"Who told you to come here?" Julissa pressed.

Victor shook his head from side to side, realizing he had no idea who his uncle had spoken to, considering his mother's absence.

"Take me there, NOW!" Julissa ordered.

"Ohhhhkayyy. Ohhhkayyy," Victor agreed.

Julissa kept her arms wrapped around Victor's as she escorted him down the depleted hallway. Rita remained unconscious and Mack was still sprawled out on the floor. Mack turned his head to the opposite side and chuckled as he watched Julissa escort Victor away from the scene. He stretched his arm as far as he could to pick up the picture of Peerless. Mack brought the photo within view and chuckled while soaking in his grandson.

Chapter 45

Pressure Busts Pipers

A police unit speeds through Crescent City. Drivers are pulling over in response to the lights and sirens, but the vehicle continues down Tulane Avenue without pause. The unit doesn't shift gears until it approaches the corner of LaSalle Street. The car comes to a complete stop once it is next to the tall and tarnished building surrounded by a fence.

Morial exits the vehicle and runs to the gate. He notices the lock on the fence and walks around the perimeter for the opening few know exists. Morial checked his surroundings, making sure no one would see him breach the premises. Not an onlooker in sight; the coast outside was clear. Morial walked around the corner of LaSalle Street and stopped midway to Gravier. He looked down either side of the path before grabbing a wedged portion of the gate, separating it slightly. Lieutenant Morial ducked under the zip ties and slid into the fenced area. He walked to a side entrance of the massive, heavily stained building. The mildewed walls were telling of the impending interior stench.

Morial entered the building, wholly aware his lungs

were compromised, but in his line of work, his internal organs often were. He slowed his breathing to control how much of the stench entered his airways while dedicating a load of effort into pushing the saturated air out.

"Hello? Anybody here?" Morial yelled.

The echo carried down the hall, beyond the area marked by light. Along the building were stained glass panes, too murky to see inside. Morial scaled the hallway slowly until he heard a door slam. Morial turned around and took out his gun.

"Somebody answer me, dammit! Come on out!" Morial screamed toward the sound.

Another door slams, this time on the opposite end of the structure. Morial strafed down the hall, weapon still pointed forward while he scanned side-to-side. The aroma becomes more profound as he passes a stairway. The stairway door lies on the floor and water nearly crests the lower levels.

"Theeeeohhhhhhhhhhh," a male's voice whips through the empty halls.

The lieutenant halted his feet, but his head remained on a swivel. A set of double doors flapped back and forth simultaneously.

"Who are you? Come on out, you son of a bitch," Morial commanded.

"I won't argue with that," the voice dispelled.

A vein bulged from Morial's head as his heart rate increased. He heard a gust enter the hall and saw water seep onto the floor from the stairwell. Morial fixed his sights on the frame of the stairwell door and crept toward the water. He began to sweat profusely, his shirt becoming as damp as the bottom of his boots. The stairwell door scraped across the floor before becoming airborne. Morial was nearly impaled but he dodged the object. Morial rose to his feet after he heard the door crash into the wall. Morial stared into the stairwell, taking notice of the water trickling in.

"What is it that you seek? Is it a deeper meaning? A sense of purpose?" the male voice intervened behind Morial.

"I came to s—" Morial began but ceased as he confronted the figure behind him.

Morial viewed a young male, cloaked in an all-black sleeveless jumpsuit. Morial was familiar with the gentleman, but not his current stature. His arms gleamed in the pale hall light as shades covered his post-pubescent face. He was forming a goatee, but it was thinner in some areas and not fully connected.

"*Michael?*" Morial uttered.

"Theodore?" the young man mouthed back.

Morial pursed his lips together, taken aback by the figure placed before him.

"You uh...you alright, boy?" Morial offered.

"One always knows the answers to that which truly concerns them," Michael stated.

Morial tilted his head forward, tightened his brows, and dug his teeth into his bottom lip. He took one step toward Michael, who took one step back in return. Morial sighed at Michael's retreat.

"They treatin' you right here? Look like you been eating pretty good," Morial pandered.

Michael provided the feeblest shrug as he continued gawking at the lieutenant. Morial withdrew his firearm and placed it back into his holster, hoping Michael was more gun shy than rude.

"It's been a while, ain't it? Sure miss seeing you around," Morial stated.

"I assure you it's been longer for me than it has for you. Hasn't it, lieutenant?" Michael challenged.

"Son...I...," Morial began.

"Don't 'son' me. You traded away that one privilege for the many you have now. Are we having visitations today? You donating another child to The Order? Why are you here, Lieutenant Morial?!" Michael berated.

As Michael became frustrated with Morial, the double doors down the hall began to sway. This time slamming louder and often.

"It's...It's...," Morial struggled over the clatters.

"I'm sorry, it's hard to hear you over the slamming doors. In fact, the last time I saw you, you disappeared behind a pair," Michael blasted.

Morial's eyes began to fill with tears. The lieutenant regretted giving Michael away, but it was a decision in desperation. Though he didn't expect complete forgiveness from Michael, he also hadn't bet on such crassness.

"I regret that, son! I have checked on you many, many, many times over the years," Morial pleaded.

"THEEEEEOHHHHHHHH," a soft female's voice swept through the stairwell.

"Shit!" Morial muttered.

Morial clasped his palms together and leaned them toward Michael. Michael looked down at Morial's gesture and mildly scoffed.

"Do you desire some form of reprieve for your actions? I suggest you search elsewhere for an altar. You won't find one suitable to your kind here!" Michael insured.

"Now you hold on just a got damn minute!" Morial directed.

The Morials locked eyes, each refusing to back down or acknowledge the room: water slowly pushed in from the stairwell, the air became still, and the double doors slowed their velocity. The lieutenant took one index finger and pointed it north of Michael's dome.

"You wanna be mad at me, that's fine, I deserve that. What I will not stand for is this constant disrespect! You gonna be cloaked and cold cocked if you keep fucking wit—" Morial was interrupted by double doors slamming simultaneously.

The abrupt disruption caused both Morials to twist their necks towards the sound. The lieutenant returned his attention to his son, but the offspring's head remained turned as he dipped his chin into his own clavicle and murmured at his father.

"You don't stand for very much, old man. You didn't stand for me when it mattered, and now you get to sit down and make everybody else do your leg work. Including me," Michael muttered.

Morial's hands clutched Michael's clothing before his eyes could register what he'd done. Michael smirked at the sight of his father's clasped fists pressed upon his chest. Michael grasped one hand and stroked it with his thumb. The lieutenant pushed Michael away, with the progeny cackling at his father's discomfort.

"Boy, I done cleared many a field just so you could have a path to stroll. You don't have to approve of what I've done, but you damn sure better acknowledge it when you reap the rewards," Morial warned.

"Unless you have some candy in your pocket, I don't think you come bearing gifts. So why the hell are you here?" Michael discredited.

"Your uncle Reggie," Morial uttered.

Michael glared at the lieutenant, unaware of what his father meant. He gawked at the officer, waiting for further information.

"What about him? What did y'all do to him?" Michael accused.

Morial lightly snorted and shook his head. He turned as if he planned on walking away only to return, steadily shaking his finger in the young man's direction. Morial then retracted his hands and placed them on his hips.

"He was shot," stated Morial painfully.

"For what? Some old beef?! This fucking city is a disease," Michael estimated.

"Naw, man. It wasn't his beef at all. He took a bullet for somebody else," Morial explained.

Michael began to breathe rigidly before his tear ducts moistened. Morial attempted to embrace him, but Michael dodged the support.

"Who the fuck was it?! Tell me, Dad!! TELL ME!" Michael howled.

"I have something to tell you," a woman's voice seeped.

Morial checked his perimeter but couldn't pinpoint another soul. Michael remained dazed and immobile. Morial reached for his hip, but Michael secured his hand and spastically whipped his head from side to side. Morial glared at Michael before removing his hand from the holster.

"How may we serve you? Would you like to get started

on your next promotion?" The woman's voice sounded again.

"Theresa? I'm not here for you. I am here for my boy. I don't have shit to say to you!" Morial clarified.

"HAHAHAHAHAHA! He may be your son, but I'm his reason to rise!" the voice teased.

Morial spun around to nothing more than the darkened hall. When he turned to face Michael, he found a middle-aged ebony woman standing next to him. Morial nearly stumbled at the sight of a woman he had not encountered in years: *Mother Rampart*!

She wrapped her arm around the back of Michael's neck while utilizing her body to shield one side of his. She stared at Morial as she stood on her tippy toes to relay a message into Michael's ear. She rubbed her hand across Michael's chest, straightening the ruffles his father left.

"I must beg of you not to put your hands on the merchandise. This one does some pretty good work for me, though we have some things that can be...well... improved," Rampart taunted as she gently cupped Michael's face inside her hand.

"He may be valuable, but he ain't nobody's property. We need to get that straight right now, Theresa!" Morial boasted.

Mother Rampart watched Morial as she ran her hand down Michael's neck to the chest plate. Morial squinted at Rampart intently, rather offended by Rampart's display of endearment towards Michael. Morial could feel the liquids in his stomach turning nearly on cue with the water saturating the floor.

"What brings you here, dear Theodore? That lieutenant position not as glamorous as you once imagined?

You prefer chief instead?" Rampart scolded.

"Theresa, I'm not fucking talking to you! I'm here for Michael!" Morial gritted.

Mother Rampart positioned herself chest to lower chest with Michael while leaning back to gawk at the lieutenant. Morial reached to remove Rampart, but she swiveled, grabbed his arm, and came face-to-face with him instead. As he pulled his arm away, Rampart scraped her fingernails along his elbow and forearm. Morial was protected by his long-sleeved shirt but still felt violated.

"Well, I'm talking to you, big boy. You don't come into a lady's domain and fail to address her. It's rude... egotistical...and chauvinistic. Not that I'm at all surprised," Rampart scoffed.

"I don't need you or this—'skanctuary'—I am just here for my boy!" Morial defended.

Rampart folded her arms below her bosoms and delivered a hearty laugh. She nearly fell into Michael while tilting her head back to fill the dingy emptied hall with comedic joy. Rampart covered her mouth as if she was blushing before uniting her hands at the fingertips.

"He was your boy when you brought him to me. He is now a man. More of a man than you were likely to make him on your own," Rampart chimed.

"What, with your hoodoo and fool's gold magic? Well, I must be a damn Geppetto! Thank you for removing his wood and making him all natural!" Morial barked.

"Now I would never sacrifice or waste good wood, Mr. Morial. If anything, I have made him more solid, more educated, and FREE! Free of the prison that is the average mind. Free of the insolent expectations of a world ruled by images instead of ideas. Free of falsehoods and false idols,"

Rampart preached.

"False idols? Are you kidding me?! You practically praise witchery and sorcery, none of which can be explained or proven. You damn right about y'all literally upholding ideas instead of true morals," Morial attacked.

Rampart cut her eyes at Morial, looked at the floor, snickered, then cackled once, engaging Morial's eyes again. Rampart rolled her eyes and began to walk down the hall, away from the Morials. She stopped mid-stride, raised her right hand and fanned her fingers as she twisted her wrist. Illumination appeared at the gloomy end of the hall. Rampart spun around to address Morial once more.

"You read from the bylaws of a book that made it okay for our people to be enslaved. We value a practice that teaches one to explore freely. You live from a book that contradicts itself regularly and limits your intuition. We practice an art that allows for one to examine the reach of their power *without* limitations. You put your faith in miracles you have never seen while we bear witness to teachings that have been long discovered...practiced...and repeated. Christians pretend to be an advocate of the sick and shut in, only to mock and monetize their struggles. We use the roots around us to make them rise again! While your only way of convincing others to follow you began from wars on other religions, our believers stay because of the peace afforded to them!" Rampart announced.

Morial stomped down the hall toward Mother Rampart, whose back was to the men while shaking her head. Morial was within reach of Rampart when a random door along the hall slammed, causing him to stir. He completed a 360-degree spin while searching for the source. Upon return to his original position, Morial landed in the clutches of the Brood Mother. Morial tried to break away, but she'd practically hooked him with her claws.

"Unhand me, you harlot!" Morial screamed.

Mother Rampart flashed a grin at the lieutenant before raising herself to his ear. She blew in the canal, causing his frenzied movements to cease. Apparently paralyzed by Rampart's calming hiss, Morial's eyes traveled the corner near his ear.

"Theo, Theo, Theo, shhhh. You are but a man looking for answers in a world you constantly have to question. You already see the truth. I am but every woman: if you give me a seed, I'll give you a garden. For the garden to continue its flourish, I'm going to need more seeds," Mother Rampart instructed.

Mother Rampart released the grasp on Morial and walked to his rear. Water rushed onto the floor as Theresa Rampart sauntered down the halls.

"The fall from grace is often the hardest, Lieutenant. If you still like the sound of that title, you will replace the fruit to elongate the harvest. Otherwise, everything we made a reality for you will become a dwindling nightmare. I already have somebody in mind, and you are going to help us get him!" Rampart warned.

Morial frantically spun around to find nothing more than the light going out down the hall. No Michael. No Rampart. And....no resolution for the one issue he intended to resolve.

Chapter 46

Unforeseen Circumstances

The car comes to a screeching halt near the entrance of Beech Grove Manor. Julissa hadn't paid much attention to her surroundings as she continued to fish her finger through Victor's open wound for his compliance. When she looked out at the long white building and covered breezeway, Julissa nearly ripped her seatbelt off.

"WHO DID YOU TALK TO? Did *she* tell you where to find me?!" Julissa accused.

"Iliiii spoke with nooooooo onnnnnnne," Victor pleaded.

Julissa didn't believe him. She knew she'd been set up and the culprit behind it. Julissa plunged her digit into Victor's arm again, arguably deeper than earlier. Victor released a horrendous howl. He reached over with the unaffected arm and pulled Julissa's wrist until her entire hand was removed.

"Take me to her, you overgrown bastard. Walk me in there right now!" Julissa ordered.

"Iiiiiiiiiiiii've nevvvvverrr beeennnnnn innnnnn therrrrrre," Victor admitted.

Victor's head hung while he gasped for air. Julissa's

eyes tightened as she carefully examined Victor for filth. For some inexplicable reason, she believed him. Julissa could tell the Baron was gargantuan, yet gentle. She looked into his eyes, noticing that once she took her focus away from his deteriorated features, he held a certain warmth inside.

"Well, how did you get to me?" Julissa inquired.

"Iiiiiii jusssst fahhlowwwwwwed instructionnnns," Victor stated.

Julissa stared at Victor to ensure he wasn't bluffing. *He wasn't.* She could tell by the way he avoided looking at the building but for a few seconds at a time. Julissa shoved the passenger door open to exit. Her eyes were glued to the entrance as she walked over to the driver side and pulled Victor's door open as well. Victor's head twisted gingerly as he watched Julissa from the open door. Julissa outstretched her arm to Victor, who appeared puzzled before flashing a slight grin.

Victor stood up and followed Julissa to the speaker unit near the door. Julissa pressed the button as Victor stood near the glass pane window. He witnessed the startled stare of the front desk staff as they gawked at his gargoyle-like frame.

"We are beyond visiting hours at this time, ma'am," the clouded voice stated from the box.

"It's an emergency; I have to meet with someone immediately," Julissa reported.

"Who are you here to see, ma'am?" the attendant asked.

"It's me, Mrs. Julissa...Brown...Julissa Brown," Julissa faltered.

"Yes, ma'am. And is that a trick-or-treater behind

you?" the attendant inquired.

Julissa was puzzled by the question initially...until she turned her focus to Victor. She looked at his sunken head and mangled skin, feeling a fit of remorse for her escort. Julissa inhaled the night air before continuing with her request.

"No, he is a friend of mine and may be familiar to one of the other patients," Julissa declared.

"Hmmm. Okay," The attendant reluctantly conceded.

The door buzzed and Julissa pulled it open. She planned on going in first but saw Victor pause at the entrance. Julissa opened the door wide and invited Victor in. Victor's eyes raced back and forth between Julissa and the front desk, surprised he would cross the door seal for the very first time. Julissa motioned for Victor to go in. He walked in but went no further than the midpoint between the door and the front desk. Julissa glared at Victor as she went ahead of him to address the attendant.

"Hey, Mrs. Brown, are you here to see....," the attendant began.

"Yep, you know it. We're both here to see her," Julissa fudged.

The attendant scanned to Victor before returning her judgmental gaze to Julissa. Her eyes whipped back to Victor as Julissa stared her down. Julissa knocked on the tabletop with her knuckles while placing herself directly into the attendant's line of sight.

"I'm sorry. As I just stated, ma'am, it is a little late for visitation," the attendant recited.

"And as I told you, 'ma'am'...it's a family emergency," Julissa announced.

Victor inched closer to the faceoff while attempting to

calm an agitated Julissa. Julissa looked over her shoulder at the towering associate as the attendant stepped back from the table.

"Myyyy motherrrrr wassss herrrrrre," Victor shared.

The attendant cocked her head to the side and bunched her brows. She grabbed a clipboard, flipped the top sheet over, and grabbed a pen. As she walked toward the odd couple, Julissa struck her palm through the board and slid it to the other side of the desk. The attendant was mortified by Julissa's actions and rushed to the printer behind her to grab another sheet. Victor walked over to the clipboard and found the pen nearby. Victor picked up both items as his eyes met with the attendant's. He gazed upon her before scribbling on the paper. Once done scribing, Victor gently laid the apparatus on the table, spinning it so the statement was clear for her to see. The attendant leisurely walked to the post to review Victor's handiwork. She lifted the clipboard from the table as she twisted her neck back and forth between the statement and the man. Julissa watched the attendant's face become unsettled.

"*That's* your mother?" the attendant queried.

"Yesssssss," Victor confirmed.

The attendant reached under the desk and pressed the button to the door. Julissa remained puzzled but led Victor towards the opening. The attendant nearly climbed onto the desk while watching Victor and Julissa proceed through the door. Once in the hall, Julissa hurried along until she heard sounds of civilization. Once amongst the patients, Julissa skimmed the room for a familiar face. Victor trailed behind her but became engrossed with the nurse technician. He was drawn to her eyes and examined her from afar.

Julissa weaved in and out of the area searching for one individual. Victor tried to keep pace but lost momentum as she approached the patients. Victor was stunned as no one appeared outwardly threatened by his appearance. A couple of patients walked past Victor, but none were moved by his stature. Victor moved toward a wall and observed the patients in their environment. He found their sense of community refreshing. Despite the varying mental health possibilities before him, Victor still shallowly considered himself the most flawed individual in the room.

Julissa continued her search of the premises while Victor settled at a spot near the hall. He continued his admiration of the patients performing in their habitat, until he accidentally became a piece in the exhibit. A young lady bumped into him from his blind side, nearly knocking the statuesque observer from his perch. He turned to find a baffled yet beautiful bronzed face to his rear. She sat with her mouth agape while she marveled at Victor.

"You new around here?" the patient asked.

"Somethiiiiiing liiiiiiiike thaaaaat," Victor answered.

The bronzed bombshell took a closer look at the Baron, quietly processing the speech impediment she encountered. She examined the specimen further, deciding there was much more to the being than his speckled pigment and mangled voice.

"You must be from Central Louisiana," the patient heckled.

She drew a quaint chuckle from the Baron. It was enough for Victor to loosen up and lean against the wall. The woman smiled at Baron as she occupied the space directly across from him. She traced his entire frame with her eyes, treasuring his obscured appearance.

"Not quiiiiite. Howww abowwwwt youuuuu?" Victor finally answered.

"I get around. Well, I used to anyway," the patient chimed while pointing to the ceiling.

She drew a heartier laugh from Baron. Enough for him to draw both Julissa's and the technician's attention. Julissa became invested in the patient garnering Victor's admiration. She began making her way toward them as the banter persisted.

"So, what's your name, mister? They call me Honey around here," Honey revealed.

"Victorrrr," the Baron elaborated.

"Well, it's definitely nice to meet your acquaintance. What family member forced you into this fine establishment?" Honey nudged.

"My muh-therrr," Victor answered.

"Seems we have something in common," Honey deflected.

Honey then felt a tap on her shoulder she initially disregarded. The hand then grasped her shoulder and spun her around, where she came face-to-face with Julissa. Honey's mouth dropped as if she'd seen a ghost.

"Miss me, bitch?!" Julissa asked.

Honey shook her head before attempting to flee. Julissa swung her into the wall near Victor, causing him to straighten his posture and nearly abandon his post. Julissa delivered a right hook that sent Honey underneath a nearby table.

"Get the fuck up, Ramona! You sent a madman to my job? *Really*?!" Julissa berated.

Honey looked up at Julissa, wiped her lip, and laughed. Julissa grabbed Honey with one hand while she stared at Victor. Victor didn't understand what had just occurred but noticed Julissa fuming.

"You lied to me? You told me you had no idea who sent you. I should lay your ass out too," Julissa threatened Victor.

Victor extended one arm out front to maintain the distance between himself and Julissa. He took the other hand and made the shape of an "x" across the left side of his chest.

"Weeee jusssst met," Victor confessed.

"He's right, bitch. I was just introducing myself," Ramona reiterated.

Julissa remained suspicious of their claims but recognized a glimpse of sincerity in their answers. Though she believed Ramona, she was no less disappointed.

Chapter 47

Mixed Signals

"So, you just told a random old coot where to find me? You really hate me *that* much?" Julissa asked.

Ramona leaned her head to one side and shrugged. Julissa grabbed ahold of Ramona's smock, threatening to strike her again.

"Youuu spoke with myyyyy uncullll? Youuu knowww myyy motherrrr?" Victor asked Ramona while trying to restrain Julissa.

Ramona squinted her eyes at the broad-figured man, slowly piecing the puzzle together. She wandered from her sister's grief-stricken face long enough to get a good look at Victor.

"Wait, that means you're—" Ramona began prior to interruption

The nurse technician in all her ivory glory came to break up the ruckus caused by the visitors. The technician placed her hands on top of Julissa's and pried them off Ramona. Victor aided by wrapping himself around Julissa and pulling her away. Even while tending to Julissa, Victor began to examine the tech methodically. The technician helped Ramona to her feet before chastising Julissa.

"Ma'am and sir, I'm going to have to ask you both to leave. What you are doing here is disruptive to the treatment of these patients," the technician announced.

Victor stood frozen as he gazed into the technician's eyes. The technician avoided eye contact and turned her attention to Julissa's firelit pupils. Ramona stuck her head out from the technician's arm, but she was careful not to expose enough of herself to be struck again.

"How could you?! I am your family!" Julissa cried.

"You're a reminder two families cast me aside!" Ramona shouted.

A tear ran down Julissa's eye as she helplessly watched Ramona become incensed. The technician went from protecting Ramona to arguably guarding Julissa. Ramona ripped herself from the technician's clutches and began to tug at her own hair. Ramona sat down, rocking back and forth. The technician closed in to comfort her, but Ramona frantically swung one arm to keep her away.

"The sirens, the sirens, the sirens. Those DAMN SIRENS!!" Ramona spewed.

"Honey? Dear...I don't hear any sirens," the technician said.

"Shit," Julissa whispered.

Julissa's comment garnered Victor's attention. Julissa dug her fingernails into Victor's forearm, so he'd let her loose. Once free, she attempted to join Ramona at her side, but Ramona shunned her away.

"You *stay away* from me. *You* are one of the reasons why I'm here. *You could have saved me*! All you had to do was tell the truth. The truth, Lisa!" Ramona blared.

"I tried. I really tried, Ramona. No one believed me. Mama and Daddy acted like I nev—," Julissa squeaked.

"THEY DIDN'T WANT TO! They had everything to lose if they believed us! I fought them and you just went along with their shenanigans. And for what? For them to enjoy a big house in Destreland while I stay in a five-star mental home and you parade around with Detective Brown?!" Ramona clarified.

Julissa froze in place as she witnessed her sister spiral into a fit. Ramona rose to her feet while gawking coldly at her sister. Ramona covered her ears and wobbled her head as she walked away from the technician. Once he could see her full profile, Victor ran over to the technician and braced her by her arms.

"*Mama!*" Victor murmured.

"Sir, I believe you have the wrong person. Now if you could please unhand me...," the technician denied as she wrestled away.

Ramona remained rocking while covering her ears. Julissa monitored Ramona from the corner of her eye while giving direct attention to the developing situation between Victor and the technician.

"They gave you a job? They didn't lock you up here like uncle said? Mama, you changed your hair?" Victor tallied.

"Sir, I must caution you again. I am not your mother. It's very sweet you see me as a nurturing soul, but I am not who you seek," the technician warned again.

"You don't remember me, Mama?" Victor sobbed.

Julissa inched closer to Victor as she saw him becoming unraveled. The technician looked up in dismay. Julissa wanted to pull Victor away, but he was statuesque in frame and mass. Victor dipped his head as he released his grip. The technician watched in horror as the Baron began to weep.

"Caaan weee goo nowww?" Victor asked Julissa.

Julissa peered at Ramona, who now sat with her arms folded. Julissa quickly forgave Ramona for the trouble she instigated as she sought to keep Victor sane. Julissa agreed to walk him out of the common area, latching onto his arm to carry him away. Despite the intended effort, Victor was not quite done with the technician.

"HOW COULD YOU! Don't you care?! The rest of the world doesn't love me and you feel like them?! *Look right through me*? Pretend I don't even exist?! What have I ever done to you? What have *they* done to you to make you forget about me?!" Victor poured.

As tears streamed down his face, Victor turned to cloak himself. Julissa was humbled by Victor's sentiments, believing Ramona's sentiments were similar. Though most close to the altercation showed sympathy, the technician remained sullen. Ramona too stared upon the technician awaiting a reaction. It was when Julissa began to comfort Victor, as a mother would, as he hoped the technician could, that the technician began to shiver. Her stature began to rupture as if the tears would depart in boulders. Julissa flashed a deadly stare at the technician as she began to escort Victor from the scene.

"It was the only way," the technician squeaked.

"What?" Julissa asked while turning toward the tech.

Other patients became invested in the conversation. Ramona planted herself near the tech as a means of support. Victor continued to look away from the tech, attempting to hide the tears of defeat and shame.

"IT WAS THE ONLY WAY! To forget what they did to you. I could never forgive it. I could never accept it. To forget what *he* did to me," the technician, Lavender, revealed.

Victor peeked over his shoulder to the technician...his mother...Lavender Baronne. His face was still sunken from the heft of his journey, but internally he was flushed with joy. Julissa snickered to herself as she patted Victor on the back. Victor delved into Julissa's eyes, searching for his next move. Julissa declared her approval with a nod. Victor began to walk towards his mother but was stifled by a kerfuffle in the main lobby. Lavender heard it as well and moved towards Victor, leaving Ramona in place.

As she approached Victor, Lavender reached up to grab his face. Victor turned his torso toward his mother and gave in as she pulled his head toward hers. She kissed him on his forehead and guided him off to the side. Julissa stared blankly at the spot where Victor and Lavender once stood, until she noticed Ramona attempting to get away.

"I'm not done with you, Ramona!" Julissa yelled.

"Well, that's funny, cuz I'm damn sure through wit' you," Ramona replied.

Ramona attempted to flee but was met with Julissa's will to find answers. As Ramona stumbled through the common area toward the technician's desk, Julissa sprinted between tables and beat Ramona to her spot.

"You don't think you owe me a little more than that? You could have gotten me killed!" Julissa blamed.

"A life for a life," Ramona blurted.

Julissa bit her lip and dipped her chin towards the floor as she gazed upon Ramona. Ramona tilted her head to the right and examined Julissa. Their staring contest was interrupted by bodies busting through the door leading to the main lobby. The Monroe sisters turned their attention to multiple C.C.P.D. uniformed officers entering the room, led by Detective Rita Barrios. Rita scoured the room until she locked eyes with Julissa. She looked at two officers and directed them to the left. Julissa attempted to grab Ramona's hand, but she pulled away and walked towards the officers.

"Where is Victor, Julissa?" Rita asked, perturbed.

Julissa pointed in the general direction Lavender escorted Victor to, but they were nowhere in sight. Julissa scanned the room but found no signs of the pair.

"They were here, somewhere," Julissa answered.

"They?! Who the hell is they?" Rita demanded.

"Lavender! Victor and Lavender. I'm sure you and your pigs in black can find them," Ramona cleared.

"Dammit! You mean to tell me you not only let a man with a mallet go running around freely, but you also possibly let out a mental patient in the process? You are just stirring up all kinds of shit, ain't ya, Mrs. Brown?" Rita diagnosed.

Rita stirred her head as Julissa tilted her own. Ramona chuckled at each of them as she occupied a seat at a nearby table.

"What do you mean by patient? The lady he left with worked here. She had an I.D. badge and everything," Julissa described.

"This shit might be worse than I thought. You two, go and search down that hall. Get a couple more of your buddies to accompany you in case there are some adjacent halls that way," Rita directed.

As the officers obliged their directives, Julissa began to move toward Ramona. She was stalled by a hand grabbing her wrist, which Julissa regarded by pulling her hand forward until her elbow tagged the sternum of a C.C.P.D.

officer. She apologized for her error but was placed into handcuffs regardless.

"What is this about? What the hell, Rita?" Julissa barked.

"Aiding and abetting, mostly. You helped a madman with a mallet escape your office without consequences. Let's try not to add any batteries of an officer or other felonies in the meantime, mmm-kay?" Rita ordered with a grin.

"The bitch hit me! What can she get for that?" Ramona blurted with her hand raised high.

Julissa twisted her neck to glare at Ramona. Ramona placed her hand under her chin and wiggled her fingers towards Julissa.

"Really? You gonna do me like that? Your own flesh and blood?" Julissa begged.

"Don't be surprised. You chose those voodoo bitches over me a long time ago. Did you feel sorry for me when everyone cast me to the side? Hmm? Did you even give a fuck? NO! You were too busy dabbling in sorcery to love anyone but yourself!" Ramona pegged.

Julissa's vision was compromised by her own weeping. Ramona was unaffected by Julissa's overwhelming rush of emotions. Ramona stopped feeling compassion a long time ago, when the world didn't possess enough to share with her.

"We are sisters. I always cared about you. ALWAYS! I did what I did for the family. *You know* what they put me through!" Julissa recalled.

"Family? What family, Julissa? You're not even a Monroe. You are nothing more than a Brown...a brown... widow!" Ramona proclaimed.

Julissa's mug was drenched with tears. How could she? How could anyone? Why would anyone say anything so *spiteful*? *Hateful*! *Egregiously erroneous*! And more importantly, exactly what she needed to hear...The thin line between blood and water was now blurred. She chose not to despair over the spilled stock, but rather, irrigate it in a way to purify her legacy. Julissa was no longer a Monroe, she hadn't been since the day she was married, but she desired a buffer between herself and Cortissa long before. She now had the chance to break the cycle before it became a generational curse. Julissa looked back at her kin and simply uttered:

"Brown Widow? Shit, I kinda like that!" Julissa chimed as the officers guided her toward the exit.

As Julissa was being escorted out of Beech Grove by the officers, she glimpsed at Rita, who met her gaze just to roll her eyes and look away. Julissa then sought Ramona, who stared back at her plainly, with a certain gloss to her lids. Julissa was taken into the main corridor, where she was handed over to additional officers who transported her away from the building.

Epilogue

Hanging Around

"You love them more than me?" A woman's voice enters Rance's slumber.

"No, I don't even know them. I was just doing a favor," Rance defended.

"You tried to save them. You were sad when you thought they were lost. You never tried to save me. You gave up on me. *You gave up on us!*" the voice blamed.

Rance tossed and turned in his bed, sweating profusely. He tried to fight off his nocturnal intruder, but he couldn't wake. He tried to pinch himself within the delusion, but it was to no avail. The woman in his vision, a green-eyed brunette with a volition, reached her hand within her chest. Rance covered his eyes to decline whatever horror she had in store.

"No, Dru, don't," Rance screamed.

"You don't know how tired I get of hearing you say that. Just open your eyes and accept your gift. It comes straight from my heart," Drusilla stated.

Rance refused to comply with Drusilla's request. Rance continued to veil himself. Drusilla grabbed Rance's wrist to guide his hand to her chest. Rance began to panic.

392

"There is no one else! Okay, I was lonely without you here. *You know* why we can't be together," Rance implored.

Drusilla became infuriated and her eyes bulged as Rance cowered. She threw the object in her hand down to an unsettling "crack." Rance uncovered his eyes to find that which he desired the most on the floor: the Recluse Vision glasses. He brought his eyes up to Drusilla's disappointed gaze.

"It's not that we *can't* be together. You won't allow it. You let the opinions of others fill your head. Who loves you, Rance? Who loves you more than me, hnuh?" Drusilla challenged.

Rance dropped his head into his hands, massaging his temples in hopes of clarity. He heard the crunch of Drusilla's foot stepping on what remained of the Recluse Vision spectacles. As Rance cringed, Drusilla grabbed one of his hands in both of hers and peeled it from his face.

"Accept the things you cannot change, my love. But be wise enough to change the things you can. As for there being no one else, I kind of like the curly haired woman you've aligned yourself with lately. I find her abundantly delicious," Drusilla indicated.

Rance removed his other hand from his face as he gazed upon Drusilla's ominous grin. The sound of her sadistic laugh was a mix of beauty disguising sheer terror. "Wha... How...What do you know about her?" Rance clamored.

Drusilla maintained her smile while placing both hands on Rance's bare chest. She then draped one arm around his neck while the other hand's fingers traced his chest plate. Drusilla's smile dwindled once she looked up at Rance.

"My dear...I may have disappeared, but I'd never stray. Not from you. Not from *us*. What we have is inevitable, irreplaceable..." Drusilla began, as the remaining hand went from his chest to his neck, causing Rance to choke. "...and real!" Drusilla concluded.

Rance thrashed about in his bed while clutching at his neck. He choked as he wrestled with malice none other could see. He screamed as he fell from his bed, dreaming he'd been thrown off a cliff. Rance found sudden comfort from his body crashing onto his bedroom floor. Rance was awoken by his plodding plunge, still grasping at his throat and gasping for air. His eyes rolled into the back of his head while Rance made a last-ditch effort to escape The Cliffhanger's grasp...

Before falling comatose, Rance's lungs expanded with high velocity, pumping a "miracle from thin air" through his compromised cavity. He blinked feverishly while sucking in a boisterous gasp. As his own palm drummed his chest, he rolled onto his side and reached the opposite arm onto the nightstand. Rance ruffled various items before sliding his hand across his prize. Rance rolled onto his back and carefully brought the loose object into view. The frames were bent with one lens shattered, but Rance held the Recluse Vision Glasses with much adoration.

Rance carefully placed the spectacles on his face while staring at the ceiling. Rance blew a little breath upward before wiping the glasses with the base of his shirt. This time, Rance whistled and began to laugh while adjusting the frames for fit.

"Okay, Dru, I hear you. Every...last...word," Rance muttered, through the frames of a shattered lens, and a fiendish grin.

About Atmosphere Press

Atmosphere Press is an independent, full-service publisher for excellent books in all genres and for all audiences. Learn more about what we do at atmospherepress.com.

We encourage you to check out some of Atmosphere's latest releases, which are available at Amazon.com and via order from your local bookstore:

Twisted Silver Spoons, a novel by Karen M. Wicks

Queen of Crows, a novel by S.L. Wilton

The Summer Festival is Murder, a novel by Jill M. Lyon

The Past We Step Into, stories by Richard Scharine

Swimming with the Angels, a novel by Colin Kersey

Island of Dead Gods, a novel by Verena Mahlow

Cloakers, a novel by Alexandra Lapointe

Twins Daze, a novel by Jerry Petersen

Embargo on Hope, a novel by Justin Doyle

Abaddon Illusion, a novel by Lindsey Bakken

Blackland: A Utopian Novel, by Richard A. Jones

The Jesus Nut, a novel by John Prather

The Embers of Tradition, a novel by Chukwudum Okeke

Saints and Martyrs: A Novel, by Aaron Roe

When I Am Ashes, a novel by Amber Rose

About The Author

K.E. Robinson is a Louisiana native who has called Marrero, New Orleans, Shreveport, and Baton Rouge home. Now as an admirer from the outside he hopes to present Louisiana to the rest of the world the way he envisions it: Not a tourist site...but a main stage all on its own!! Through expansion of the "Crescent Mooniverse", K.E. hopes to firmly plant his vision in rooms he hasn't occupied, minds he never mentored and classes that expand beyond the bell.

CPSIA information can be obtained
at www.ICGtesting.com
Printed in the USA
BVHW040833270522
638300BV00006B/93